IRON WARRIOR, IRON WILL

Nate roused himself when a pair of Crows entered, hoisted him to his feet, and pushed him outside.

Pierce and a dozen warriors were waiting. "Enjoyed your little rest?" Pierce asked. "I was going to have you run a gauntlet, like I wanted to do with your friends. But then I got to thinking. I can use you to teach the Crows a little lesson."

"Killing me won't teach them anything about you they don't already know," Nate responded. He wasn't about to submit meekly. He dug in his heels and tried to tear free.

More warriors came to the assistance of those holding him. His arms were pulled to full extension and his wrists secured.

"Not so cocky now, are you, King?"

"Go to hell," Nate declared.

"After you, I'm afraid," Pierce said, drawing his butcher knife. The blade gleamed brightly in the sunshine as he sank to one knee. "I'm fixing to make me a new ammo pouch. And you get to supply the hide."

SAVAGE REVENGE

Sawyer blinked a few times. "You're here too? Well, isn't this something? All my friends are showing up. How did you hear about my wife and my precious sweethearts? About the murdering sons of bitches who killed them and nearly killed me. I'm going to get them. You watch."

Nate darted between his friend and the animals. "Hold on, Jeremiah," he said kindly, putting a hand on the man's chest. "You're not going anywhere right this minute. You need food; you need some sleep. And we have to talk."

Sawyer's features clouded and his spine went rigid. "Get out of my way, Nate. I can't afford any more delays. Those butchers have a lot to answer for."

"You're not leaving," Nate ~~said~~

It was plain ~~~~ is friend was extremely ~~~~ ument. What he didn't ex~~~~ take a swing at him.

"No!" Jer~~~~ go! Those bastards have~~~~

WILDERNESS

IRON WARRIOR/ WOLF PACK

DAVID THOMPSON

LEISURE BOOKS NEW YORK CITY

To Judy, Joshua, and Shane.

A LEISURE BOOK®

April 2000

J M

Published by

Dorchester Publishing Co., Inc.
276 Fifth Avenue
New York, NY 10001

If you purchased this book without a cover you should be aware that this book is stolen property. It was reported as "unsold and destroyed" to the publisher and neither the author nor the publisher has received any payment for this "stripped book."

IRON WARRIOR Copyright © 1994 by David L. Robbins
WOLF PACK Copyright © 1995 by David L. Robbins

All rights reserved. No part of this book may be reproduced or transmitted in any form or by any electronic or mechanical means, including photocopying, recording or by any information storage and retrieval system, without the written permission of the Publisher, except where permitted by law.

ISBN 0-8439-4722-5

The name "Leisure Books" and the stylized "L" with design are trademarks of Dorchester Publishing Co., Inc.

Printed in the United States of America.

IRON WARRIOR

Author's Note

Transcribing the King journals is a challenge at times. The archaic spellings and grammar are easy enough to change, but his frequent use of Indian terms and names poses a translation problem.

Consulting the tribes in question doesn't always help because King spelled phonetically, and it is sometimes hard to determine exactly how he meant a particular name to be pronounced. Then too, some of the names have to be shortened for convenience's sake. (Examples: Daunts Him by Blows to the Face, or Paints His Ears and Nose Red.)

I mention this because of one of the individuals who plays a prominent part in this excerpt. His Crow name, as recorded by Nate King, translates roughly as He Who Can Not Be Killed in Any Way, which I have taken the liberty of shortening to the Invincible One.

I hope historical purists will forgive me.

Prologue

It was in the autumn of 1836 that Jacob Pierce became invincible.

Pierce had no inkling of the bizarre twist of fate that lay in store for him on that fine fall day. At first light he started a fire so he could partake of his morning coffee, one of the few luxuries he allowed himself. He donned his low-crowned wool hat, wedged a flintlock pistol under his wide leather belt, and strolled to the nearby stream to fill his coffeepot.

Although the sun had yet to blaze the eastern sky with golden glory, the magnificent Rocky Mountains were already astir with a myriad of life. Sparrows, jays, and ravens warbled and cawed in raucous chorus. Chipmunks were out, scampering madly abroad with their tails twitching. In a clearing by the stream grazed several elk that looked up as Pierce approached, then promptly melted into the dense underbrush.

Jacob Pierce was in high spirits, as well he should be considering he had caught many more beaver than he had at the same time the year before. If they continued to be so plentiful until winter made trapping impossible, he stood to earn upwards of two thousand dollars at the next Rendezvous, more than he had ever earned at one time before. After he outfitted himself with provisions, he'd have about fifteen hundred dollars left. A very tidy sum indeed to add to his already large poke.

Unknown to anyone except Pierce, he had already saved close to three thousand dollars. It was his personal hoard, his treasure, as it were, which he valued more highly than life itself. It was his means of overcoming the poverty that had molded his youth back in New York, his way of escaping the humdrum existence his adult life had become before he left civilization for the frontier.

Another few years and Pierce would have enough to go back to the States and live in grand style. A fifty-acre estate, a fancy carriage, a beautiful, elegant woman—they would all be his. Of such lofty designs had his dreams been composed for the better part of four years, and often at night he would toss and turn in restless anticipation of the good life awaiting him once he traded in his buckskins for city clothes.

At least once a day Pierce took his poke from its hiding place, poured the money into his lap, and counted it, fondling it as he might a lover. The money was all that mattered to him. It was the sole reason he'd ventured into the Rockies, the sole reason he tolerated the dangers and hardships. Few other jobs in that day and age paid as well. Common laborers earned less than a dollar a day. Masons, carpenters, and the like only earned a dollar and a half daily. A trapper, though, earned three to four times as much. Lucky trappers even more. And so far he had been one of the luckiest.

Little did Jacob Pierce realize that his luck was about to change drastically. He sank to one knee on the bank of the stream and lowered his coffee-pot into the icy water. There was rustling in the brush on the other side. Pierce figured the elk were to blame, and paid little attention until he heard a low cough.

Stiffening, Pierce glanced up. Deep in the trees, figures moved. He counted two, possibly three Indians, and dropped flat on his stomach. Rather than lift the coffeepot and have the splash inside be heard, he let go and scooted backwards until he was well hidden. Parting thin branches, he saw five warriors strung out in single file, moving parallel to the waterway. As yet there wasn't enough light in the forest to distinguish details, so he had no idea whether they were hostiles or not.

Pierce flattered himself that he knew all there was to know about heathen redskins. In his opinion they were all just so much worthless trash, to be disposed of or avoided as the occasion demanded. He looked down his nose on the whole lot of them. Unlike many of his fellow trappers, he shunned even the friendly tribes and had never taken an Indian woman for a wife. Some trappers thought he was peculiar in that regard. They simply didn't understand that the only love in his life always had been and always would be money.

The warriors continued on to the southeast. Pierce stayed where he was until they were long gone, then he hurriedly crept to his lean-to and began gathering his belongings. Where there were five Indians, there were often 20 more, and he had no inclination to stay around and risk facing a large war party.

The possibles bag went over Pierce's arm and across his chest, as did his powder horn and ammo pouch. He squatted and pulled the unlit ends of burning brands from the fire, then poked the burning ends on the ground until the flames went out. Thin tendrils of smoke wafted sluggishly skyward, dispersing before they rose higher than the tree under which he had wisely situated his camp.

As a matter of course, Pierce always kept his bundled plews near his pack animals. He loaded them swiftly, saddled his mount, and claimed his poke. His blankets rolled up easily and were tied on behind his saddle. Ever watchful, he gathered the rest of his things, making as little noise as he could.

Pierce was all set to climb on when he remembered to take his special precaution. His first winter in the high country, an old-timer, who had spent more years in the mountains than most, had given him advice on how to live to the same ripe old age. At the time Pierce had thought the suggestion ridiculous, but later, after a skirmish with the Bloods in which his trapping partner at the time had been shot in the gut and died a horrible, lingering death, Pierce had decided to heed the old man's words and do what was necessary to render himself "damned near invincible," as the mountain man had put it.

As yet, Pierce had not had to test his "precaution," nor, if the truth be told, did he want to. He was a trapper, not a fighter, a man devoted to wealth, not to warfare. He would rather avoid war parties than clash with them. And so far he had been remarkably successful in doing just that. Until today.

Pierce took the lead rope to his pack animals in hand and slowly headed northward. He stayed away from open spaces and stopped frequently to listen, troubled by the fact the birds and animals had fallen silent.

From the small valley where he had camped, Pierce made his way steadily higher until he came to the crest of a ridge. From here he enjoyed a bird's-eye view of the surrounding countryside. The sun had risen, bathing the stark peaks and pine forests in brilliant sunshine. He could see black-tailed deer on a mountain slope across the way. He saw a lone bald eagle soaring on outstretched wings. And he spotted the five warriors far down the stream.

Pierce relaxed a little. The Indians clearly had no notion he was anywhere in the vicinity. He decided to wait until they were out of sight, then return and retrieve his traps. The stream was about played out anyway, he reflected, so he might as well go on into the next valley and begin anew. Another valley, another 50 plews. That was how Pierce viewed it. A typical valley yielded that many, only a half dozen of which were kittens.

Opening his tobacco pouch, Pierce filled the bowl of his pipe. Presently he was puffing contentedly, his left leg curled on top of his saddle, his rifle across his thighs. He congratulated himself on outwitting the heathens, and grinned at the thought of the story he would tell at the Rendezvous. With proper embellishment, he could turn the incident into a hair-raising tale that would tingle the hackles of every greenhorn in attendance.

Pierce chuckled at the idea, but the chuckle died in his throat when he happened to glance to his left and set eyes on a large party of warriors on the next ridge over. There had to be 20 or more, and every last one of them was staring straight at him.

Unbridled fear rippled down Pierce's spine. He was petrified, certain the time had come for him to meet his Maker. He noted five riderless horses with the band, and guessed that the five warriors he'd seen earlier were scouts sent ahead to search for enemy villages.

As yet the Indians hadn't moved. Pierce casually upended his pipe and stuck it, still hot, in a pocket. He lowered his leg, gripped the reins, and turned his bay to go down the opposite slope. No sooner did he do so than unholy howls erupted from the throats of the savages and most applied their quirts to their mounts.

"Oh, God!" Pierce cried, jabbing his heels into the bay. The dependable animal sensed the extremity of the moment and broke into a trot. To his mind, unbidden, came all the stories he had ever heard about the many and varied atrocities committed by the Blackfeet and other tribes. He imagined himself being skinned alive, or having his eyes gouged out, or being shot so full of arrows he'd resemble a porcupine, and he wished he had wings, like that eagle, so he could fly to safety.

At the bottom Pierce turned to the left, sticking to open country now to make better time. He glanced back repeatedly, hoping against hope the Indians would let him escape. When the fleetest appeared on the ridge he had just vacated, he uttered an inarticulate cry and goaded the bay to go faster.

The Indians rapidly gained. Pierce was being held back by the pack animals. Burdened as they were, they couldn't run fast for any length of time. Either he stubbornly tried to keep possession of his furs, and lost his life, or he released the lead rope and lived to trap another day.

The first pack animal slowed the instant Pierce's fingers slipped off the rope. He bent low, prodding the bay with his rifle. The Indians whooped with bloodthirsty glee, some veering to claim the packhorses while others, those more interested in counting coup, veered toward him.

Pierce gulped and rode for his life. He had great confidence in the bay. It was a good-gaited horse with more stamina than most. Barring a mishap, he just might make it.

The land became rockier, more open. Pierce saw a canyon ahead and debated whether to swing around or go on through. Since doing the former would allow the foremost warriors to cut the gap' even more, he clattered into the canyon, dirt and stones flying from under the bay's hooves.

Jacob Pierce anxiously scanned the high walls for a trail to the top. By getting above the Indians, he reasoned he might be able to hold them at bay by rolling boulders down on their heads. But the walls were too sheer. He went over a quarter of a mile and swept around a bend.

A solid rock wall reared before him. It was 60 feet high if it was an inch, and no man living could scale it, let alone a horse. Pierce reined up and looked around in frantic desperation. He was trapped! His stomach knotted and he felt lightheaded.

The war whoops of the onrushing warriors echoed loudly. Pierce wheeled the bay and raced to the bend, then drew rein sharply again. The wily savages had fanned out across the canyon floor and were closing in on him in a ragged line. They stopped when he appeared, and one said something that made the others smile and laugh.

Pierce was certain he would die. He faced the reality all must eventually face, and inwardly he struggled with himself to decide the disposition of his soul. Would he die a craven coward, cringing from their onslaught? Or would he fight to the last, knowing no one would ever know how bravely he met his end, knowing there was no one in the

States to mourn his passing? He glanced at a parfleche hanging from his saddle, the parfleche containing his prized wealth, and he made his decision. "I'll be damned if the bastards will take my money without a fight!" he declared aloud.

One of the warriors suddenly yipped and charged, notching a shaft to a sinew bowstring.

Pierce raised his rifle. He'd expected them to swarm over him, not to challenge him one by one. Taking a careful bead, he waited until the warrior was well within range and fired. At the same time, the warrior loosed his shaft. Pierce was only able to glimpse the Indian catapulting backward because he was struck a jarring blow squarely in the center of the chest and catapulted rearward himself.

He hit the ground brutally hard. Jarred to his core, dazed, Pierce blinked and sucked in air. So that was it, he mused. One measly shot was all he got off! He looked down at himself, dreading the sight of the arrow jutting from his body. Only it wasn't there. He blinked, then spotted the shattered shaft near the bay.

Shaking his head in disbelief, Pierce shoved unsteadily to his feet. The old mountain man's idea had worked better than he'd dared hoped it would. He looked at the warriors, whose amazement matched his own, then at the brave he had shot, lying dead in a spreading pool of blood.

Pierce saw his rifle and went to pick it up. He was denied the chance, as two warriors abruptly roared in rage and sped forward to avenge their companion. Straightening, Pierce jerked out the two flintlocks at his waist. He never had been much of a pistol shot, so he was forced to permit the Indians to draw much closer than he liked in order to be sure of dropping them.

The one in the lead held a lance, the second a fusee. Pierce put a ball through the forehead of the first man and shifted to shoot the other one. He was a hair too slow. The fusee blasted, spewing smoke and lead, and Pierce was hit full in the sternum. The impact bowled him over, and he lay in the dirt, stunned. He heard the drum of hooves, heard the war horse stop and footsteps approach. His senses sharpened as his hair was gripped by iron fingers and his head was yanked upward. Above him gleamed a scalping knife.

With a quick twist, Pierce thrust his pistol into the warrior's ribs and squeezed the trigger. The man staggered, clutched himself, gaped in astonishment at Pierce, and died on his feet.

Gritting his teeth against the pain, Pierce stood. He touched his chest, thinking his fingers would be coated with blood, but there was none. His special charm had worked again. He was bruised but not mortally stricken. Yet.

Venting strident yells, the war party swooped toward him in a body.

Jacob Pierce calmly drew his Green River knife and prepared to make them pay dearly for the right to claim his hoard.

Chapter One

Several years passed. The beaver population in the valley multiplied until there were nearly as many as there had been before the coming of the white man. The other wildlife likewise thrived. To an outsider, the valley appeared serene, inviting, yet another pocket paradise in the vase expanse of the rugged Rockies.

Into this paradise rode three new trappers. Like Jacob Pierce, they were attired in buckskins. Each wore a possibles bag, powder horn, and ammo pouch slung across his chest. Each wore knee-high moccasins. Two of them wore hats made from beaver fur, the third a blue wool cap.

In the lead rode the oldest, a white-haired veteran of decades in the mountains, his flowing beard lashed by the strong gusts of wind blowing from the northwest. His eyes were sea-blue, his skin as bronzed and weathered as the skin of an Indian.

Next in line came a strapping young mountaineer whose striking green eyes swept the terrain with bold confidence. A pair of matching pistols were tucked under his belt. On his left hip nestled a keen butcher knife, on his right a tomahawk. Tied to the back of his long black hair was a single eagle feather, slanting out from under the bottom of his hat. With his broad shoulders and muscular frame, he was the perfect picture of masculine vitality, as elemental in his own way as a mountain lion or a grizzly bear.

Third in line rode the youngest of all, a man whose beard was more fuzz than hair. He cast nervous glances right and left and started at the loud cries of birds and beasts. Often he licked his lips and looked at his partners as if for reassurance that all was well. His brown hair was the shortest of the three and brushed so that it exposed his ears instead of covering them as was the case with the other two.

The trio descended to the gurgling stream and sat scouring its length in both directions. The black-haired young giant nodded, then remarked to the older man, "I'd say it's worth trapping. How about you, Shakespeare?"

"This coon has to agree, Horatio," Shakespeare McNair said. "See those lodges down yonder? And up there a ways? A few weeks here would prove right profitable."

The third member of their party coughed to clear his throat. "Pardon me for asking, McNair, but why the dickens do you call him Horatio half the time when you know as well as I do that his real name is Nate King?"

"His memory is failing," Nate answered before Shakespeare could reply. "Why, sometimes he looks at his own reflection and doesn't know who in the world it is."

"Ha!" declared McNair, and then quoted from the writings of the English bard whose name he now bore as his own. "Swounds, I should take it! For it cannot be but I am pigeon-livered and lack gall to make oppression bitter, or ere this I should have fatted all the region kites with this slave's offal!"

The youngest trapper looked at Nate King. "What did he just say?"

Nate chuckled. "It was his way of putting me in my place." He saw lingering confusion in the other's eyes, and had to remind himself that Tim Curry was a greenhorn, new to the mountains and new to them. Curry had not yet learned of McNair's passion for William Shakespeare, a passion legendary among the trapping fraternity. "If you're going to stick with us, you'll have to get used to McNair rambling on the way he does. Every chance he gets, he quotes from that big book he lugs all over creation."

"Big book?" Curry repeated.

Shakespeare twisted and gave a parfleche a resounding whack. "The complete works of old William S.," he said. "The best investment I've ever made. If you want, I'll read you one of his plays after supper."

Nate leaned toward Curry. "Try not to encourage the old rascal or you'll never get a moment's peace." He turned his stallion up the stream. "Now let's find a spot to camp for the night."

The sun hung low in the western sky. Already the shadows had lengthened on the valley floor and the temperature had dropped a few degrees. Nate trotted briskly along, eager to rest after a hard day's travel. He glanced back at Curry and hoped they wouldn't regret allowing the newcomer to tag along with them.

Greenhorns were dangerous, not only to themselves but to those they worked with. Their ignorance made them prone to mistakes, and mistakes in the wilderness often proved deadly. A man might make too much noise or build a fire too big and draw a war party down on his head, or he might not pay as much attention as he should and blunder onto a grizzly or a panther. There were a thousand things greenhorns could do wrong, and did, as the bleached bones of far too many testified.

Nate well knew the difficulties greenhorns faced. He'd been one himself once. But thanks to the patient teaching of his mentor, McNair, he had gone on to become one of the most skilled trappers around. Few men caught as many beaver in a single season as he routinely snared. Few men had tangled with as many hostiles and beasts and lived to tell of the clashes.

Nate was one of the best at what he did, and now he had a chance to help someone else as he had once been helped. Which was why he had offered Curry the opportunity to join them when they encountered the younger man several days ago near Clark's Fork of the Yellowstone River. Since then he had learned enough about Curry to know the youth wouldn't last long alone.

Timothy Curry was from Maine, the son of a blacksmith. He had chafed at the idea of following in his father's footsteps, instead craving adventure and excitement. So when he'd read *The Trapper's Guide*, a manual put out by a firm that made traps, he knew he'd found the ideal career for him. The life of a trapper, boasted the manual, was for men "looking out for pleasant work and ways of making money." The manual had gone on to portray the profession in the same glowing terms as it might the life of European royalty, complete with drawings that were supposed to represent how real trappers lived, but were more in keeping with a boar hunt by an English earl.

Young Tim Curry had blithely accepted the distortions as the real article. Taking all his savings, he had headed west without delay despite the loving protests of his parents. In St. Louis he had outfitted himself according to the advice of a trapper in from the mountains to "guzzle at the trough of polite society." Then, in keeping with his reckless audacity, Tim had ventured beyond the mighty Mississippi into the depths of the unknown.

Miraculously, Tim had crossed the plains without being discovered by the Pawnees, Sioux, or Cheyenne. His luck had held as he ascended into the Rockies, pushing high into the remote regions where beaver were most abundant. And it was there Nate King and Shakespeare McNair had found him after spying his oversized campfire from miles off.

Just thinking about the youth's good fortune was enough to make Nate shake his head in wonder. Most men would have perished long since. He'd once heard a seasoned mountaineer, as the trappers like to call themselves, calculate that well over a hundred trappers began each new season, and less than twenty were alive one year later. Death was a daily prospect for the men who chased beaver, and only the hardiest survived.

The sight of a clearing brought Nate's reverie to an end. He reined up, and was about to swing down when he saw a crude lean-to under a lofty pine on the north side. Firming his grip on his heavy Hawken, he rode over to investigate.

Right away it became apparent the lean-to was old. Pine needles and dust coated the back and one of the supports was cracked almost clean through.

Nate dismounted and checked for tracks, but time and the elements had long since erased any. He turned as the others climbed down. "Looks like someone else passed this way a few years ago."

Tim Curry walked over. "Injuns, you figure?" he asked.

"No, white men. Or more likely just one."

"How can you tell?"

"Indians prefer conical forts," Nate explained, "the same shape as their lodges."

"Oh. I didn't know. I've never seen a lodge."

Shakespeare was beginning to strip off his saddle. "You will, son. Once the cold weather sets in, we'll go visit the Shoshones. After months of sleeping under the stars, you'll swear their lodges are more comfortable than the finest mansions."

"Are they friendly?"

It was Nate who answered. "The friendliest tribe there is. I should know. I'm married to the most beautiful Shoshone of all."

"You took a squaw as your wife?" Tim blurted out in surprise, and barely were the words out of his mouth before Nate towered above him, those green eyes smoldering like molten jewels.

"Since you're new to the mountains, I'll let your remark go. This time. But keep in mind that some of us don't like to have our wives called that. Only those who think of Indian woman as being little better than dogs call them squaws."

"I'm sorry," Tim said sincerely. "I didn't know. Please believe me when I say I didn't mean any insult." To hide his embarrassment, he turned away and worked at removing his saddle and unloading his supplies from his packhorses.

Tim was more upset than he let on, and not just because of his blunder. It was becoming more and more apparent as time went on that he had a lot more to learn about life in the mountains than he had gleaned from the manual. A trapper's life wasn't the life of ease he had envisioned. Several times during his arduous trek across the prairie he had nearly perished from lack of water and food. The sun had burned him brown. The wind had chafed his skin. Frequently the packhorses gave him trouble. It had been a constant struggle to keep things on an even keel ever since leaving St. Louis, and from what he had learned from his new friends, the worst was yet to come.

Many times Tim had doubted the wisdom of continuing on, yet always he had, goaded more by pride than determination. He had boasted to his family and friends that he would return to Maine a well-to-do man, and he'd be damned if was going to crawl on back in defeat, penniless. His father would shake his head in that way fathers had, and his friends would mock his foolhardy scheme.

Tim hadn't said anything to King or McNair, but he'd tried laying out traps several times before meeting them, without success. On finding streams rife with beaver, he'd lowered his steel Newhouses into the water with every hope of coming back the next morning to find each contained a dead animal, only to haul them in empty. It was as if the beaver knew the traps were dangerous and avoided them like the plague. Yet the manual claimed beaver would fall all over themselves in their eagerness to be first to step into the jaws. He'd realized he was doing something wrong but had no idea what.

Just when it seemed certain Tim would have to give up, along had come the two more experienced men. How overjoyed he had been to have other souls to talk to! He'd gratefully jumped at their offer to join them, and so far had found them marvelous company. The old man, McNair, was a bit strange, and at times King could be downright moody, but overall it was better than being alone. The last thing he wanted to do was offend them and have them tell him to go his own way.

Tim glanced at Shakespeare and was given a reassuring smile. Nate King was leading his horses toward the stream, so Tim said quietly, "I really didn't want to upset him. Will he hold it against me?"

"Horatio isn't the kind to hold a grudge for more than a month or two. Don't fret yourself."

"A month!" Tim declared.

"I was only joshing you, son," Shakespeare said, holding in an urge to laugh. "It helps to make the time go faster if a man has a sense of humor." He toted his saddle under the pine tree and set it down next to the lean-to.

"Easy for you to say," Tim responded. "You've grown accustomed to this sort of life. You must know all there is to know about trapping and Injuns and such."

"I wish I did." Shakespeare sighed, then gazed wistfully skyward. "There are more things in heaven and earth than are dreamt of in our philosophy."

"More William S., as you call him?"

"Sort of." Shakespeare walked to his horses to gather up the reins and the lead rope. "There isn't a man alive who knows all there is to know about anything. Some like to flatter themselves they do, and they let their heads swell as big as the hind ends of buffaloes. But what comes out of their mouths is the same hot air you hear coming out of buffaloes when they've eaten too much sweet grass."

Curry mustered a smile. "You sure do have a way with words."

"There's more," Shakespeare said. "It seems to me that the surest way for a man to keep from putting his foot in his mouth is to keep his mouth closed except when he has something important to say." He put his hand on Curry's shoulder. "I don't often give advice unless it's asked for, but in your case I'll make an exception. I'll teach you the three words told to me by the old French-Canadian who took me under his wing for a spell when I first came to this neck of the country, words that have served me well ever since and helped me to avoid making more mistakes than I did." He paused for effect. "Look. Listen. Learn."

"That's it?" Tim said, somewhat disappointed the advice hadn't been a trifle more profound.

Shakespeare nodded.

"Why, any child can do as much."

"I beg to differ. Children seldom look before they leap, they talk when they should be listening, and they only want to learn when it suits them. Do better than they would and you'll do better in these mountains." Shakespeare made for the stream, wishing there was more he could say, some magical combination of words that would impart his stockpile of wisdom to the novice. Unfortunately, though, wisdom was a lot like money. It had to be earned, and commonly the only way to earn it was the hard way.

Nate King stood by his horses, scanning the valley while they drank. He heard Shakespeare coming and shifted. "Sorry I got so testy with him. I just hate to have anyone insult Winona."

"There's a lot to be said for a man who will stick up for his wife," Shakespeare commented. "Of course, there's a lot more to be said for a man who knows when she really has been insulted and when she hasn't." He positioned his animals along the bank and sank to one knee to take a sip himself.

"Ever worked this stream before?" Nate inquired, with good reason. McNair was more familiar with the mountains than any man alive, white or red. Sometimes it seemed to Nate as if his mentor knew every square inch of the Rockies from Canada to Mexico. Not even the redoubtable Jim Bridger knew them as well.

"Can't say as I have," Shakespeare said. "Near as I can tell, we're in country no tribe claims as its own. We've got the Utes to the south of us and the Crows to the north, but the only time they go through this area is when they're raiding one another."

"We'll have to keep our eyes peeled," Nate said. "I don't care to meet with either." The Utes were a war-like tribe, nearly as feared as the Blackfeet, who had a long-standing policy of driving all trappers from their domain. The Crows weren't so openly hostile, but they had been known to steal from trapping parties on occasion, and had killed a few whites foolish enough to enter their territory alone.

"It's not us I'm worried about," Shakespeare said, gazing at the greenhorn. "We'll have to keep him on a short tether or he's liable to cost all of us our hair."

"There's an easy solution."

"Impress me."

"One of us must be with him at all times. He can't do much harm if we're always looking over his shoulder."

Shakespeare grinned. "Now why didn't I think of that?" He pointed at the water, at his reflection, and quoted, "A fool, a fool! I met a fool in the forest! A motley fool, a miserable world. As I do live by food, I met a fool." His mouth curved upward. "See, Horatio? You claimed I wouldn't know me when I saw me. But if that's not me, there is someone walking around who deserves to be."

"Your brain is addled," Nate observed. "One of these days someone is going to hear you babble on so and give you a sound knock on the noggin to set your mind right again."

"Though this be madness, yet is there method in it," Shakespeare countered somberly.

Nate knew better than to joust with words with McNair. He stretched to relieve a kink in his lower back, then suddenly went rigid on seeing movement high on a mountain to the west. He looked closely and saw a huge brown shape plowing through a bramble patch. Thankfully, the monster was going up the slope, not coming down. "Damn," he muttered.

Shakespeare looked, and frowned. "We'll have to keep the horses close at night and never leave them untended during the day. A grizzly that size could kill half the string before we bring it down. They're awful hard to die."

"As I well know," Nate responded. It had been his misfortune to tangle with the fierce brutes on more occasions than he cared to recollect, and each time he'd had a closer shave than the time before. Not for nothing had he been given the name Grizzly Killer by the Cheyennes. If he wasn't almighty careful, sooner or later one of the beasts was going to rip him open from neck to groin. The thought sent a shiver down his spine, as if he had just had a premonition of his final fate.

Timothy Curry picked that moment to join them. "What are you both looking so grim about?" he asked.

"Grizz," Shakespeare said, nodding at the mountain. The gigantic predator had vanished into an aspen grove.

"Grizz?" Tim said, puzzled.

"As in bear," Shakespeare clarified.

"As in the scourge of the mountains," Nate amended. "Next to hostiles, they're the one thing we have to always be on our guard against. If a grizzly attacks you, aim for the eyes and then climb the handiest tree as if you were born a squirrel and not a man."

Tim patted his rifle. "I'm not scared," he blustered. "Believe it or not, gentlemen, I'm a good shot. Let one of those overgrown groundhogs pester me and I'll make worm food of it."

"Have you ever fought one before?" Shakespeare inquired.

"No, but I've hunted black bears back in Maine. Killed one, in fact, with a clean shot to the head."

"A black bear is only half the size of a grizzly," Nate pointed out. "And not a tenth as mean."

"Straight tongue," Shakespeare said.

The young trapper glanced from one to the other, then stepped to the water's edge. He failed to see what all the fuss was about. The clerk who had sold him his rifle had spoken eloquently of the gun's stopping power, saying that it could kill "any animal this side of the veil." Buffalo, panthers, bears, it mattered not. One shot from his flintlock and they were as good as dead.

Shakespeare noticed the look on the greenhorn's face, but said nothing. Cockiness, in his opinion, went hand in hand with youth.

Nate also noticed, and almost took Curry to task for doubting him. He held his tongue, though, since he had already give the youth a hard time once and didn't want to make a habit of it. Removing his beaver hat, he ran a hand through his tousled hair and gave his head a vigorous shake. The wind felt cool on his neck.

"Say," Tim Curry spoke up. "Why do you wear that feather? Is it because of your wife?"

"No." Nate reached behind him and touched the feather. "This was given to me by a Cheyenne warrior named White Eagle as a token of his respect after a fight I had with some Kiowas."

"Cheyennes. Kiowas. Shoshones. How do you keep them all straight?" Tim wondered.

"Irish. Scots. Italians. How do you keep them all straight?" Nate retorted. "All Indians aren't the same. Get that through your head and spare yourself grief later on."

"How so?"

"If you don't learn to tell the Sioux from the Piegans or the Mandans from the Pawnees, your scalp is liable to wind up hanging from a coup stick or a lodge pole." Nate hunkered down, cupped his left hand, and lowered his fingers into the chill water. He was lifting the hand to his lips when he spied a stake beside his left foot, buried so deep only the top showed. He swallowed, then said, "What have we here?"

Tim moved closer for a better look. "I don't see anything," he stated.

"This," Nate said, brushing dirt and grass from around his find. "Strange that a trapper would go off and leave his stakes behind. Good ones can be used again and again."

"Maybe he was in a hurry," Tim suggested.

"Or maybe he was killed," Shakespeare said.

Nate had exposed the uppermost inch. He dug further, trying to find a chain. If the trap was still there, it meant the former owner had met an untimely end. Traps cost 12 to 16 dollars apiece, depending on the kind, making them far too costly to be carelessly left behind. Not to mention that they were essential to a trapper's livelihood. Without them a man couldn't earn a cent.

Tim Curry had stepped to one side and was peering into the water. He abruptly cried out, "Look! I'd swear that's a coffeepot!" And then he stepped into the water.

"No!" Nate and Shakespeare warned simultaneously, but they didn't yell in time. The greenhorn suddenly arched his back and screamed in abject agony. As well he should. In his haste, Tim Curry had stepped on an abandoned trap.

Chapter Two

Nate King reached Curry in two long strides, sending a spray of water in all directions. He reached for the youth, but Curry doubled over and began hopping on one foot while trying to get at the trap clamped on the other. Spurting blood turned the stream a dusky crimson. "Hold still, darn you!" Nate said. "Let us help."

Tim heard the words, but they were eclipsed by the incredible pain shooting up his leg. The pain was all he could think of. It obliterated conscious thought. He wanted to tear the trap off, but couldn't get a grip on the slippery steel. The sight of the blood made him nauseous, but even that could not take his mind off the pain.

Shakespeare had started into the stream, then stopped so as not to get in Nate's way. "Pull him out," he directed, "or he might bleed to death before we can get him stitched up."

Nodding, Nate swooped in close, looped an arm

29

around the greenhorn's waist, and bodily lifted Curry clear into the air. The young man thrashed and squealed, his fingers slapping ineffectually at the muddy trap. In his anguish he dropped his rifle, which would have sunk to the bottom had Nate not snatched it up.

"Set him here," Shakespeare said, motioning at the bank and stepping backward to get out of the way. He could appreciate the young man's torment, but he was more interested in the trap. All beaver traps were not the same. Some were small, some were quite large. Some were barely strong enough to hold an adult beaver, others strong enough to hold a bear—or a man. Some had razor-sharp teeth, others did not. He was relieved to see that the one fastened to Curry was not the toothed variety. However, it was a big one, five pounds or better, with enough force to crack a leg bone as if the bone was a mere twig.

Nate took a step toward shore and was brought up short by the heavy chain. He glanced down and saw that most of the chain still lay imbedded in the muck at the bottom. "Here," he said to McNair, and tossed his mentor the rifle. Then, seizing hold of the chain, he wrenched to rip it loose, but in doing so he inadvertently caused the trap to bite deeper into Curry's ankle and the greenhorn screamed louder than ever.

Nate was stymied. He didn't dare set the young man down in the waist-deep water, nor could he reach the bank so long as the chain stayed buried. Bending, he gripped the slimy links closer to where they protruded from the mud, bunched his shoulders, and heaved. He could feel the mud loosening its grip, but before he could yank the chain completely loose he had to release his hold to deal with Curry, who was kicking and struggling in a frenzied panic. "Calm down," Nate urged, without effect. He gave Curry a shake to get the greenhorn's attention. Curry only struggled harder. Exasperated, Nate did the only thing he could think of to calm the youth. He slugged Tim Curry on the jaw.

The greenhorn went as limp as a sack of potatoes. Quickly Nate bent to the chain again. He had to gouge mud from several links before his handhold was adequate. Then, muscles rippling, he pulled until his face turned beet red and the veins in his neck bulged. The clinging mud was reluctant to give up its prize, but ever so slowly the chain slid free. Finally he had enough lose links to loop them around his wrist for extra purchase. Within a minute the battle was won, and Nate strode from the water and placed the unconscious youth at McNair's feet. "What do you think?"

Shakespeare knelt to inspect Curry's leg. The knee-high moccasins had been sheared clean through on both sides, as had Curry's socks. The jaws had bitten half an inch into his flesh, but a careful inspection showed that the bone wasn't broken. "He was damned lucky," Shakespeare remarked.

They carried the greenhorn to the clearing and propped him on his saddle. Nate got a fire going while Shakespeare filled a pot with water and cut strips from a blanket to use as bandages.

Curry didn't revive until the fire was blazing. He groaned, then his eyes snapped wide and he sat up with a start. "What happened?" he blurted out, staring at his naked lower leg. "Now I remember!" He look at Nate. "You struck me!"

"It was either that or let you bleed to death."

Tim Curry was about to give King a piece of his mind when a fresh wave of pain washed over him. He cried out and pressed his hands to his leg above the ankle. "Oh, Lord! It hurts!"

Shakespeare checked the pot to see if the water was boiling, then fixed a critical eye on the greenhorn. "If you intend to earn the respect of others out here, you can't go around blubbering like you do."

"You wouldn't be saying that if it had been you the trap caught," Tim responded. "I bet you'd be acting the same as I am."

"In the first place," Shakespeare said, "I know enough not to go traipsing into water near a trap stake. In the second place, I've been hurt far worse than you and as a general rule I didn't blubber. Pain is part and parcel of life. Accept the truth of that and you won't be so bothered by little accidents like this one." He picked up one of the strips and dipped it in the bubbling water, mindful of his fingers.

"Little?" Tim grumbled. "I nearly lost my foot!"

"You didn't even come close," Shakespeare said. "Had it been a bear trap, that would be a whole different story. We'd be cauterizing the stump right about now."

Tim hugged his leg to his chest, appalled by the mental image of his foot being severed. "How was I to know a trap was there? Neither of you told me."

Nate was in the act of changing from his wet leggings to a spare dry pair. He looked up and said, "We tried, but you walked out there too fast. You have to learn to look before you leap in these mountains, or one of these day you'll be sorry."

"Who would have thought stepping into a stream would be so dangerous?" Tim whined.

Shakespeare pulled the soaked strip out. "You just don't get it, do you, young coon? *Everything* you do in the wilderness can be dangerous if you don't pay attention. Something as simple as putting an edge on a knife could cause you to lose a finger if your hand slips. Or you might be loading your rifle and accidentally blow your head off. Or maybe you'll go into the bushes to heed Nature's call and forget to take a gun and a grizzly will spot you and decide you look right tasty."

"Surely you exaggerate," Tim said. "It can't be as bad as all that."

"I don't blow about words when someone's life is at stake," Shakespeare said with rare irritation. "I'm trying to help you, you dunderhead, but your head is thicker than most."

"I'd listen to him, Tim," Nate threw in. "The only reason I'm alive today is because I took his advice to heart." He stood, fully clothed again. "I know it goes against the grain to think you don't know it all, but you don't, hoss."

Tim elected to say nothing. He was mildly upset with himself. He'd tagged along with them to learn, yet here he was giving them such a difficult time. What was the matter with him? Didn't he have the brains God gave a turnip?

Shakespeare moved nearer holding an end of the strip in each hand. "This will smart some," he announced. "You might want to bite down on a stick."

"Do what you must," Tim said, resolved to show them he wasn't the pampered coward they thought he was. "I can handle it." He gritted his teeth and tensed, prepared for the worst. Or so he thought. The scalding-hot material seemed to sear right through his skin and sent bolts of fire boiling up his leg. He involuntarily squawked, then choked it off by biting his lip.

"If you'd used the stick, Troilus," Shakespeare casually remarked as he wound the strip around the gash, "your lip wouldn't be bleeding."

"What did you call me?" Tim grunted through clenched teeth.

"A character from one of old William S.'s plays," Shakespeare said.

"Any reason you picked *him?*" Tim asked in order to take his mind off the discomfort.

"The two of you have a lot in common."

"Such as?"

McNair finished looping the material and dipped a second bandage in the scalding water. "Troilus and you"—he paused to swirl the fabric before quoting—"are weaker than a woman's tear, tamer than sleep, fonder than ignorance, less valiant than the virgin in the night, and skilless as unpracticed infancy."

"That's an insult," Tim huffed.

"It just means you have a lot of growing to do," Shakespeare said, unruffled. "As do we all."

Nate walked off to tether the horses. His mentor's bluntness surprised him. Usually McNair was much more tactful in dealing with those unfortunate enough to be suffering from the lingering effects of civilized society. But he could understand why McNair wasn't mincing words. Young Curry had to learn fast or he wouldn't last out the season.

Every horse had to be tethered for the night. Trappers who failed to tie their animals invariably spent most of the next morning rounding up their stock. It wasn't bad enough that horses strayed off on their own accord. Any loud noises, such as the caterwauling of panthers or the roars of grizzlies, might spook them into terrified flight. And there was always the constant threat of Indians, who accorded high honors to warriors brave enough to steal mounts right out from under the noses of their enemies. As a result of all these factors, the trappers had a popular saying: "It's better to count ribs than tracks." Which simply meant it was better to tie a horse and be able to count his ribs the next day instead of the tracks the animal made as it fled or was led away.

Nate took his time. When done, he strolled to the fire and sat down to enjoy a cup of steaming black coffee. Tim Curry lay on his back, resting, while McNair read from his book of Shakespeare. Overhead, the firmament was liberally sprinkled with sparkling stars. A strong breeze rustled the treetops and fanned the flames. Off in the distance an elk trumpeted. The tranquil setting brought a sigh of contentment to Nate's lips.

"It looks as if Troilus will be laid up for a day or two," Shakespeare announced. "One of us will have to set his traps for him."

"I'll go out first," Nate said, eager to venture abroad after so many days in the saddle.

"I'll let you," Shakespeare said. "It'll give me a chance to catch up on my reading."

"You've already read every play three times over."

"I'm working on the fourth."

Nate settled back, looking forward to a nice, restful night. He should have known better. For from the mountain slope across the stream came a guttural grunt that caused all the horses to prick their ears and some to fidget.

"I was hoping it hadn't seen us," Shakespeare said.

"What?" Tim asked, propping himself on his elbows. He'd heard similar grunts before, but had never been able to learn what made them. Wild pigs, he'd assumed. "What's out there?"

"That grizzly we saw earlier."

Tim sat up and placed a hand on his pistol. "Will it bother us, do you think?"

"There's no predicting how grizzlies will behave," Shakespeare said. "They're some of the most cantankerous, fickle creatures in all of God's creation. No two ever act the same. Some will run if they so much as catch a whiff of man scent. Others will go out of their way to hunt a man down." He tossed a new log on the fire. "All we can do is hope this one has never gotten a taste of human flesh."

"Why's that?"

"Once they do, they can't seem to get enough. Maybe we're tastier than most other creatures. Or maybe we're just easier to kill. Whatever, it's a known fact that once a grizzly has filled its belly with human flesh, it craves more."

Tim Curry suddenly felt more frail and vulnerable than he ever had before. In his condition he wouldn't be able to run very far or very fast and would be easy prey for any predator. He stared at the gloomy wall of darkness ringing them and longed for daylight so nothing could sneak up on them unnoticed.

The grunt was repeated, only much closer. Nate took his Hawken and walked to the edge of the clearing nearest the stream. The brush on the far slope was so thick a man would be hard pressed to move through it without making noise, yet the huge grizzly didn't break so much as a twig.

Nate went all the way to the bank and knelt, cocking the Hawken. Although he waited for ten minutes, the grizzly never gave its location away. He convinced himself the bear had opted to find game elsewhere and rose to return. It was then, in a thicket directly across from where he stood, that a bush shook as if with the ague. He crouched and tucked the stock to his right shoulder.

A vague shape materialized in the night, a massive form that blotted out the bush and the lower third of a sizeable pine tree. Nate wanted to fire, but held off because he couldn't pinpoint the bear's head and anything less than a fatal head shot would bring the monster down on him in a flash. The beast moved a few feet and Nate heard loud sniffing. A second later it turned and lumbered into the vegetation, making an exceptional amount of noise.

Nate followed its progress and determined that the bear was moving northward parallel to the stream. He hoped it would cross, since its silhouette against the lighter backdrop of the water might give him a reasonably clear shot. The grizzly plodded on, though, still creating a racket, almost as if it was deliberately stomping the underbrush for his benefit. Then, of a sudden, the forest fell silent.

Puzzled, Nate shifted position a few feet to the north. He remained motionless for minutes on end, until certain the grizzly had gone elsewhere. Lowering the hammer on the Hawken, he walked toward the fire, vastly relieved. But his relief was premature.

A tremendous splashing broke out in the vicinity of where Nate had last heard the bear. Spinning, he dashed to the stream and beheld an enormous shadow disappearing into the pines on his side of the stream. Instantly, Nate raced for the camp, shouting, "Shakespeare! It's coming! It's coming!"

Nate ran for all he was worth. He saw McNair leap erect, rifle at the ready. Tim Curry lifted a pistol, which was as useless against a grizzly as a slingshot. The horses had caught the bear's strong scent and were rearing and kicking while neighing loud enough to rouse the dead. Nate went past them on the fly and stood by McNair. "See it yet?"

"Not hide nor hair," Shakespeare replied, moving so they were back to back and could cover both sides of the clearing. "But I've heard him once or twice."

A loud snap accented the statement. Nate concentrated on fir trees to the east, and observed several shake even though the wind had temporarily died. Flicking firelight danced on the limbs, lending the woods an ominous aspect. He thought he glimpsed a hairy mass moving slowly southward and deduced the beast was circling them. The fire was keeping the bear at bay for the time being, but might not do so for long.

Tim Curry glanced every which way, his arm shaking a little as he tried to hold the flintlock steady. "Where is the thing?" he whispered.

Nate was too busy trying to spot the bear to bother answering. McNair was equally occupied. The horses were becoming more and more frantic, apparently sensing the grizzly had drawn closer to them. Nate was worried that some might break free, so he took a few paces in their direction, thinking he should attempt to calm them down.

Tim Curry was a nervous wreck. He saw shaggy behemoths in every flickering play of light. The fact that neither of the mountain men had answered him only served to confirm his conviction the situation was desperate. So when another crisp snap shattered the nerve-racking stillness, he spun, thought he saw the bear peering at them from under a pine, and fired.

The shot had unforeseen effects, the most immediate of which was the terror it provoked in the already scared horses. Several became uncontrollable. One broke loose and galloped madly into the forest. Another effect was an abrupt series of snarls to the southwest, followed by the heavy crashing of foliage as the grizzly ran off.

Nate began to run after the fleeing horse, but stopped on realizing the futility of his gesture. He had no hope of catching it, but ran a great risk of stumbling on the bear. Halting close to the trees, he listened to the rapidly dwindling sounds of the pell-mell flight.

Shakespeare hastened to the rest of the horses and went from animal to animal, soothing their frayed nerves by speaking softly and stroking their necks. Nate soon lent a hand, and between the two of them they quieted the entire string. As they went to reclaim their seats, Shakespeare saw the stern look in Nate's eyes and touched Nate's elbow. "Let me handle this," he requested softly.

Tim was trying to reload, but his hands shook so badly he spilled most of the black powder he poured down the muzzle. He glanced up and asked excitedly, "Did I get it?"

"With that?" Nate responded angrily. "Mister, you'd do better throwing marbles. The bear wouldn't get quite so riled."

Rebuffed, Tim lowered his pistol, spilling more powder. "Why are you so upset? I saw the brute, clear as day. What else was I supposed to do?"

Shakespeare sat next to the greenhorn and took the flintlock. "Allow me," he said. As he opened his powder horn, he said, "Remember what I told you about looking, listening, and learning? You should have paid attention to us, and if you had you would have noticed that we were holding our fire until we could see what we were shooting at."

"But I . . ." Tim began, and stopped when the older man held up a hand.

"Let me finish, son," Shakespeare said. He wagged the pistol. "A piece like this is no good against a grizzly. Their skulls are so thick, the balls bounce off. And if you'd wounded that bear, as sure as you're sitting there, it would have charged us." Shakespeare paused. "You ever had a grizzly come at you from out of the dark?"

"No."

"I have, and it's not something I'd rate as one of life's great experiences. In the time it takes you to blink your eye, a grizzly can swat you twenty feet or rip you apart with one swipe. And believe me, that's not a pretty sight."

Tim bowed his head. Now that he had a moment to reflect, he wasn't so certain he'd seen the bear. His imagination might have gotten the better of him. "I made a mess of things again, didn't I?"

"We're still alive, so no real harm was done," Shakespeare said, offering a kindly grin. "The loss of a horse will be bothersome when it's time to pack out our plews, but we can live with it."

"True," Nate chimed in. Curry was so downcast, Nate regretted snapping at him. "And I'm a fine one to be mad. You should have seen some of the dunderhead stunts I pulled when I was green to the Rockies. My being here today is proof that fools and simpletons have their own guardian angels."

Shakespeare clapped the youth on the back. "I'll vouch for that. So cheer up, Troilus. Another day, another lesson learned."

"I'll try," Tim said. But deep down he was worried. For the first time since leaving Maine his mettle had been seriously tested, and his insides had turned to mush. He'd always believed he was as brave as the next man, but now he had his doubts. Would he act the same if hostile Indians showed? Would he be so rattled he couldn't load a gun?

Nate had taken his seat on the other side of the fire. He leaned the Hawken on his saddle, then reached behind him to pull the lower half of the eagle feather into view. "Recollect me telling you about the Cheyenne who gave me this?"

A dull nod was Tim's response.

"I didn't tell you the whole story," Nate said. "The same warrior also saw me tangle with a grizzly. He thought I handled myself well. But I don't mind admitting that I was never more scared in my whole life than when that hairy devil came at me."

"You were?"

Nate nodded. "And that wasn't the last time I've been scared hell and cooked. We all suffer a fright now and again. The trick is to find your grit and bounce back."

The youth settled down on his blankets to ponder. Not in a hundred years would he have suspected King of being afraid of anything, man or beast. And if someone of King's caliber knew fear on occasion, he figured he shouldn't be so hard on himself for the same failing. He had to give himself time to adjust, to find his grit, as King put it. Then he'd show them. He'd show everyone that Timothy Curry was a man to be reckoned with.

Shakespeare pulled out his pipe. He was mightily pleased at how Nate had handled the situation. It justified his trust in Nate's judgment, and his decision years ago to take Nate under his wing and do for Nate as he would have done for the son he'd never had, the son he'd always wanted.

For Nate's part, he laid back discontented. The incident had confirmed that greenhorns were unreliable, and some more unreliable than others. He wanted to help Curry learn the ropes, but not at the expense of his life and McNair's. Something told him that unless he was extremely careful, the youth would bring more hardship down on their heads. And in the raw, savage wilderness, where survival of the fittest was the unwritten law for all, hardship had a nasty habit of leading to the ultimate affliction; death itself.

Chapter Three

Nathaniel King spent the entire next day setting traps by himself. Prior experience had honed his skills to where he was a master at locating ideal places and putting the traps where they would be the most effective.

Trapping was never done in a haphazard fashion. There was a science to the procedure that every mountain man made sure to know intimately since his livelihood depended on his ability.

First off, a trapper had to find a stretch of stream beaver frequented. Their marvelous dams and intricate domed lodges were dead giveaways. Then came the next, critical step.

Not many people back in the States knew much about the habits of beaver. Few knew, for instance, that beaver had a way of marking their territory, much like dogs. In the case of beaver, the marking was done by the animal bringing a small amount of mud up from the bottom, smearing it on the bank, and then dabbing the mud with a sticky yellow substance secreted from its glands. Whenever other beaver caught the scent, they invariably made straight for the spot to dab on their own mud and secrete castoreum.

This was their weakness, the Achilles heel the trappers exploited. For it was by smearing mud and gland extract on the banks of waterways, and submerging traps at points where the beaver would climb out to investigate, that trappers snared their prey.

Nate stored his castoreum in a small wooden box he kept in his possibles bag. On this particular morning he had set five of the six traps he'd toted from camp, and was opening the box to dip the tip of a stick inside for more castoreum when he had the distinct feeling that he was being watched. Seasoned trappers knew the sensation well. A prickling at the nape of the neck combined with a tingling in the mind, an instinctive alarm that something was amiss.

Nate knew better than to leap up and scour the landscape. Whoever, or whatever, was out there would duck down and he'd never spot them. No, he continued to work, applying a small amount of castoreum to a large patch of mud, while at the same time, shifting from side to side, he looked out the corners of his eyes.

Waving grass gave the culprit away. Nate saw it move, 20 feet to his left, but didn't let on. He made a show of closing the castoreum box and replacing it in the possibles bag. He still had to establish whether he was being watched by a human or an animal. Standing, he stepped to the last trap and bent to grip the chain. The grass parted, and he was astounded to see the face of a small Indian boy peeking at him.

Acting as if he hadn't noticed, Nate carried the trap to the end of the bank. On the one hand, he was relieved it was only a child. On the other, the boy's presence meant a village must be near-by, much too close for comfort. Should the boy's people prove to be Utes, he would have to alert McNair and get out of there before they lost their hair. If Crows, the situation was little better since the Crows were notoriously unreliable.

Nate had to talk to the child. In order to trick the boy into thinking he wasn't aware of anyone being nearby, Nate set the trap. He stood with a foot on each spring, bent, and opened the jaws. It was delicate work to adjust the pan so that the dog caught in the notch. Then he carefully lowered the trap to the streambed, stretched the chain to its full length, and firmly drove a stake into the bottom. His stake, like the one left by the mys-terious trapper who had abandoned the trap Cur-ry stepped in, had been chopped from hard, dry wood. Using freshly cut wood invited failure since it was a favorite fare of the beaver.

Wading to shore, Nate clambered out and shook his legs. He contrived to move close to the patch of high grass. A hint of buckskin assured him the boy was still there. So whipping around, he dived.

The boy was jackrabbit-quick. He came up off the ground in a rush and turned to flee. Nate bare-ly caught hold of an ankle, and held fast. The boy shrieked and tugged on his leg, but he was no match for Nate's vast strength. Holding on, Nate lunged and grabbed the boy around the waist. He almost missed seeing the knife that arced at his chest, and caught the boy's wrist at the last second. The wildcat kicked and clawed, trying to gouge Nate's eyes out. Nate merely swiveled, swinging the boy over his hip, and tossed the spunky youngster to the earth. The boy, groggy, tried to stand, so Nate pinned him with one knee, then wrested the butcher knife loose.

Clarity returned to the boy's dark eyes. He vainly tried to move the big knee astride him, then gave up and glowered, his expression saying more eloquently than words that he expected to die but would die as a true warrior should.

Nate tested the blade on his thumb and found it razor sharp. Tossing the knife aside, he addressed his captive in the universal Indian tongue, sign language. "Question. How are you called?"

The boy seemed surprised that Nate could communicate. He twisted, slapped at Nate's knee, and finally subsided, signing, "My name is known far and wide as the name of a fierce fighter, white dog! Kill me if you will, but know that Gray Badger, the son of Two Humps, does not fear you."

"I am known as Grizzly Killer," Nate signed. "I kill grizzlies, not boys too small to climb on horses by themselves."

Gray Badger puffed his cheeks like an enraged chipmunk. "I have seen twelve winters, white man! I can ride better than you."

Nate held back a smile. He knew that Indian boys were plunked on horses at the tender age of four, and by the time they were ten, they were adroit riders. "Perhaps you can," he signed, "but I can run faster than you can. So I can catch you easily if you try to run off." He paused. "Will you give me your word that you will not try to flee if I let you up?"

The boy's brow knit. "I really am not going to die?"

"Not today. Not by my hand." Nate uncoiled. He grasped the youngster's wrist and pulled the boy upright. "Do I have your promise?"

Gray Badger regarded him suspiciously. "Question. Why would you take the word of your enemy?"

"Even enemies can have a sense of honor," Nate responded, trying to identify the boy's tribe from the child's clothes and hair style. Neither revealed much. Gray Badger wore his hair long and loose, not braided in any particular fashion. His buckskin leggings might have been made by a woman belonging to any of a dozen tribes. The boy's moccasins, however, were different from most. "And I have no reason to call a Crow my enemy unless he shows me that he has a bad heart."

"How did you know I am a Crow?"

"No two tribes make moccasins the same," Nate signed. He stared off down the valley, seeking columns of smoke. "How far off is your village?"

"I do not know."

"Are you lost?"

"A Crow does not lose his way in the woods."

"Then how can you not know where your village is?"

"Maybe I do know," Gray Badger allowed. "Maybe I do not trust you enough to tell you where to find my people."

That made sense, but Nate suspected there was more to the boy's reluctance to answer than Gray Badger let on. He wondered if possibly the boy was on a family outing. "Where is your father and mother?"

"Far away from here."

"Then who are you here with?"

"No one."

"Straight tongue?"

"Whites lie, not Crows," Gray Badger signed indignantly.

Nate was unwilling to accept the boy's assertion.

Gray Badger was too young to be permitted to wander any great distance from a village alone. So either the Crow had lied to protect others who were close at hand, or there was much more to this than met the eye. "Where is your horse?"

"I do not have one."

Now Nate was doubly skeptical. The Crow nation had acquired horses shortly after the early Spanish exploration of the Rockies, and had adapted to them as readily as the Sioux and the Cheyennes. Crows never went any great distance unless it was on horseback. And boys were given their first ponies when they were barely old enough to walk. "Your family must be very poor," he signed.

Gray Badger bristled as if insulted. "My father is one of the richest men in our tribe. He has three hundred horses all his own. And that does not count the many horses he has given away to those in need."

"Two Humps is a chief," Nate deduced, basing his judgment on the knowledge that only prominent warriors owned so many animals.

"My father is a man of great importance," Gray Badger boasted. Strangely, his countenance fell, as if the admission saddened him. "He does not let his sons want for anything."

"Except horses."

The boy's temper made him careless. "Had I wanted, I could have taken any animal my father owns. But I needed to leave quietly, on foot."

"You snuck away from your own people?" Nate signed. "Why? Were you in trouble with your parents? Were you being punished and you did not think the punishment fair?"

Gray Badger lifted his hands to reply, hesitated, then dropped them to his sides.

"Very well," Nate signed. "As you have made

clear, your affairs are not my concern. Go in peace. I wish you well." He picked up his trap sack, slung it over his shoulder, and headed northward, hoping he wasn't making a numskull mistake that would cost him dearly. If there was a village near, the boy would take off like a shot. If there wasn't, if he was right about there being more to this than seemed apparent, then the boy might tag along with him, out of curiosity if for no other reason. He refrained from glancing back until he came to the first bend, and he grinned on discovering the Crow youngster a dozen paces behind.

Going on, Nate debated whether to lead the boy all the way to camp or to try to get to the bottom of things beforehand. He hiked a quarter of a mile and stopped beside a log perched on a cutoff. There he sat, pretending to rest.

Gray Badger had halted. He made no attempt to hide or flee, nor did he approach any closer.

Nate opened his possibles bag and took out some venison jerky. He broke off a piece and chewed lustily, smacking his lips as if it was the best meal he'd eaten in ages. The boy licked his lips and fidgeted, taking a step forward, then a step back. "Question. Would you like to eat?" Nate signed.

The young Crow was in the grip of a quandary. His hunger was obvious, yet his pride prevented him from giving in.

Taking another, bigger bite, Nate made as much noise as a hog at the feed trough, thankful his wife wasn't there to hear him or he'd never hear the end of it. He was the one who always insisted their children eat with their mouths closed. New York upbringing did that to people.

Practically watering at the mouth, Gray Badger advanced. "I would be grateful to share your food," he signed with all the dignity of a warrior invited to attend a grand feast. He took a seat at arm's length and accepted a thick piece of jerky. Rather than wolf it, he bit off a small chunk and chewed slowly, savoring the morsel.

Nate was impressed by the boy's self-control. He finished eating in silence, then signed, "I am with two friends. Our camp is not far, and you are welcome to come with me and share the rabbit stew we will have later. There will be more than enough for everyone."

The boy had frozen in the act of taking a nibble. "There are more white men?" he signed, unable to hide his apprehension. "Are they like you or like him?"

"Who?"

Gray Badger suddenly crammed half the piece into his mouth and chomped down. He gazed at the stream, clearly stalling. "How do I know your friends will be as kind as you?"

"You do not," Nate admitted, "but you have my pledge that no harm will come to you while you are under my protection." He didn't press the issue of the other white man the boy alluded to. All in good time, he told himself. To further soothe the young Crow's fears, he added, "I have a son about your age. You remind me of him."

"I do?"

"Both of you are more fond of food than you are anything else," Nate signed, grinning to show he meant it as a joke. The boy smiled for the first time. "Once, my son, Stalking Coyote, ate a whole buffalo at one sitting."

"He did not," Gray Badger signed, laughing.

Nate beckoned and resumed his journey. Now that he had an opportunity to examine the youngster at his leisure, he observed that the boy's leggings and moccasins were grimy with dirt, a condition no mother would abide. The boy's face also bore more smudges than regular washing would allow. The only conclusion Nate could reach was that Gray Badger had indeed been on his own for quite a while. But why? What had driven the boy to flee his own tribe? "Question. Was your village attacked by the Utes or another war party recently?"

Gray Badger appeared surprised. "No. Why do you ask me this?"

"Just a thought I had," Nate signed. They had to go around a sharp curve in the stream, past a gravel bar bordered by thick mud. Nate was half-way across when he spied several gigantic prints in the mud that hadn't been there when he went downstream. Halting, he measured the length and breadth with his hand, then whistled in amazement. The grizzly's front paws were seven inches long, the hindpaws 14 inches in length. The claws were fives inches alone. A truly gargantuan beast by any standard.

"I am glad I did not meet this bear," Gray Badger signed. "He would have swallowed me whole."

Nate grinned to be polite. Deep down, though, he was immensely troubled. Bears were roamers by nature, foraging far afield to fill their stomachs. Often when they encountered humans and were shot at, they went elsewhere until the humans left the area. This one had stayed, indicating the grizzly regarded the valley as its home. Bears always had one place they liked to come back to, a special den where they holed up in cold weather and bore their young. There must be just such a den somewhere in the valley.

Nate ran a finger along the bottom of one of the prints, guessing how long it had been there by the texture and dryness of the mud. Under an hour, he concluded, and scanned the mountain flanking the gravel strip in case the grizzly was watching them from on high.

Gray Badger was doing the same. "I lost an uncle to a great bear two winters ago. My favorite uncle, and he was slashed in half, his face eaten. My father and others wanted to go after it and kill it, but he would not let us."

"Who would not?" Nate signed absently while scouring the underbrush.

"He who is High Chief of all the Crows."

Had Nate been paying more attention, he might have attached more importance to the comment. But since tribes often had several chiefs, he let the remark go by. Later he would regret not prying to obtain more information. For now, he hurried to camp to let Shakespeare and the greenhorn know about the bear. The stream widened into a wide pool, and out in the middle sat a large beaver lodge. He hardly noticed, but the boy did.

"Question? Will you tell me something, Grizzly Killer?"

"If I can," Nate signed.

"Why are beaver hides so important to you whites? Why do you leave your own country and come to ours to catch them?"

Thinking the questions stemmed from the youth having seen him set traps, Nate answered as simply as he could. "Our women like beaver as much as Crow women like beads and red blankets. Our men use beaver to trade for things they want, much as Crow men do with horses."

"But why beaver, of all the animals?" Gray Badger asked, still perplexed. "Buffalo robes keep us warmer, bear hides are thicker and last longer, deer hides smell better when wet. Beaver hides are not special."

"True," Nate said. He wanted to explain about the white man's sense of fashion, and how beaver fur was all the rage in the States and over in Europe, but the concept was alien to Indian thought. There was no sign language equivalent for the English word "fashion." Indians were primarily interested in functional clothes, which was why the vast majority wore buckskin shirts and leggings and dresses.

"Then why?" Gray Badger persisted, his tone implying it was of earthshaking importance.

Nate glanced at him. "Some things are hard to explain. The best I can do is tell you that whites value beaver as highly as Crows value buffalo."

Through the trees the clearing appeared. The boy missed a stride, recovered, and moved a little closer to Nate. "Are you sure your friends will welcome me in peace?"

"No one will harm you."

McNair was rummaging in a parfleche. Tim Curry was honing his knife on a whetstone. Both looked up on hearing footsteps and both did a double take.

"We have company," Nate announced.

"So I see," Shakespeare said, smiling at the Crow. "Where the dickens did you find the whippersnapper?"

"He found me."

Tim sat straighter, studying the boy with ill-concealed mistrust. "What's he doing here? Are we close to a village and don't even know it?"

"I haven't been able to get a whole lot out of him," Nate admitted. "But I think we have a runaway on our hands."

"Do tell," Shakespeare said, pulling pemmican from the parfleche. "Maybe I'll have better luck. I speak Crow fairly well."

"You never have told me about the time you spent among them," Nate mentioned. The last he'd counted, McNair was conversant with five Indian tongues and knew another three or four well enough to get by in a pinch.

"My abject apology," Shakespeare said with mock gravity. "Had I known you were supposed to know every little thing about me, I would have sat down long ago and made you a list of all I've done and learned over the years." Twisting, he saw the boy hungrily eyeing his pemmican. "Care for some?" he asked in the Crow tongue.

Gray Badger took a step backward and put a hand over his mouth, expressing astonishment.

"Yes, I know your language," Shakespeare went on amiably. "It is one of the easiest tongues for white men to learn. We can use it without twisting our tongues into knots." He took a bite of the pemmican, a popular Indian food made by pounding dry meat to a fine consistency and mixing it with melted animal fat.

Nate guessed what McNair was up to and commented, "I've already fed him jerky."

"Oh?" Shakespeare held out the pemmican and the boy snatched it. "I haven't met a coon his age yet who doesn't have a bottomless pit for a stomach."

Tim Curry was troubled and voiced his feelings. "Should we be doing this? What if he was sent by a war party to spy on us? For all we know there are hordes of braves lurking in the woods right this instant, waiting for this boy's signal before they pounce."

"You missed your calling, Troilus," Shakespeare responded. "With the imagination you have, you should be a fiction writer like James Fenimore Cooper instead of a trapper."

"I'm serious. I've heard tell Indians try tricks like this."

Shakespeare slowly stood. "Your life will be a whole lot happier, son, if you believe only half of what you see and a third of what you hear."

Annoyed at being taken so lightly, Tim turned away and folded his arms across his chest. "Fine," he said. "Treat me like an idiot. But don't say I didn't warn you when we're set upon and wind up being burned at the stake."

Neither Nate nor McNair felt compelled to inform the greenhorn that they had never heard of a single instance in which a white man had met his end in that particular manner. Nate poured himself a cup of coffee while Shakespeare watched the famished boy eat.

"What are we going to do?" Nate inquired. "We can't just keep him around. Sooner or later a search party is bound to show up." He took a sip. "If only we knew what brought him to the valley."

"Let's find out," Shakespeare said, and switched to the Crow language. "We are very curious, my young friend. We would like to know what you are doing here. And where we can find your village."

The boy had been chewing heartily. He stopped, suddenly downcast, and fixed his gaze on the ground. "If I tell you, you will make me go back. He will be mad and punish me. I will be beaten."

"Who will? Your father?" Shakespeare asked, convinced the boy was lying. Many years ago he'd spent two winters living with Crows and learned that it was against tribal custom for parents to use corporal punishment on their children.

"No. Invincible One will order it done."

"Is that the name of your chief?"

"It is the name . . ." Gray Badger began, lifting his head, and abruptly stopped, fear lining his smooth features as he looked over McNair's right shoulder.

Shakespeare spun, dreading the grizzly had returned. Instead, he found the clearing partially ringed by a score of somber Crow warriors.

Chapter Four

Nate King was in the act of removing six traps from a pack so he could set them later in the day when he heard the boy's sharp intake of breath. He glanced up, then swiftly rose, his Hawken in hand. As yet none of the Crows had brought a weapon to bear, but their expressions did not bode well. Sidling closer to the sulking greenhorn, he nudged Curry with a toe.

"What do you want?" Tim asked brusquely while staring off in space.

"We have more visitors."

Tim shifted, cursed, and went for one of his pistols. His hand was closing on the butt when Nate's hand clamped on his shoulder.

"Don't be a fool. There are too many. They'd fill us full of arrows before you got off a shot."

"What do we do, then?" Tim whispered.

"We let them make the first move," Nate said, "and pray to high heaven they're friendly."

"Maybe we should make a run for it," Tim proposed. "If we can get to the horses before they do, they'll never catch us. They're all on foot."

"You're not up to running with your ankle in the shape it is," Nate reminded him. "And for all we know, their mounts are back in the trees."

"We can't just do nothing!"

"That's exactly what we will do," Nate said. "We don't want to provoke them if we can avoid it. We have too much to lose."

"Don't worry on my account."

"I was thinking of the horses and all our gear." Nate took a step to the left so he would have a clear shot as the Crows warily advanced. He pegged a stocky man with an arrogant strut as the leader of the band, and he didn't care for the way the man openly sneered at them.

Shakespeare's rifle lay propped on his saddle. He edged toward it while proclaiming, "Greetings to our Crow brothers! Come, join us for coffee and pemmican. There is plenty to go around."

On hearing their own tongue, the Crows halted to a man. The stocky brave, who held a fusee, cocked his head and demanded, "Who are you, white man, and how do you know our tongue?"

"My Indian name is Wolverine," Shakespeare disclosed, "and I learned the ways of the Crows when I lived among the people of the great chief Long Hair many winters ago."

"Many is right," the spokesman declared. "Long Hair was killed by Blackfeet when I was half the age I am now." He touched his chest. "I am called Whirlwind Hawk."

"You are welcome at our fire."

Whirlwind Hawk motioned, and all the Crows came several feet nearer. None made any threatening gestures. Neither did they smile or give any other indication of being overly friendly.

Nate grew uneasy. Not only did he have no idea what was being said, he was now hemmed in on three sides and there were too many warriors for him to hold at bay with just three guns. Moving so that his back was to the fire, he tried to keep them all in sight at once.

"You have done us a favor, Wolverine," Whirlwind Hawk told Shakespeare, and pointed at the boy. "We have been searching for Gray Badger for six sleeps. His father will be pleased to have him back."

"Is his father named Invincible One?"

Whirlwind Hawk scowled. "No. Two Humps." He paused. "What did the boy tell you about Invincible One?"

"Only his name. Is he a chief?"

"Invincible One rules our people."

"Interesting," Shakespeare said. "I thought I knew all the high chiefs of the Crow nation by name if not on sight, and yet I have never heard of this man."

"Invincible One is not chief of all the Crows. He is chief of our village alone."

"Your chief has a very unusual name."

"Invincible One is a very unusual man," Whirlwind Hawk said. Again he took a few steps, and at his cue so did the rest. A mere six feet separated the crescent of Crows from the three free trappers.

Nate fingered the hammer of his rifle. "Shakespeare," he interrupted, "I don't like this one bit. What do they want? Are they after the boy?"

McNair turned to answer, and Whirlwind Hawk chose that moment to yip like a coyote. At the signal all the warriors sprang forward. So swift was their attack that they were on the vastly outnumbered trappers before a shot could be fired.

Nate King tried. He brought the Hawken up and was leveling it at one of the braves when he was rammed into by two more, one tackling him low, the other catching him in the chest with a stony shoulder. Nate tumbled backwards, losing his grip on the Hawken. With a start he realized he was falling into the fire, and he threw himself to the right to escape the flames. The Indian holding his legs let out a squawk and let go, allowing Nate to scramble to his knees as more warriors swarmed in.

Nate had a glimpse of Shakespeare fighting madly and Tim Curry being overwhelmed by four adversaries. Then he had to devote all his energy to preserving his own life. A warrior grabbed his left arm and he buried his right fist in the man's stomach. Another Crow pounced on him from behind, looping an arm about his neck. Nate bent, flipping the man clear over him into another onrushing brave.

Momentarily free, Nate rose and tried to unlimber his tomahawk. He was set upon by two assailants who grabbed his shoulders in order to fling him to the ground. Nate planted knuckles on the mouth of one, then kicked the other in the knee. Both crumpled.

Ducking under an awkward punch thrown by a skinny Crow, Nate retaliated with a sweeping right cross that rocked the man on his heels. He landed another blow to the midsection of a warrior, who staggered aside. Skipping to the left, Nate suddenly realized that not one of his attackers had relied on a weapon. There could only be one explanation: The Crows wanted to take them alive! Already Tim Curry was down and being bound at the wrists. Nate couldn't see Shakespeare, but from the commotion McNair was putting up one hell of a fight.

Suddenly Whirlwind Hawk himself appeared. He barked words that Nate didn't understand, then launched himself at Nate with both arms extended. Nate slipped out of the way, seized Whirlwind Hawk's wrist, and swung with all his might, flinging the stocky warrior into two others.

Pivoting, Nate spied his Hawken and started for it. A Crow was faster. Since further resistance would result in certain capture, Nate decided to make a break for it and come back to help his friends later. He sprinted toward the horses, going less than ten feet when he was overhauled by several fleet warriors. Hands gripped his shirt, his arm, his right leg.

The ground leaped up at Nate's face. He managed to twist so that his shoulder bore the brunt of the impact. Then he was on one knee and slugging fiercely, raining punches on Crow after Crow, dropping one after another only to have more take their place. He shoved to his feet, was hit low in the back. Pain lancing his spine, he spun and clipped the man responsible on the chin.

From all directions at once sped more Crows. Six, seven, eight warriors buried Nate under their combined weight. He punched, kicked, pumped his elbows into faces and necks. Crows grunted, cried out, roared in frustration. Iron fingers found his wrists and ankles and held on. Gradually his strength ebbed and his limbs were pinned. He looked up at a circle of bloody, battered faces.

Shakespeare McNair still fought on. Not for nothing had the Flatheads named him Wolverine decades ago when he first came to the vast Rockies. He had been one of the first white men to set foot in the pristine realm the Indians called home, and all the tribes had been impressed by the strange newcomer whose honesty was beyond reproach and whose savagery in battle was memorable.

Few of the current crop of hardy free trappers knew much about Shakespeare's past. The same even applied to Nate, who had been taken into the mountain man's confidence. Most had heard stories circulated by Indians belonging to the four tribes who claimed McNair had lived among them at one time or another. Of his early exploits, the most persistent were about his prowess in battle.

Many of the younger trappers rated the tales as so much nonsense. They would hear of the time Shakespeare supposedly slew eight Bloods in personal combat using nothing but a tomahawk, and they would look at the white-haired legend with his slightly drooped shoulders and seamed features and would shake their heads in wry amusement.

But the stories were true, as the Blackfoot Confederacy, the Comanches, and the Apaches could all attest. McNair was the most peaceable of men most of the time. Until riled. Then he transformed himself into a raging wolverine.

This day the Crows were finding it out the hard way. Strive as they might, they couldn't subdue McNair. Despite his years, he was panther-quick and coiled steel. Hitting and kicking and gouging and biting, he held them off. Slippery as an eel and as sinuous as a snake, he slipped out of their grasp again and again.

Only four Crows had converged on him at the outset of the fight. He was the oldest, Whirlwind Hawk had reasoned when spying on the whites from the brush, so he would be the easiest to capture. But it was the youngest trapper who had succumbed first after hardly offering any resistance. The next oldest had put up a terrific struggle, but now was bound. Leaving only the old man, who put the Crows to shame with his tenacity.

At a command from Whirlwind Hawk, all the warriors except for two formed a circle around Shakespeare. Whirlwind Hawk wiped a trickle of blood from his throbbing bottom lip, then held his hand aloft. "Will you come quietly now, Wolverine? You have my word that you will not be harmed."

Shakespeare McNair was covered with sweat and panting heavily. The exertion had drained him of energy, sapped his vitality. He girded his reservoir of stamina and straightened, adopting a grim front for the benefit of the Crows. "You expect me to trust a man who took advantage of our hospitality and attacked us without reason? You have no honor, and the Blanket Chief will know as much when he finds we have been made prisoners."

"The Blanket Chief is in this area?"

"He is, with sixty others," Shakespeare lied with a straight face. He referred to the one trapper nearly all Indians knew, Jim Bridger, whose firm dealings with them on behalf of the Rocky Mountain Fur Company had earned him a widespread reputation as a man of integrity and courage. Actually, Shakespeare had no idea where Bridger had elected to trap that season. For all he knew, Bridger's brigade was hundreds of miles away. But the Crows would be less likely to do anything to Nate, Curry, and him if they thought a whole company of vengeful trappers would swoop down on their village in retaliation.

"Where is the Blanket Chief's camp?" Whirlwind Hawk wanted to know.

"On the moon."

"We will find out in time. You might as well tell us now."

"And deprive you of all that hard work?" Shakespeare forced a laugh. "I hope you do find him. The Blanket Chief is smarter than I am. He will not fall for the same trick. Your bones will be left for the vultures to pick clean."

"You are a fool, old one."

"And you are a lying pile of buffalo droppings."

Whirlwind Hawk flashed his arm downward. The warriors charged, coming from every direction, too many for any one man to withstand no matter how strong or crafty or slippery he might be. Shakespeare was literally buried under bronzed bodies.

Nate King saw and tried to stand, to go to his mentor's aid. His wrists were tied behind his back, but his legs were free. He was halfway erect when the sharp tip of a lance jabbed into his side. The muscular Crow beside him grunted and gestured for him to sit back down.

Resentment coursing red-hot through his veins, Nate was on the verge of lashing out when he realized he would be endangering himself needlessly. It was too late to help Shakespeare, who was being trussed up. Nate sank to his knees and held his anger in check. He made a mental vow that come what may, he was going to see the Crows pay for their vile deceit.

The band swiftly prepared to depart. Packs and plews were tied on horses. Nate, Shakespeare, and Tim were hoisted on mounts, each with personal guards who led their animals by the reins. All was in readiness when an argument broke out among the Crows.

"What is the racket all about?" Nate asked McNair.

"They're squabbling over which one of them is the biggest jackass," Shakespeare said, and chuckled. "In all the confusion, the boy vamoosed."

Only then did Nate realize Gray Badger was missing. He was glad, for the boy's sake. Gray Badger couldn't have much of a father if Two Humps let others hunt the boy down instead of doing it himself.

There was a delay while the Crows spread into the surrounding forest in search of the runaway. Young Tim Curry watched them go, then slumped in abject misery, certain his end was near. His quest for excitement seemed a deluded craving in light of the harsh reality of wilderness life. He remembered how his family had warned him he would suffer just such a fate if he was foolhardy enough to travel beyond the frontier, remembered laughing at them and assuring them he was capable of dealing with "ignorant heathens and dumb beasts." Little had he known.

Within half an hour the warriors returned empty-handed. Whirlwind Hawk led the party to a meadow a hundred yards away where the Crows had left their war horses. There the warriors huddled and argued in low tones. Presently half the band was trotting to the northeast with the prisoners while the rest stayed to continue to look for the boy.

Nate was pleased. Now there were only ten Crows. He had been secretly working at his bounds, alternately straining against them and letting his wrists go limp, and had loosened the loops a little. Not enough to slip free yet, or to seize the reins and ride off. The thought caused a thrill to shoot through him. He didn't need his hands to ride. A skilled horsemen could control a mount using leg pressure alone. He looked at the warrior leading his horse. The man held the rope lightly, carelessly. It would be child's play.

Nate bided his time for over an hour. They had just started down the slope of a jagged mountain after negotiating a high pass when he put his plan into effect. The warrior in front of him went around a large boulder and for a moment was out of sight. The warrior behind him had lagged a dozen yards. There might never be a better opportunity.

Nate jammed his heels into his horse and the animal took off, racing around the boulder and breaking into a gallop as soon as it was in the clear. He bent low, guiding the sorrel with his knees. He saw the warrior holding the rope twist and try to tighten his grip, but the fleeing horse ripped it loose, tearing off skin in the process.

Strident yells erupted. Nate angled toward thick timber and reached the tree line as an arrow nipped a branch to his left. Eight of the Crows were in pursuit, two with bows raised. Nate plunged into underbrush, cut to the right, covered 50 yards, then cut to the left, down slope. Low limbs tore at his face, his shoulders. One scratched his cheek, drawing blood. He had to clamp his legs hard against the animal's sides to keep from being pitched off.

The Crows were howling like incensed wolves. They had spread out and the fleetest were trying to get ahead of him to cut him off.

Nate desperately tugged at his bounds. He could only go so fast without his hands. In order to escape he must break free. The rope bit into his flesh, slicing the skin. He felt blood, and smiled grimly. Blood would make his wrists slippery, would hasten his release. He redoubled his efforts.

A Crow warrior closed rapidly on the right. The man rode a superb paint that skirted trees and leaped logs at breakneck speed. Grinning in anticipation, the warrior hefted a war club, anxious to be the one to bring the white man down.

Nate was making painful but steady progress on the ropes. He turned his wrists furiously, the loops chafing deeper and deeper, the blood flowing thickly. Suddenly his left wrist jerked loose and he swung both hands in front of him to seize the sorrel's mane. None too soon.

The warrior with the war club roared in feral delight as he broke from a thicket not ten yards away. Waving the club overhead, he raced alongside the sorrel.

Nate ducked under a vicious swing that would have caved in his skull like an overripe gourd. The Crow raised the club for another swing. Shifting, Nate kicked, driving his foot into the man's chest. The blow sent the warrior flying from the paint; he let out a yip as he collided with a prickly pine.

Inspiration struck Nate even as the Crow fell. For several fleeting seconds the paint brushed against the sorrel, and in that span he tensed all his limbs and pushed off from the sorrel's back. The paint began to pull ahead and for a few anxious moments Nate thought he would tumble earthward. Then he came down astride the Crow's mount, gripped the trailing reins, and applied both heels.

In a burst of speed the paint streaked past the sorrel. Nate veered to the right to avoid a fir tree. A meadow unfolded before him. He was a third of the way across when two Crows appeared behind him, side by side, one with a bow.

Nate reined sharply to the left as a glittering shaft sought his back. The arrow missed by yards. Nate reined in the opposite direction and kept on weaving until he regained cover. The Crows gradually lost ground, their inferior mounts unable to sustain the pace.

Renewed confidence brought a smile to Nate's lips. He would eventually lose his pursuers, then circle around to pick up the war party's trail. From there on, he would stalk them until he could free Shakespeare and Curry.

The timber thinned little by little. More and more boulders dotted the mountainside. Nate wasn't worried because he was well beyond bow range. The Crows didn't have a prayer of catching him. Or so he thought until a cliff reared directly ahead.

Nate slowed, scouring the barrier. It seemed to extend endlessly on either hand. He knew there had to be a break somewhere, so he bore to the left and hugged the base for the next half a mile. Repeatedly he checked his back trail without seeing sign of the Crows. He had about accepted that they had given up when wisps of dust hovering in the afternoon air showed otherwise. They were five or six hundred yards off, and closing.

Below Nate lay a steep, barren slope littered with small boulders and loose gravel. He couldn't go that way. The footing would be too treacherous and there was no cover. No, he had to reach the end of the cliff, and do it quickly. Whipping the paint with the reins and pumping his legs, he galloped along until the barrier was abruptly replaced by the narrow mouth of a canyon.

Nate didn't like the notion of entering, but he had no choice. The Crows were much nearer, the slope below still open. Stones clattering under the paint's hoofs, Nate wound into the depths of the canyon. High walls shaded him from the sun. Occasionally he saw massive boulders perched on the rims, and hoped they wouldn't come crashing down on top of him.

One thing was encouraging. Nate found dozens of animal tracks, proof wildlife passed through on a regular basis. There must be a way out, he figured.

The canyon floor climbed. Nate looked back often but as yet couldn't see the Crows. The dust now hung in the canyon so they had to be close. He wished he had a weapon, any weapon. The warriors had stripped him of everything, including his possibles bag. Making a fire would be no problem since he could do without his flint and steel, but bagging game would be a challenge. To say nothing of defending himself if the Crows caught him.

The walls became shorter the higher Nate ascended. Soon he could hear the echoes of hoofbeats from below. He came to a wide shelf where a waist-high boulder sat near the edge, and drew rein. Swinging off, he ran to the boulder and knelt. It appeared to weigh upwards of two hundred pounds, only a bit more than he did. Bracing himself, Nate pushed and moved it a few inches. It was much heavier than he has estimated, more like three hundred. Digging in his moccasins, he tried again, his muscles quivering as he strained to his utmost. Slowly the boulder slid, inch by laborious inch, to the edge of the shelf.

Suddenly the Crows rode into view, a lanky warrior at the forefront scouring the ground, reading his tracks. Nate braced both feet, wedged his fingers as far under the boulder as they would go, and heaved. With a resounding thud the boulder flipped onto the incline and rolled downward, gaining momentum as it went.

The Crows heard and glanced up. Instantly they wheeled and fled, trying to reach the first bend before the boulder brought one of them low. All but one gained safety. The last man was mere yards from the turn when the heavy projectile rammed into the back of his horse and the animal spilled earthward, dumping the Crow.

Nate didn't wait to see the result. He had bought himself a few minutes, at most, and he meant to take advantage of them. Rising, he whirled, and his heart missed a beat. For the crash of the boulder had sent the paint fleeing on up the canyon. He was afoot, unarmed, and hemmed in by the canyon walls. In short, he was as good as dead!

Chapter Five

Nate King rose and sprinted after the paint. He went 20 yards before it sank in that he'd need the speed of an antelope to catch the fleeing horse. Giving up, he turned and ran to the rim of the shelf. The Crows were gathered around their fallen fellow, tending his broken, bloody body.

Moving back so they wouldn't spot him, Nate cast about for a means out of his predicament. The rock walls were too sheer and smooth to scale. Nor were there any large boulders to hide behind. Once the warriors swept over the rim, he wouldn't last five seconds.

Then Nate's gaze drifted to the bottom of the wall to his right and a spark of hope was kindled in his breast. Carved out of the rock by the wear and tear of erosion over countless years was a niche approximately five feet in length and three feet wide. Nate dashed over and hunkered down for a closer look. There was barely enough room for him if he contorted himself just right.

Harsh yells heralded the oncoming Crows. Nate dropped onto his right side with his back to the opening and scooted into the niche, wriggling to squeeze his wide shoulders under the upper lip. Rough stone scraped his skin, gouging flesh. He put both hands flat and squirmed and shoved until his buttocks touched.

Nate could only hope that none of the Crows looked down as they streaked past or they might catch a glimpse of him. The hammering of hoofs pealed off the walls. He swore the ground under him shook when the leading riders rushed into sight. From where Nate lay, all he could see were the legs of horses, yet he dared not peek out. He'd be wholly at their mercy if they found him.

At a full gallop the war party sped on up the canyon. Only when the last warrior had disappeared did Nate crawl out and stand. Now he had to reach the canyon mouth before the Crows overtook the paint and discovered they had been duped.

Breaking into a run, Nate went down the incline. The warrior thrown by the horse was sprawled in a spreading pool of blood that seeped from a nasty gash in his chest. The cause of death, however, had been a broken neck. The man's head was bent at an unnatural angle, his tongue sticking between his parted teeth.

Nate was more interested in the warrior's weapons. In their haste to overtake him, the rest had ridden off without stripping the dead brave's knife and tomahawk. Both Nate hurriedly appropriated. Then he rose and ran to the bend. He doubted that he'd be able to reach the mouth before the Crows returned, but he wasn't about to give up so long as breath remained in his body.

Nate raced around the bend, and had to leap to

the right to avoid colliding with the dead brave's mount. The horse stood with head low, more shaken than battered by its fall. Bleeding cuts marred its legs and flanks, and its hind end had been bashed badly by the boulder. Otherwise, it appeared fine. There were no broken bones that Nate could find, so, seizing the reins, he vaulted astride the dazed animal and prodded it down the canyon at a canter.

Nate didn't look back until he was almost out. Reining up, he twisted and spied the Crows on a ridge adjacent to the canyon. They had seen him and were waving their lances and bows in impotent rage. To rub a pinch of salt into their wounded pride, he smiled and waved as if bidding close friends so long. Then he trotted to the open slope and descended to verdant woodland. His prospects were looking up. He had a horse and two weapons. And unless the Crows were as good at tracking as Apaches, he would soon give them the slip.

To that end, Nate spent the time until sunset riding a zigzag pattern through the thickest brush and over the hardest ground he could find. Periodically he dismounted and used small branches to wipe out his tracks, then sprinkled leaves and bits of grass on the marks the branches made.

As the sun set in the west, Nate halted beside a ribbon of a creek. He allowed the weary horse to drink, tied it to a brush, and climbed a nearby tall pine. From 80 feet above the ground he enjoyed a panoramic view of the countryside. Nowhere were there any Crows.

Safe at last, Nate collected two old bird nests on the way down and used them as kindling for his small fire. He had to go without food, but a grumbling stomach seemed such a paltry problem after the ordeal he had just been through. He only hoped his mentor and the greenhorn were faring half as well.

At that very moment, Shakespeare McNair lay on his left side near a crackling fire, his arms and legs tied tight. He shifted a few inches to glance at the man from Maine, and remarked, "Why so downcast, my young friend? You're still alive, and where there's life, there's hope."

Tim Curry had been staring sadly at the dancing flames. He looked at the mountain man and said bitterly, "Please, McNair. There's no need for you to treat me like a child. I might be new to these mountains, but I'm not an idiot. I know we'll be killed as soon as we reach the Crow village."

Shakespeare made a clucking sound, then quoted, "He does nothing but frown. As who should say, 'if you will not have me, choose.' He hears merry tales and smiles not. I fear he will prove the weeping philosopher when he grows old, being so full of unmannerly sadness in his youth."

"How can you prattle on so?" Tim snapped. "Your silly words do nothing but make me feel worse than I already do."

"It's human nature, son, to be as happy as we make up our minds to be."

Tim snorted. "No sane man could be happy at a time like this. We're staring death in the face and you want to make merry!" He shook his head in disgust. "My parents were right. I never should have left Maine."

Shakespeare saw no point in trying to cheer the greenhorn. He arched his back so he could see the Crows, who were clustered together across the fire. They were a quiet, gloomy bunch, no doubt because of the death of the warrior killed by Nate. The body had been brought back and draped in blankets, and now lay over by the trees, as far from the horses as possible.

Just then Whirlwind Hawk rose and walked over. "I have decided we will all go on to our village tomorrow instead of spending more time searching for your friend. Invincible One can send warriors to look for him, if he chooses."

"You will never find Grizzly Killer," Shakespeare predicted. "He is not about to let himself be caught a second time. He seldom makes the same mistake twice."

"We will see." Whirlwind Hawk squatted. "Your friend is very clever. I will admit that much. It took great skill to elude Stalking Fox and the others."

Shakespeare rolled onto his back so he could look at the warrior without having to bend his neck. "Even as we speak, Grizzly Killer is on his way to the camp of the Blanket Chief. Every trapper in the region will be after you before too long. You would be wise to let us go before there is more bloodshed."

"Let them come. Invincible One fears no man, not even the Blanket Chief."

"This chief of yours must be very brave."

"His medicine is the greatest of all. No one can kill him."

McNair wasn't sure if he had heard correctly. "Everyone dies."

"Not him," Whirlwind Hawk repeated. "When he first came among us, some doubted. He agreed to be tested, and let men stab him and shoot him with arrows and guns. One even tried to pierce him with a lance. Nothing hurt him. So he was named the Invincible One because his body is as hard as iron."

"How can any man have a body made of iron?" Shakespeare responded skeptically.

"I did not say it is made of iron," the Crow corrected him. "It is *like* iron."

"The meaning is the same. Unless you speak in riddles."

"If you knew what I know, you would not think so," Whirlwind Hawk said. "Soon all will be made clear. Invincible One will decide what to do with you and the young one. If he does as he has done with the others—" The warrior did not finish the statement.

"What others?" Shakespeare prompted. "Have you taken more trappers prisoner?"

"Invincible One will answer all your questions."

Shakespeare was getting nowhere with the direct approach, so he tried to learn more by saying, "This Invincible One of yours is going to bring a lot of misery down on the Crows if he makes war on the Blanket Chief. Just ask the Blackfeet and the Piegans. They have been trying to defeat him for years."

"Your threats are empty," Whirlwind Hawk said, but his tone lacked conviction.

"Keep on believing that and lives will be lost on both sides," Shakespeare said, continuing to bluff. "And once the whites know the truth about your people, there will be no more trade between us. The friendly tribes will get guns and blankets and steel knives, but not the Crows."

Again McNair had struck a nerve. Whirlwind Hawk was most displeased. "Without guns and steel knives we will not be able to fend off the attacks of our enemies. Already the Blackfeet and their allies have many more guns than we do. If they obtain more, my people might be driven from our land."

"Just as they once drove the Snakes off to take this territory," Shakespeare said. "Perhaps your people

will be able to find new land to the west. I hear there
is plenty of desert no one claims as their own."

"You would be wise not to mock us, Wolverine."
So saying, the warrior rose and walked stiffly off.

Shakespeare chuckled while making himself as
comfortable as possible. His wrists ached abominably and his feet were practically numb, but neither bothered him much. They couldn't hold a can-
dle to the terrible wounds he'd once sustained during a trip to the Mandan country when a grizzly
had about ripped him apart. He'd survived that;
he'd survive this.

"McNair?" Tim Curry unexpectedly whispered.

"What?"

"I just had a thought."

"Thinking is a good habit to get into."

"Do you reckon King will try to rescue us?"

"As sure as I'm lying here."

"Tonight?"

"There's no telling. He'll make his move when he
figures he has the best chance. Whatever you do,
don't give him away if you should see him snaking
up on us to cut us loose."

"I'd never do that. What do you take me for?"

Shakespeare merely smiled and lay back to rest.
There were times when keeping one's mouth shut
was wisest. Curry was miserable enough without
being told he didn't appear to have the tempera-
ment necessary to be a successful trapper, that
perhaps he should go on back to Maine and take
up clerking for a living.

The thought gave Shakespeare pause. Who was
he to judge others? So what if the young man was
headstrong, rash, and moody? Shakespeare well
remembered another young man with a similar
disposition who had gone on to become a first-rate
mountaineer. He had to extend the benefit of the

doubt until Curry was able to prove himself, one way or the other.

Closing his eyes, Shakespeare allowed himself to drift asleep. He entertained no fear of having his throat slit in the middle of the night. The Crows wanted them alive, for the time being, at least. And he'd need his wits sharp on the morrow, especially if they reached the village and he met the mysterious Invincible One face to face.

But as things turned out, the journey to the Crow village required four days of hard riding. Whirlwind Hawk refused to say exactly when they'd arrive, so Shakespeare was as surprised as Tim Curry when they surmounted a rise and saw spread out below them scores of painted lodges. The village was nestled in a verdant valley, southwest of a small lake. Hundreds of horses were in evidence, along with yapping dogs, playing children, and too many women and warriors to count.

"The Lord preserve us!" Tim Curry blurted out. It was the first Indian village he had ever seen, and while he was impressed by its orderly arrangement, and even impressed by its picturesque beauty, he was filled with dawning horror at the thought that soon, very soon, he would be slain in the most gruesome manner conceivable.

Shakespeare saw the younger man's expression and advised, "Don't show that you're afraid, Troilus. Indians don't respect a man who is yellow. They'll grant a brave man a quick death. But cowards they torture just to hear them squeal."

"I won't let on," Tim said, and swallowed hard. For the life of him he couldn't understand how McNair could be so calm.

Sentries alerted the encampment to the arrival of the search party, and by the time Whirlwind Hawk guided his party in among the lodges a considerable body of curious Crows had gathered. Shakespeare rode straight and tall, smiling at the children and women and nodding respectfully at warriors, particularly the older warriors. He hoped there were some who would know him and speak on his behalf at the tribal council that would decide their fate.

Shakespeare was mildly puzzled when they were taken to a small lodge instead of to the large lodge of the chief, conspicuous by its location and size. He offered no protest when several strapping warriors hauled him from his horse and rather roughly shoved him inside. He quickly moved aside, and moments later young Curry stumbled through the entrance and collapsed in the very spot he had vacated.

"What now?" Tim asked.

"I reckon we sit and wait."

"That's all?"

"Unless you'd rather sing. Do you know the words to 'Rock of Ages'?"

"You *are* insane, McNair. Joking? *Now?*"

"There's a method to my madness," Shakespeare replied. "When they hear us singing they'll think we don't have a care in the world. It will show them we're brave men deserving of fair treatment."

"I can't."

"Try."

"Maybe later," Tim said. He saw Crows filing past the opening to peer in at them. "Damn," he muttered. "They're acting as if we're on exhibit."

"In a sense we are," Shakespeare said. "It isn't every day they see white men. The same thing would happen if you were to take five or six of them for a stroll through New York City."

"That's different. They're savages."

Shakespeare sat up and frowned. "Son, if you

truly believe that, then you're worse off than I thought. Indians are people like you and me. No more, no less. There are good and bad, kind and wicked, rich and poor. They live, eat, make love, and die much as we do. They're allotted this earth for the same one brief lifetime, and are as scared of the veil as we are."

"How can you say we're the same? They scalp whites, for God's sake."

"And whites scalp them for money's sake."

"They live in the wild in a primitive state."

"Does living in cities and towns, cramped up like too many prairie dogs in a colony, make us smarter or better than they are? As for being primitive, since when is living in harmony with Nature a crime? Isn't that what Adam and Eve did before they were cast out of the Garden?"

"You make them sound better than our own kind," Tim said testily. "Maybe that comes from having lived among them so long."

"I'm not saying any such thing," Shakespeare said. "I'm just trying to get the point across that we don't have a right to brand them as savages when we're not all that refined ourselves."

"You can talk until you're blue in the face but you'll never convince me," Tim declared. "Maybe some of them are good. It hardly matters. Because they're all heathens, every last mother's son of them."

Shakespeare lapsed into silence. It would be a study in futility to try and make the greenhorn understand. Some of life's lesson had to be learned through experience. He was toying with the idea of taking a nap when outside the lodge a commotion broke out. A shadow darkened the opening, and a Crow warrior with high cheekbones and a cleft chin poked his head in.

"One of you speaks our tongue, I am told."

"I do," Shakespeare confessed. "Are you Invincible One, the chief?"

For a few fleeting moments the warrior's features underwent a startling change, reflecting intense, bitter hatred. He seemed to wrestle with inner demons, then composed himself and said, "I am a chief, but I am Two Humps."

"The father of Gray Badger."

Two Humps entered and squatted in front of McNair. "Then it is true," he said anxiously. "You have seen him. How is he?"

"Fine, the last I saw," Shakespeare answered. "He was half starved when we found him so we gave him some food. I tried to find out why he was all by himself, but before he could tell me anything we were interrupted by Whirlwind Hawk." Shakespeare paused. "I got the idea he had run away from your village. He was afraid we would bring him back."

"Afraid?"

"He claimed he would be beaten."

A cloud flitted across the warrior's face and he clenched his fists until the knuckles were white. "I do not beat my children," he said harshly.

Shakespeare believed him. The raw emotion the father showed was genuine. "Your son told me that Invincible One would order him to be beaten."

Two Humps glanced darkly at the entrance. "I would die before I would let him go so far," he said half to himself. "There are limits."

"I do not understand," Shakespeare said kindly, hoping to elicit more information. "Since when do chiefs have the right to order a boy whipped? I lived among your people once, and I never heard of such a thing."

The warrior glowered, but not at McNair. "There have been many changes in our village since the Invincible One came to live among us. Few of them have been for the better."

"Where did he come from? Another Crow village?"

"No," Two Humps said. "He is not a Crow."

The revelation shocked McNair. It was unthinkable for any tribe to accept as chief one who was not of their blood. The Invincible One's medicine had to be great indeed to have accomplished such a miracle. "How can this be?" he asked. "When I lived among you, a Crow had to prove himself worthy over many winters before he became a chief. He had to demonstrate his bravery by earning many coup, and show his generosity to his people by giving often to those in need. Has this outsider done all that?"

"He counted four coup when he led a raid on the Piegans to punish them for attacking us," Two Humps said.

"Four? That is all? Most chiefs I know have counted twenty or thirty."

"And he does pass out coffee and sugar and blankets to those in need."

"How does he get them? Trading with whites?"

The Crow appeared reluctant to discuss the issue. After a bit he said, "It is not wise to question the Invincible One's actions. Since no one can kill him, he can do as he pleases."

"Including beating a small boy if he wants?" Shakespeare asked.

Two Humps abruptly stood. "I thank you, white man, for being kind to my son. If the decision were mine to make, I would restore all of your belongings and allow you to go your way in peace, as a friend. But Invincible One has other plans for you. There is nothing I can do." Stooping, he went out.

The interview had left Shakespeare more confused than ever. He wished he had thought to inquire about which tribe the Invincible One hailed from. He moved to the opening, expecting to find the Crows had begun to disperse. To his consternation, he saw the warriors huddled to one side while the women and children waited in an expectant group as if for an important decision.

"What's happening?" Tim asked.

"I'm not sure."

"What did that warrior want?"

"He was the boy's father," Shakespeare said absently. He was more interested in the tall figure at the center of the knot of warriors, a figure to whom all the others were listening. It had to be the Invincible One. Shakespeare shifted, trying to get a better glimpse, but too many Crows blocked his view.

"Listen, I've been thinking again," Tim said. "What if we try to buy our freedom? We'll offer them five rifles for each of us in exchange for letting us go."

"We don't have ten rifles."

"So we'll pretend we can get our hands on them. We'll tell the Crows that if they'll take us to Fort William, the guns will be theirs. As highly as they value firearms, they're bound to go for the deal. And once we're there, we're safe."

"It won't work. They wouldn't trust us."

"Where's the harm in trying?"

"Once the Crows learn we've tricked them, there will be one hell of a fight. A lot of good men would die on our account." Shakespeare glanced at the greenhorn. "I for one wouldn't want their deaths on my conscience."

"You'd rather be killed?"

Amazement froze the reply on Shakespeare's lips. The clustered warriors had suddenly parted, revealing the tall figure in the middle. The man strode in lordly fashion toward the lodge, the warriors following like dutiful children.

It had to be the Invincible One.

And he was white!

Chapter Six

About the time that Shakespeare McNair was making the shocking discovery that would shortly embroil him in a desperate fight for his life, Nate King was nearing the Crow village from the southwest. He spied a rise ahead, and stopped in the shelter of a pine in case the war party had stopped on the crest to scour the area for enemies. After making certain there were no silhouettes on the skyline, he started around the tree, then drew up in alarm and dropped his hand to his knife.

Voices carried on the breeze, mingled with low laughter. Nate had to lean forward to see through the woods to his left. A pair of Crow warriors were 40 yards off, moving parallel with the trail he followed. One had a dead buck hanging over the back of his mount. Judging by the noise they were making, neither had any idea there was anyone else close by.

Nate smiled. For the warriors to be so relaxed and noisy indicated they were close to their village. He observed them climb the rise and disappear beyond. Then, hugging all available cover, he rode to the top himself.

From behind a row of pines Nate gazed down on the Crow village. The entire populace was gathered near a small lodge, where quite a tumult was taking place. The press of people prevented him from learning the exact cause, but the racket did not bode well for McNair and Curry.

Wheeling the horse, Nate rode to the bottom of the hill and slanted to the west. He intended to circle around until he could locate his friends. As he drew abreast of a small stand of shimmering aspens, the horse glanced into the stand and whinnied.

Nate looked but didn't see anything. He rode on, passed the aspens, and trotted toward high brush. A low growl snapped him around, and this time he saw a village mongrel bristling in feral anger while behind it stood three small boys armed with small bows. They gaped in astonishment at him. Then one gave a shout and the trio pivoted on their heels and fled through the aspens with their dog at their heels.

Instantly Nate turned into the forest and galloped westward away from the village. The boys would spread the alarm and within minutes there would be anywhere from 50 to 100 warriors spreading out across the countryside after him. He went over two miles, then climbed a switchback to an upland bench. There he halted to rest his mount and ascertain if the Crows were tracking him.

There wasn't much daylight left. The lengthening shadows plunged the lower slopes in gloom. Nate surveyed them without result. He feared greatly for the safety of the others, but was not about to do anything rash. If he was caught, the others had no hope at all.

In due course the sun sank. The Crows never appeared. Nate became restless and paced back and forth, unable to explain their absence. He had been in such a hurry to escape he hadn't bothered to hide his tracks, so they should have had no trouble sticking to his trail. Either they hadn't been interested in catching him, which he didn't believe for a minute, or else the boys hadn't told anyone they'd seen him, which seemed highly unlikely. Whatever, he was not going to delay any longer.

Picking his way carefully, Nate threaded a roundabout route through the woodland. The bench fell far behind, and he presently saw pinpoints of light in the distance. Since he had the wind at his back and didn't care to have the dogs detect his scent, he angled to the south, then eastward. Approximately a quarter of a mile from the encampment, he halted and secured his horse to an oak tree.

Holding the butcher knife in one hand, the tomahawk in the other, Nate crept forward, stopping repeatedly to listen. The village was quieter than it should be. Absent were the night singers, the beat of drums, the muted drone of voices. He advanced until he could see individual lodges, then flattened and crawled. All the dwellings were lit from within, and in addition a few outside fires blazed. The latter might give him away should the light reflect off his pale skin at the wrong moment, so he paused to smear dirt on his cheeks, brow, and chin.

Snaking into a thicket, Nate stalked to the very perimeter of the village. He saw horses behind every lodge, but not nearly as many as there should be. And suddenly the odd lack of activity made sense. Most of the warriors were gone.

Nate was thoroughly mystified. Where had the Crow men gone, if not after him? What else could have drawn them all from the village? An enemy war party perhaps, or a report by a scout of a big group of trappers nearby. Yet he had seen no sign of either.

He decided not to look a gift horse in the mouth. With the majority of warriors gone, his task was less dangerous but far from a cinch. The lodge he must reach stood 60 yards off. In between were 14 other lodges, and there was no cover whatsoever.

Boldly rising, Nate tucked his weapons under his belt and entered the Crow village. He strolled along as if he didn't have a care in the world, prudently holding his head low so his features were in shadow. From a distance he might be mistaken for a Crow, but a close scrutiny would give him away. Above all else he must hide his beard.

Nate passed the first three lodges without mishap. In each people talked softly. There was no yelling in a village at night, none of the rowdy noise one associated with certain establishments in towns and cities. Neighbors were respectful of one another, and violators were subject to being disciplined by the tribal police, members of a warrior society appointed for just such a purpose.

The fourth lodge reared before him. Nate swung wide so as not pass too close to the entrance, and as he did the flap parted and out came an elderly woman supporting herself with a cane. She glanced at him and he quickly looked away, but gave a little wave and went on, hardly daring to breathe until he had gone far enough to justify safely looking over his shoulder. The woman had trudged to another teepee and was just entering.

Nate congratulated himself on his narrow escape and quickened his pace. He went by two more lodges, and was halfway to the sixth when a bulky shape detached itself from the side of the teepee and came straight toward him. In a flash he guessed the truth. As was customary with many tribes, two unwed lovers were taking a stroll with a buffalo robe thrown over their shoulders. Kneeling, he fiddled with his left moccasin, pretending to be adjusting the binding. Out of the corner of his eye he saw the pair come closer, ever closer. Then they were a yard away and he heard a soft giggle and the tinkle of a tiny bell. Raising a hand to his chin as if scratching it, he risked a look, and had to check an impulse to exhale in relief when the lovers went on into the night without so much as acknowledging his presence.

Nate hastened on. The small lodge was the only dark dwelling in the camp. He half expected to find guards, but there were none. Drawing his knife and holding it next to his right leg, he walked to the entrance and sank to one knee. The flap was tied up. With a sinking feeling in his gut, he slid inside. "Shakespeare?" he whispered. "Curry?"

The total blackness took a few seconds for Nate's eyes to penetrate, and when they had, he understood why he received no reply. The lodge was empty. At a loss to know what to do next, Nate turned and scanned the village. He had no idea whether his friends were already dead or whether they had been moved to another lodge. The only thing he did know was that he couldn't very well go from teepee to teepee searching for them.

Nate moved to the opening to leave, but stopped when he saw an inky form walking toward him. He darted to one side to wait for the Crow to pass. Moccasins crunched on the dry earth, drawing nearer. To his dismay, they halted in front of

the lodge and a warrior spoke, apparently address-
ing him. With a start he realized the Crow had gotten a glimpse of him and mistaken him for another
warrior. No doubt the man wanted to know why
he was in there.

The Crow spoke again, more insistently. Nate
clasped the knife hilt firmly and grunted an inarticulate answer. He heard the rustle of buckskin.
The black outline of a human head and neck poked
into the interior. The Crow said a single word. Then
Nate pounced. He grabbed the warrior's hair and
yanked, hauling the man inside even as he drove
the keen blade into the Crow's throat. The warrior
stumbled to his knees, wheezing horribly as blood
gushed from his severed jugular. Nate stabbed
again, sinking the knife in the Crow's chest. The
man grabbed Nate's arm and tried to pry it loose
while simultaneously opening his mouth to shout
or scream.

Nate slammed the Crow to the bare earth and
leaped on the man's back to keep him pinned
down. The Crow gurgled, thrashed, and flailed in
a frenzied effort to shake Nate off and stand. Slowly
but surely his movements weakened, then subsided
altogether. Nate stayed on top another minute for
good measure.

A peek outside verified no one had heard the
scuffle. Nate ran his hands over the warrior's waist
and found another knife and a small pouch. Both
he appropriated. After dragging the corpse to the
back of the teepee, he cautiously stepped outside.
Rather than walk all the way around the lodge circle, Nate opted to make a beeline and cut across
the open middle space. Tucking his chin to his
chest, he hastened off. Somewhere close a dog
barked, making him jump. He looked, saw no sign
of it, and walked briskly on.

Nate was halfway to the other side when he saw a couple under a buffalo robe. It must be the same pair he'd seen earlier, he thought. They were bundled in the hairy folds, their heavy breathing clearly audible. Nate intended to give them a wide berth. But as he swung to the right to go around them, the robe unexpectedly fell to their shoulders. Before he could avert his face, the pretty young woman saw him.

Nate was on them as the woman's scream blasted his eardrums. The young warrior twisted. The robe bulged as he moved his arms to grab a weapon. Nate slugged him full on the jaw, then spun and raced for the trees. On all sides there were shouts and Crows spilled from every lodge, seeking the source of the disturbance. Most were women.

Nate was about to pass between the two teepees nearest the thicket when someone spotted him and had to let the whole village know. To his right were tethered war horses, some grazing, unfazed by the uproar. He swerved and jumped onto the back of a chestnut.

A sleek warrior carrying a war club sped around one of the lodges and launched himself at Nate as Nate wheeled the horse. The club arced at Nate's head and Nate jerked aside and kicked, dumping the warrior on his backside. Poking his heels into the chestnut, Nate galloped into the forest and fled for his life.

The din being raised by the Crows was loud enough to be heard for miles. Nate didn't know if any would give chase but he was taking no chances. He pushed the chestnut despite the ever-present peril of the horse stepping into a rut or animal burrow and suffering a broken leg.

Nate was greatly upset by the outcome of his rescue attempt. He had lost the element of surprise. If the Crows still had McNair and Curry, they would take steps to ensure another such try was thwarted. His prospects of saving them would vanish completely.

On into the wilderness Nate rode for over 15 minutes. He had not been paying much attention to his direction of travel, and reined up to get his bearings. From the position of the North Star he knew he was riding due east. The forest had gone completely silent, and in that silence he couldn't miss hearing the drumming of hooves hundreds of feet to the rear.

It was hard to tell how many there were. Nate galloped to the southeast, pleased when the woods ended and a lowland plain stretched out before him. He flew through high grass, the wind whipping his long hair, on the lookout for roving beasts. Panthers, grizzlies, and wolves were partial to hunting their prey at night, and the last thing he needed was to stumble on one of them with the Crows breathing hot and heavy down his neck. Yet that was exactly what happened.

Nate came to a rocky knoll and angled to the left to pass it. He saw a large animal rear up on the slope. A rumbling snarl identified the creature, and with the speed of thought it gave chase. The chestnut didn't seem to fully appreciate the danger until a paw the size of a melon took a swipe at its tail. Fear lent renewed vigor to its limbs.

Nate glanced over a shoulder and saw the gaping jaws and glistening teeth of the grizzly. It wasn't as big as the one in the valley, a small consolation given that it was nearly the size of the chestnut and could disembowel the horse in an instant if it caught up. Nate would have given anything for a loaded flintlock.

Full-grown bears were capable of astonishing speeds that belied their immense size. They rivaled horses over short distances but lacked endurance. This one was typical of the breed, and for ten harrowing seconds Nate thought he would be torn from the chestnut's back and ripped to pieces on the dank earth. The bear's fetid breath filled his nostrils as its claws shortened the chestnut's tail even further.

Then the horse pulled ahead. A growl of bestial fury was the grizzly's reaction, and it stopped. Nate made no attempt to slow his mount until they had gone over half a mile. At a walk he rode to the top of a hill. From there he could see clear to the village. He thought he had shaken the Crows, but he was wrong. A lone warrior was two hundred yards off, paralleling the course he had taken.

Nate was impressed by the brave's skill. Most men would have lost track of him long before this. He trotted down the hill and into a tract of forest to make it difficult for the Crow to use a rifle or bow. He also sought a spot to ambush his pursuer. No favorable sites presented themselves, and in a short while the trees ended.

Nate went 15 feet out and drew rein. Sliding down, he left the chestnut standing there and sprinted back to the forest. A young spruce tree afforded him the hiding place he needed. He drew one of the hunting knives, then pressed an ear to the ground. The dull thud of hooves indicated the Crow was a lot closer.

Practically hugging the spruce, Nate crouched and held the knife poised to strike. He figured the rider would emerge about ten feet to his right. He could see the pale horse but the warrior was hidden in shadow. Suddenly, as if suspecting a trap, the Crow stopped.

Nate's skin prickled. He wondered if the warrior could see him, if there was a rifle being trained on him or a bow being drawn back. Then the Crow approached slowly. Nate lowered himself until his chin brushed the grass. The horse's head hove into sight. Nate could see its legs but not much of the man astride it. Again the Crow halted and Nate knew the warrior was staring at the chestnut.

In a lithe motion Nate surged erect and sprang. He had taken two steps and was in midair when he saw that he had erred. The rider wasn't a man after all. Unable to stop, Nate caught the boy around the waist, propelling both of them into the weeds. He managed to land on his shoulder and absorbed the brunt of the impact. Rolling, he released his hold and rose partway.

Gray Badger was shaken but unhurt. He stood, his posture suggesting he would flee at any more sudden movements.

Nate wedged the knife under his belt and employed sign. "I am sorry, son of Two Humps. I thought you were a warrior come to kill me. Are you hurt?"

The boy sniffed as if insulted. "Crow men are not weaklings." He nodded at the chestnut. "That was a fine trick, Grizzly Killer. I must remember it when I go on the war path."

Standing, Nate gazed westward. "Are you alone?"

"Yes. I have been following you ever since you were captured by Whirlwind Hawk."

Gray Badger walked to his horse, which Nate now recognized as one of the pack animals belonging to Tim Curry. In all the confusion back in the valley, Nate had never noticed it was missing from the string. Understandable, given his predicament.

"I slipped off during the fight," the boy confirmed. "No one saw me go, and I hid on the other side of the stream until they gave up looking for me. Then I trailed them, keeping far back. Much later I saw that you had broken away and were also trailing them, but I could not catch up to you before you reached the village."

"You were spying on the village and saw me leave?" Nate signed.

"Yes. My horse is not as fast as yours or I would have been with you sooner." Gray Badger gave the animal a light whack on the side. "I am glad you were the one the bear tried to eat and not me. It would have caught me easily. When I heard it chase you, I went far around."

"You are brave beyond your years," Nate signed, and meant every word. It took courage for anyone to brave the wilderness alone. For someone of the boy's tender years to dare the feat was rare. Gray Badger's pluck reminded Nate of his own son, Zach, and he almost reached out and tousled the boy's hair.

"Question. Did you find your friends?" Gray Badger asked.

"No," Nate signed, the reminder kindling anew his anxiety over his mentor's plight. "I have no idea where they are. Do you?"

"I did not get too close to the village," the boy signed. "The Invincible One might see me."

Nate brought the chestnut over and moved under the overspreading limbs of a tall fir. Sitting with his back to the trunk, he watched the young Crow tie the packhorse, then signed, "Would this Invincible One have my friends killed?"

"He kills all whites," Gray Badger answered, and added hastily, "Many of my people want him to stop but they are afraid of him, afraid of his powerful medicine." He paused. "How do you fight someone who can not be killed?"

Believing the boy was exaggerating, Nate inquired, "Has anyone tried?"

"Eight warriors so far. I saw one of them try. His name was Black Shield, and he had counted eighteen coup. He challenged Invincible One in front of everyone, then shot an arrow into Invincible One's chest."

"What happened?" Nate asked when the boy fell silent.

"I could not believe my eyes," Gray Badger signed slowly. "The arrow hit Invincible One but bounced off. He laughed, as he often does when he hurts others, and he shot Black Shield through the head. No one has dared go up against his medicine since."

Nate did not know what to make of the story. He'd expect such an outrageous tale from a half-drunk trapper, but the boy was sincere. Maybe, he reasoned, he could get at the truth another way. He knew that the Crows, like other tribes, had a strong belief in talismans, as the trappers called them, everyday articles believed to bestow good medicine on those fortunate enough to possess them. It might be something as simple as an eagle claw, or a piece of wood, or a stone or a seed. Whatever, it would be wrapped in a piece of skin and worn touching the owner's body so that the power of the charm was most potent. "What gives Invincible One his great medicine?" he asked.

"No one knows."

"Has he always been invincible?"

Gray Badger yawned. "We have not been told. He will not talk about his power with anyone."

Nate felt an urge to yawn himself and fought it off. "How many whites has he killed?"

"Nine or ten, I think." The boy lay on his side. "It might be more. I cannot remember. I am too tired."

Nate wanted to learn more, but it was evident the little Crow was exhausted. For that matter, so was he. He'd slept fitfully at best the past few days. "Tomorrow I must try to find my friends. Will you help me?"

"I will do what I can," Gray Badger signed wearily.

"Perhaps your father would aid us."

The boy's eyes shot wide and he swiveled to glare at Nate. "Do not think such a thing. He would be in too much danger. Invincible One would be very mad if he found out and might harm him."

Nate smiled. "So you do care for him."

"Of course I do."

"Then why did you run away?"

"I had to. I made Invincible One angry."

"How?"

"I would rather not say," Gray Badger signed, then tried to make himself comfortable.

"What harm can it do?" Nate pressed.

Gray Badger pondered a few moments. "Very well. I was curious, like all the boys. I wanted to learn where Invincible One gets his medicine. So when Lame Elk, my friend, dared me, I spied on Invincible One by cutting a hole in the side of his lodge."

"And he caught you?"

"Yes, and came running out, very mad. I shamed myself by running. He yelled for men to catch me so he could beat me. Since there are some who do whatever he asks, and since I knew they would have to fight my father to get to me, I left."

More pieces of the puzzle fit into place. Nate was more impressed than ever by the boy's maturity.

"You left to protect your father. You did not want him clashing with Invincible One."

"What else could I do?" Gray Badger lay flat. "Now excuse me. I must sleep."

In under a minute the young Crow was lost to the world. Nate tried to stay awake a while longer to mull over the best course of action for him to take, but he was unable to keep his eyes open. It seemed as if he had hardly closed them when chirping sparrows brought him around to find the sun peeking over the horizon. Nate stretched as he stood.

Gray Badger slept on undisturbed. The packhorse was trying to get at a patch of nearby grass. But there was no sign of the chestnut, which had wandered off during the night.

Nate had a good idea where the animal had gotten to, but before looking he untied the packhorse so it could get at the grass. A short run brought him to the narrow plain. His hunch proved accurate, for 40 yards out grazed the chestnut. Nate started to fetch it, then froze.

A quarter of a mile beyond the horse a large body of Crows had appeared, evidently all the warriors missing from the village the night before. And they were heading right toward him.

Chapter Seven

Shakespeare McNair's astonishment at discovering the Invincible One to be white was compounded by a second shock when the man came close enough for Shakespeare to see his features. "Well, I'll be damned!" he exclaimed.

"What's the matter?" Tim Curry asked, moving closer.

"Why, he is the prince's jester," Shakespeare quoted. "A very dull fool."

Tim peered out and blinked several times. "As I live and breathe, we're saved! That trapper must be friendly with the Crows! I bet they'll let us go if he asks them."

"I'd take that bet but I'd be stealing your money," Shakespeare said. He moved aside as the Invincible One bent to enter. He studied the man's harshly angular features, and saw recognition in the other's darkly smoldering eyes. "Fancy meeting you again," he commented.

Jacob Pierce knelt in the opening and gave them both a look of utter disdain before focusing on Shakespeare. "Greetings, McNair. I never figured you would be careless enough to be taken by the Crows or anyone else. Must be your years catching up with you."

Tim Curry was so overjoyed to see a fellow trapper that he didn't notice the man's expression or tone. He leaned forward and twisted to reveal his bound wrists, declaring, "I don't know who you are, friend, but I'll be eternally grateful if you would cut us loose and convince these savages to release us. You have no idea of the nightmare we've been through. Until I saw you, I thought we were doomed."

Pierce reached out and touched the rope. Without warning, he gripped Curry's forearms and gave them a brutal wrench, causing the greenhorn to cry out. Curry tried to pull loose but couldn't. "Who is this fool, McNair?" Pierce sneered, and shoved Curry to the ground.

"Allow me to introduce young Troilus," Shakespeare responded. "His heart is in the right place but he left his mind back in Maine."

"Troilus?" Pierce repeated, then frowned. "Oh. More of your nonsense. Well, the coons at the next Rendezvous will be spared from having to listen to your silliness."

"You've gone that far over the line, have you?"

"All the way and then some."

Tim Curry was rising to his knees, his cheek scraped from his fall. Complete confusion dominated him. He had no idea what to make of the cruel trapper's attitude and actions. "Why did you do that to me?" he demanded. "I haven't done you any wrong. We should be sticking together. The real enemies are the heathens."

Jacob Pierce laughed, a low, rumbling mockery of the greenhorn's remarks. "You're more of a jackass than I thought, hoss. Don't be fretting over the Crows. They're not the ones you have to worry about. *I* am."

"You?" Tim said in bewilderment. "But you're white, like us. Surely you don't want us to come to any harm."

"Just because someone has the same skin color as you doesn't make him your brother," Pierce said. "Out here in the wilderness it's every man for himself, boy. The stupid and the slow don't last long." •

"I still don't understand. Why would you hurt us?" Tim asked. "Why would any sane man want to hurt another?"

"Bootle."

"What?"

"Come with me. I'll show you."

Shakespeare followed the other two out. The Crow women and children were gathered to the right, waiting expectantly. In front of the lodge two dozen warriors had arranged themselves in two long parallel rows about eight feet apart, each man holding a war club or tomahawk or knife. At sight of them, Shakespeare involuntarily tensed. "Damn you, Pierce," he said.

The Invincible One only chuckled. "As last words go, they're not very original." He walked to the next teepee, a larger dwelling, and opened the flap. "Take a gander, Troilus," he told the greenhorn, "and maybe then you can go to your grave knowing why you have to die."

Curry tentatively stepped to the opening. Inside were stacked bales of beaver fur, a fortune in plews nearly filling the bottom of the lodge. "My word," he blurted. "There must be hundreds!"

"Thousands," Jacob Pierce corrected. "A few more seasons and I'll be one of the richest men on the continent." He bent and touched one of the hides, stroking the fur as if caressing a lover. "A lot of hard work went into raising these plews, and not one lick of it was mine."

"Then how . . . ?" Tim began, and stopped, the awful implication hitting him with the force of a physical blow. "Sweet Jesus! You're killing trappers and stealing their catch!"

"At last! To think, I thought you were dumb!" Pierce put his hands on his hips and roared.

Shakespeare had taken all of the abuse he was going to tolerate. He squared his shoulders and announced, "If you're fixing to kill us, you turncoat son of a bitch, then do it. I'm sick of listening to you crow just to hear yourself flap your gums."

Pierce's humor vanished in a twinkling, to be replaced by scarlet wrath. "As you wish, McNair," he said gravely. "Although if I was in your shoes, I wouldn't be in such a hurry to meet my Maker." He motioned at the twin rows of stalwart warriors. "Have you ever seen a man run a gauntlet before? It's not a pretty sight. By the time you reach the end, if you live that long, you'll beg me to put you out of your misery."

"I've never groveled in my life," Shakespeare countered. "And as you pointed out, I'm too blamed old to start now." He wagged his arms. "Cut me loose and let's get cracking."

"McNair, no!" Tim butted in, aghast.

Shakespeare faced the greenhorn. "When a man's time comes, son, he has to meet it squarely, with all the gumption he can muster. Dying with dignity is one of the few graces afforded us, and I for one don't aim to pass up the chance to show I've learned more from life than not to sit downwind of men who have eaten beans for supper."

Pierce grinned. "And you had the gall to claim I like to hear myself talk! Have you ever listened to yourself, old-timer? At the Rendezvous you go on for hours reading that miserable book of yours aloud." He glanced at a third lodge, where all of the plunder the Crows had confiscated was stacked for his inspection. "Come to think of it, that damn book must be in one of your bags. It will make dandy kindling."

"You're lucky I don't have a gun," Shakespeare responded, "or I'd show these Crows that you're about as invincible as a bowl of mush."

"Am I indeed?" Pierce laughed, then gestured at a knot of warriors, among them Two Humps, who hurried to do his bidding. Seizing McNair and the greenhorn, the Crows hauled the pair to the end of the gauntlet. Both had their bounds removed, at which point the Crows formed a small ring around the two trappers and leveled rifles or drew knives.

"Just in case you get any crazy notions about trying to get away," Pierce said. He stood with his brawny arms folded, his brow knit, for half a minute. "It occurs to me, McNair, that I ought to demonstrate why the Crows gave me the name they did. You see, I once raised beaver in the same valley where Whirlwind Hawk found you. Then a war party trapped me, and I figured I was a goner for certain. But when they shot me, I wasn't hurt. Not so much as a scratch. That convinced them I was something special, so they brought me back for everyone else to see. Put me to the test, you might say."

"And you've had them wrapped around your finger ever since," Shakespeare said. "It must be a whopper of a trick you have up your sleeve."

"Oh, it's no trick," Pierce said. "You couldn't kill me if you wanted to."

"Care to let me prove you wrong?"

"Yes, as a matter of fact." Pierce unexpectedly drew one of the pistols at his waist. "But I'm not about to turn a gun over to a crafty bastard like you. Let's have your idiot friend show you I'm speaking with a straight tongue." He offered the flintlock to Curry. "Take this and shoot me."

The young man from Maine gaped at the piece, then at the madman who held it. Nothing in Tim's prior experience had ever prepared him for a situation so outlandish as this. He wished he was dreaming, wished he would wake up and find he had been slumbering in his own bed at his parents' home in Maine. "I've never killed anyone before," he said meekly.

"Then here's your chance," Pierce said, shoving the pistol at him. "Hell, everyone should kill somebody at least once just to know what it's like."

"You're insane."

Taking a short step, Jacob Pierce rammed the flintlock into the greenhorn's stomach. Tim Curry doubled over in excruciating torment and felt his stomach start to heave. Shakespeare moved to help, but a rifle muzzle blossomed in front of his nose.

"Now then, boy," Pierce said, grabbing Curry's chin. "You're going to do exactly as I say without any more of your guff or I'll have one of these Crows put a ball through your private parts. Savvy?"

Tim could scarcely breathe. He gulped in air, nodding briskly when Pierce raised the pistol to strike him again. "I'll do whatever you want," Tim said, and suddenly had a thought that electrified him into recovering swiftly. Pierce was the one responsible for killing and robbing trappers. Therefore, if he killed Pierce, the Crows might be willing to permit Shakespeare and him to depart unmolested. He listened to Pierce bark words at the Crows in their tongue.

"Take the gun," the murderer ordered.

Dutifully, Tim obeyed and put his thumb on the hammer.

"Don't cock it until I say," Pierce directed. "If you do, the Crows will make wolf meat of you." He backed up a half-dozen long paces, then held both arms out from his sides. "Now pull back the hammer."

Tim did.

"Aim at my heart."

Tim did, annoyed when his hand shook uncontrollably. He tried to steady his nerves through sheer force of will. Several of the Crows had trained rifles and bows on him, which didn't help his state of mind any.

"Come on, you dunderhead," Pierce taunted. "You can do it. Just think of me as your worst enemy."

Tim had no trouble in that regard. At length the shaking subsided and he took deliberate aim, centering the bead on the middle of the rogue's chest. Sweat broke out on his palm and his mouth abruptly went dry.

"When I count to five, squeeze the trigger."

Nodding once, Tim licked his lips and stilled the fluttering of his heart. He was so high-strung he nearly jumped when McNair spoke.

"What happens if he kills you, Pierce?"

"He won't."

"But what if he does?" Shakespeare said. "I want you to tell these Crows of yours to let us collect our fixings and leave if you go under."

"I hold all the cards here, McNair. Not you."

"Do you?" Shakespeare responded. "The only reason you want Troilus to shoot you is so you can prove to the Crows that not even other whites can kill you. This stunt is a big show you're putting on for their benefit. Survive, and they're liable to think you're all-powerful, a god in human form." Shakespeare took a step toward the greenhorn. "But if we don't do as you want, they might get the notion into their heads that you're not as high and mighty as you make yourself out to be. It might give a few an incentive to test your invincibility on their own."

"You always were a clever son of a bitch," Pierce said. "Too damn clever for your own good." He sighed. "All right. If I'm killed, you can go. My word on it."

"Tell them," Shakespeare said, and paid close attention as Pierce relayed the order. He was strongly tempted to make a grab for the flintlock in Curry's hand, but knew he'd be shot dead before he could. The greenhorn was pale, yet radiated a somber air of resolve. Shakespeare knew Curry would do it, and he had to admit that he was intensely curious to learn how Pierce pulled the chicanery off. Because it had to be deception of one kind or another. No man could live after being shot in the heart at such close range.

Pierce motioned impatiently. "Now can we get this over with? Shoot, boy, before I lose my temper and have the Crows separate you from your hair."

Tim closed his eyes for a moment and reached deep within himself for the spark of willpower needed to take the supreme step. He aimed again, then touched his finger to the trigger. Flame and smoke belched from the flintlock.

Jacob Pierce was flung backward, his arms flapping, to smack hard onto the ground. A great, collective gasp went up from the assembled Crows, and a number of warriors hastened toward him. They all stopped dead when Pierce abruptly sat up, a hand pressed to his chest, pain etching his features. He looked down at himself, at his blood-less hand, and smiled in personal triumph.

The greenhorn gawked, unable to accept the real-ity of the tableau.

And Shakespeare McNair so forgot himself as to snatch the empty pistol from Curry's grasp so he could sniff the barrel. There was no denying the gun had contained plenty of powder. "You didn't put in a ball," he guessed. "That's your secret, Pierce. You put in powder but no bullet."

"Think so, do you?" Pierce glanced at one of the warriors. "Let him load the pistol using your powder horn and ammo pouch. Keep a close eye on him. If he tries anything, kill him."

Shakespeare took the proffered items and set about reloading. First he added the right amount of powder. Too much, and the barrel would burst. Too little, and the bullet wouldn't penetrate. Then he wrapped the ball in a patch and tamped both down on top of the powder using a rod handed him by another Crow. When he was done he looked up and saw Jacob Pierce standing 15 feet away, waiting.

"I've heard tales about your marksmanship, McNair. They say you can shoot the eye out of a chipmunk at three hundred yards. Here's where you prove them right." Pierce slowly turned and spread his arms out. "Let's see if you can put one through my heart from the back. Put your shot smack between my shoulder blades."

Shakespeare straightened and cocked the flint-lock. He wanted nothing more than to put an end to Pierce's bloody spree, but he had never shot anyone in the back and wasn't inclined to start. "Turn around. I'd rather see your face when I pull the trigger."

"No, you'll do it through my back or not at all."

Everyone was watching intently. Shakespeare sighted halfway between Pierce's shoulders. In his mind's eye he envisioned the ball shattering the spinal column, ripping through Pierce's flesh into the heart, and exploding out the chest in a spray of blood and gore.

"I don't have all day."

Shakespeare hesitated. It went against his grain to shoot an unarmed man, no matter how vile the man might be. He had to remind himself of all the trappers Pierce had wiped out, all the innocent lives destroyed in the name of blatant greed. Then he stroked the trigger.

Jacob Pierce hurtled forward, stumbled to his knees, and collapsed. Shakespeare took a few steps, confident a spreading red strain would dampen the back of the renegade's shirt. To his consternation, no blood appeared. He saw Pierce twitch, then put both hands on the ground and push to his knees. Wearing a smile of pure evil, Pierce slowly turned.

"Nice shooting, McNair. If I was an ordinary man, I'd be gone beaver."

"Impossible," Shakespeare breathed. "I loaded the pistol myself."

"And you shot me yourself," Pierce bated him. "Maybe now you see why the Crows think I'm so special. They don't want to rile a man with medicine as strong as mine." He rose unsteadily, took a few deep breaths, then walked back. "Still, that packed quite a wallop. I hurt like hell."

Shakespeare stared at the flintlock in his hand. For the life of him he couldn't figure out how Pierce still lived. Could it be, he wondered, that the man actually *was* invincible? The very notion seemed preposterous, yet what other explanation was there? The next moment one of the warriors snatched the pistol from him and handed it to Pierce.

"I should thank you and the greenhorn, McNair. Now that the Crows have seen with their own eyes my medicine works on whites too, they'll be more agreeable to doing my bidding than ever before."

"And a lot more trappers will die," Shakespeare said bitterly.

"Another ten or twelve ought to give me enough plews to set myself up for life," Pierce boasted. He nodded at the plunder taken from McNair, King, and Curry. "The three of you hardly had any. I keep telling the damn Crows to only capture whites who have a lot of hides, but they can't seem to get it through their thick skulls. Twice now they've brought back trappers who hardly had a plew to their name." He tucked the spent pistol under his belt, beside another flintlock. "Now let's end this so I can get on to other things."

"End it?" Tim said, dread piercing him like a lance. For a while there he had forgotten all about the fate awaiting them. "You mean, kill us."

Pierce stepped to the gauntlet and bobbed his chin at the aisle between the rows of Crows. "Which one of you wants to go first? I can flip a coin if you can't make up your minds."

Tim glanced at the glittering knife in the bronzed hand of the first strapping warrior, and gulped. "What if we won't cooperate? What if we refuse to run?"

"Then I'll shoot you dead myself and have your bodies dumped in the woods for the coyotes and vultures to feast on," Pierce said.

Shakespeare boldly moved to the aisle and halted, his shoulder almost brushing Pierce. The warriors covering him likewise moved, two taking up positions on his right, the others behind Pierce. One of those on his right was Two Humps.

"I knew you'd be the noble sort and let the greenhorn go last," Pierce said sarcastically. "And to show you I can be just as noble, I'll grant a last request. Would you like a smoke? A chew? A cup of coffee?"

"I'd like a minute to make my peace with the Good Lord, if you don't mind," Shakespeare said.

Pierce's eyebrows arched. "I never took you for the religious type. Thought you had more sense than most." He shrugged. "If that's all you want, be my guest."

Folding his hands at his waist, Shakespeare bowed his head as if to pray and closed his eyes, but not all the way. Through cracked lids he watched those around him. He saw the Crows relax a bit, saw the pair with rifles lower the barrels a few inches. He saw Pierce shift to sneer at the greenhorn. And it was then, while they were all off guard, that he sprang into action, spinning and grabbing Pierce's second pistol before Pierce could think to stop him and whirling and shoving the cocked flintlock against Two Humps's temple before Two Humps or any of the other Crows could so much as move. "Lift a finger against us and he dies!" he shouted in their language.

A woman in the crowd screamed. Some of the warriors had started to lift their weapons and close in, but they halted on perceiving the consequences. They looked uncertainly at one another, and at the Invincible One.

Pierce had not batted an eye. Acting more amused than angry, he held out his hand. "Save us all some trouble. Give me the gun, McNair, and run the gauntlet."

"I'm not bluffing," Shakespeare bluffed.

"What do I care if you shoot him? He means nothing to me."

"But he means something to the Crows," Shakespeare said. "He's one of their chiefs, so he must have a lot of friends, a lot of influence. Let him die, and what will they think?"

Pierce's humor faded. "You keep trying to turn the tribe against me. Haven't you learned yet that I have them eating out of the palm of my hand?"

"Only so long as you keep them happy with fixings and baubles stolen from trappers. And only so long as they don't have to pay a high price in Crow blood." Shakespeare stepped behind Two Humps, who had not moved a muscle since being taken by surprise. The warrior held a knife, which Shakespeare plucked loose. "I want three horses brought over, Jacob. Then I want everyone to stand back or you'll have a heap of explaining to do as to why your medicine wasn't powerful enough to keep the chief from being killed."

"Damn you, McNair!"

"The horses. Now."

Pierce snapped commands and three mounts were promptly produced. Shakespeare had the greenhorn climb on first, then Two Humps. He moved the third animal, a stallion, next to the chief's horse and swung up while keeping the barrel pointed at his hostage. Many warriors fingered weapons but none proved foolhardy.

"We'll ride out slowly," Shakespeare said in both English and Crow. He walked the stallion alongside Two Humps until they were past the lodge circle. Looking back, he spied three boys talking to Pierce. Crow men were running every which way to fetch their war horses.

"What now?" Tim Curry asked.

"We ride like hell," Shakespeare said, and had Two Humps do just that, keeping pace beside him. They were a quarter of a mile from the encampment when a horde of wrathful Crows poured out in hot-blooded pursuit.

Chapter Eight

Jacob Pierce was fit to be tied. Just when he thought he had proven to all the Crows that his medicine was greater than any man's, and shown the few remaining doubters among them that his invincibility was beyond question the genuine article, Shakespeare McNair had turned the tables and made him out to have no medicine at all and the brains of a turnip to boot. By getting the better of him, McNair had demonstrated that he could be beaten, and it might give some of the warriors who opposed him the wrong ideas.

So Pierce had one thing and one thing alone on his mind as he swept out of the village at the head of the ravening horde. He was going to kill the old mountain man in the most painful manner he could devise, and thereby show the Crows the fate of any who dared oppose him. By the time he was done, no warrior would dare think of crossing him.

Far to the east were the fleeing figures of the three men. Pierce whipped his horse with his reins and drove his heels into its flanks to goad it to go faster. There were so many Crows behind him, the combined thundering of countless hoofs was almost deafening. He tried not to think of the result should his mount trip and go down before the unstoppable wave of horseflesh.

And as if Pierce did not have enough to worry about, there was the report of the three boys who had been out shooting birds with bows. They claimed to have seen another white man in the vicinity of the village, a white man who had ridden westward after encountering them. Pierce had thanked them for the information, but had decided not to act on it until after the McNair affair was settled. First things first, as the saying went. Besides, a lone trapper was hardly cause for concern.

As time passed and Pierce realized he wasn't gaining on his quarry, his anger steadily mounted. He wanted to kick himself for not making the two trappers run the gauntlet sooner. Had he not seen fit to put on a grand performance for the Crows, he wouldn't be in the fix he was in.

Presently the trio entered heavy woodland. Pierce slowed when he came to the spot, and called for the best trackers to come forward. Five warriors were soon following the sign eastward as rapidly as they could, but not rapidly enough to suit Pierce. It soon became apparent McNair was as canny as an old fox. The trail led through thorny thickets and over the rockiest of ground, often doubling back on itself. Time and again the whole party had to sit and wait while the trackers scoured the ground for prints.

Pierce chafed at the delays, but the thought of giving up and turning back never entered his head. He didn't dare, not until McNair and the greenhorn were stone-cold dead. If either escaped and spread word of his activities, every trapper in the Rockies would be after his skin. He wouldn't live out the month.

The sun gradually dipped ever lower in the blue vault of sky and hovered above the pink horizon. Pierce grew correspondingly more anxious as twilight approached. The Crows wouldn't ride at night, so unless McNair and company were caught soon, Pierce must resign himself to a fitful night spent sleeping on the ground and would have to resume the chase at first light. Neither prospect appealed to him.

Just when the outlook seemed bleakest, he had a lucky break.

A short while earlier, Shakespeare McNair had galloped down the slope of a ridge to the edge of a shelf. He fully expected to keep on going to the bottom of the low mountain he had crossed, but when he was yards shy of the rim he discovered to his chagrin that the shelf ended abruptly in a sheer drop-off over 60 feet high. At the bottom, buried in shadow, lay a murky lake.

"There's no way down!" Tim Curry wailed.

"We'll find one," Shakespeare said, reining to the right and trotting along the rim. Several small rocks rolled out from under his mount's hooves and plummeted over the precipice. So intent was he on locating a way of reaching the bottom that he didn't notice the Crow come up on his right side.

"Wolverine, there is a trail not far from here that will take you to the lake."

Shakespeare glanced at him. "Why tell me? You should want us dead after what I did."

Two Humps smiled. "A man who intends to shoot another man usually puts his finger on the trigger of his gun."

"Noticed, did you?"

"I wanted to be ready to jump aside if you started to shoot. The others were all watching you, not your hand." Two Humps paused. "You have great courage, white man. I hope you get away from the butcher who has led my people astray. Then they will see he is not as mighty as he claims."

A sudden thought made Shakespeare slow down. "Speaking of getting away, you have a son in need of your help. Swing wide of the village and head southwest until you reach the valley where your people first found Invincible One. Your boy should be somewhere in that area."

"You will permit me to ride off?"

"I will chase you off if you delay any longer."

The Crow's face betrayed baffled amazement, and something deeper. He leaned over to put a firm hand on McNair's shoulder. "From this moment on, we are brothers. Whatever I have is yours. You are welcome in my lodge any time, and your enemies are my enemies."

"Does that include Invincible One?"

Two Humps never hesitated. "It does. I have held my tongue long enough. After I find Gray Badger, I will appeal to my people to cast Invincible One out. He might be bullet-proof, but he can not stand up to all of us at once." He lowered his arm. "May the Great Spirit permit your moccasins to make tracks in many snows." With that, he tugged on his reins and galloped off into the timber.

Tim Curry was quick to draw abreast of McNair. "Why the devil did you let that heathen go? Now what will we do if Pierce catches us?"

"Fight."

The greenhorn muttered something.

"What was that, young Troilus?"

"My name is *Curry,*" Tim snapped, "and I said that I'm sick and tired of all you crazy mountaineers. Each and every one of you doesn't care a whit whether you live or die."

"On the contrary, I wouldn't have all these white hairs if I wasn't extraordinarily fond of breathing," Shakespeare disagreed. "But when a man's back is to the wall, he has to give as good an account of himself as he can, not for posterity's sake, mind you, but on his own behalf."

"What the hell are you raving about now?"

"Dying, Tim."

"A gloomy subject, and one you talk about a lot."

"Only because out here dying is part and parcel of our lives each and every day," Shakespeare said. "Until you come to terms with how you're going to go out, you won't be able to deal with the wilderness on its own terms." He paused. "You came out here expecting paradise, and instead found that life in the raw demands hard work and constant attention. It's not for the weak or the squeamish or those who'd rather spend their time strolling about in cities than in virgin forest."

"Are you saying I don't fit in, that I might as well go on home?" Tim asked.

"I'm saying . . ." Shakespeare began, and froze when his gaze drifted to the ridge above them where scores of lances and rifles glittered dully in the fading sunlight. "Damn my stupidity," he said.

Tim twisted, sucked in air. "Oh, God! We shouldn't have slowed down! They have us now!"

"Maybe they do," Shakespeare said, facing the drop-off, "and maybe they don't." He reined up and rose as high as he could for a better view of the cliff. It was sheer, the aquamarine water below unmarked by the shadows of submerged boulders. "We just might make it."

"Make what?" Tim said. He saw where the older man was looking, and recoiled as if someone had just suggested that he shoot himself. "You're crazier than I thought if you expect me to do what I think you expect me to do."

"It's either that or let the Crows lift your hair."

"I can't, I tell you!"

A tremendous outcry erupted across the ridge as the Crows hefted their weapons and vented war whoops. With Jacob Pierce in the lead, they swarmed down the slope in bloodthirsty glee.

"Oh, Lord!" Tim bawled.

"Follow my lead," Shakespeare said, turning his horse toward the onrushing Crows. He galloped 20 yards, then reined up in a spray of dust. Higher up, rifles popped, and bullets thudded into the nearby earth. Shakespeare wheeled his mount and galloped straight at the rim. The horse, accustomed to obeying without hesitation, was flailing air before it quite awakened to the peril in which he had placed it. Wind whipped Shakespeare's hair as he pushed off from the animal's broad back and fell free. He saw the surface of the lake growing larger and larger until it seemed to be the whole world, and then he hit, feet first, and cleaved into the water like a blade into flesh, sinking so fast he was completely enveloped in a frigid liquid cocoon in the span of mere heartbeats. The effect was like having a cold fist rammed into his gut, and he almost made a fatal blunder, almost opened his mouth to cry out.

The horse had hit at the same time, the explosion of its impact like the blast of a cannon. Shakespeare saw it above him and to one side, kicking and straining to regain the surface. His momentum had slackened enough that he could do the same, so he drove his legs and arms in short, steady strokes to propel himself upward.

Shakespeare marveled that his bones were still intact. The plunge had rendered the pistol useless but he held onto the gun anyway in case he found a use for it later. The murky depths gave way to lighter water with terrible slowness. His lungs began to ache, and it was all he could do not to gulp in water.

Just when Shakespeare thought he might expire, his head broke through and he gratefully inhaled crisp fresh air. The horse was close by, swimming toward shore. From on high wafted the pop of rifles. Shakespeare glanced up, wondering if the greenhorn would have the gumption to make the jump, and a shadow fell across his upturned face.

With a start, Shakespeare bent at the waist and dived, swimming frantically downward at a sharp angle. He hadn't gone nearly far enough when a second explosion rocked the lake. An invisible hand buffeted him seconds before something more tangible slammed into his shoulder and sent him spinning out of control. He lost all sense of direction. When the spinning stopped, he looked around, trying to determine which way was up. He saw a human figure drifting limply toward him and swam to it. Draping an arm around the greenhorn's chest, he rose to the surface a second time.

Tim Curry came to life, sputtering and wheezing. He coughed in racking sobs and spat water. "Damn you!" he railed. "I nearly got killed!"

"Hush!" Shakespeare warned, letting go. "Follow me. And don't dawdle! We're not out of the woods yet." Instead of making for land, which both horses were now doing, he swam to the base of the precipice and hugged the wall.

The greenhorn paddled up beside him. "What the hell are we doing this for? The shore is in the other direction."

"Keep your mouth shut and take a gander at the rim," Shakespeare said softly.

Tim looked, but saw nothing. He was about to wade into McNair for being the biggest fool in all of creation when over a dozen coppery faces appeared, scanning the lake for sign of them. Tim instantly pressed flush with the smooth rock surface and whispered, "Do you think they'll spot us?"

"Maybe not," Shakespeare said. "We're in the shadow of the cliff. If we're lucky, they'll figure we drowned."

Prominent among the faces was one crowned by a dark beaver hat and wreathed by a bushy beard.

"There's Pierce!" Tim whispered, terrified at the thought of falling into the renegade's clutches again.

"What I wouldn't give for a rifle," Shakespeare said.

The Invincible One and the Crows were most persistent. For ten minutes or better they scoured the lake, only giving up when the setting sun brought darkling twilight to the wilderness. When they disappeared, Tim started to swim out from the cliff wall.

"Not yet," Shakespeare cautioned. "We'll wait another five minutes to be on the safe side."

Treading water, Tim looked landward. "I don't see the horses," he commented. "What if they've gone on back to the village?"

"Then we have a heap of walking to do. But I doubt they've gotten far. A fall like that would have rattled them so badly they'll stay close for a spell."

"At least the savages are gone."

"Not far, they haven't."

"What? Why not? Are they still looking for us?"

"No. Some tribes, the Crows included, think it's bad medicine to be traveling at night. They'll make camp close by and head on back come daylight."

The answer brought home to Tim yet again how very little he knew of the wild and the ways of its inhabitants. Back in Maine he'd often roamed the woods and flattered himself that he was a competent woodsman. His trek westward had been illuminating in that it had demonstrated his ignorance far exceeded his knowledge. Where the Rockies were concerned, he was a virtual babe in the woods. He had grown to doubt the wisdom of his decision to become a free trapper, and thought longingly of the simple, safe life that was his for the asking in the States.

From the forest across the lake wafted a feral shriek that echoed eerily off the cliff. Shakespeare paid it no mind, but Tim Curry glanced at the trees in alarm.

"Was that a mountain lion?"

"Bobcat."

"Are the horses in any danger?"

"Not unless they've shrunk to the size of colts since we saw them last."

Quiet minutes went by, broken only by periodic gusts of wind and the lapping of water against rock. When Shakespeare was satisfied the Crows were long gone, he stroked toward shore at a point where thick brush sloped to the lake's edge. By then a few stars had blossomed in the heavens and the water was as black as pitch.

Tim tired swiftly. His drenched buckskins weighted him down as though they were made of lead and not deer hide. He was vastly thankful when his feet at long last brushed the gravel-strewn bottom. Panting heavily, he shuffled into the undergrowth and sank down beside the older man, who had squatted to wring water from his clothes.

"Once we find the horses, we'll head north, then swing westward until we reach the village."

Astonishment brought Tim up off the ground in a crouch. "I was wrong about you. You're not crazy. You must want to die if you're so all-fired eager to go back into the lion's den." He gestured irritably. "What could possibly be important enough to justify the risk? Our supplies? We can replace them. Our rifles and pistols? We'll manage until we can buy others."

"I don't care a lick about any of that stuff. It's Nate King I'm thinking of," Shakespeare answered, and rose to search the immediate area for their horses.

"But he got away."

"And so have we, but Nate's probably not aware of it. And Hamlet isn't the kind to rest until he's freed us. Even as we speak, he might be spying on the Crow village, waiting his chance to sneak on in. He'll be endangering his life for no reason." So we're going to find him before he does."

"Maybe he saw us ride off."

"I can't take it for granted he did. That boy means too much to me."

"He's a grown man, not a boy. He can take care of himself," Tim commented. He didn't like the idea of going anywhere near the Crow village no matter what the reason might be, and if not for the fact he'd be next to helpless on his own without provisions, he would have parted ways with McNair on the spot.

Shakespeare faced the Easterner and replied gruffly, "Get one thing straight, Troilus. Nate King means more to me than you and all the other free trappers put together. I tend to regard him as the son I wish to hell I'd had, and I'd gladly throw my life down for him. He'd do the same for me, for both of us if it came down to it. He's the best there is."

"I didn't mean to upset you."

"Forget it," Shakespeare said, working hard to smother his vexation. The greenhorn's whining and contrary attitude were getting to him, a sure sign he needed rest and recuperation. He walked into the woods, moving silently in order not to spook their mounts. Curry trailed along, and from the racket he made he was doing an outstanding job of stepping on every dry twig in their path.

Movement off to the right drew Shakespeare's interest. A large shape materialized, moving to intercept them. The dull plod of heavy hooves assured him it wasn't a bear. He stopped until the horse halted in front of him, its head hanging. "There, there, fella," Shakespeare said gently. He rubbed its neck and bent to examine its front legs. Neither were broken. Nor were the back ones. The rope reins dangled on the off side, and seconds later he had grabbed them and hooked a leg over the animal's back.

The greenhorn stood gazing forlornly up at him, the perfect picture of city-bred incompetence.

"Here," Shakespeare said, offering a hand. He pulled Curry on behind him, then turned and commenced a systematic hunt of the area around the lake for the other horse. After half an hour he had to concede the animal had strayed off or headed for the village.

"Are we going to look all night?" Tim asked. "I don't mind admitting, I'm bushed. I need rest, McNair, or I'll be of no use to anyone."

Shakespeare would rather have gone on to the village. Unfortunately, their horse was as worn out as the greenhorn. Unless they rested the animal until morning, it wouldn't last long bearing both of them. He rode into a stand of spruce. "You're in luck, Troilus. Pile some pine needles into a pillow and get some sleep."

"Thank you, McNair," Tim said, sliding off.

"Don't thank me. Thank the horse." Shakespeare dismounted and tied the animal where it could graze if it so desired. Out of habit he made a circuit of the stand, verifying all was well. Or as well as things got in the wild, where a man never knew from one minute to the next what new threat would appear. Temporarily, they were safe. They could rest, but they couldn't let down their guard, not unless they didn't care if they wound up in the belly of a roving bear or big cat.

Shakespeare rejoined his companion and found the young trapper snoring lightly. He gazed down on the helpless novice and thought of all the others like Curry who had traveled to the mountains in search of adventure and wealth and wound up as worm food. If their bleached bones were to be stretched out end to end, the skeletal line would reach halfway to St. Louis.

Yet no one could talk them out of throwing their lives away. Shakespeare had sometimes wished there was a magical combination of words that would impress on greenhorns the hard truths of wilderness living. Like sheep flocking to the slaughter, they came west thinking they were fit to deal with Nature on their own terms, only to find out, often too late, that Nature was a tyrant with deaf ears and a heart of ice.

Shaking his head, Shakespeare sat with his back to a trunk and rested the pistol in his lap. He felt along his belt for the knife he'd taken from Two Humps, but it was gone, undoubtedly resting on the bottom of the lake. Since it wouldn't do to be defenseless, he rose again and hunted until he found a broken limb that made a suitable club. Propping it against the tree, he sank down, bowed his chin to his chest, and willed himself to relax so he could fall asleep. The tension filling his body drained, but not the anxiety gnawing at his mind. He was too worried about Nate.

Finally, much later, Shakespeare dozed. He awoke five or six times that night, and would look and listen for a while before drifting off again. His fitful state had one advantage he hadn't foreseen. He was up well before dawn, raring to go.

Shakespeare had to shake the greenhorn vigorously before Tim Curry roused to partial wakefulness. "Rise and shine, Troilus. We have a long ride ahead of us."

Tim smacked his lips while trying to keep his eyes open. "How many times do I have to tell you, McNair? I don't like to be called that."

"Some folks would regard it as an honor to be named after one of old William S.'s characters, but I won't quibble. On your feet."

The horse behaved sluggishly the first mile, but loosened up thereafter. Shakespeare held it to an energetic walk to conserve its strength. He stayed well to the north of the route they had taken the day before and avoided skylines. By the middle of the morning they were winding among a series of low hills laden with briars. Suddenly Shakespeare heard hoofbeats ahead, the drumming of dozens of horses, and reined up.

"It sounds like the Crows," Tim whispered.

Shakespeare eased the horse forward until he could see around the next hill. A large group of Indians were halfway across the narrow plain beyond, bearing to the southwest. The painted symbols on their mounts and their bodies as well as their glittering lances and rifles showed the reason they were abroad. It was a Ute war party. And they were heading for the Crow village.

Chapter Nine

The very instant that Nate King saw the large body of Crow warriors coming toward him, he threw himself backward into the underbrush and ducked low. Ears pricked for an outcry, he tensed to flee should they have discovered him. But there was no reaction; as yet they were too far off.

The chestnut, meanwhile, continued to graze, chomping loudly, unaware of the Indians.

Nate debated whether to crawl to the wayward animal and try to lead it under cover without being detected. He decided it would be unwise to risk being caught in the open, so he cupped his hands to his mouth and called out just loud enough for the horse to hear, "Come this way! Over here, damn your bones! Amble over to the trees!"

The animal looked up, saw him, flicked its ears, and resumed eating.

Just then loud yells broke out. The Crows had spotted the horse. Nate saw some of the warriors peel away from the main group and race forward. He quickly melted into the forest, and ran to the sleeping boy. He gave Gray Badger a shake. The young Crow jumped up as if launched from a catapult and looked around in confusion. "Many warriors from your village are coming," Nate signed. "Do you want them to find you?"

"No," Gray Badger replied.

"Then we must hurry. We will ride double," Nate signed. He turned toward the pack animal, and was flabbergasted to discover the critter was gone. He realized it had strayed off while he searched for the chestnut, and he wanted to kick himself for being so careless, for not tying it again before he left.

Taking the boy by the shoulder, Nate trotted deeper into the woods. He knew the Crows would conduct a search of the immediate vicinity, so he cast about for someplace to hide. There were several thickets, but none dense enough to withstand a close scrutiny. He came to a shallow furrow eroded by rainfall, jumped over it, and kept on going.

Suddenly an idea struck Nate. Turning, he went back to the furrow and examined it closely. Not quite a foot deep and three feet wide, it just might do. Working rapidly, he gathered a number of fallen limbs and broke off several others. "I want you to lie down," he signed to Gray Badger, "so I can cover you."

The boy divined the scheme, and grinned. Reclining on his back in the middle of the furrow, he folded his arms across his chest and held still while Nate aligned branches across the top, hiding him.

Next Nate lay down and covered himself from head to toe. From a distance the branches would blend into the background and appear part of the forest floor. He could only hope none of the Crows came close enough to see that something was amiss.

Shouts presaged the arrival of the warriors. Nate imagined them milling around the horse and trying to figure out what it was doing there and where it came from. One of them was bound to remember his escape and put two and two together. Sure enough, moments later the brush crackled to the passage of horses as the Crows fanned out to scour the woods.

Nate tilted his head to glance at the boy. Gray Badger was as still as stone, a credit to his father's teachings. From an early age Indian boys were taught that the keys to being a successful hunter were patience and the ability to stay motionless for long periods at a time. He was confident the youngster would do nothing to give them away.

Nate shifted again, peering at the trees to the left where the riders were bound to first appear. Presently they did, five somber Crows who probed behind every sizeable bush and poked their lances into every thicket. They were going over every square inch.

Nate held his breath as a skinny brave rode within several yards of the furrow. The man circled a tangle of undergrowth, thrusting with a long lance. Then the Crow moved to the south, his gaze sweeping the woodland ahead but not the ground almost under his mount's hooves.

The warriors hollered back and forth. Nate had no idea what they were saying, nor could he ask the boy. The braves shortly vanished in the vegetation. He prayed that would be the last of them, and was disappointed when three more appeared. Two of the trio came straight toward his hiding place.

Nate closed his eyes until they were slits so the whites wouldn't betray his presence. The farthest Crow slanted to one side, but the nearer Crow rode to the edge of the furrow and there reined up. The man carried a rifle which he rested across his thigh as he arched his back to relieve a kink.

Nate watched the warrior's eyes. They were the key. He saw them swivel right, saw them swivel left. The Crow idly glanced skyward, then shifted and looked down, straight down at the pine boughs covering the furrow, straight at Nate's face. The man's eyes narrowed, his brow furrowed. And then they began to widen in dawning comprehension.

Surging upward, Nate burst through the layer of branches and seized the Crow by the arm. A deft twist, a sharp swing, and the brave sailed through the air into a tree trunk. The warrior's rifle went flying. Nate turned to go get it, but strident yells told him he had already been spotted. In a long stride he reached the man's war horse and swung into the Indian saddle. An arrow streaked past his head as he yanked on the reins.

Nate planned to flee and lead the Crows away from the boy. His good intentions were ruined when Gray Badger abruptly rose, shaking branches from him, and extended his arm. Bending outward, Nate grabbed the boy's hand and swung Gray Badger up behind him as a second arrow fanned his hair. He quickly brought the horse to a gallop, racing for their lives.

Crows seemed to be everywhere. Their whoops and yips resembled a pack of ravenous predators on the blood trail. Nate spotted some on the left and cut to the right. More appeared, so he bore to the right again. And still there were others. The earth seemed to disgorge them in droves.

Nate spotted a warrior raising a rifle. He had nowhere to hide, no way to avoid the shot, so he braced for the searing sensation of the slug ripping through his body. Salvation came from an unexpected quarter as someone bellowed in the Crow tongue, causing the warrior to reluctantly lower his gun. Another brave, about to throw a lance, let his arm drop.

It didn't take a genius to figure out why. Nate guessed that they wanted to take him alive, and they certainly had the odds in their favor, but he'd be damned if he was going to make his capture easy. A Crow came at him with a clawed hand reaching for his arm. Nate dodged, then backhanded the Crow across the mouth and sent the man tumbling.

A shout from Gray Badger drew Nate's gaze over his shoulder. Yet another warrior was bearing down on him with an upraised knife. Nate yanked out the tomahawk he had taken from the dead Crow in the canyon and swung as the knife arced at his face, blocking the swing. The jolt rocked his shoulder. He slashed before the Crow could, slicing deep into the man's chest, and the warrior retreated, bleeding profusely.

Riding with skill surpassed by few, wheeling the horse this way and that, Nate avoided additional enemies. He thought he was doing a fine job of eluding them until his mount suddenly broke from the forest onto the very plain where the chestnut had been grazing and he beheld dozens of warriors clustered directly ahead. They promptly spread out, seeking to enclose him in a howling ring.

Nate reined to the left and galloped northward. The fastest Crows were gaining rapidly, closing in from several different angles. He whipped the tomahawk at one and the man slowed. Another

Then fists rained on him without letup and the whole word spun and danced drunkenly.

Dimly, Nate was aware of iron fingers on his arms and of being brutally yanked to his feet. He sagged and would have fallen if not for the Crows holding him up. His vision slowly cleared to reveal a circle of hostile faces surrounding him, while in front of him stood a bearded white man whose expression was innately more cruel than that of any Crow.

"I lose two, I find two," the man mentioned, evidently talking to himself. "I'd call that a fair swap, I reckon." He jabbed a thick finger at Nate. "You're the one who got away from Whirlwind Hawk, aren't you? What's your name, friend?"

Nate licked his bleeding lips. The Crows must be on amiable terms with some whites, he mused, if this stranger was able to move among them with impunity. So perhaps if he could convince the man that he meant the tribe no harm, they would see fit to release him and restore his possessions. "I'm Nate King," he disclosed. "Who are you?"

"Jacob Pierce."

"Are you a free trapper like me?"

Pierce's mouth curved in a lopsided grin. "This hoss is a trapper, sure enough, but I'm not a thing like you or any other Mountainee Man."

The sarcasm was uncalled for, but rather than take umbrage, Nate said, "Do me a favor and assure these Crows I'm no threat to them. My pards and I weren't even deep in Crow country when Whirlwind Hawk jumped us without cause and took us captive. All we want is to get our fixings back and go on our way in peace."

"I'm sure you do."

Nate scanned the Crows. "I hear tell that a chief by the name of Invincible One has been stirring them up against all whites. Is that true?"

"It sure is."

"Are you a friend of his? Do you know him well?"

"I know him real well."

"Is he crazy? Or just plain stupid?"

Pierce frowned.

"Doesn't he realize that it's better for the Crows if they're our friends, not our enemies? Hasn't he heard about Pierre's Hole, or the Missouri Legion?" The former referred to a pitched battle in which over two hundred whites, two hundred Flatheads, and three hundred Nez Perces had set upon a large force of Blackfeet who had been making trouble for the trappers. The latter referred to the army raised in Missouri to punish the Arikaras for attacking whites. "Talk to him on our behalf and persuade him to smoke the pipe of peace."

"I doubt it would do any good."

"What harm could it do?" Nate persisted. "He has everything to gain and nothing to lose from being on friendly terms with us." Out of habit, Nate lowered his voice. "Is the bastard here now?"

"Yes-sir-ree."

"Which one is he?"

Jacob Pierce shifted in his saddle and seemed to be studying the Crows. He raised a finger and began to point at one, then apparently changed his mind and began to point at another.

"I thought you claimed that you know him," Nate said.

"And I do."

"Then which one is he?"

"This one," Pierce responded, and beamed wickedly while touching the fingertip to his own chest. "I'm the bastard who killed your partners, McNair and Curry."

Nate stiffened in horrified outrage. "Shake-speare? Dead?"

Pierce leaned forward, his features reflecting insolent disdain. "Mercy me. Were you close to the old-timer, King? What a pity." He snickered. "If you can breathe water, you're more than welcome to give the son of a bitch a proper burial."

Where the strength came from, Nate couldn't say. But he abruptly exploded, heaving the Crows from him as if they were feathers, and leaped, getting his hands on Pierce's shirt. Whipping around, he slammed the callous killer to the ground and thought he heard an odd clang. He started to wade into the killer with his fists flying, but the Crows were on him in a flash. Once more he fought them tooth and nail. Fueled by his fury, he knocked down four of them before the others were able to grasp his arms and pin them at his side.

Jacob Pierce had risen, a nasty bruise on his forehead. He took a step forward, eyes blazing, and snaked out his pistol. His thumb curled the hammer back as he pointed the flintlock at Nate's face.

Nate stared death in the face. He squared his shoulders to show the Crows he was unafraid, and met Pierce's glare with a defiant stare of his own. For an eternity the muzzle of the pistol loomed inches from his nose.

"No," Pierce snapped, dropping the hammer. "This would be too simple. You deserve more, King. You deserve to feel pain such as you have never felt before." Pierce jammed the pistol under his belt. "I won't deprive myself of the pleasure of listening to you beg for mercy."

"It will never happen," Nate vowed.

"We'll see."

At an order from Pierce, the Crows slung Nate onto his horse and the whole party trotted westward. Escape was rendered impossible by a living wall of warriors. Nate stayed beside a brave who rode double with Gray Badger, and when they had gone a ways he turned to the boy and signed, "I am sorry. I tried to keep you from falling into their hands and could not."

"You fought like ten men, Grizzly Killer," the boy answered, then added the supreme compliment. "You are as good a warrior as my father."

A Crow riding behind them pulled closer, his hands flowing. "Question? Why does he call you Grizzly Killer? That is an Indian name."

"The Shoshones adopted me into their tribe many winters ago," Nate explained, and would have let the matter drop but the man became surprisingly curious.

"You are Shoshone? We did not know. There has been peace between our two peoples for a long time, and we would not like to have a quarrel with them."

"Tell that to Invincible One."

The Crow dropped back and spoke in hushed tones to several others. Soon the word was being spread among them. Jacob Pierce, unaware of what was going on, rode at the head of the war party with his chin high and his posture rigid, as if he was a victorious Roman centurion returning in triumph.

Nate was pleased by the development, for it could only work in his favor. The Crows and Shoshones, who occupied adjoining territory, had a long-standing truce that neither cared to see violated. Both tribes already had enough enemies to contend with, without having another in each other.

And although Nate was a white man, by being adopted he had become, to all intents and purposes as far as all Indians were concerned, a Shoshone. Indians never did anything halfheartedly. They put their hearts and souls into every enterprise, including adoption. When someone was admitted into a tribe, no matter the color of his skin or his race, then he became a bona-fide member of that tribe subject to the same privileges and discipline as everyone else. The tribe would do anything for him, and he was expected to give equally in return.

Would the Crows risk war with the Shoshones by allowing Pierce to kill him? That was the crucial question Nate pondered as they traveled mile after mile. Pierce did not deign to glance at him even once, not until the village appeared.

"Take a good look, King. You'll never leave it alive."

The moment Pierce faced forward again, Nate used sign language to translate for Gray Badger. Naturally, some of the Crows noticed, and soon Pierce's threat was being passed from man to man.

The entire population turned out for their arrival, the women and children studying the new captive with great interest. Nate was escorted to the same small lodge in which his mentor had been held. His wrists were tied and he was pushed inside and left to his own devices.

Since Nate no longer had to put on a stalwart front for the benefit of the Crows, he moved close to the wall and slumped against it. All the emotion he had kept pent up inside since learning of McNair's death now gushed out from his innermost being, threatening to drown him in profound sorrow. *Not Shakespeare!* Moisture rimmed his eyes, and the only thing that prevented him from bawling like a baby was the knowledge the Crows would hear and think him weak because grown warriors were expected to control their feelings at all times.

Still, the anguish was like a red-hot poker burning through Nate's core, and he had to bite down on his lower lip hard enough to draw blood to keep from sobbing aloud. Sweet memories filtered through his mind, of wonderful times spent in the company of the man he had come to regard as more of a father than his own had been.

True friends were as rare as gold and were to be as prized as precious gems. The average person might have a handful in a whole lifetime, usually less. An affinity of souls, Nate's grandmother had called such friendships. Rare moments in time when two people were in harmony. The next best thing to being married.

Nate knew he would never meet another like Shakespeare. For all the jesting he had done over McNair's fondness for the playwright, he would have given anything to have Shakespeare seated beside him at that very moment, spouting quotations as glibly as if he had been the one who wrote the plays.

How much time went by, Nate couldn't say. Mired in misery, he only roused himself when a pair of Crows entered, hoisted him to his feet, and pushed him outside.

The Invincible One and a dozen warriors were waiting. "Enjoyed your little rest?" Pierce asked.

Nate merely glared, his dislike of the man flaring into fiery hatred. Had his hands been free, had no one else been there to stop him, he would have clamped his fingers on Pierce's thick neck and squeezed until the killer was as lifeless as McNair.

"I was going to have you run a gauntlet, like I wanted to do with your friends," Pierce mentioned. "But then I got to thinking. I can use you to teach the Crows a little lesson. They've been acting a mite uppity of late and I need to put them in their place."

"Killing me won't teach them anything about you they don't already know," Nate responded.

"That's where you're wrong," Pierce said. "They believe my medicine is greater than any man's since I've already demonstrated that I can't be killed. Now I need to show them that I'm as hard inside as I am outside."

"You can't be killed?" Nate scoffed. "Cut me loose and I'll prove you wrong."

"Do you really think I'd be jackass enough to give you the chance?" Pierce said.

The cutthroat spoke in the Crow tongue, and several warriors propelled Nate toward the center of the village. Word must have already spread because it appeared that every last Crow had gathered for the spectacle. Nate foresaw his fate on seeing four stakes imbedded in the shape of a large rectangle. Beside one of them stood a brave holding four long pieces of rope.

Nate wasn't about to submit meekly. He dug in his heels and tried to tear free. More warriors came to the assistance of those holding him, and he was lifted and carried the rest of the way. Nate knew they would have to cut his wrists loose in order to spread-eagle him to the stakes, so he was ready when the loops parted. So were the warriors. The second he began to whip his arms around, four of them were on him, pinning him flat with their combined weight. He heaved and bucked, but his struggles proved useless.

Nate fiercely resisted their attempts to tie him, yet once again their numbers prevailed. His arms were pulled to full extension and his wrists secured. The same was done with his legs. He yanked at the stakes, but couldn't budge them at all. The Crows stood, then moved aside.

Jacob Pierce reared over Nate, wearing a sadistic smile. "Not so cocky now, are you, King? In a few minutes you'll be blubbering hysterically."

"Go to hell," Nate declared.

"After you, I'm afraid," Pierce said, drawing his butcher knife. The blade gleamed brightly in the sunshine as he sank to one knee. "I'm fixing to make me a new ammo pouch. And you get to supply the hide."

Chapter Ten

Nate King had heard stories about men skinned alive. The excruciating torment was said to be unbearable, so overwhelming that some victims went insane from the pain before the skinning was done. Some claimed that it burned, like having the body set on fire after being doused with kerosene. Whatever the case, no trapper in his right mind wished such a terrible fate on his worst enemy.

Nate watched the blade dip toward the bottom of his left leg. He felt a hand grasp his pants, heard the buckskin being slit. The breeze touched his flesh as high as his knee. Then a sharp pang lanced his ankle and he could feel blood trickling down his foot.

Suddenly there was a shout and a quartet of warriors advanced. Two of them addressed Pierce, who jumped up and angrily replied. The warriors, in turn, countered with sharp words and gestures.

At a loss to explain the interruption, Nate craned his neck in order to glimpse his ankle. The knife had just pricked the skin, nothing more. He listened to the argument, trying to determine from facial expressions and motions why the warriors had interferred. As near as he could figure, the Crows didn't want him slain. He suspected it had something to do with the seed he had planted about being an adopted Shoshone, and shortly he had his hunch confirmed when Pierce turned to him in vile wrath.

"What the hell did you tell them, King?"

"I don't know what you mean," Nate said innocently.

"You damned liar!" Pierce fumed, and before Nate could guess the renegade's intent, Pierce hauled off and kicked him in the ribs.

Intense agony speared through Nate's chest. He gritted his teeth to keep from crying out and trembled uncontrollably.

"Pretty damned clever!" Pierce snarled. "Claiming that you're Shoshone because you know the Crows and the Snakes are on friendly terms! Now they don't want me to touch a hair on your head!"

"I am Shoshone," Nate found the strength to say.

"Like hell!" Pierce said, and drew back his leg to kick again. Instead, he glanced at the Crows and slowly lowered his foot. "You're lucky I can't afford to get on their bad side right now, or I'd stomp you to death." Bending over, Pierce grabbed Nate by the throat. "But don't think this lets you off the hook, bastard. You've bought yourself a little time, is all. Tonight I'm holding a council with the chiefs, and when I'm done convincing them, they'll skin you themselves."

Nate didn't respond. Crows cut him loose and hauled him to the small lodge, where he was bound hand and foot and rolled through the doorway. He wormed his way over to the side and pushed himself into a sitting posture. For the time being he was safe, but he couldn't count on the Crows prevailing in the long run. Somehow he had to escape.

Over the next several hours Nate worked diligently at doing just that. He rubbed and rubbed until his wrists and ankles were raw and bleeding. The blood helped to loosen the rope, but not quite enough to permit him to slip a hand free. His feet were another matter. The knife wound added more blood, making his ankles twice as slick. By wriggling and shifting his feet, he was able to finally slide one foot loose.

Now Nate could stand if he wanted, but the exertion had left him weak and woozy. He moved close to the entrance and peeked out. The village lay quiet under the late afternoon sun. A few children played with a hoop. Women were busy at various tasks. One was removing tissue and hair from a buffalo hide. Another was engaged in scraping a hide stretched taut on a square frame. Others were getting an early start on supper by boiling water in buffalo-paunch cooking pots. A few warriors were gambling using buffalo-bone dice.

The Crows were so confident Nate couldn't escape, they had failed to post guards. Not that he would get far if he made a break for it while the sun was up. There were too many Crows abroad, not to mention numerous dogs.

Nate devoted himself to his wrists, chafing them worse as he twisted and slid them back and forth and up and down. The blood flowed thick over his palms and fingers, rendering them sticky. Yet try as he might, he still couldn't free them.

At length the sun hovered above the stark mountains to the west. The village quieted even more as most of the Crows went into their lodges to enjoy their evening meal.

Nate knew the council session would soon be held in the biggest lodge of all. He noticed several warriors dressed in their finest buckskins go in, but saw no sign of the so-called Invincible One. Then, as he shifted for a better view of the council lodge, he detected movement in trees bordering the encampment to the north. Focusing, he saw approximately a dozen warriors, and for a moment assumed they were a hunting party on their way back, until he observed they were moving far too stealthily, slinking from tree to tree, and saw their painted faces and the weapons they held ready for use.

It was a war party! Nate realized. Utes, most likely. And they had slipped past the perimeter sentries and were about to attack. Without thought for his own life, he rose and darted outside, bellowing at the top of his lungs the one word the Crows would understand because it was the same in their tongue and in English. "Utes! Utes! Utes!"

The Crows still outdoors glanced at him, most in puzzled bewilderment. A few, more astute, rose to look around, while from many lodges came curious warriors wanting to know what the uproar was about. And in that frozen moment before the Crows awakened to their plight, the Utes launched their attack.

Screeching and howling like banshees, scores of Utes poured out of the forest in a bloodthirsty wave, clubbing and shooting and stabbing every Crow caught in their path. Over 20 were slain in the first few seconds. Crow warriors were swiftly rallying to defend their loved ones, but as yet the Utes had the upper hand.

Nate was 50 yards from the onrushing line. He knew the Utes would slay him without hesitation. In fact, they would be more eager to kill him since they prized whites' scalps more than those taken from other enemies. So he spun and ran to the south, frantically struggling to slip his wrists from the rope. He passed Crow men charging to the fray. Women and children were fleeing in panic in the same direction he fled. He rounded a lodge, and was on the verge of being in the clear when the high-pitched shriek of a young boy made him look back.

A lone Ute, well in advance of the rest, had clubbed a Crow woman, and was trying to do the same to a young boy resisting furiously. The Ute had the boy by the hair, and was trying to hold him still long enough to slit his throat. The boy was Gray Badger, and there were no Crows nearby to help him.

Whirling, Nate barreled to the rescue. He had no idea what good he could do with his hands bound, but that didn't stop him.

Genuinely brave men never take their own welfare into consideration when they commit acts of raw courage. They simply do what has to be done without regard for the consequences.

The Ute was so busy trying to firm his grasp on the boy that he didn't look up until Nate was almost upon him. Lowering his shoulder, Nate rammed into the Ute's chest, knocking the man into the side of a lodge. The Ute slipped, almost fell, then rallied, and thrust at Nate's heart. Nate jumped backward, and was spared a fatal blow, although the tip of the blade nicked his chest. The enraged Ute came after him, slashing wildly, forcing Nate to retreat before the vicious onslaught. Nate ducked, weaved, leaped aside, always backing away, never slowing. He only had eyes for the glittering knife seeking his life. So it was that he failed to see the aged woman behind him until he collided with her. She had been fleeing, heedless of all else, and had not seen him. Together they toppled in a tangle of legs.

Nate tried to rise quickly, but was hampered by being unable to use his hands. The old woman stood first. She looked down at him and smiled, then bent to grip his shoulders to help him to stand. To Nate's horror, the Ute abruptly appeared behind her, seized her by the hair, and drove his knife into the back of her neck. Nate saw the bloody point slice through the front of her throat, and recoiled as a crimson geyser sprayed him.

The Ute wrenched the knife out, then flung the aged Crow aside. Uttering a bestial growl, he raised his arm for another killing stroke.

Flat on his back, with no time to roll out of the way, Nate did the only thing he could. He drove his right foot into the Ute's knee. There was a loud crack and the warrior staggered to the left. Nate coiled his legs under him and pushed erect just as the Ute recovered sufficiently to stab at him. He skipped out of reach. And when the Ute shuffled in pursuit, he bounded to the right, dropped low, and kicked again, this time into the warrior's other knee.

Hissing like a serpent, the Ute fell. He was in great distress, but not willing to give up. Lunging, he cut at Nate's legs, and Nate leaped high into the air to save himself. On coming down, Nate lashed out with his foot, catching the Ute in the elbow. The man howled when the bone shattered.

Nate danced out of reach and crouched. He tried for the hundredth time to slip his wrists free, but the rope wasn't loose enough. The Ute, teeth grinding, tried to stand, and couldn't straighten his legs. Anxious to end their clash, Nate darted in close to try to kick his enemy in the face. The Ute drove him off with a low swing of the knife.

Desperate circumstances called for desperate measures. Nate had to do something before more Utes appeared. He took a running step forward as if to kick at the warrior's body, and when the Ute attempted to bury the knife in his leg, Nate vaulted high into the air, over the Ute's arm, and rammed the sole of his foot into the Ute's nose. The warrior buckled.

Nate kicked twice in rapid succession, each time planting the sole of his foot on the other's jaw. Groaning, the warrior went limp, and the knife fell from his fingers. Nate crouched beside it, and bent way down so he could grasp the hilt. Reversing his grip, he frantically sawed at the rope.

Meanwhile, a general melee had erupted. The Crows had rallied and were slowly driving the invaders off, but at a high cost. For the most part the battle was being waged man-to-man, although here and there small groups clashed fiercely.

Nate made aggravatingly slow progress. His palms were slippery from blood and sweat, preventing him from getting as firm a hold as he would have liked. Bending his hands as sharply as he could, he cut and cut. Suddenly a hand fell on his shoulder.

With a start, Nate glanced around, dreading it was a Ute out to kill him or a Crow intending to recapture him. But it was neither. Gray Badger took the knife and bent to the ropes, and in seconds they parted. He gave the knife back to Nate, then gestured urgently, signing, "We must get away while we can!"

The crack of guns and the riotous clamor of war whoops had reached a crescendo. Mingled in the din were screams, loud whinnies, and vociferous barking. The Utes had been driven northward to the last line of lodges, but had taken a high toll of the defenders.

Nate ran alongside Gray Badger toward the trees. They passed a dead Crow and Nate saw a rifle lying nearby. It was Shakespeare's Hawken, which Nate promptly claimed. Rolling the Crow over, Nate found Shakespeare's powder horn and ammo pouch. He stripped both off despite the heated urging of the boy to flee.

Once rearmed, Nate sped into the woods. They ran for hundreds of yards, glimpsing clusters of frightened women and children. No one challenged them. The women were too afraid of the Utes to bother about an escaping prisoner.

Once Nate was in the clear, he halted and reloaded the Hawken. It felt grand to have a gun in his hands again. He would have liked nothing better than to encounter Jacob Pierce and demonstrate to the Crows their folly in believing any man impossible to kill.

"We must keep going," Gray Badger signed. "Once the Utes have been driven off, Invincible One will send men to hunt us."

"I am not running," Nate signed.

"What will you do?"

"Find Invincible One and kill him."

Gray Badger clutched at his throat in dismay. "He can not be slain! Many have tried, many have died. We are better off running."

"There comes a time when a man must stand and fight if he is to be worthy of being called a man," Nate said. "My belongings, my horses, and my guns were taken from me because of Invincible One. The only way I will get them back is if I show your people that my medicine is more powerful than his."

"You will be killed," Gray Badger signed sadly, "and then I will be all alone again."

"We will find your father."

"Why?" the boy responded. "If he cared for me, he would have searched for me before now."

"Maybe Invincible One would not let him," Nate speculated. "Until we learn the truth, you must trust in your father to do what is right." He gave the young Crow a pat of encouragement on the head, but Gray Badger was beyond being cheered by words or gestures.

"I want you to stay here until I return," Nate signed. "If I am not back by dark, you will be on your own."

"I do not want you to leave me."

"I have no choice," Nate signed, and ran northward. He assumed Pierce would be helping the Crows drive off the Utes, and since it sounded as if heavy fighting still raged on the north side of the village, he figured that was where he would find the renegade. He passed a few bunches of women and children who either fled or cowered in brush until he had gone by.

As the tumult increased, Nate slowed and angled toward the lodges. He came to a log and hunkered behind it to survey the landscape ahead. Five or six of the teepees were in flames. Dozens of Crows and Utes lay scattered about, some moving, some not, some groaning or wailing, others bearing their wounds in stoic silence.

Beyond the northernmost dwellings a running fight was underway. The Utes were retreating in an orderly manner, pockets of them keeping the Crows at bay while the majority gained ground on their vengeful pursuers.

The raid had been different than most, Nate reflected as he advanced again. Usually a warring tribe conducted a lightning foray, fleeing before many lives were lost. Some tribes considered it the very worst of calamities for a single brave to die on a raid. But this time the Utes had been out for blood, and hadn't seemed to care about losing many of their own. Nate didn't know what to make of their strategy.

About 60 yards away a half-dozen Utes were putting up stiff resistance against twice that many Crows. Arrows and lead flew back and forth.

Nate stopped at a fir tree, braced the Hawken against the trunk, and took precise aim on a Ute with a bow. His shot felled the man as the Ute started to release a shaft. Nate was reloading when the Crows made a concerted rush and put the Utes to flight.

Treading warily forward along the tree line, Nate sought sign of Jacob Pierce. He was beginning to think Pierce had elected to remain out of the fray when a familiar raspy voice bellowing orders in the Crow tongue drew him toward a jumbled maze of downed timber. Somewhere in there, he knew, was the rogue.

Alert for Utes, Crows, and Pierce, Nate cautiously clambered over downed trees and crept through dense growth. The acrid scent of gunsmoke hung heavy in the air. He found a dead, scalped Ute, then another with eyes gouged out. From the trampled vegetation and puddles of fresh blood, it was clear a ferocious clash had taken place.

Presently, through the trees, Nate saw several Crows stalking to the northeast. Pierce wasn't among them. Nate moved to the left, around a large stump, and halted, his blood chilling, as 30 feet off the killer appeared. Pierce shouted more instructions, then worked at reloading a rifle.

Nate didn't dare miss the golden opportunity fate had presented. He tucked the Hawken to his shoulder, sighted down the barrel, and pulled back the hammer with his thumb. Very carefully, he fixed the front bead on Pierce's back, and hesitated. Shooting a man from behind was a cowardly act, plain and simple. He wanted Pierce to turn, wanted Pierce to know what was coming.

The Invincible One finished loading and straightened. He shouted, started to walk deeper into the woods. In another few steps he would be lost in the vegetation.

Nate sucked in his breath, steadied the Hawken, and yelled, "Over here, you son of a bitch!" Pierce, predictably, whirled, and the instant the bead settled on the center of the killer's chest, Nate squeezed the trigger. He grinned as Jacob Pierce was lifted from his feet and flung into high grass.

"So much for being invincible!" Nate said under his breath. Dashing behind the stump, he reloaded, then glided toward the spot where Pierce had fallen. He couldn't wait to show the Crows that no one deserved so lofty a name, and to persuade them to return all of the goods stolen from his trapping party. He would take all of McNair's possessions to his friend's Flathead wife. Curry's things he would sell and send to the greenhorn's next of kin.

Nate came to where Pierce had been standing and looked down, expecting to find drops of blood. There were none. He went further, into the grass, to where the body should have been, but there was no body, just an impression in the grass where something heavy had fallen.

"What in the world?" Nate blurted out, and raised his head to scour the area. The glint of sunlight off metal saved his life, for it gave him the fraction of

a second warning he needed to dive to the right. A
rifle boomed and the slug whizzed overhead.

Nate rolled in among small pines and rose
partway. He was amazed Pierce had survived.
At that range Nate rarely missed. But obviously
he had, or else the ball had merely grazed the
killer and not drawn much blood. Either way, he
intended to put a stop to Pierce's bloody career then
and there.

Bearing to the right, Nate sank onto his elbows
and knees and crawled. Pierce would need up to
a minute to reload, giving Nate time to sneak in
close enough for a fatal shot. He snaked through
the pines to more grass, through the grass to a
tall bush. Tucking both knees up under him, he
rose high enough to catch sight of someone moving through waist-high weeds 20 feet away. He
took a hasty bead, but never saw the figure clearly
enough to tell who it was, and held his fire.

Lowering to the ground, Nate crawled to the
northeast, to a pine. He stood in the shelter of the
wide trunk and peered out. The wily Pierce was
nowhere to be seen. Nate wondered if the renegade
was hiding somewhere, waiting for whoever had
taken the shot to show. Glancing down, he saw a
short piece of broken limb and picked it up. The
trick he was about to try was as old as the hills,
but sometimes still worked.

Nate hurled the stick as far as he could to the
south, then brought the Hawken to his shoulder
while scanning the vegetation on all sides. The
stick hit with a thud, rustling some weeds. Almost
immediately a dark shape materialized beside a
spruce to the west and the man shot at the weeds.
The shooter's face was in shadow, but a stray ray
of waning sunlight bathed his head, revealing a
beaver cap. Nate aimed and fired. The Hawken

belched a cloud of gunsmoke that momentarily hid Pierce. By the time the smoke cleared, Pierce was gone.

Pressing his back to the pine, Nate reloaded rapidly. He had no idea whether his shot had been accurate, and there was only one way to find out. Crouching, he raced in a half circle that brought him up on the spruce from the rear. He probed the grass at its base and nearly cursed aloud. Again there was no body!

Mystified, Nate cat-walked to the left, to a small boulder. Squatting, he examined the Hawken's sights, but they were fine. He couldn't understand how he could have missed a second time. A troubling notion, unbidden, filled his head: What if Jacob Pierce really was invincible? He shrugged, dismissing the idea as lunacy. Yet how else could he account for the rogue's deliverance? He had never thought to inquire why the Crows believed Pierce to be immortal, and they must have had a good reason.

Nate might have stayed there pondering for minutes had a twig not snapped. Twisting, he gazed in the direction the sound came from, but saw no one. He propped the rifle on the top of the boulder, and pulled the hammer to be ready in case it was Pierce or an Ute. Then he thought he saw something move, but he couldn't be sure.

Brush suddenly parted, revealing a buckskin-clad forearm. For a minute nothing else happened. At last the forearm moved, parting the brush wider, and Jacob Pierce showed himself from the waist up. He was staring north of Nate's hiding place, at a thicket he evidently believed harbored Nate.

This time Nate had the butcher right where Nate wanted him. He willed himself to calm down, to still his speeding pulse. He took twice as long as he normally would to set the bead on the exact middle of Pierce's torso. His finger delicately touched the cool metal trigger, and he held the Hawken rock steady for all of five seconds before he fired.

Pierce clutched at his chest and fell backward into the brush. Nate sprinted madly toward the spot, afraid he would get there and find Pierce had once more evaporated into thin air. He was yards off when he saw the foot, and smiled. Plunging into the brush, he stood over Pierce and beamed in elation at his victory. Only belatedly did he see there was no blood. Only belatedly did he see that Pierce still held a rifle. He leaned down to pry the gun from the dead man's fingers, and as his fingers closed on the barrel Pierce's eyes snapped wide open and the killer's other hand closed on his ankle.

Chapter Eleven

Total paralyzing shock held Nate King in place, and Jacob Pierce was quick to take advantage. The killer gave a vicious wrench, causing Nate's leg to sweep out from under him. As Nate crashed down, Pierce shifted, trying to bring his rifle to bear. In sheer reflex Nate swung the Hawken, and swatted the renegade's rifle aside just as the gun discharged.

They both rose to their knees. Pierce growled and attempted to smash Nate in the head, but again Nate parried. Angered by his failure, Pierce began raining blows down in a furious attempt to smash Nate's skull to a pulp. The two barrels tinged together repeatedly. Then, swiveling, Nate lanced the muzzle of the Hawken into the killer's gut, doubling Pierce over in sputtering agony.

Seizing the initiative, Nate gained his knees and drew back the Hawken to club his foe. But Pierce was far from defenseless, and he abruptly let go

of his rifle and leaped, clamping his arms fast on
Nate's chest and bearing Nate to the ground. Pierce
grabbed the Hawken, and they struggled mightily
for possession. Nate was about to wrest it loose
when the killer kneed him in the groin.

Racked by a welling wave of anguish, Nate
sagged, weakening. He clung to the Hawken for
dear life as Pierce tugged and jerked. The renegade
bent toward him to get a better purchase on the
rifle, and the moment Pierce did, Nate rammed
his forehead into the other's face. Pierce slumped,
blood oozing from his nose, and Nate rammed him
again.

Jacob Pierce lost his grip on the rifle and fell
to one side. Nate would have sorely liked to bash
in the man's brains, but his groin still throbbed
abominably, the misery rendering him too feeble
to lift the Hawken. He fell back onto his haunches,
and resisted an instinctive impulse to bend over
and cup his privates. He had to keep fighting! He
mustn't give in to the pain or he would die!

Pierce was slowly pushing off the ground. Nate
forced his legs to cooperate, and beat the rogue to
the punch. Swaying, he held the rifle as if it were
a club and streaked it overhead. Pierce glanced
up just as Nate swung, and hurled himself aside.
The stock clipped the killer on the temple, stun-
ning him.

Nate took a shambling stride and lifted the
Hawken again. Pierce looked up in horror, aware
of Nate's intention but incapable of doing a thing.

"Here's where I end it," Nate said. He looked
into Pierce's eyes and saw a sight that gave him
deep, personal satisfaction: fear, raw, unbridled
fear. He began his swing.

Unexpectedly, the underbrush crackled and three
Crows were there. They leaped on Nate, knocking

him off his feet, trapping him under them as they smashed him flat. He hit one with the stock, and was punched in the cheek by another. In concert they held his arms down and the Hawken was ripped from his grasp. Nate kneed the warrior astride his chest, then tried to kick the man on his right.

From out of the woods dashed a fourth Crow, holding a fusee. Cocking the trade gun, he touched the barrel to Nate's nose and barked words in his tongue.

Nate didn't need a translator. He stopped resisting and was yanked erect. He saw a tall Crow offer Pierce a hand, but Pierce angrily slapped it away and stood on his own.

"I'm making you a promise here and now, King. Before the sun comes up tomorrow, you're gone beaver."

Nate stared at the renegade's shirt, looking for blood or bullet holes. All he found were two tiny rips level with the sternum.

"Did you hear me?" Pierce snapped when he received no answer. "Don't you have anything to say?"

"How?" Nate asked.

"How what?"

"I put three balls into you. Had you dead to rights each and every time. Yet there aren't any wounds. How can that be?"

Some of Pierce's former bluster returned. "Wouldn't you like to know, you rotten varmint! But it'll be a cold day in hell before I tell you. The secret of my medicine goes to my grave with me."

At a command from the Invincible One, the Crows shoved Nate toward the village. By now the battle was over, the attackers having been routed, but not before wreaking a terrible toll on the defenders. Crows were going from body to body, helping hurt friends and taking the few Utes found alive back to the village.

Halfway to the village the four warriors escorting Nate were approached by several others and a heated debate broke out. Nate had no idea why they were arguing, but soon suspected he was the cause when several pointed at him while making statements. Then Pierce appeared and sent the newcomers packing. As they left, the Invincible One spun and jabbed Nate with a finger.

"You think you're so damn clever, don't you?"

"I have my moments," Nate quipped, when in truth he didn't have the vaguest notion what Pierce was talking about.

"Well, it's not going to work. I won't let you turn these stupid savages against me, not when I'm just a few trapping seasons away from being one of the richest men in the country. Your killing a few Utes won't change a thing."

Nate was ushered onward, giving him time to reflect on the comment. Apparently some of the Crows had seen him trying to save Gray Badger from the Ute in the village, or else had witnessed him shooting the Ute with the bow. If word spread, it would reinforce the case of those Crows who wanted him spared.

Nate reached the edge of the trees, and observed women and children returning in droves. Mournful cries filled the air as loved ones were found lying in pools of blood. One elderly woman knelt beside her slain son, beating her temples with her fists. The next moment she had taken her son's knife, poised it over her hand, and sliced off one of her fingers as a token of the depth of her grief.

At the small lodge Nate received a surprise. Instead of being tied, he was simply pushed inside, and one of the Crows addressed him in sign language.

"We will leave you on your honor, Grizzly Killer, if you will promise not to escape."

"Why would you do this for me?" Nate asked.

"We have heard how you fought to save the young boy. We know now that you are not the enemy Invincible One would have us believe you are."

"Then I give you my word," Nate signed, "but on one condition."

"Speak."

"Tell everyone you meet that I am a friend and hold no ill will against the Crows for the way I have been treated. It is Invincible One who is to blame, for he has filled your heads with lies and deceived you into thinking he cannot be killed."

"We have seen with our own eyes that weapons have no more effect on him than drops of rain."

"He tricks all of you."

"How?"

"That I do not know, but I will before too long."

The Crow grunted. "I am Big Hail. Two Humps is my friend. I will do as you want, and so will some of the others. At the council later I will speak in your behalf."

"If Big Hail does this for me, then is he my friend as well," Nate signed, and received a warm smile. He watched the warriors trot off, and took a seat just inside the entrance, his shoulder leaning on the lodge. The events of the past hour or so had left him greatly fatigued, and he dearly wanted to lie down and sleep. Yet he couldn't, not when he didn't know if he would wake up again; he wouldn't put it past Pierce to slit his throat while he slept.

The general lamentation had grown loud enough to be heard a mile off. As was typical among most tribes, the women were the ones who expressed their grief vocally. The men reflected their sorrow in sad countenances, but did not cry out.

Both sexes indulged in other practices as well. One was the chopping off of fingers from the first joint up, as the elderly woman had done. Another custom was for mourners to take arrows and lightly stab themselves in a straight line across their foreheads from ear to ear. The men also pricked their arms, legs, and torsos, and some did it so many times their bodies were covered with thin scarlet rivulets. The females made a point of smearing their faces with blood, a tradition that demanded they must not wash until the blood had completely faded.

A few chose less painful methods. Shaving the hair close to the head was done, but infrequently. The war horses of chiefs and prominent warriors were also shaved, and the manes and tails wrapped in bundles and buried with the deceased, it being a Crow belief that the hairs would turn into horses in the spirit realm.

Presently all the wounded Utes, seven in number, were brought into the village. And then Nate was treated to an uncommon spectacle as the Crows took revenge on their enemies. Easterners would have branded the treatment the Utes received as barbaric in the extreme, but the Crows did no worse than would have been done to them had the situation been reversed.

The Utes were laid out in a row and completely surrounded. The Crows held the first captive down while one of their number wielded a razor-sharp knife with marvelous dexterity. The Ute's ears were sliced off and dangled in front of his eyes. Then came at him from the opposite side. Nate drove the tomahawk at the Crow's head, but the man jerked away.

Suddenly Gray Badger yelped and his arms slid from around Nate's waist. Nate twisted. A warrior had torn the boy loose and was bearing him off. Without hesitation Nate wheeled his horse to go to Gray Badger's aid, but in doing so he made a grave mistake.

A brash young Crow astride a bay, his face painted red with yellow lightning bolts on both temples, deliberately rode into Nate's mount, the bay's shoulder striking Nate's horse with such gut-wrenching force that Nate's animal crashed to the ground.

Nate leaped clear at the last instant. He scrambled to his feet and drew back the tomahawk to hit his attacker, but had the tomahawk wrenched from his grasp by a warrior who came up on him from the rear. Drawing his knife, Nate leaped and caught hold of the man. The warrior tried to batter him senseless with the tomahawk's haft. Nate thrust at the Crow's stomach, but only succeeded in nicking the skin.

The warrior got a hand on Nate's wrist, then sprang, bearing both of them to the earth. Nate rolled and tried to pull loose. He rose to one knee, and almost had the leverage to rise all the way when additional Crows pounced, flying from their speeding war horses like birds of prey swooping in for the kill.

Nate was buried under an avalanche of warriors. The knife was ripped from him so he fought with fists and feet, knees and elbows. It was a repeat of the fight in the valley, and as in that instance he was doomed to lose. He cracked a jaw, split a lip, and sank knuckles into an unprotected groin.

his nose was chopped off, and each finger and toe, one at a time. He was scalped prior to having his stomach slit and his intestines pulled out. Last, the Crow gouged the Ute's eyes from their sockets and threw them to the onlookers, who played catch with them until the novelty wore off.

The whole time the carving took place, the Crows kept up a scornful verbal abuse of their prisoners. There was much yelling and whooping, and those so inclined picked up discarded body parts and tossed them in the Ute's face.

Most amazing of all to Nate was the captive's ability to endure the torture without complaint or sign of weakness. Not once did a sound pass the Ute's lips, not even when the lips themselves were hacked off. Until the very end the Ute showed his courage and manhood. He finally expired when his heart was cut from his chest.

The other Utes had observed everything. Yet not one flinched when his time came. Not one called out, or cried, or did anything that would besmirch the reputation of his tribe.

At the end, all the heads were chopped off and jammed onto poles which the women took and waved about. When they'd had enough, they smashed the heads on rocks and scattered the brains outside the camp for beasts to eat. The same was done with the bodies of the Utes, except for one. It was tied to a tree, and the children were allowed to amuse themselves by shooting arrows and throwing small lances into it. By the time the children tired of their sport, the body resembled a porcupine.

Night had descended when the Crows dispersed to attend to their own dead. Nate's eyelids were growing heavy, and he put a hand to his mouth to stifle a yawn. Suddenly a small figure appeared and boldly stepped up to him.

"Good evening, Grizzly Killer. I saw them bring you in and have come to stand by your side."

Nate blinked in surprise, grabbed Gray Badger's shoulders, and pulled the boy in. "What are you doing here?" he signed. "You should have been far away by now."

"I started to go," the boy responded. "But your words hung in my head and I could not shake them out." He paused, then repeated the statement Nate had made earlier. "There comes a time when a man must stand and fight if he is to be worthy of being called a man."

"But I did not mean you should put yourself in danger on my account."

"What kind of friend would I be if I left you to face Invincible One alone?"

Nate didn't know whether to be flattered or angered. He glanced out, but saw no indication that anyone had noticed Gray Badger arrive. "I want you to leave. Go find your father. I am sure he will stand up for you."

"I will stay with you, my friend," the young Crow signed.

"Like hell," Nate said aloud, and gripping Gray Badger's wrist, he hauled the boy through the opening and gave him a push. "Go before you are seen. You can do more good for me if you tell your father that I am your friend and ask his aid."

"My father no longer cares about me."

"You are wrong. I am a father. So I know that in their hearts all fathers care for their sons, even if they do not always show it as often as they should." Nate put a hand on Gray Badger's shoulder. "There is something else you must keep in mind. A man can be measured by the quality of his children. You are a boy I would be proud to call my own, which means your father must be a wise man to have raised you so well. And no man could raise so well who loves so little. I think you do him an injustice, and I think it is time you found that out for yourself. Go home."

Gray Badger hesitated.

"Go home," Nate repeated. He folded his arms, and watched the boy run toward a lodge at the far end of the circle. A half-dozen fires had been lit, providing more than enough illumination for him to see that Gray Badger made it safely. The Crows were preparing for a special ceremony to commemorate the passing of their fellows, and would be up until dawn dancing and singing and chanting. Over in the council lodge a meeting was underway, the purpose of which wasn't hard to guess.

No one was paying Nate any regard. He could have left if he wanted, could have turned and faded into the forest without any of the Crows being the wiser. But he had given his word, and he solemnly believed that once a man had done so, nothing short of death must make him break it. He moved back into the small teepee and sat with his back to the wall.

The drone of voices and crackling of flames had a soothing effect. Nate dozed despite himself, and would not have awakened until morning, or perhaps never if Pierce had gotten to him first, had a small hand not gingerly touched his wrist. He snapped upright and shifted.

Gray Badger knelt next to him. The boy's features were in shadow, but there was no mistaking the glistening streaks on his cheeks.

"I thought you went home," Nate signed. "Why are you back so soon?"

"My father is gone."

"Where?"

"He is searching for me," Gray Badger replied, his hands shaking a little as he formed the symbols. He made a choking sound and went on. "My mother told me he has been out of his mind with worry. He wanted to come after me, but he is one of the few men brave enough to stand up to Invincible One, and he was worried about what Invincible One might do in his absence. So he sent his friend, Whirlwind Hawk, to find me."

"I told you."

"There is more," Gray Badger signed, and had to stop to clear his throat. "Invincible One has accused my father of having a hand in helping your friends escape."

Nate was all interest. "Why?"

"My mother says that Wolverine used my father as a hostage to keep the other men from shooting. Later, the warriors found tracks that showed my father had parted company with your friends without being harmed. Some tried to follow his trail, but lost it."

"You met Wolverine. He is not the kind to kill a hostage for no reason. He just let your father go his way in peace."

"Invincible One will never believe that."

Another possibility occurred to Nate. Since Two Humps had been a thorn in Pierce's side for some time, Pierce might have been looking for any excuse to turn the Crows against him. But the incident Pierce had picked smacked of desperation, for the Crows were not about to turn on one of their own chiefs without convincing proof of wrongdoing on the chief's part.

"I am afraid for my father," Gray Badger signed.

"You have nothing to fear. Two Humps would not be a chief if he was not a skilled warrior. He can stand up to Invincible One."

"But what if Invincible One challenges my father in public? My father would be killed as so many others have been."

The thought that struck Nate brought a somber smile to his lips. "I have an idea," he signed, and then went on to detail a request.

"Your mind must be in a whirl for you to think of such a thing," Gray Badger remarked. "No one can kill him. I know. I have seen his medicine work with my own eyes."

"My medicine is stronger," Nate boasted. "And I can prove it if you will do as I say."

The boy looked out at the council lodge. "It is forbidden for anyone to interrupt when the council is meeting," he signed nervously.

"Would you rather have your father come back and be accused by Invincible One of being a traitor to his own people?"

Gray Badger gnawed on his lower lip. "Are you doing this to save my father? He would not want any man to fight his fights for him."

"I am doing this for me," Nate said as he stood, "and for every other trapper in these mountains. Invincible One must be stopped before more whites lose their lives and their furs." He paused. "But most of all I am doing this for Wolverine. He was the best friend I have ever had, and I can not let his death go unpunished."

"You cared for him very much."

"We all make a lot of friends during a lifetime. But a few, a very few, are so special they are too deep for words to describe. Wolverine and I were like that."

"Then you should have your chance to avenge him," Gray Badger said, and hastened away.

Nate stepped outside, into the inky shadows to the right of the flap, and sat cross-legged with his back to the lodge. He imagined he would not have long to wait, and he was right. Within minutes a heated quarrel had broken out in the council lodge. Many Crows stopped whatever they were doing to listen.

In due course warriors began filing out. Jacob Pierce was the last to emerge. He had a firm hand on Gray Badger's arm, and roughly shoved the boy ahead of him every step of the way as the entire party came to the small lodge. Pierce pushed Gray Badger so violently that the boy stumbled, then knelt to look inside.

"I'm over here," Nate said softly.

Pierce spun and stabbed a hand at one of his pistols. He stopped when he saw that Nate posed no threat, and slowly straightened. "What the hell are you up to now, King? You ought to be ashamed of yourself. Sending the brat to do a man's work!"

"What's your answer?" Nate asked.

Pierce folded his arms and glowered. "I'm in no mood to humor you. My answer is no. Why should I soil my hands when you're not worth the bother? You proved that earlier."

"Showing your true color at last," Nate taunted, and regarded the gathered members of the council. "What did the Crows have to say about my challenge?"

"Most of them side with me."

"Do they?" Nate said, and before the renegade could intervene, he resorted to sign language to address the Crows. "Honorable warriors, I greet you in friendship," he began formally. "I came to this country wanting only to trap beaver, yet because of Invincible One I have been forced to strike at those my people regard as brothers. Is this right, I ask you? Should you let Invincible One carry on as he has, killing whites without cause and antagonizing those who are your friends?"

"Why you . . . !" Pierce snarled, advancing. He almost had his pistol out when one of the Crows said something that caused him to abruptly halt.

"In your hearts you know that he has led you astray," Nate continued. "You know that your people would be better off without him. If you will let me, I will rid you of him once and for all. I will show you that his medicine is an illusion."

Jacob Pierce could bear no more. Leaping, he caught hold of Nate's shirt with one hand and whipped out his flintlock with the other. He jabbed the barrel at Nate and pulled back the hammer, but before he could fire Nate batted the gun aside, swept up off the ground, and gave Pierce a powerful push that propelled the renegade back into the Crows. The pistol discharged into the ground. A few of the warriors tried to grab Pierce's arms, but the furious rogue shook them off and stormed forward.

"All right, King! You get your wish! But since you issued the challenge, I get to pick the weapons. And I choose tomahawks!" Pierce tramped off, shouting over his shoulder. "In one hour in the middle of the village. I'll be waiting."

The confused Crows stared after him, then at Nate, who signed, "Invincible One has accepted. In a short while we will fight with tomahawks." He went inside as murmuring broke out behind him. Soon the news would spread from one end of the village to the other. The entire population was likely to turn out to see the fight, which didn't bother Nate in the least. What *did* bother him was Pierce's choice of weapons. Why tomahawks, he wondered, when Pierce had already demonstrated that bullets had no effect on him?

A small form filled the doorway. "I hope you know what you are doing, Grizzly Killer," Gray Badger signed. "I would not like to lose the first white friend I have ever had."

Nate grinned. "Thank you. As to whether I know what I am doing, ask me when it is over."

"You sound worried."

"I am." Nate beckoned the young Crow to take a seat. "You mentioned seeing Invincible One fight before. Have you ever seen him use a tomahawk?"

"No. But he went on a raid against the Blackfeet once to show us that they could not kill him. My father went along. During the raid he saw a Blackfoot swing a tomahawk at Invincible One's chest."

"What happened?"

"Invincible One was knocked down but got right up again. He hit the Blackfoot on the mouth with his fist and the Blackfoot fell. Then he took the tomahawk. As the Blackfoot went to stand, Invincible One buried the tomahawk in his head."

"Was Invincible One bleeding afterward?"

"No. But he did walk slowly for a while."

Nate began pacing, a habit of his when under great stress. Evidently the renegade was as impervious to tomahawks and knives as he was to rifles and pistols. But there had to be a way to kill the bastard, and he would find it or die trying.

"Is there anything I can do to help you?" Gray Badger signed.

"Only one that I can think of," Nate responded, and crouched in front of the boy. "You can do me a great favor if I am slain."

"How?"

"Find a way of getting word to the Shoshones, to the village of Chief Broken Paw. I would like my wife and children to know my fate."

"You can depend on me," Gray Badger signed.

"I thank you. Now leave me. I have much to think about."

The boy complied, but it was clear he was loath to do so. Nate lowered the flap and sat in the darkness reminiscing, thinking of his loved ones, of his life in general. It was rare for him to have such a luxury before a conflict. The dangers of wilderness living were so plentiful and so varied that usually he was embroiled in a fight for his life without any advance warning whatsoever. He'd often dreaded that one day he might be shot from ambush, or ripped in half by a ravenous grizzly before he had time to so much as blink, and he'd wind up dying without having time to think about Winona or Zach or Evelyn.

The hour elapsed swiftly. Immersed in fond recollections, Nate had no idea it had gone by until he heard his name being bellowed. Stepping to the flap, he shoved it wide open, and wasn't at all taken aback to behold scores upon scores of Crows formed into a wide circle with an opening on the side facing the small lodge. Through the gap he could see his nemesis, waiting with a tomahawk in each hand.

Nate strode briskly to meet Pierce. The renegade had changed into a baggy buckskin shirt several sizes too big. Why, Nate had no idea. He walked up to the Invincible One and held out his right hand. "I'm ready if you are."

"You think you are, but I'll soon show you otherwise," Pierce said, extending his left arm. "This one is for you."

Gripping the haft, Nate hefted the tomahawk a few times, gauging its weight and balance. It was a superior weapon, made by a Crow expert at the craft.

"I can't tell you how much I've looked forward to this. Once I dispose of you, things can go back to the way they were," Pierce declared bitterly.

"Big talk when you haven't even gotten in the first lick yet."

"Then it's time I did," Pierce said, and executed a lightning strike that would have split Nate's face had Nate not skipped backward with a hair to spare.

Thus the fight was joined. Nate countered by swinging at Pierce's legs, but the renegade jumped from the blade's path. Pierce aimed a terrific blow at Nate's head, which Nate blocked. Then, in a downward motion, Nate tried to rip open Pierce's abdomen. Again Pierce evaded the swing.

The two combatants separated and circled, taking the measure of one another. Nate was slightly bigger, but he didn't delude himself into thinking that gave him any sort of edge. He feinted, forcing Pierce backward, and it was then, when Pierce raised his tomahawk to ward off the presumed attack, that Nate noticed he had been duped. *The handle of Jacob Pierce's tomahawk was four or five inches longer than his!*

The discovery jolted Nate so severely that he almost had his head separated from his shoulders. Only his pantherish instincts saved him. He backed off an extra stride, mad at himself for not realizing it sooner. Four or five inches wasn't much, but it was enough to give Pierce a longer reach, a wider swing. It was enough to cost Nate dearly in flesh and blood.

Pierce wore that aggravating smirk of his as he waded in close once more. He drove his tomahawk at Nate's chest, and when Nate spun out of reach,

Pierce reversed direction and went for Nate's neck. Their tomahawks clashed, parted, clashed once more.

Nate ducked to the right, staying well beyond the radius of his foe's reach. His tactic appeared to upset Pierce, who was transparently eager to end their fight quickly. Pierce's tomahawk cleaved the air, narrowly missing the top of Nate's head. For a second Pierce left his chest exposed, and Nate instantly struck. The edge of his tomahawk tore into the baggy buckskin shirt but *glanced off Pierce's body!*

The renegade staggered rearward, regained his balance, and sneered. "You'll have to do better than that, bastard!"

Nate was at a loss to know what to do. With his shorter reach he would be hard pressed to wound Pierce in the arms or legs. And with Pierce's chest virtually invulnerable, it seemed as if the outcome was foreordained. Then he remembered the one time he had hurt Pierce, when they had first met and he'd bruised Pierce's forehead. In a flash of inspiration the simple answer to his dilemma exploded full-blown in his brain and made him grin.

"What can you possibly find so funny?" Pierce demanded.

"Just this," Nate said. He had been circling to the right. Suddenly he circled to the left instead, throwing Pierce off stride. Dropping into a crouch, he swung at the renegade's knees. Pierce automatically hopped backward, and as he did, Nate flung himself forward, his left forearm rising to block Pierce's counter-swing even as he slashed his tomahawk in an overhand blow that ended with the blade cleaving into Pierce's skull. It sheared through hair, through skin, and deep into the underlying bone, so deep Nate couldn't pull it out again, so he let go and backed away.

Jacob Pierce's eyelids fluttered as he tottered to the left, his arms swinging feebly, a dull groan coming from his parted mouth. Blood poured down over his face, covering his eyes, his nose, his lips. He sputtered, began to reach upward, then froze for a few seconds before keeling over with a loud thud.

The Crows gaped in astonishment, and it was obvious from their expressions that many fully expected the renegade to rise and continue the fight.

Nate inhaled slowly, calming himself. He stepped to the body, pulled Pierce's knife from its sheath, and slit Pierce's buckskin shirt up the middle. In the pale glow of the flickering firelight a large, thin sheet of steel was exposed, attached by leather straps to Jacob Pierce's chest and shoulders. The sheet bore dozens of nicks, scrapes, and dents where it had been hit by knives, arrows, and bullets. "Well, I'll be damned," Nate said to himself. Rolling the body over, he pulled up the shirt high enough to reveal a similar sheet that covered Pierce's back from the shoulder blades to the waist.

A small Crow detached himself from the throng and walked over. Nate glanced at Gray Badger, tapped the steel, and signed, "So much for the Invincible One."

"He will never rise again?"

"Not in this life."

"No one will miss him. His medicine was as bad as his heart. What good can be said about a man like him?"

"In the end, he got what he deserved."

Epilogue

It was one week later that Nate King, Shakespeare McNair, and Tim Curry rode from the Crow village with all their horses and their possessions intact. McNair and Curry had shown up the day after the death of the Invincible One, after Shakespeare had spotted Nate strolling about the village as if he owned the place. And in a sense, Nate did.

The Crows could not apologize often enough to suit them. They did their best to accord him all hospitality, and assured him again and again that they were staunch friends of the trappers and the Shoshones.

To make matters perfect, on the second evening after the fight, Two Humps rode in from the south, dejected because he had failed to find his son. The reunion brought tears to many an eye. And with Pierce's deceit proven, Two Humps's public esteem rose higher than ever.

Now, with the sun shining down on the verdant countryside, Nate reined up on a hill for a last look at the village. "I suppose it was all worthwhile in the end," he commented.

"If nothing else, we've shown those Crows that not all whites are no-account, murdering sons of bitches," Shakespeare said.

"This nightmare has taught me something as well," Tim Curry said. "I hope you won't be upset, but I plan to head on back to the States and take up where I left off in Maine. There's a nice, safe job waiting for me there, and I can take a walk in the woods whenever I want without having to worry about being parted from my hair."

Shakespeare chuckled. "Do you mean to tell us you'd give up all the excitement of wilderness living for a plain, safe, civilized life?"

"Do you hold it against me?"

"Not at all, young Troilus." Shakespeare patted his parfleche. "If there's one thing old William S. has taught me, it's this." He paused to sort through his memory. "This above all, to thine own self be true."

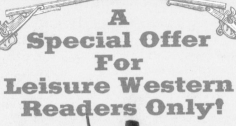

A Special Offer For Leisure Western Readers Only!

Get FOUR FREE* Western Novels

Travel to the Old West in all its glory and drama—without leaving your home!

Plus, you'll save between $3.00 and $6.00 every time you buy!

EXPERIENCE THE ADVENTURE AND THE DRAMA OF THE OLD WEST WITH THE GREATEST WESTERNS ON THE MARKET TODAY... FROM LEISURE BOOKS

As a home subsriber to the Leisure Western Book Club, you'll enjoy the most exciting new voices of the Old West, plus classic works by the masters in new paperback editions. Every month Leisure Books brings you the best in Western fiction, from Spur-Award-winning, quality authors. Upcoming book club releases include new-to-paperback novels by such great writers as:

Max Brand   Robert J. Conley   Gary McCarthy   Judy Alter
Frank Roderus   Douglas Savage   G. Clifton Wisler
David Robbins   Douglas Hirt

as well as long out-of-print classics by legendary authors like:

Will Henry   T.V. Olsen   Gordon D. Shirreffs

Each Leisure Western breaths life into the cowboys, the gunfighters, the homesteaders, the mountain men and the Indians who fought to survive in the vast frontier. Discover for yourself the excitment, the power and the beauty that have been enthralling readers each and every month.

SAVE BETWEEN $3.00 AND $6.00 EACH TIME YOU BUY!

Each month, the Leisure Western Book Club brings you four terrific titles from Leisure Books, America's leading publisher of Western fiction. EACH PACKAGE WILL SAVE YOU BETWEEN $3.00 AND $6.00 FROM THE BOOKSTORE PRICE! And you'll never miss a new title with our convenient home delivery service.

Here's how it works. Each package will carry a FREE* 10-DAY EXAMINATION privilege. At the end of that time, if you decide to keep your books, simply pay the low invoice price of $13.44, ($14.50 US in Canada) no shipping or handling charges added.* HOME DELIVERY IS ALWAYS FREE*. With this price it's like getting one book free every month.

AND YOUR FIRST FOUR-BOOK SHIPMENT IS TOTALLY FREE*! IT'S A BARGAIN YOU CAN'T BEAT!

 LEISURE BOOKS A Division of Dorchester Publishing Co., Inc.

GET YOUR 4
FREE* BOOKS NOW—
A VALUE BETWEEN
$16 AND $20

Mail the Free* Book Certificate Today!

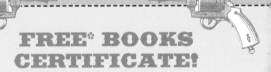

FREE* BOOKS
CERTIFICATE!

YES! I want to subscribe to the Leisure Western Book Club. Please send me my 4 FREE* BOOKS. Then, each month, I'll receive the four newest Leisure Western Selections to preview FREE* for 10 days. If I decide to keep them, I will pay the Special Member's Only discounted price of just $3.36 each, a total of $13.44 ($14.50 US in Canada). This saves me between $3 and $6 off the bookstore price. There are no shipping, handling or other charges.* There is no minimum number of books I must buy and I may cancel the program at any time. In any case, the 4 FREE* BOOKS are mine to keep—at a value of between $17 and $20!

*In Canada, add $5.00 Canadian shipping and handling per order for first shipment. For all subsequent shipments to Canada the cost of membership in the Book Club is $14.50 US, which includes $7.50 shipping and handling per month. All payments must be made in US currency.

Name _____

Address _____

City_____ State_____ Country_____

Zip_____ Telephone_____

If under 18, parent or guardian must sign. Terms, prices and conditions subject to change. Subscription subject to acceptance. Leisure Books reserves the right to reject any order or cancel any subscription.

Tear here and mail your FREE* book card today!

Get Four Books Totally
FREE* –
A Value between
$16 and $20

Tear here and mail your FREE* book card today!

PLEASE RUSH
MY FOUR FREE*
BOOKS TO ME
RIGHT AWAY!

LeisureWestern Book Club
P.O. Box 6613
Edison, NJ 08818-6613

AFFIX
STAMP
HERE

WOLF PACK

Chapter One

Jeremiah Sawyer had lived in the Rocky Mountains for over five years. He knew them as well as he knew the palms of his hands. The ways of the wild beasts, the ways of the various Indians tribes—they were all familiar to him.

So when a red hawk soaring high to the southeast uttered a piercing cry, Jeremiah looked up from the snare he was in the act of setting along a rabbit run.

Hawks made different sounds. There were the low whistlelike cries made by mating pairs as they whirled in aerial ballet. There were the occasional throaty cries of challenge issued by males. And there were those piercing cries of warning such as Jeremiah had just heard.

Straightening, the burly free trapper scanned the adjacent mountain slopes. He saw a few mule deer to the south, several mountain sheep on the craggy heights to the north. Other than the hawk, which had sailed to the east over the entrance to Jeremiah's little valley, nothing else moved.

Jeremiah sank to one knee to finish the snare, then froze, deeply troubled. He'd learned to rely on his gut instincts during his years of wilderness living, and his intuition was telling him to get back to his lodge as quickly as possible. Scooping up his rifle, he adjusted his possibles bag under his left arm and took off at a trot.

The hawk might have seen riders coming, Jeremiah reflected. Visitors were rare to the remote valley he called home. Every now and then some of his wife's people, the Crows, would stop by. And every blue moon another mountain man would show up to share a drink or three and a plug of chaw.

There was another, more disturbing possibility.

Jeremiah's sanctuary was nestled along the border of Crow country. To the south lived Utes, perennial enemies of the Crows. To the east lived Arapahoes and Cheyennes, who sometimes raided deep into Crow land. And well to the north lived the Blackfeet, who were at war with all tribes not belonging to their confederacy.

Jeremiah had long lived with a secret dread of the valley being found by an enemy war party. He had picked the isolated site because it was so far off the beaten path that getting into a racket with hostiles was unlikely. But a man never knew when fate would rear its ugly head.

The sun hung high in the afternoon sky. Soon, Jeremiah knew, Yellow Flower would begin making supper. She and the girls had spent the morning gathering berries and roots, and the last Jeremiah had seen them, they had been pounding stakes into the ground so they could stretch out the hide of a black bear he had killed the day before and scrape the hide clean of tissue and hair.

If anything ever happened to them, Jeremiah did not know what he would do with himself. Before he met Yellow Flower, he had been a wanderer and a bit of a rake. Now, she was his anchor, the source of the greatest happiness he had ever known—a happiness so deep and so intense that he gave thanks every day for the blessing of her love. Together with his daughters, she gave his life meaning.

Suddenly the air was rent by a faint scream, punctuated by a gunshot.

Fear rippled down Jeremiah's spine. He poured on the speed, running as fast as his legs would fly. In his mind's eye he imagined his family being set upon by Blackfeet or Bloods. Yellow Flower was fearless and a fair shot, but she was no match for a war party of seasoned warriors.

The high grass lashed Jeremiah's legs. He could see the stand of pines in which the lodge was located, but as yet was unable to catch a glimpse of the clearing where it stood. His possibles bag and ammo pouch slapped against his chest as he ran, and he had to keep one hand on his pistol or risk having it slip out from under his belt.

Jeremiah was within 50 yards of his goal when another shot rang out. He thought he heard gruff laughter, but couldn't be sure.

Convinced hostiles were definitely to blame, Jeremiah slowed as he neared the trees. It would do his loved ones no good if he were to blunder in among his enemies and be slain outright.

He cocked his rifle when he entered the pines. Gliding from trunk to trunk, Jeremiah strained his ears to catch more sounds, but heard only a vague rustling. Then he saw the lodge, awash in a beam of sunlight, and in front of it were seven horses he had never seen before.

Jeremiah halted behind the last trunk to survey the clearing. A thin tendril of smoke wafted from the top of the lodge, as it always did when Yellow Flower cooked a meal. The flap hung open. As he watched, a shadow flitted across the opening.

The next moment a tall man emerged.

To say that Jeremiah was surprised would be an understatement. The visitor was a fellow trapper, a company man, an employee of the Rocky Mountain Fur Company. Jeremiah had run into him at the last rendezvous. Holding his rifle level, Jeremiah boldly strode into the open. "Lassiter?"

The tall man turned, a smile creasing his rugged features. "So there you are. I was wondering where you had gotten to, hos. After I came all this way just to see you, I was afeared you were off on a gallivant and wouldn't be back for weeks."

"I never leave my family except during trapping season," Jeremiah said. He glanced at the lodge, then at the horses. "Who are you with? Where are the others? What was all the shooting about? I thought I heard a scream."

"My, my, aren't you a bundle of questions?" Lassiter said. He sat down on an old stump and rested his rifle across his thighs. "Have a seat, friend. We have some talking to do."

"I'd rather check on my family first," Jeremiah

said, moving toward the tepee.

Lassiter made a clucking sound. "Maybe your ears are plugged full of wax. I want to palaver and I want to do it right this minute."

Jeremiah didn't care for the man's tone. "I'll do as I damn well please, thank you. You can just hold your horses a minute or two." At the opening he lowered his rifle, bent at the waist, and went to enter. The next moment he found himself staring down the barrel of a gun held by a huge man in greasy buckskins.

"I'd do as Lassiter says, mister, were I you."

Caught flat footed, Jeremiah backed away, careful not to elevate his rifle. The huge man squeezed through the gap, revealing a shock of black hair as greasy as his clothes.

"Don't plug him, Bear," Lassiter said. "We need him alive."

From out of the pines came more strangers, five in all. Three wore garb typical of mountaineers. One appeared to be a half-breed. The last, incredibly, was a Blood Indian.

"What the hell is going on here?" Jeremiah demanded. "Where's my family?"

"You'll see them soon enough," Lassiter said smugly. "Provided you cooperate with us, hos."

"Cooperate?" Jeremiah said. He could not help but notice that the other men had fanned out to form a ring around him. He was completely hemmed in and dared not lift a finger or he would be instantly cut down.

Lassiter scratched the stubble on his chin. "Let me explain, Sawyer. At the last rendezvous I heard tell that you always trade a goodly number of your plews for gold coins. The word is that you have a big stash cached somewhere. I want them."

The audacity of the man would have been laughable if not for his six menacing companions. Jeremiah tried a bluff. "I don't know what in the hell you're flapping your gums about. If I had a stash of gold, I wouldn't be living in the middle of nowhere in a buffalo-hide lodge. I'd be back in the States, set up proper in a fancy mansion with servants at my beck and call."

A cruel grin creased Lassiter's mouth. "I didn't say that you were as rich as old King Midas. The story is that you have a few thousand socked away, is all."

"And who fed you this lie?" Jeremiah said. "Someone three sheets to the wind, I reckon."

"His name doesn't matter," Lassiter said. "All that need concern you is giving us the money. Do it now and spare yourself a heap of grief."

"You just waltz in here and steal me blind, is that it?"

"More or less."

Jeremiah flushed with anger when several of the men snickered at his expense. "Are all of you company men? What do you think will happen when your employers find out what you've been up to?"

"Really, Sawyer. Are you dunderhead enough to think that I still work for the Rocky Mountain Fur Company?" Lassiter shook his head. "It wasn't for me. Long hours and working like a dog for a pittance. No thanks. I've found a better way."

"You've turned to robbery."

"Among other things."

The sinister tone the man used sparked raw

fear in Jeremiah. Not for himself, but for those he cared for most. Shifting, he tried to peer into the lodge but he was at the wrong angle.

"Drop the rifle," Lassiter said abruptly. No sooner were the words out of his mouth than the other five trained their weapons on Jeremiah's chest. "And do it nice and slow unless you're partial to the notion of being turned into a sieve."

Reluctantly, Jeremiah obeyed. He was so furious he could barely think straight. All he wanted was to get his hands around the bastard's throat.

"That's being smart," Lassiter said. "Now tell us where we can find this gold of yours?"

Without hesitation Jeremiah squared his shoulders and said, "I don't have any."

"Think again. Believe me when I say you don't want us to pry the information from your lips."

"I'd like to see you try," Jeremiah said, poised to draw the flintlock if a single one of them came toward him. He would rather die fighting for his life than submit meekly like a weakling.

"Suit yourself," Lassiter said, and he made a gesture with his right hand.

Jeremiah was tensed to strike. Years of wilderness living had turned his body into iron whipcord, and he was certain he could draw and fire before any of the cutthroats reached him. He glanced from one to the other. The one called Bear took a step toward him and Jeremiah whirled, his hand clawing for the polished butt of a smooth-bore pistol. Too late he realized it was a ploy, a trick to divert his attention.

Like a pair of striking serpents, the Blood and the half-breed pounced, closing from different directions as once. Out of the corners of his eyes Jeremiah saw them coming and tried to turn to confront them but they were on him in an instant. Steely fingers seized his. He winced as his arms were savagely wrenched behind his back. A moccasin flicked out and caught him across the shin. The next thing he knew, he was on his knees in front of a smirking Lassiter.

"Some folks just have to learn the facts of life the hard way."

"Go to hell!"

Lassiter slowly rose, his lean form resembling that of a rattler rearing to strike. "I'm afraid you'll be suffering the fires of damnation long before I will. For the last time, Sawyer, where's your gold?"

Jeremiah preferred to die than reveal the secret. But he had his wife and daughters to think of. Rather than keep up the pretense, he asked bluntly, "What about my family? If I tell you, will you let them go?"

Some of the ruffians laughed.

"You still haven't seen the light, have you?" Lassiter said. "You're going to tell us one way or the other. As for your family, they're not worth fretting yourself over."

The sadistic gleam in the tall man's eyes caused an icy knot to form in Jeremiah's breast. "What do you mean?"

"Show him, boys."

Bear came over and grabbed hold of Jeremiah's hair. The Blood and the breed held onto his arms. Between the three of them, they hauled Jeremiah over to the lodge and Bear pushed his head low enough for him to see the interior clearly.

At the sight of the three bodies, each lying in a

spreading pool of blood, Jeremiah was overcome by dizziness and his limbs turned to mush. Bitter bile filled his mouth. It was all he could do to catch a breath.

Yellow Flower was naked, lying on her side by the fire she had started. Her torn beaded dress lay nearby. There was a bullet hole in her left breast.

The two girls were at opposite sides of the tepee. The oldest had been knifed, slit open from navel to chin. The youngest had been shot in the stomach. Both girls, mercifully, were clothed.

Harsh, grating mirth shattered Jeremiah's daze and brought him back to the land of the living. A potent rage gripped him, rage such as he had never known, and without thinking, he twisted and slammed his right foot into Bear's left knee even as he whipped the Blood into the breed.

Jeremiah found himself free. He could have turned, wrested a gun from one of them, and tried to slay Lassiter before the rest made wolf meat of him. But he was too canny for that. He wanted revenge on all of them. So the moment they let go, he streaked around the lodge and into the trees while to his rear Lassiter bellowed.

"After him, you jackasses! Don't let him get away!"

Limbs snatched at Jeremiah's face and hands. He didn't care. Blood flecked his cheeks and wrists. It didn't matter. In all the world only his vengeance mattered.

Then the lead started to fly.

Chapter Two

Nathaniel King was on his way home after a successful hunt. Packed on the three extra horses he had brought along were the remains of an elk he had picked off at 200 yards. He was rightfully proud of the shot, made in heavy timber when the bull was on the move. Few men could have made it.

Nate was a member of the trapping fraternity, a man who caught and sold his own hides rather than work for a fur company.

Typical of his hardy kind, Nate wore buckskins and moccasins. A Hawken rested across his saddle. A pair of matching flintlocks adorned his waist, as well as a long butcher knife and a tomahawk. He was armed for bear, as the saying went, and with good reason.

A lone white man never knew when he might wind up beset by Indians or animals determined to deprive him of his life. The rate at which trappers perished was fearsome. In any given year, out of scores who ventured into the wild to make their fortune laying traps for beaver, a quarter of them fell victim to the random perils so common in the mountains.

Only the toughest survived for more than two or three seasons. Exceptional were those who lasted longer, men like Nate King, men who became as hard as their surroundings.

On this day Nate rode along a spine connecting two high country slopes. He had chosen the high lines so he could keep his eyes skinned for movement below. It paid for a man to have eyes like an eagle, as his mentor Shakespeare McNair so often said.

Thinking of McNair brought a smile to the big man's face. It had been a spell since last he saw his best friend, so a visit was long overdue. It would do their wives good to get together, and Nate's kids never tired of the antics of their Uncle Shakespeare.

The black stallion that Nate rode pricked its ears and swung its head to the west. Nate looked and immediately reined up.

Crossing the next valley were four riders. At that distance it was impossible to note details. Nate recognized them as Indians though and drew into the shadows to keep from being seen.

They might be friendly Shoshones, Nate's adopted tribe. They might even be Crows. But it had been Nate's hard experience never to take anything for granted. The warriors might just as well be unfriendly and he didn't care to tangle with them if it could be avoided.

Nate observed them carefully. They rode in single file, Indian fashion, two on pintos, another on a bay, the last on a sorrel. Their angle of travel would take them south of the spine and put them between him and home.

Only when the quartet had vanished into thick timber did Nate ride from cover and descend the far side of the spine, threading among tightly packed firs and deadfalls. At the bottom he swung to the south, holding the stallion to a walk. The three packhorses plodded along wearily, no doubt as anxious to reach their small corral as he was to reach his cabin.

Often Nate stopped to look and listen. The stock of the .60-caliber Hawken rested on his right thigh. Made by the master craftsmen Jacob and Samuel Hawken of St. Louis, Hawkens were rapidly gaining a reputation as the most reliable guns ever made. Nate's sported a smooth 34-inch octagonal barrel, a crescent-shaped butt plate, low sights, and a percussion lock.

His pistols were also works of quality. Single-shot .55-caliber flintlocks, they were almost as powerful as the Hawken at short range.

All three were vastly superior to the trade guns given Indians. Fusees, as they were called, often blew apart or misfired or broke readily. They were of such poor workmanship that most Indians preferred to rely on their bows and arrows rather than the white man's weapon of choice.

Crowning Nate's shock of black hair was a beaver hat. A Mackinaw coat lay draped over the back of his saddle. He was glad it was there and not on his person. A red coat stood out in a green forest like the proverbial sore thumb.

The woodland thinned. Far ahead figures moved. Nate halted, his eyes narrowing against the glare of the high sun. The Indians were there, all right, heading due south now, the same direction he had to take.

"Damn," Nate said to himself and pulled in behind a briar patch. He had a choice to make. Should he play it safe, camp there until morning, and then go on? Or should he try to swing around ahead of them?

As if he truly had much of a choice. The disturbing fact was that he happened to be less than ten miles from the cabin. If the warriors kept on as they were going, they'd probably get there before nightfall.

Nate wished Shakespeare was along. The two of them had licked their weight in hostiles more times than he cared to count. As it was, he would have to rely on a sizable portion of pure luck if he hoped to save his family.

Prodding the stallion with his heels, Nate angled to the left, moving parallel to the warriors. Mentally he reviewed the lay of the land in front of them—countryside he had traveled through so often he could ride across it at a full gallop in the dead of a moonless night and avoid every obstacle in his path.

Nate marked the position of the sun, then turned his attention to the ridge ahead. That ridge overlooked the domain he had claimed as his own, a verdant valley three times the size of most, watered by a lake rife with fish and fowl, a virtual paradise.

Presently Nate came to a hillock. Stopping shy of the crest, he dismounted, ground hitched the stallion, and crept to the top. From his vantage point he saw the warriors plainly. His mouth became a thin slit and his eyes as flinty as quartz.

They were Utes.

Like the Blackfeet, Piegans, and Bloods to the north, the Utes had made no secret of their dislike for whites. They regarded trappers as invaders and either ran off or slew every mountain man they found in their territory.

Nate's valley happened to be at the northern limit of the Ute range. Years ago, when Nate first settled there, the Utes had made annual raids in an effort to drive him off. They had failed.

It was doubtful the four warriors were part of a war party; none were painted for war. Nate figured it was a hunting party, maybe younger warriors eager to count coup who had decided to test the mettle of the white devil they had heard so much about from older men.

Nate had to stop them before they reached his valley. And since he would find no better spot to make a stand, he pressed the Hawken to his shoulder and fixed a bead on the back of the last warrior. It would be an easy shot. The Ute would never know what hit him.

But Nate lowered the Hawken and stood. He had never been a backshooter by nature, a weakness some of the other free trappers had mocked him for having. To them, shooting an enemy in the chest or between the shoulder blades was all the same. As one voyager from Canada had so succinctly put it, "A dead enemy is a dead enemy. *C'est la guerre, mon ami.*"

Swallowing hard, Nate planted both feet, made

sure his ammo pouch and powder horn hung
loosely across his chest, and cupped a hand to
his mouth. From his lips issued the lusty war
whoop of his adopted people, the Shoshones.

The Utes wheeled their mounts and sat staring
at him. Evidently suspecting a trick, they made
no move to come toward him.

Nate tensed, ready to leap for cover when they
charged. They were just out of bow range. By
the time they got close enough, he would be flat
on his stomach, picking them off as fast as he
could.

The huskiest of the warriors broke ranks, riding
slowly forward, his bow slung across his back, a
lance held low at his side. He acted calmly, as if
he were riding into his own village.

Keeping one eye on the others, Nate cradled
the Hawken in the crook of his left elbow. He
wouldn't put it past the Utes to try a trick of
their own.

The warrior drew near enough for Nate to see
the man's features clearly, and Nate allowed himself to relax. Grinning, he strode to the bottom of
the hillock and used sign language to say, "It has
been many moons, Two Owls."

The Ute chief whom Nate had befriended years
ago reined up and smiled in genuine friendship.
"Too many moons, my brother. Question. Your
family is well?"

"And growing. I have a girl now."

"Does your son follow in your footsteps?"

"He tries."

"Then he will grow to be a man of honor, as
is his father." Two Owls turned somber. "Question, Grizzly Killer," he signed, using the name

by which Nate was known by a goodly number of tribes. "Have you had any trouble with my people in the past few moons?"

The query surprised Nate. Ever since he had arranged a truce between the Shoshones and the Utes, who had been squabbling over a remote valley special to both peoples, the Utes had left him alone. They no longer made annual raids against him. "No. Why do you ask?"

"Some of the young hotheads think that you are to blame for the death of a warrior named Buffalo Hump and his family."

"I have not rubbed out a Ute since the truce."

Two Owls signed, "I believe you. But the younger ones do not know you like I do, Grizzly Killer. They still see all whites as our bitter enemies. Were it not for my influence, they would already have paid you a visit."

The knowledge made Nate wonder how long his family would be safe if anything were to happen to the chief. "Tell me of this Buffalo Hump."

"He was an old warrior, well past his prime. In his time he counted over twenty coup, and he was widely respected." Two Owls lowered his hands a moment, his sadness obvious. "Every Thunder Moon he liked to journey to Dream Lake, where he went on his first vision quest when he was only fourteen winters old. He would take his wife and two daughters with him."

Nate knew of Dream Lake, a small, pristine jewel fed by runoff, one of the highest lakes in the Rockies. It was located about 15 miles from his cabin.

"This last time Buffalo Hump did not return as expected and warriors were sent to learn why,"

Two Owls signed. His gestures became sharper as anger crept over him. "They found him and his family butchered. Things had been done to him that even we would not do to our enemies. His wife had also been mutilated. As for his daughters—" Two Owls stopped.

"There is no need to go on," Nate signed.

For a minute the chief simply sat there, glowering at the sky. At last he sighed. "It was a great loss, Grizzly Killer. Buffalo Hump and I were very close. I relied on his wisdom during councils."

"There were no clues to who did it?"

"One," Two Owls signed, staring Nate in the eyes. "The warriors found a strange knife. It is no longer than my longest finger and folds in half so that the blade fits into a groove in the wooden handle."

The revelation was deeply disturbing. Until that moment, Nate had suspected that other Indians were responsible for the old warrior's death since few whites ever ventured anywhere near Dream Lake. But based on the description, the knife found had to be a jackknife, and only whites carried them. Warriors preferred big-bladed butcher and hunting knives. Indian women liked smaller knives, but the blades needed to be rigid and thin for the sewing and hide work the women did.

"Those who trap beaver carry this kind of knife," Two Owls signed.

"I know."

"Since Wolverine and you live closest to Dream Lake, the two of you were blamed. I came to talk to both of you. We went to Wolverine's wooden lodge first but he was not there."

Wolverine was none other than Nate's mentor, Shakespeare McNair, who in his younger days had been a regular hellion in battle and thereby earned the name.

"I have not seen Wolverine in over a moon," Nate signed, suddenly worried that whoever slew Buffalo Hump might have done the same to Shakespeare and Shakespeare's Flathead wife, Blue Water Woman.

Two Owls pursed his lips. "You did my people a great service when you helped us settle matters with the Shoshones. I am in your debt, Grizzly Killer. But I do not know how long I can hold the young warriors back. Many of them thirst for vengeance. The only way to put out the fires in their hearts is to find the ones who are truly to blame. Since your kind are the culprits, you would have a better chance of doing so than I would."

The chief was being as polite as could be, but the underlying message could not have been more sinister had he made a declaration of war. Either Nate tracked down the real culprits or the Utes would come against him in greater numbers than ever before, and there was nothing Two Owls could do to prevent it. His family wouldn't stand a prayer.

"I am sorry, Grizzly Killer," Two Owls signed. "You have taught me that not all whites are bad medicine, but my people do not see you through my eyes."

"How much time do I have?"

"There is no way to tell. I will try to get word to you if an attack is planned."

Nate made the sign for gratitude, which was

done by extending both hands flat, palms down, and sweeping them in a curve outward and downward.

The war chief of the Utes grunted and rode off to rejoin his fellows. The quartet then trotted to the southwest. Nate stared until they were out of sight, his mind awhirl with the life-or-death situation his family faced. He wasn't about to move, no matter what. Yet how was he going to find the guilty parties when they were long gone, their tracks no doubt long since obliterated by the elements?

Hurrying over the hillock, Nate mounted the black stallion and applied his heels. He no longer cared how tired the packhorses might be. Winona, Zach, and Evelyn were more important.

Twilight veiled the majestic Rockies in a gray shroud when Nate paused on the lip of a ridge overlooking his valley. The sight of the familiar emerald lake brought a sense of relief. He was almost home.

Descending to the valley floor took over half an hour. He expected to see smoke curling from the stone chimney of their cabin, but when the log structure came into view, it appeared deserted. There was no smoke. The door was closed. The leather flaps to both windows were drawn.

A kernel of fear formed in Nate—fear that he was too late, that a band of young warriors had already struck. He fairly flew the last quarter of a mile and sprang from the saddle before the stallion came to a standstill.

Hawken in hand, Nate threw open the door and burst inside. The single large room was empty. No fire had been kindled in the fireplace. The supper dishes had not been placed on the table.

"Winona?" Nate called out. "Zach?"

Dashing back outside, Nate ran around to the corral he had built. It was as empty as the cabin. All the other horses were gone: Winona's mare, Zach's calico, and their extra pack animals.

There could only be one explanation, and it practically froze Nate's blood in his veins. A Ute band had struck, carted off his family, and stolen their stock.

Racing to the stallion, Nate vaulted into the saddle and made a hasty circuit of the cabin, seeking sign. Thanks to the expert teaching of Shakespeare and Shoshone friends such as Touch The Clouds and Drags The Rope, Nate could track as well as any man alive.

At the southwest corner of the corral Nate found where a lot of horses had made off briskly into the forest. The freshness of the tracks, indicated by clods of earth which had not yet had time to dry out, gave him hope. He figured the attack had taken place within the past hour. So the Utes couldn't have gotten all that far.

At a mad gallop Nate raced in pursuit. He left the packhorses standing near the cabin. They wouldn't stray off, not with plenty of grass and water handy.

By now the twilight had faded to the point where Nate could barely see the well-marked trail. He worried that darkness would force him to curtail his pursuit until morning. Thinking of his wife in the clutches of hostile warriors was almost enough to give him fits.

Suddenly Nate sped into a meadow. At the opposite end something moved in the shadows.

On looking closer, he beheld riders and seven or eight horses. Elated that he had come on the Utes so soon, he whipped the Hawken to his shoulder and charged, throwing prudence to the cool wind.

The nearest rider raised a rifle. Nate curled his finger around the Hawken's trigger and fixed a quick bead. He was about to apply enough pressure to discharge the black powder when the oncoming rider whooped in delight.

"Pa! Pa! It's great to have you back!"

Nate King snapped the Hawken down and broke out in a cold sweat. In his unreasoning fear and haste he had almost put a lead ball into his own flesh and blood.

The boy galloped to his father's side, so over-joyed that he cackled crazily and slapped his thigh. "Land sakes, Pa. It took you long enough. Ma was getting a mite worried. I told her you'd probably gone plumb to Canada. You've always wanted to visit the North Country."

Laughing, Nate reached out and affectionately rubbed the youngster's tousled dark locks. "You're pretty near right, but I had to go up, not north. This time of year it's hard to find elk at the lower elevations. I had to climb a mountain so high I could have spit on the moon from where I stood before I found the herd I was looking for."

"Shucks, Pa. There ain't no mountain that high. Don't try your tall tales on me. I'm getting too old to believe those preposterous stories of you."

"Preposterous?" Nate said, pretending to be flustered. "Where'd you learn a two-dollar word like that? Have you been hanging around that no-account McNair again?"

"Pa!" young Zachary said. "Don't let him hear you talk like that or he's liable to get his feelings hurt."

"Son," Nate said, "that old coon has a hide thicker than a bull buffalo's. He's happiest when he can be as feisty as a riled bantam rooster, and he's feistiest when I'm picking on him. Trust me. Insults slide off his back like water off a duck."

Just then Nate smelled a tangy minty scent and looked up. The aromatic fragrance was one he had inhaled countless times since marrying the loveliest maiden in the Shoshone nation. Eleven years later, he still felt that way.

Winona King's features were as smooth as the day she had taken Nate for her husband. She wore a finely crafted buckskin dress, which she had made herself. Her raven tresses had been braided so she could strap a cradleboard to her back. Her white teeth flashing, she bent to give her man a warm kiss on the cheek. "We have missed you, husband."

"So I gather," Nate said, pleased by her show of emotion. As a general rule, Indians seldom went in for such public displays. Matters of the heart were confined to behind lodge walls.

"Did you bring back as much meat as we need to tide us over until winter?" Winona asked in her perfectly precise English.

It was a source of pride to Nate that she had mastered his tongue much more thoroughly than he had mastered hers. She was exceptionally intelligent. Shakespeare liked to say that Nate had married her for her intellect instead of her beauty, it being McNair's belief that a man who wed a woman smart enough for two came out even in the long run.

"I've brought plenty of meat," he said, "but I've also brought word of a heap of trouble. We have to talk."

"First greet your daughter."

Nate moved the stallion forward a step so he could lean to the right. A small bundle of joy beamed at him from out of the cradleboard. She cooed when he pecked her cheek. "Goodness gracious, precious. How you keep growing. The next time I come back from a hunting trip, I expect you'll have a beau."

Winona had the missing pack animals on a long lead. She swung her mare beside her son's mount and together they headed across the meadow.

"What the blazes are you doing out here anyway?" Nate asked as he fell into step beside her. "Did the packhorses get out of the corral?"

"No," Winona said. "They had been cooped up so long they were restless. We brought them out to the meadow and let them graze and wander a while."

"We would have been back sooner, Pa, but for that darn painter," Zach said.

"What painter?" Nate asked, all interest. Recently he'd nearly lost his life tangling with a panther, or mountain lion as some of the mountaineers called the big cats, and he had no interest in doing so again.

Zach bobbed his chin at a slope to the south. "Up there yonder. A little before sunset it set to hollering and screeching and spooked two of the horses. I had to fetch them before we could head on home."

"We haven't heard it in a while," Winona said. "I imagine it has wandered elsewhere by now."

As if to prove her wrong, in the pines directly ahead of them, a caterwauling cry rife with menace rent the night.

Chapter Three

Men and women who are genuinely brave do not think of themselves in a time of crisis. It is an undeniable mark of true courage that, when danger strikes, the courageous are more concerned with the welfare of others.

So it was to Nate King's credit that, the instant he heard the feral challenge of the savage cat, he goaded the black stallion out in front of his wife and offspring so that he was in a better position to protect them should the painter attack.

And it was equally to young Zach's credit that he did the same. Ablaze with excitement, the boy hefted his heavy Hawken to his shoulder and cocked the hammer.

"Don't shoot unless you see the varmint," Nate said. "A man who shoots at shadows can wind up with an empty gun when he needs it the most."

The cry had issued from an inky stand of trees

where the undergrowth was especially dense. Nate glued his eyes to the tract, seeking a telltale tawny flash that would be all the forewarning he had of the beast's onslaught. High grass rustled, but whether from the wind or the passage of a large form, he couldn't tell.

Nate was not about to give the painter the chance to spring on them from ambush. Sometimes the best way to handle a contrary critter, he had learned, was to give the critter a taste of its own medicine. With that notion in mind, he urged the stallion into a trot, straight at the high grass. Whooping and yipping like a demented coyote, he flapped his arms and legs.

The panther was there, all right. A feline shape streaked from concealment, but instead of charging, it made off to the south in smooth bounds that covered 15 feet at a time. In the bat of an eye it was lost among the vegetation.

Nate reined up and elevated his rifle but he held his fire when he saw there was no need for it. He spotted the mountain lion for a fraction of a second as it crossed a clearing; then it was gone for good.

"Darn," Zach said. "I was hoping to have me a new painter hide."

"Just be grateful it didn't draw blood," Nate said. He waited for Winona to catch up and took the lead rope from her. "Now let's get home before that cat has a change of heart and comes back for its supper."

Once the horses were safely bedded down and the elk meat lay on a counter in the corner of the cabin, Nate could finally unwind. He took a seat at their table and propped his feet on top. "I dried the strips proper, but ran out of salt before I was done," he said for his wife's benefit.

Winona was examining the jerky closely. "None of it spoiled. We will eat the unsalted meat over the next few days." Opening a cupboard he had constructed from soft pine, she removed a parfleche and began stuffing the jerked meat inside. "You did well, husband."

"I have my days," Nate said.

"You mentioned something about trouble, Pa," Zach said. He was seated on the bed, tickling Evelyn with a jay feather.

"That I did," Nate said and launched into the full story of his encounter with the Ute leader and the information that had been imparted.

"It was kind of Two Owls to warn us," Winona said afterward. "You are supposed to go off trapping soon. We would have been alone when the Utes came for us."

Zach straightened up. "But what do we do now that we know? We can't hardly fight off forty or fifty warriors at a time."

"There is only one thing we can do," Winona said. "We must find the ones who slew Buffalo Hump before the Utes drive us off or wipe us out."

It shouldn't have surprised Nate that his wife made the suggestion. Bred from infancy to be worthy partners of their warrior husbands, Shoshone women could be as fierce as their mates when the need arose. He had seen firsthand how they fought like tigers when their villages were attacked. But he was unwilling to put her in danger when there was an alternative. "What's this we business? I aim to go after them by my lonesome."

"And what will we be doing?" Winona asked. "Are we supposed to stay here doing nothing?"

"No. I figured that the kids and you can stay with your uncle while I tend to whoever brought this aggravation down on our heads."

"I see," Winona said, clipping the two words as if spitting them out rather than speaking them. "You would feel better if we were safe in a Shoshone village."

"I'm glad you understand." Nate grinned, trying to appease her, although he knew full well he was in for a dose of her temper.

Winona gave him the sort of look that could melt ice at ten paces. "You want us to cower among our kin while you risk your life on our behalf?"

"Who said anything about cowering?" Nate asked. "I just think it's for the best, what with you having Zach and Evelyn to look out after and all."

"We have them to look after, husband." Winona walked to the table. "In the past, when they were younger, I was content to stay here while you went off time and time again. But no longer. This time I will not stay behind. Our whole family is in peril, so we will deal with the problem as a family."

"But what about the boy and Evelyn?"

"Zach is old enough to handle himself. Didn't he save you from those Gros Ventres a while ago? And who was it who escaped from the Blackfeet all on his own?"

"True, true," Nate said. "But this is different."

"Tell me how."

Nate opened his mouth to speak, but for the life of him he couldn't think of a convincing argument. Truth was, she had a valid point. In frontier terms, Zach was on the verge of manhood. Sheltering the youth would do him more harm than good in the long run. A body had to learn to stand on his own two feet at an early age or he never would.

Nate glanced at his son and saw the earnest appeal in the boy's eyes. Zach wanted to help, to prove he could carry his weight. It would be wrong to deny him.

Then there was Winona. Nate knew she had an independent streak in her a yard wide, and once she set her mind to something, only an act of the Almighty could change it.

In this case Nate couldn't blame her for wanting to lend a hand. She had every right. Her family and home were at risk. What sort of husband would he be if he raised a fuss over her doing what came naturally?

"Well?" Winona said.

Sitting up, Nate regarded his wife and son soberly. "I must be as crazy as a loon. But I'm not about to try to buck you on this. The danger is to our whole family, so as a family we'll clear ourselves of blame."

Zach came off the bed as if shot from a cannon and leaped so high into the air his head nearly brushed the ceiling. Like a virile young wolf reveling in being alive, he howled and spun. "Thank you, Pa! I'll pull my own weight. You'll see. Whatever you want, whatever you say—"

"Calm down, son, before you bust a gut," Nate

said grinning. "I know you'll do right fine." His grin evaporated as he pondered how best to proceed. Their first step was to find those responsible for the grisly deaths. But how, when they lacked a single shred of information that might identify the guilty party or parties other than the jackknife? "Maybe we'll have to make a trip to Dream Lake."

"What could we hope to find after all this time?" Winona said. "It has been over a month."

"I'm open to a better idea," Nate said.

Zach was listening intently. Now that he had been given a chance to show his folks that he was no longer the small boy they all too often treated him as, he was bound and determined not to let them down. "I have an idea," he said tentatively.

"What is it?" Nate asked.

"Well, Two Owls thinks whites are to blame. If there have been any strangers in this neck of the woods in the past month or so, doesn't it stand to reason, Pa, that some of the other mountain men have seen them?"

The insight was so obvious that Nate was amazed he hadn't thought of it himself. There were at least two trappers he knew of who lived within a few day's ride of Dream Lake. Paying them a visit might prove rewarding. "I think you've got the right idea, son. We'll head for Old Bill's place at first light."

"Bill Zeigler's?" Winona said sharply.

Nate nodded. "He lives closest to Dream Lake."

"But is it safe? You know the horrible stories told about him. What if they are true?"

"It's a risk we'll have to take."

* * *

Miles from the King cabin, six men sat around a crackling fire. Several held tin cups filled with black coffee. One chewed loudly on jerked buffalo meat. A string of tired horses had been tethered nearby.

Earl Lassiter sank to one knee to refill his cup. He cursed when he accidentally rubbed the back of his hand on the scalding pot and pain lanced up his arm. One of the others snickered but fell abruptly silent when Lassiter glared at him. "Do you think it's funny that I burned myself, Yost?"

The stringbean addressed shook his scarecrow head vigorously. "No, sir, Earl. Not on your life. I just sort of thought the look on our face was a little bit comical, is all."

"Oh?" Lassiter's voice was as cold as ice, as hard as granite. "Maybe I should shove the pot down your britches and see how comical you act."

Yost gulped. Every member of the gang knew it wasn't very smart to rile their leader. There was no telling when he might unexpectedly snap and fly into a fit of violence that made grizzlies seem tame by comparison. "I didn't mean anything. Honest. You've no call to be so testy."

"I don't like being laughed at," Lassiter growled.

He never had. As a boy, he'd been notorious for pounding anyone who had the gall to poke fun at him. To his way of thinking, to be mocked was the ultimate insult. It reminded Earl of all those awful childhood years when his drunkard father had belittled him every time he turned around. He'd been jeered, slapped silly, and called all kinds of names: jackass, idiot, good for nothing, plumb worthless, and many, many more. The memory was enough to make Lassiter clench his fists in budding rage.

One of the others noticed. He was much older than his rough companions, his hair the hue of freshly fallen snow. Ben Kingslow was his name, and he took it on himself to avert possible bloodshed by clearing his throat and saying, "I swear! That squaw sure did put up a scrap, didn't she? It's too bad we couldn't have kept her alive and brought her with us."

"Why?" asked a stocky man partial to a blue cap. "So she could slit our throats in our sleep the first chance she got? No thank you. I'm glad that Earl had Bear put a ball into her."

The giant with the greasy hair and clothes chuckled. "Did you see the way she squirmed after she was shot, Dixon? I saw a snake do that once after its head had been chopped off."

Ben Kingslow was studying Lassiter on the sly. "I just meant it would be nice to have a woman or two to accommodate those of us who might be inclined at night. None of us have been getting it regularly since we left the States."

Dixon chuckled. "I didn't know old goats your age could still get a rise."

"My age?" Kingslow snorted. "Haven't you heard, you young pup, that the older the wine, the better it is? I'll have you know that, the last time I was with a woman, she compared me to a tree."

A scrawny man whose lower lip had been split long ago in a knife fight spoke up for the first time. "A dead tree, I'll bet."

At this there was rowdy laughter.

"That's putting the geezer in his place, Snip," Dixon said. "To hear him talk, you'd think he had females fawning over him everywhere he goes."

Kingslow was pleased to note a smile curl Lassiter's lips. For the time being trouble had been averted. But sooner or later someone would say the wrong thing and he wouldn't be there to bail whoever it was out.

Only one soul there did not join in the mirth. The half-breed sat apart, his arms folded across his chest, his rifle in his lap. "I do not care about women," he said gravely in his heavily accented English. "I want my share of the gold."

Bear thumped his thigh in irritation. "So did I, Cano. It got my dander up when we couldn't find that bastard's cache."

"Don't fret yourself," Lassiter said. "There are a lot more sheep out here waiting to be fleeced. One of these times we'll strike it rich so we can all go back to civilization and live like kings."

"That would be fine by me," Dixon said, "but I doubt all the mountain men combined have that much money."

"They have proved slim pickings," Lassiter said, "leaner than I counted on. So maybe it's time we did like all good hunters do when the game they're after proves scarce."

"Which is?" Bear asked.

"Go after different game," Lassiter said, leaning back and propping an elbow under him. "I've heard tell that a lot of pilgrims have taken to heading for the Oregon Country by way of South Pass and the Green River Valley region."

Snip poked a stick into the flames. "What makes you think we'll be any better off?"

"Think for a minute," Lassiter said. "Most of these pilgrims travel in big old wagons piled high with all their worldly goods. Odds are they also tote all their money along, since it's not likely they'd leave their nest eggs behind."

Greed sparkled in Dixon's eyes. "I'll bet you that some of those goods are worth a lot, besides. Why, we could have full pokes in no time."

Lassiter took a long sip of coffee. "My notion exactly, hos. So what say we drift up toward the Green River and keep our eyes skinned for plump wagons ripe for the plucking?"

"This is your best idea yet." Kingslow saw fit to compliment the plan to make up for his blunder earlier. "We'll be hip deep in bootie."

Dixon twisted and scanned the surrounding forest. "What about the Blood, Earl? Think he'll go along with the scheme?"

"Brule has stuck with us this far," Lassiter said. "I doubt he has anywhere else to go."

Scrawny Snip gave a little shudder. "I don't mind admitting that he gives this coon a bad case of the fidgets every time he looks at me. I don't rightly see why we keep him around when he might up and scalp the bunch of us one night while we're sleeping. It's no damn secret that his kind hate our kind worse than anything else."

"Usually that's the case," Lassiter said. "But you have to remember that Brule hates his own people just as much because they booted him out of the tribe. It was a lucky day for me when I stumbled on him up by the Tetons."

Ben Kingslow had heard of that fateful meeting several times since throwing in with Lassiter's wild bunch. Lassiter had been trapping during the spring season when he'd come on the Blood at the top of a precipice.

The warrior had been on the verge of throwing himself off. Apparently Brule had been so shamed at being made an outcast, he hadn't cared whether he lived or died.

"We need the buck," Lassiter said, bringing Kingslow back to the present. "He's a better tracker than any of us will ever be. And he has an uncanny knack for sniffing out trouble."

"It's like having a caged panther," Snip said. "You never know when it might turn on you."

Dixon appeared afflicted by the same unease. "Where is he anyway? Why does he always go off by himself at night? Ain't our company good enough for him?"

"He's a loner at heart," Lassiter said. "But he's always by our side when we need him the most, so I don't want any of you saying anything to him. If you have a grievance, you go through me."

"Think I'm loco?" Dixon said. "I'm not about to get into a racket with that red devil. He's the meanest son of a bitch alive. You can tell just by looking into his eyes."

Earl Lassiter set down his empty cup. "Maybe he is. So what? Think of the bright side."

"What bright side?"

"If anyone comes after us, I'll just sic Brule on him. As much as that Blood enjoys shedding blood, no one will last two minutes."

Bold strokes of pink and yellow framed the pale eastern horizon when Nate King stepped from his warm cabin into the chill morning air and around to the rough-hewn corral. Hardly half an hour was required to saddle the three mounts and load provisions onto three packhorses. When he led the animals around front, he found his loved ones waiting for him. Winona and the baby were bundled in a heavy green shawl he had traded for at a prior rendezvous.

There were no locks to make secure, no bolts to be thrown. The door was simply closed, the windows covered.

This was the high country, where thievery was rare. Anyone caught stealing was likely to be shot on sight, which served to discourage those inclined to step over the line.

In New York City it had been different. How well Nate remembered the growing epidemic of robbery and assaults that had made life there so miserable. Footpads had roamed at will, secure in the knowledge that if they were apprehended they would likely get off with a slap on the wrist or a small fine.

Nate never tired of thinking about the startling contrasts between life in the States and life in the wilderness. In New York the people were crammed together like rats in a run-down tenement. Small wonder they snapped at one another all the time and couldn't get along except during emergencies, when their common humanity forged a temporary bond.

In the Rockies, men and women were truly free. They behaved as they pleased, doing what they wanted when they wanted. There was no overcrowding. There were no power-hungry politicians dictating how folks should live. None of the pressures New Yorkers experienced every single day of their sad lives existed.

Consequently, Nate had never met a happier lot of people than the mountaineers and Indians who inhabited the mountains. As a rule, if one excluded the hostile tribes, they were friendlier than their counterparts back east. They were more trusting. Best of all, they respected one another. There was none of that casual contempt Easterners unconsciously cultivated.

Nate would never go back to live in the States. He had ventured to the frontier for all the wrong reasons and discovered the right reasons to stay. Personal freedom, individual happiness, robust health—they all mattered more than the few conveniences civilization had to offer.

Such was Nate King's train of thought as he led his family northward out of their precious valley. Once on the ridge, he bore to the northwest.

From the lofty rampart, they watched the golden sun rise into the azure sky. Nate always found dawn to be invigorating. The rosy splendor, with its promise of life renewed for another day, caused him to regard the world in which he lived with abiding respect and reverence.

From the ridge Nate descended into a verdant valley where a small herd of shaggy mountain buffalo grazed. Deer moved among the trees. Ravens soared with outstretched wings on uplifting air currents.

Nate reveled in the grandeur. He took a deep breath, and heard a horse trot up next to his.

"Pa, I wanted to thank you for bringing me along," Zachary said. "It means a lot to me."

"So I gathered," Nate said. "I suppose I'd better

get used to having you do more and more as you get older. It's hard though, son. I can't stand the idea of you coming to harm, so I try to protect you more than I should."

"Do all fathers feel the same way?"

"Most do, I expect," Nate said. "My pa was the kind who never let me do anything for myself. I always had to do things his way, whether I liked it or not. Why, I was ten before he'd let me go to the store alone."

"You're joshing."

"I wish I was," Nate said. He pulled his beaver hat lower so the wind wouldn't snatch it off at an inopportune moment.

"I've been meaning to ask you," Zach said. "Last night ma acted upset when you mentioned going to visit this Zeigler feller. Doesn't she like him?"

"She's never met the man."

"Then why was she so bothered?"

"There are some who say Old Bill isn't quite right in the head."

"How so?"

Nate looked at his son. "Some folks claim he's a cannibal."

Chapter Four

Zachary King had heard of cannibals, of course, but he had never in his wildest imaginings suspected he would actually meet one.

Tall tales were a staple of the mountain men; swapping yarns around a campfire was a favorite entertainment. Most of them had to do with living in the wild. Trappers told of vicious beasts they had slain, of narrow escapes from hostiles, of which streams were best for catching beaver and which were trapped out.

Now and then, however, the talk had nothing to do with the mountains. Men spoke of the places they hailed from, the varied sights they had witnessed in their travels. Several of the trappers had been seafaring men before they took to raising beaver for a living, and their exotic and thrilling accounts were some of Zach's favorites.

One night in particular Zach had never forgotten. It had been at the rendezvous, four years earlier. A lumbering slab of a man by the name of Gristle Jack had riveted the boy with chilling stories of outlandish peoples in other lands.

"Let me tell you about Africa," Gristle Jack had said, his eyes alight with the reflection of dancing flames. "I was there once, you see. On board a slaver. And the things I saw and learned, you wouldn't believe."

"Tell us," a trapper said.

"Well, why do you think everyone calls Africa the Dark Continent?" Gristle Jack said. "It's the natives. There are as many black men in Africa as there are whites in this country. More, I'd say. And they're as different in their ways as we are in ours. Some are as civilized as we are. They're the ones who sell slaves to plantation owners in the South. Others run around half naked and carry spears and clubs. They're the ones a man has to watch out for."

"How so?" someone had asked.

"Why, some of the tribes are cannibals. They like to plunk their captives in huge pots and boil the poor souls until the flesh is nicely cooked. Then they all sit down to a fine feast, chewing away with their pointed teeth."

"Pointed teeth?" a scoffer said.

"As the Lord is my witness," Gristle Jack said. "I heard that they file their teeth to make them as sharp as daggers. And some of them stick bones through their ears or else through their nose. I swear! I saw them with my own eyes!"

Now, four days after leaving the cabin, Zach gazed anxiously down on the narrow, shadowy valley where Bill Zeigler lived and felt a shudder go through him. He pictured Old Bill with filed, tapered teeth and bones in his pierced ears and nose, and he wondered if the old man had a huge pot in which to cook his victims.

"Are you all right, son?" Nate asked.

Zach glanced around and self-consciously cleared his throat. He was embarrassed that his father had seen the worry on his face and tried to explain it away by saying, "I was just thinking that maybe we should go down there alone, Pa. It might not be safe for ma and sis."

Winona overheard. "I was taking care of myself long before you were born. If Old Bill is not careful, you will see how capable I am."

It was a continual source of amusement and irritation to Winona that the males in her family treated her as if she were a fragile flower that would fall to pieces at the slightest touch. Shoshone warriors never regarded women so.

Having mulled over the matter at length, Winona had reached the conclusion that Nate did not think of her as inferior in any way. Time and again he had admitted that she was a fine shot, a skilled rider, and a competent provider.

No, her husband's attitude stemmed from his upbringing. Winona had questioned him and learned most white men shared his view. At an early age the idea was instilled in them that women were in need of constant protection. It was ridiculous.

Winona knew that her husband tried to see her more as a Shoshone warrior would, but it was hard to break habits so old, so ingrained. Unfortunately, at times Zach seemed to be afflicted with the same attitude. She could only hope that one day they both came to their senses.

A few yards in front of her, Nate stood in the stirrups to survey the valley closely. He had never been there before, but he had been told how to reach it by a trapper who had. Mountain men routinely swapped information having to do with routes of travel, the locations of streams and lakes, and more.

Bill Zeigler had chosen a forbidding spot in a remote chain of stark peaks. If it was privacy he craved, he had found it. There was no more isolated valley in all the Rockies.

Thanks to the high summits ringing Zeigler's sanctuary, it lay in shadow most of the day. A game trail meandered to the valley floor through densely packed pines standing like silent sentinels along the pathway.

Nate assumed the lead, the Hawken propped on his thigh. According to an acquaintance of his, Frenchy Smith, Zeigler lived in a dirt dugout on a knoll overlooking a deep stream. Nate was on edge. He didn't like taking his family down there but he would be wasting his breath if he tried to persuade them to stay on the slope.

As Nate rode, he recollected the story told about Old Bill. Ten or 12 years earlier—no one could remember exactly when—Bill and his partner, Yerby, had gone off after beaver and been trapped in the high country by the first heavy snow. They had ended up being snowbound all winter. Came the spring, and only Bill made his way down to the rendezvous. Many asked about Yerby and were told that he had died in an avalanche.

Somehow, whispers got started. Loose lips

speculated that maybe Yerby had died differently, that maybe the sole reason Old Bill had survived was too ghastly to be believed.

Nate had never taken the tale seriously. Old Bill wasn't the first to be branded a cannibal. Every so often it would happen, and in nearly every instance, the rumors turned out to be nothing more than the gory handiwork of mountaineers with too much free time on their hands and too much alcohol in their systems.

Still, Nate felt uneasy. He wasn't a friend of Zeigler's, and Old Bill was known to be touchy about people dropping in on him out of the blue. Zeigler might be inclined to shoot first and learn who they were later.

The pines were eerily quiet. The wind whispered through the jade-green needles, but the birds and beasts who dwelt in the forest were as quiet as the great slabs of rock on the heights above.

Halfway down, Nate spied the stream, flanking a mountain to the north. To reach it, he had to cross a lot of open ground. They would be exposed, vulnerable.

So intent was Nate on the grassy flatland, he almost missed hearing the faint tread of a human foot to his right. Almost, but not quite. Twisting, he saw a buckskin-garbed figure hurtle at him from out of the brush. He tried to bring the Hawken to bear but the figure had already leaped atop a small boulder and from there sprang straight at him. He heard Zach's cry of warning even as his attacker slammed into him. The rifle went flying when he was bowled from the saddle.

Nate shoved free of the man's clutching grasp

as he fell. He hit on his right shoulder and rolled into a crouch, his left hand stabbing for a pistol. His assailant pounced before he could draw and they both went down. A knife glittered above him.

Thrusting his arms out, Nate sought to prevent the blade from sinking into his flesh. He finally saw the craggy, grizzled face of Old Bill Zeigler poised against the backdrop of foliage, his features aglow with bloodlust, his eyes gleaming with demonical intensity. For a harrowing moment Nate thought that the tales must be true, and he braced himself as the older man's arm tensed to arc downward.

Then there was the drum of flying hooves and from out of nowhere swept the smooth stock of a rifle. It caught Zeigler on the side of the head and toppled him into the weeds.

In a flash Nate was on his feet, a flintlock filling each brawny hand. A few feet away stood Zach's calico, the boy holding the Hawken he had used to brain old Zeigler.

"I'm obliged, son," Nate said.

Zach swelled with pride. He had acted without thinking, doing the first thing that came to mind. His mother, he noticed, was gazing fondly at him in that way she often did when she was enormously pleased by something he had done.

When a low groan emanated from the weeds, Nate strode over to the shabby pair of patched moccasins jutting into the open and whacked one with a foot. "Get up and explain yourself."

The groan was repeated, louder and longer. Old Bill Zeigler slowly sat up, both hands pressed to his head, his eyes squeezed tight shut. "Oh,

Lordy. My achin' noggin. What the devil happened? Did a tree fall on me?"

"You tried to kill me, damn you," Nate said.

Zeigler lowered his arms, revealing a nasty knot where the stock had slammed into him. He cocked his head and squinted at the four of them, focusing on Nate. "I know you. Met you at the rendezvous, as I recollect. King, ain't it?"

"Nate King."

"This must be your family," Old Bill said pleasantly. Shaking his head as if to clear cobwebs, he pushed upright. His knees nearly buckled and he swayed a few seconds, then cackled and slapped his thigh. "Which one of you walloped the daylights out of me?"

"I did, sir," Zach said nervously. He felt a little guilty having hurt the man until he reminded himself that his pa's life had been at stake.

"You're a dandy walloper, lad," Old Bill said without a trace of malice. "You must go around whippin' the tar out of grizzlies in your spare time."

Zachary laughed, pleased there were no hard feelings. "No, sir. My pa is the one they call Grizzly Killer. He's rubbed out more than any man alive, white or Indian."

Old Bill shifted his attention back to Nate. "That's right. Kilt about a hundred, I heard tell."

"Hardly," Nate said dryly. The old-timer had dropped the knife and wasn't armed with pistols or a tomahawk, so Nate felt safe in wedging his flintlocks under his wide leather belt. "Now suppose you tell us why you tried to bury that pigsticker in me."

The grizzled mountain man looked down at the ground and shuffled his feet from side to side as if embarrassed. "I'm plumb sorry about that, King. To tell the truth, I mistook you for hostiles."

"In broad daylight?" Nate said skeptically. "I'll admit that a greenhorn might mistake me for an Indian, but a seasoned mountaineer like you should be able to tell the difference."

"Should be," Old Bill said, frowning. "I don't rightly know if I should let the cat out of the bag, but I guess it can't do no harm."

"What are you talking about?"

"My peepers." Bill raised a finger to his eyes. "They're not what they used to be. Why, once I could see a sparrow on the wing half a mile away. Nowadays I'm lucky if I can make out a darned elk at twenty feet." He mentioned at the trail. "When I first spotted you folks, you were all a blur. I figured you must be some of those pesky Utes who have aggravated me something fierce over the years." Bill paused. "I'm just glad I didn't have my rifle. I'm not the shot I once was, but I might have hit one of you anyway."

The mention of a rifle set Nate to searching for his Hawken. He found it lying a few feet away. "I'm sorry to hear about your problem," he said. A man needed all his senses intact to survive in the wild. "If you're that bad off, maybe you should give some thought to moving down out of the mountains."

"And do what? Live at one of the forts? I'd go crazy being cooped up all the time. And I'm sure as blazes not going back to the States. I'm not about to spend the rest of my days sitting on some street corner, begging for pennies. I may not have much, but I've got my dignity."

Nate saw the knife lying seven feet away and retrieved it for the man. "Here."

"Thanks." Old Bill wiped the blade on his leggings, then shoved it into a sheath that had seen better days years ago. His buckskins were also in dire need of mending. "Listen. What say I make it up to you by having you folks for a meal? I managed to bring down a buck yesterday so there's plenty of fresh meat. It's early yet, I know, but I don't often get company. And the older I get, the less I object to having people stop by."

"We'd be grateful," Nate said, although he would have preferred to ask a few questions and be on his way. There was a touch of melancholy about the older man that tugged at his heartstrings. He looked at Winona for confirmation and she nodded.

"I'm the one who's grateful." Old Bill brightened. "I haven't had a soul to talk to in weeks."

Nate opened his mouth to glean more details but the old mountain man moved off down the trail as quickly as a jackrabbit.

"Come on! Don't dawdle! I'll scoot on ahead and have the coffee on before you get there. Just follow the stream west a ways. You can't miss my place."

"There's no need—" Nate said and stopped. Bill was moving with remarkable speed for someone who couldn't see very well. In moments he rounded a bend and was gone.

Zach chuckled. "He sure is excited about having us to vittles. Do you reckon he's awful lonely, Pa?"

It was Winona who responded. "He must be. Men and women are not meant to spend their days alone. That is why my people prefer village life to going off by ourselves, as your father's people do." She clucked her mare into motion. "There are many things about whites I do not understand, husband, but liking to live alone has always puzzled me the most."

"Do tell," Nate said while mounting. In all the years they had been together, she had never once mentioned it to him. "Maybe it has something to do with having different natures, sort of like buffalo and bears. Buffalo like to live together in great herds, bears like to live alone in dens."

"Which is the right way for folks to be?" Zach asked.

Nate urged the stallion and packhorse into following them. "It's not etched in stone, son. It all depends on the person. You have to do what is right for you and not care what anyone else thinks."

"I don't think I'd ever like to live all by myself," Zach said. "I'd need a family, at least, just like you, Pa."

They fell silent until they reached the gurgling stream, which ran surprisingly deep and swift. A clearly defined trail pointed the way to the knoll, hundreds of yards off. Situated at the tree line, it blended into the wall of vegetation as if part of it. A casual observer would never suspect that someone lived there.

Bill Zeigler was as good as his word. On reining up in front of the dugout, Nate smelled smoke and saw a thin tendril wafting from a small hole atop the knoll. As he tethered the horses, part of the slope swung outward and there stood Zeigler, framed in a doorway.

"Howdy again, folks!"

Zach gawked in astonishment at the cleverly concealed door. "I declare! I've never seen the like in all my born days!"

"An old cuss like you?" Zeigler said. He gave the planks a whack. "Came up with this idea all by myself. I had a heck of a time gettin' Wyeth to bring me some metal hinges from St. Louis. He claimed I was the only trapper in the Rockies who had ever ordered hinges, and there wouldn't be any profit in it since he only had to bring three."

"That sounds like Wyeth," Nate said, referring to the trader who had once supplied provisions at the rendezvous and later built Fort Hall. "That man won't do anything unless there's a profit in it."

Old Bill propped the door open with a stick he kept handy for the purpose and beckoned. "Come on in, folks. Make yourself to home and we'll chaw a while." He stepped aside to permit them to enter, then did a double take on seeing the cradleboard. "A sprout! Land sakes! I didn't know you was totin' a young'un, ma'am."

"Evelyn is her name. I'm Winona."

Zeigler was taken aback when she offered her hand. He took it gingerly, as if afraid he'd break it if he squeezed too hard. "It's a pleasure to make your acquaintance. I can see your husband is a man who likes women of quality."

Winona stepped inside and promptly wished she hadn't. A rank odor assailed her nostrils, and the interior was as filthy as it was possible to be and still be habitable. Piles of hides, some half rotten because they had not been cured properly, lined both walls. A bundle of blankets and robes at the far end served as the bed. In the center sat a small table and two stools, a stove, and a bench littered with tools and traps.

"Don't mind the mess," Old Bill said. "Every two or three years I give the place a thorough cleaning. I reckon it's about due."

"So it would seem," Winona said politely.

"Sit anywhere you like," Old Bill said. "I'm not fussy at all."

Winona did not see how any human being could live under such conditions. She picked her way with care to a stool and took a seat after removing the cradleboard so she could hold Evelyn in her lap.

The stench hardly bothered Zach. He had smelled much worse, like that time after the Shoshones conducted a buffalo surround and the prairie had been choked with carcasses being roasted by the scorching sun. The horrible stink and the swarming flies had about gagged him.

Nate, however, covered his mouth with a hand and pretended to cough. Breathing shallow, he took the stool next to his wife and leaned the Hawken against the table.

"This is wonderful, just wonderful," Old Bill said as he puttered about hanging an unlit lantern on a peg, moving some hides closer to the side of the dugout, and collecting battered cups for their coffee. "I sure am glad you folks stopped on by."

"We had a reason," Nate said. "We're trying to

find out who killed an old Ute by the name of Buffalo Hump."

In the act of setting the cups on the table, Old Bill paused. "A Ute, you say? What does it matter who killed him? They're all a bunch of murderin' skunks in my book."

"Not all of them," Nate said and detailed the reason for their visit. "You can appreciate the fix we're in. We have to find the guilty parties or risk losing everything that means anything to us."

Zeigler had listened with rising interest. "I'd like to help you, King. But the fact is that not a single stranger has paid me a visit in pretty near a year. The last man who did stop by was Jeremiah Sawyer, just about four weeks ago. He lives northwest of here in Crow country. About a two-day ride, is all. Maybe he can help you."

"I know Jeremiah," Nate said, not showing his disappointment that the visit to Old Bill hadn't panned out. Going to see Sawyer might prove equally as useless but it was better than doing nothing. "We'll head for his lodge at dawn."

"I'll be glad to guide you there," Zeigler said.

"That's all right. We'll manage."

"It'll be hard if you've never been there. His place is as out of the way as mine is. I can shave half a day off the trip if you're willing to push yourselves."

The prospect was appealing. "Let me talk it over with my wife," Nate said. Clasping her elbow, he escorted Winona from the cramped dugout. The cool evening air was downright intoxicating. He inhaled the sweet pine scent with relish.

"Thank you, husband," Winona said softly. "I did not know how much longer I could stand it in there. If a member of my tribe were to keep his lodge in the same condition Old Bill keeps his dugout, the man would be shunned by everyone."

"Should we refuse his help?" Nate asked.

Winona pondered before answering. She was glad that her husband often relied on her judgment when making decisions of importance to both of them. It wasn't a trait shared by all trappers. From other Shoshone women who had become the wives of whites, she had learned that by and large the trappers did as they pleased without regard for the feelings of the women. Several Shoshones had even been beaten for questioning their husband's actions.

"If he can save us half a day," Winona said, "we should accept his offer. It worries me, being gone from our cabin for so long. Should the Utes come while we are gone, they might burn it down to spite us."

"I was thinking the same thing," Nate said. He was also questioning how the old mountain man would be able to lead them when it would be difficult for Zeigler to keep track of landmarks. "You stay out here while I go have a few more words with him." He walked past Zach, who stood by the entrance.

Winona turned and admired the blazed of color painting the sky. She observed her son move toward the horses, then stare eastward and freeze. Whirling, she learned why, and gooseflesh erupted all over her body.

Lumbering across the stream toward the dugout was a huge grizzly.

Chapter Five

Nate King hardly got a word out of his mouth when his son bawled his name and a tremendous roar smote his ears. He was outside in a half-dozen bounds, the short hairs of his neck prickling when he beheld a veritable monster of a grizzly upright on its hind legs.

It had been many months since last Nate had tangled with a grizzly. When he first arrived in the mountains, it seemed as if every time he turned around he ran into one of the savage behemoths. More by circumstance than design he had survived time and again. But each harrowing nightmare had left him that much more anxious about future encounters.

So when Nate saw the enormous creature drop to all fours and move closer, it took him five seconds to bring his Hawken up to shoot. He knew that a single shot seldom dropped a griz.

More than likely he would only enrage the beast. But he couldn't stand there and do nothing. He had to act before his wife and children were torn to shreds.

Nate aimed at the grizzly's chest. Provided fate smiled on him, he might succeed in putting a ball into its lungs or heart.

"No! Don't shoot!"

Bill Zeigler raced from the dugout, flapping both arms like an ungainly demented bird trying to get off the ground. He leaped in front of the Hawken, blocking the shot with his body.

"Are you crazy?" Nate yelled. "Get out of the way before it's too late!"

"It's just Ulysses!" Old Bill cried. "He won't hurt any of us if we give him what he wants." So saying, the mountain man ran toward the bear.

Too flabbergasted to do anything except gape, Nate realized that Zeigler held a deer haunch. The grizzly had stopped and lifted its ponderous head to sniff the air, sounding for all the world like a bellows.

"Here, Ulysses!" Old Bill said, halting a dozen feet from the monster. "Just like always." Using both hands, he flung the haunch with all his might. It sailed end over end to plop down directly in front of the grizzly.

The bear sniffed at the meat a bit, then widened its maw and clamped down so hard the bone crunched. Its prize firmly held between its iron jaws, the lord of the Rockies ambled off across the stream and into the lush undergrowth beyond.

Nate liked to think that he had seen practically everything that had to do with the mountains and those who lived there. But never had he beheld the like of a man feeding a griz as if it were a prized pet instead of a living engine of destruction. Old Bill had to be missing a few marbles to pull such a stunt. Nate lowered the Hawken, shaking his head sadly when the old trapper waved at the departing bear.

"Thanks for not firing, King," Zeigler said. "That griz has been a friend of mine since before that boy of yours was born."

"You're playing with fire if you let that thing come around here whenever it pleases," Nate said. "Mark my words. It'll turn on you one of these days. Grizzlies are too unpredictable."

Old Bill clucked at him like a hen at an uppity chick. "Most griz are, I'll agree. But I came on that one when it was just a cub, shortly after it's ma was wiped out in a rock slide." He smiled at the memory. "I was going to blow its brains out when the thing started bawling like a baby. Then damned if it didn't waddle up to me and lick my hand. How could I shoot it after that?

"I fed it for weeks and weeks. Got to the point where the critter followed me around everywhere I went. Made trapping real hard, what with the beaver not about to go anywhere near a trap if there's griz scent in the area. Finally I had to shoo it off. But it still comes by every now and then, so I give it some grub like in the old days. It always goes on about its business without trying to hurt me."

Winona had clutched Evelyn to her bosom when the bear appeared, but now she cradled the child and said, "My people believe that only someone who possesses powerful medicine can

call the great bear a brother. We will be honored
to have you go with us tomorrow."

A peculiar grin twisted Old Bill's mouth. "Thank
you, ma'am. You have no idea how much it means
to me." He snickered for no apparent reason. "No
idea at all."

His name, as best the whites could pronounce
it, was Brule. He was a Blood warrior, a former
member of one of the three tribes that made up
the widely dreaded Blackfoot Confederacy.

He stood on a flat rock on a shelf of high
land overlooking the next valley the men who
followed him must cross, and he bowed his head
in shame—shame that tormented him every time
he thought about his former life, shame that he
would never let those behind him see.

Brule was an outcast. He had done that which
no warrior was ever allowed to do, committed
the most heinous of acts. He had killed one of
his own people.

It had been justified, in Brule's eyes. Minoka
had tried to woo the maiden Brule had craved
as his own. And when Brule had confronted him,
Minoka had been rash enough to strike Brule
across the face with an open palm.

No man could endure such an insult and still
lay claim to manhood. Brule had done what
any warrior would do. He had stabbed his rival
through the heart.

Perhaps if it had been anyone but Minoka, Brule
would still be among the Bloods. But Minoka's
father was a war chief, a man of vast influence.
That influence had been used to persuade the
people of the village to cast Brule out, to expel

him into the wilderness, where he was destined to roam until he died.

And he had roamed, for a while, until the aching loneliness had driven him to despair and he had resolved to end his existence by throwing himself off a cliff overlooking a lake in the Tetons.

Who could have foreseen that the white-eye named Lassiter would spot him and come to investigate? Lassiter had drawn a pistol and pointed it at him, but Brule had made no move to defend himself. He hadn't cared how his life ended, so long as it did.

Then the white man had asked him questions in sign language, and after Brule answered, Lassiter had put the pistol away and asked Brule to ride with him, to share in the killing and the plunder to come. For Lassiter had a great scheme to make himself rich among his kind, and in order to achieve his goal he needed to gather around him those of like minds.

Brule had not held any desire to be rich as the whites conceived of wealth. But he was a warrior born, and he did like the idea of going on the warpath against everyone and anyone—even his own people. For the more Brule thought about the injustice done him, the more he learned to despise those who had seen fit to cast him aside. Yet he could not shake the sense of shame.

Behind Brule a horse snorted. He turned and saw the breed, Cano, trailed by Lassiter and the rest of the whites. He bore no friendship for any of them. The breed, he tolerated. Lassiter, he owed a debt. The rest, he would as soon slit their throats as look at them.

Brule despised whites. His tribe, along with the

Blackfeet and the Piegans, exterminated any and all white men found in their territory.

He knew that the mountain men considered his people, and their allies, as little better than bloodthirsty animals who slaughtered for the sheer thrill of bloodletting.

Nothing could have been further from the truth, in Brule's opinion. While it was true the Bloods had always been a warlike people, they adhered to an honorable system of counting coup little different from other tribes. They were no more cruel or savage than the Sioux, the Cheyenne, or the Arapaho.

But in one major respect the Bloods did differ. They were heartily unwilling to stand idly by while their lands were overrun by the white vermin from the East.

It was a proven fact that the whites killed off wildlife at an unbelievable rate. In just a span of ten winters the trappers had severely reduced the number of beaver and mountain buffalo and were now slaying plains buffalo with an abandon the Bloods found appalling.

Brule's tribe regarded the whites as invaders who would eventually drive the Bloods from their homeland unless they were stopped before they became too numerous to resist.

For Brule to associate with whites, as he was doing now, required a measure of self-control he had rarely exercised. He couldn't stand to be near Lassiter and the others for more than a short while without feeling an urge to smash their heads in. They were filthy, arrogant, revolting. They looked down their superior noses at Brule and his kind, when in truth they were no better.

Brule had yet to make up his mind how long he would stay with them. He did know that before he left, he might slay every last one. For the time being, however, he was content to act as their scout and to share in any booty that interested him.

Already Brule had benefited. He had a new knife riding on his left hip and a steel tomahawk on his left. He carried a fine rifle instead of the cheap fusil he had formerly used. A large ammo pouch and a powder horn adorned his chest. He was better armed than ever before, which pleased him immensely.

Now, facing the others, Brule adopted a stony expression and squared his bronzed shoulder.

The half-breed addressed him in sign language. "Why have you stopped, my friend?" Cano asked.

Brule let the insult pass. He would never be friends to any bastard offspring of a white pig and a Dakota slut. But it served his purposed to pretend. Pivoting, he pointed at a column of smoke rising to the northeast. "White men," he signed.

The breed turned to Lassiter and addressed him in the birdlike gibberish the whites called a language. Brule had tried to learn the tongue, but found the chirpings almost impossible to duplicate. He knew a few words—that was all.

Lassiter moved to the edge of the shelf and studied the smoke a while. He then employed sign to say to Brule, "I think you are right. No Indian would make a fire that gave off so much smoke. Sneak down there and see how many there are. We will wait here for you."

Brule saw Cano go to speak and quickly jogged

off. He suspected that the breed wanted to go along but he would much rather scout by himself.

Perhaps because of his Indian blood, Cano liked to spend time with Brule, a feeling the Blood did not reciprocate. He came to a game trail and flew toward the grassy basin below, making as little sound as the wind itself.

The smoke rose from fir trees near the mouth of the valley, which was watered by a stream large enough to contain beaver. Brule soon spied a beaver lodge, leading him to suspect the fire had been made by trappers.

He heard their voices long before he glimpsed the camp, which was typical. Brule didn't know why, but white men always raised their voices much higher than they needed to. It was as if they were taught at an early age to bellow instead of to speak in normal tones. They talked loudly, they laughed loudly, they snored loudly—all in keeping with the loathsome creatures they were.

Brule slowed and flitted from tree to tree. Presently he saw a string of horses, eight in all. The fire blazed in the middle of a clearing. A lean-to had been erected, and under it sat a beefy man sharpening a knife on a whetstone. Two other men were by the fire, sipping coffee.

Going prone, Brule snaked to a bush at the clearing's edge. From there he spied a pile of steel traps beside the lean-to. He counted three rifles and five pistols between them.

But it was the knife that interested Brule most of all. It was extraordinary, at least three hands long, the blade sharp on both sides instead of just one, the hilt a glorious golden hue and encrusted with several sparkling stones. Brule's breath caught in his throat as he marveled at its beauty. It was unlike any knife he had ever seen, and he wanted it so badly that he tingled in anticipation.

There was only one problem.

When it came to plunder, Lassiter had the final say. Spoils were always collected into a heap and passed out as Lassiter saw fit. If any of them wanted a particular item, they were free to say so. Usually Lassiter handed it over, but not always. Brule had lost a fine red blanket and an ax he coveted to Cano.

This time would be different. Brule was not about to let anyone else lay claim to the magnificent knife owned by the beefy trapper. He would take it for himself and slay anyone who objected.

In order to have first claim, Brule knew he had to dispose of the whites himself. With the thought came action. There was no hesitation, no prick of conscience. Whites were his enemies. Enemies were to be slain. Life was as simple as that.

Brule backed into the trees and made like an eel, worming his way around the camp perimeter until he was behind the lean-to. It would have been better to wait until dark, but nightfall was hours off and Lassiter was bound to come see what was taking him so long.

The Blood placed his rifle on the ground and drew both his slender knife and the steel tomahawk. Rising into a crouch, he stalked to the side of the lean-to and peeked around the corner. One of the whites at the fire had his back to Brule; the other was busy refilling the coffeepot. The man in the lean-to was bent low, stroking that grand knife with delicate precision.

Brule's pulse quickened at being so close to the unique weapon. Its gleaming brilliance dazzled him. He had to restrain a mad impulse to dash over and snatch the knife from the man's hand.

The trappers by the fire owned rifles, which were propped on a nearby saddle. One had a pair of flintlocks, the other a single pistol. The man in the lean-to also possessed a rifle but it had carelessly been leaned against a sapling in front of the shelter. He also had two pistols under his belt.

Coiling his legs, Brule cast about for an object to throw and found a small stone that suited his purpose. Transferring the tomahawk to his left hand, he hurled the stone as far as he could into the firs on the opposite side of the clearing. It hit a high branch, then clattered earthward from limb to limb until it thudded on the ground.

Both trappers at the fire stood and warily peered into the trees. The man who owned the wonderful knife looked up from the whetstone.

In that moment when they were distracted, Brule struck. He was on the beefy man before the white could blink. His tomahawk cleaved the air and the man's skull with equal ease, shearing deep into the brain. The man died without an outcry, blood spurting from the rupture.

Without hesitation Brule whirled and charged the other pair. They both had heard the blow and turned. The nearest was momentarily paralyzed with fright but at last made a grab for a flint-lock. By then Brule was close enough to throw his knife with an accuracy honed by years of practice.

The slim blade imbedded itself in the base of the man's throat. Squealing, the trapper clutched in a panic at the hilt and wrenched. The blade popped free. A scarlet geyser followed it, pouring onto the grass at the man's feet.

Brule didn't give the man another look. He concentrated on reaching the last trapper before the white man could draw a pistol. His arm arched in an overhand blow that brought the tomahawk streaking down at the trapper's head but the man was too fast for him and dodged aside while simultaneously drawing a flintlock.

Spinning, Brule slashed sideways. The tomahawk clipped the pistol a glancing blow, just enough to deflect the barrel at the very instant the man squeezed the trigger. There was a loud blast and the ball went wide.

The trapper speared a hand at his other pistol. Brule leaped in close and swung again. This time he connected, but not with the man's face, as he wanted. The tomahawk's keen edge bit into the trapper's arm above the wrist and sliced the hand clean off.

Uttering a scream of pure terror, the last trapper tried to flee. Brule was on the man in two bounds. He swung the tomahawk a final time and was splattered with gore when it split the trapper's head like a soft melon. The man pitched forward, limp and lifeless.

Brule turned to check on the one he had wounded in the jugular. The man had tottered a few feet toward the horses and fallen to his knees. Blood gushed and gushed, soaking the trapper's buckskins and the soil. Brule stepped over and raised the tomahawk on high.

The trapper twisted, eyes wide in stark terror. He managed to croak a few words in his strange tongue, red spittle flecking his lips.

There was a loud crunch as the tomahawk split the man's forehead wide open. Brule let the white man sag, then braced a foot on his chest and tugged on the haft. The blade came loose with a sucking sound.

Brule had to work swiftly. He wiped the tomahawk clean on the dead man's leggings, then tucked it under his own. A glance at the shelf showed Lassiter and the rest galloping down the slope, drawn by the shot.

Quickly Brule dashed to the lean-to and claimed his prize. The blade gleamed brightly; the bejeweled hilt sparkled and shimmered. Brule stripped the bearded man of a large sheath, discarded his own, and strapped on the new one. Into it he slid his new weapon.

Taking his old knife in hand, Brule scalped the former owner. In turn, he scalped the other two, and was just rising with all three dripping trophies in hand when Earl Lassiter rode into the clearing and drew rein.

The men muttered among themselves. Cano appeared most displeased. Lassiter looked around, a scowl indicating his state of mind.

"It would have been better if you had waited for us."

Brule ignored the remark, delivered in curt sign. Discarding the old knife, he hastened around behind the lean-to and retrieved his rifle. Only when he could shoot the first one who lifted a finger against him did he swing toward the angry men.

"I wanted you to wait," Lassiter signed.

Brule deposited the scalps on the lean-to so he could respond. "I had to kill them," he signed.

"Did they spot you?" Lassiter asked.

"No," Brule signed.

"Did they hear you then?" Lassiter asked. "Why did you have to slay them?"

To answer honestly would invite trouble, so Brule elected not to reply. Instead he stuffed the scalps into a parfleche he carried slung over his chest. The whites took to chattering like chipmunks, snapping at one another. It was clear they were extremely upset. He observed them on the sly, ready to defend himself if need be.

Eventually Lassiter shrugged and pointed at the rifles and pistols belonging to the trappers, then at the packs. Everyone dismounted except the breed and commenced sorting through the plunder.

Brule came out from behind the lean-to and watched. He had no interest in the booty. He already had the only item he wanted.

Just then Cano kneed his bay closer and stared hard at Brule's waist. He said something that aroused the interest of all the whites.

"Where did you get that knife?" Lassiter signed.

Again Brule chose not to reply. He would not let Lassiter lord it over him. He was free to do as he wanted whenever he wanted, and he was accountable to no man, least of all a white man.

Cano chirped at the others, using many angry gestures. Bear spoke, then Dixon. Cano shook his head, growing madder and madder. At length he addressed Lassiter and the two of them argued for a minute.

Brule could see that the breed was urging Lassiter to act but Lassiter appeared reluctant. He kept his own features as impassive as the smooth face of a cliff.

Earl Lassiter gazed at the new sheath, then at Brule. "The breed is upset and I do not blame him. As leader of this band, I have the right to pass out the spoils as I want to. And I promised him that he could have the first choice of weapons the next time. He has been wanting a new rifle for some time."

"I did not take a rifle," Brule signed.

"I know," Lassiter signed. "But you did take that knife. And now Cano wants it." He paused and mustered a patently fake smile. "So why not make everyone happy and give it to him? You can always get another later."

"I want this one."

"Have you been paying attention? Cano wants it too. And since he has every right to it, I am afraid you have no choice but to hand it over."

"There is one other choice."

"Which is?" Lassiter asked.

Brule's answer was to snap his rifle up and plant a ball smack between Cano's greedy eyes.

Chapter Six

Nate King had to hand it to Bill Zeigler. The old trapper had guided them unerringly over some of the roughest terrain in the mountains to the valley where Jeremiah Sawyer lived with his Crow wife.

Old Bill had done it all from memory. He knew the location of every prominent peak, pass, mountain, and vale. He'd tell them to be on the lookout for such and such a landmark, and sure enough, they'd spot it just when he said they should.

"Now look for some pines to the north," Zeigler said as they entered the valley. "His lodge will be there."

Zach poked a finger in the air. "Over yonder are a bunch of pines. Want me to go on ahead, Pa, and let Mr. Sawyer know we're coming?" He had met Jeremiah Sawyer on several occasions and rated him the nicest trapper in the Rockies next to his own father. He was also quite fond of Sawyer's oldest daughter, Beth, and couldn't wait to see her again.

"Go ahead, son," Nate said. "Just hail the lodge before you go riding up to it so Jeremiah doesn't mistake you for a Blackfoot."

Giddy with excitement, Zach galloped toward the pines. He sorely missed having others his age to be with. If there was any one drawback to living in the mountains, it was the lack of company that came calling and the all-too-few times the family went visiting.

During the summer they always spent time with the Shoshones, and Zach loved every minute of it. He was half Indian, after all. His mother's culture was part and parcel of his being. Except for his blue eyes, which he got from his pa, he could pass for a Shoshone anywhere, anytime.

To Zach's regret, he'd had little to do with his father's people. Trappers, yes, but they were hardly typical of the people back in the States, as his father had pointed out many times. Nate kept promising that one day they would make the long trek to New York City so Zach could see where his pa had been born and bred, but so far an opportunity hadn't presented itself.

Beth Sawyer had often expressed the same wish. She yearned to visit the States, to see how folks back there lived. Zach and her had talked it over endlessly.

Now, as Zach came to a clearing, he beamed happily, eager for a glimpse of Beth. But all he saw was the charred ruin of a lodge. Shocked, he reined up.

Somewhere, sparrows twittered. In the distance

a hawk screeched. All Zach had eyes and ears for was the clearing. Nudging the paint forward, he stopped beside a stump and slid down.

Zach had seen similar sights too many times in his brief life. He swallowed a lump that formed in his throat as he imagined sweet Beth and her younger sister, Claire, being brutally slain by hostiles.

The soft tread of a stealthy footstep behind Zach made him realize his mistake. Instead of staying alert he had permitted his mind to drift. Fearing he was about to be killed by those responsible for the deaths of the Sawyers, he spun, or tried to. He wasn't halfway around when something slammed into the middle of his back, knocking him onto his hands and knee.

Racked by pain, Zach nonetheless threw himself to the right, rolling onto his back and making a play for the pistol his father had given him for his last birthday.

Zach's hand had barely closed on the smooth wood butt when a foot rammed into his sternum. The breath whooshed from his lungs. For a few seconds his vision spun. When it cleared, he found himself staring up at an awful apparition that resembled a man he knew and respected.

It was Jeremiah Sawyer. A leather patch covered his left eye, attached by a thong looped around his head, while his right eye blazed with inner light. His hair was disheveled and matted with dirt. A deep scar marred his left cheek. In his hands he held a wooden club. His leggings were torn, his moccasins in tatters, and there was a bullet hole in his left thigh.

"Mr. Sawyer?" Zach croaked. "It's me, sir.

Zachary King. Don't you remember me?"

The man whom Zach felt was most like his own father blinked and slowly lowered the club. "Zach?" he rasped, his skin pallid. "Is that really you, boy?"

"Yes, sir," Zach said, wheezing as he tried to breathe again. "My folks are with me too. Are you all right, sir?"

"All right?" Jeremiah said and did an odd thing. He laughed long and loud, a strident, wavering sort of laugh that no normal person would ever make.

The crash of horses coming through the brush emboldened Zach to sit up. He saw the stunned disquiet on the faces of his folks and thought he should explain. "I forgot to hail. He didn't know it was me."

Nate merely nodded. He could see his son was unharmed. Sliding from the stallion, he stared at the blackened circle where the lodge had stood and beyond it at three graves crowned by crude crosses. The very calamity that he had always dreaded would strike his own family had felled that of his good friend. He put a hand on Sawyer's shoulder. "Jeremiah?"

The other man averted his sole eye and voiced a low, pathetic whine. He coughed a few times, then looked up, his haggard features a shadow of their former healthy hue. "Nice to see you again, Nate."

"Have a seat," Nate said. "We'll fix coffee and a bite to eat. You look half starved."

"I reckon I am," Jeremiah said. He sank onto the stump and placed the club between his legs. "I can't quite recollect when I ate a full meal last.

I know it's been two weeks or better since—" He broke off to swallow and lick his lips.

"If you'd rather not talk about it, that's fine," Nate said. "For now, just rest."

Winona and Old Bill had climbed from their horses. Sawyer seemed not to notice them. His good eye fixed on something in the distance, something only he could see. "It's never enough, is it?" he said softly. "No matter how hard we try, it's never enough."

"How do you mean?" Nate asked, but received no response. He exchanged knowing glances with Winona, who gave the cradleboard to Zach so she could get a fire going that much sooner.

Old Bill squatted by the stump. "Jeremiah? It's me, your good pard. Don't you recognize me?"

Sawyer blinked a few times. "Bill? You're here too? Well, isn't this something? All my friends are showing up. How did you hear?"

"Hear?"

"About my wife and my precious sweethearts? About the murdering sons of bitches who killed them and nearly killed me. I'm going to get them, Bill. You watch. No matter how long it takes, no matter what I have to do, I'm going to find them and make them pay." Jeremiah absently turned toward the horses and gave a start. "Look! Just what I need! Did you bring them for me? I can't thank you enough."

The next instant the apparition was on his feet, stepping toward the stallion.

"If you want to tag along, you're welcome. But we're not stopping until we find them. We'll eat in the saddle, sleep in the saddle. If the horses drop dead, we'll find others."

Nate darted between his friend and the animals. "Hold on, Jeremiah," he said kindly, putting a hand on the man's chest. "You're not going anywhere right this minute. You need food; you need some sleep. And we have to talk."

Sawyer's features clouded and his spine went rigid. "Get out of my way, Nate. I can't afford any more delays. Those butchers have a lot to answer for."

"You're not leaving," Nate said.

It was as plain as the nose on his face that his friend was extremely upset, so he expected to get an argument. What he didn't expect was for Sawyer to haul off and take a swing at him. If Jeremiah hadn't been so weak he could hardly stand, the blow would have felled Nate like a poled ox. As it was, the punch clipped Nate's chin and made him recoil a step to ward off several other blows.

But then the punches stopped. The effort crumpled Jeremiah Sawyer in his tracks. Venting a loud groan, he feebly tried to rise, his once powerful arms trembling violently from the strain.

"No!" Jeremiah wailed. "You have to let me go! Those bastards have to pay!" Moisture rimming his eye, he tried to stand. He looked up at Nate in eloquent appeal but Nate made no move to help him. Scowling, he glanced at Zach. "Please, Zachary. They killed Beth! You liked her, didn't you? Don't you want to see her killers punished?"

Torn by turmoil, Zachary started to go to the man's aid, but drew up short at a gesture from his father.

"Winona!" Sawyer said. "Bill!"

Neither of them moved.

"Damn it all!" Jeremiah raged at Nate. "If it had been your family, you know I'd help you!"

"We'll lend a hand, but we'll do it right," Nate said. Hooking his arm under Sawyer's, he hoisted Jeremiah onto the stump and steadied him until he could sit up straight unassisted. "How long ago did this happen?"

"I told you. About two weeks, I think," Jeremiah said. "I've lost track of time." Slumping, he bowed his forehead to his left knee. His next words were barely audible. "It's a miracle I'm still alive, old friend. I remember running, with them nipping at my heels like a pack of rabid wolves. A shot hit me in the leg, and I thought for sure it was all over. Then I came to a ravine north of here." Jeremiah paused, his voice breaking. "I was looking for a way down when I turned to see how close they were and a ball caught me in the eye. That's the last I recollect for quite a spell."

There were so many questions Nate wanted to ask, but his friend was too worn down. He stripped his bedroll off the stallion and spread it out. "Here. Catch up on your rest."

This time Sawyer didn't object. He slid onto the blankets and lay on his back. "I've been sleeping on the ground for so long I'd forgotten how soft a blanket can feel."

Winona had a fire going. She filled their coffee-pot with water, then took a small bundle of herbs from a parfleche and added three slivers of root about the size of a large coin. "Toza," she said when she noticed Sawyer looking at her. "It is the root of a plant quite common in these mountains. When dug up, it resembles a carrot in shape, but smells and tastes like the celery I once tasted when my husband took me to New Orleans years ago."

"What does it do?"

"Toza is a tonic. It will help you build up your strength quickly."

"It better. I don't care what your husband says. Once I'm strong enough, I'm leaving."

Winona remembered Sawyer as a man whose poise had never been ruffled, not by wild beasts, not by enemy tribes, not by anything. It was said that Jeremiah Sawyer always kept his head, even in the midst of dire crisis.

This was a gravely different man. The deaths of his loved ones had pushed him close to the brink of mental chaos. Winona sensed it wouldn't take much to drive him over that brink, and then there was no telling what he might do.

Young Zachary stood close by, watching the man he thought he knew. Like his mother, he recognized that something was terribly wrong inside of the man's head. He wondered if Jeremiah would ever be the same carefree man he had always been. Somehow, Zach doubted it. Glancing up, he saw his father walk over to the graves.

Nate was even more troubled than his wife and son. Had circumstances been different, the situation might have been reversed. Would he burn for vengeance as his friend did? he asked himself. And being an honest man, he admitted that he would. The murder of a man's family was the one atrocity he could never forgive or forget.

Many times Nate had lain awake at night, fretting the same fate might befall those he cared for. Violent death was part and parcel of wilderness existence, but acknowledging the fact didn't make the reality any easier to bear.

Old Bill Zeigler ambled over. "I think he's driftin' off," he whispered. "Let's hope so. Sleep would do him a world of good."

"And make him harder to handle if he decides to ride out on us," Nate said.

"You can't blame him," Old Bill said. He rubbed the stubble on his chin, his brow knitting. "Say, do you reckon that the same bunch that rubbed out Buffalo Hump are the ones who paid Jeremiah a visit?"

In the tragedy of the moment, Nate had completely forgotten about the reason for their visit. "Could be," he said and checked an urge to question Sawyer more. He would just have to wait until the man was in better shape.

"If so, that means they're drifting north," Old Bill said. "I don't like that one bit. Go north far enough and we'll hit Blackfoot country."

"Maybe the ones we're after are Blackfeet," Nate said.

"I doubt it," Old Bill said. "Blackfeet may be a lot of things, but they ain't lazy. When they set about wipin' a family out, they generally do a thorough job. If they saw Jeremiah fall into a ravine, they'd climb down to be damn certain he was dead and to lift his hair."

"Maybe the ravine was too steep."

"For Blackfeet? You know as well as I do that they can climb like mountain sheep when they set their minds to it," Old Bill said. "No, if you ask me, whoever did this was a mite sloppy. And we both know Indians ain't ever sloppy."

Nate was about to go to the fire when he saw that small letters had been carved on the dead branches used to make the crosses. Hunkering down, he read the first inscription aloud. "Here lies my darling wife, Yellow Flower. My soul died with you."

"Damn," Old Bill said.

"In memory of Bethany Sawyer," Nate said, reading the second. "She met her Maker before her time."

"It must have taken him days to carve all them words."

The last was the hardest to read. The letters were fainter, as if Sawyer had become too weak to wield the knife effectively. "Here lies little Claire Sawyer," Nate read, "whose only sin was being born."

The old mountain man leaned down to run his fingers across the words. "Pitiful, ain't it? But that's the way life is sometimes. Just when we think we have it licked, it tears our innards out."

"Is that experience speaking?" Nate asked idly.

"What else? When you've lived as long as I have, you learn a thing or three." Old Bill adopted a melancholy air and raised his hand to touch below both eyes. "When I was your age, King, I was a regular hellion. Now look at me. I never figured on ending my days as blind as bat, of no use to anyone, not even myself."

"You're of use to me," Nate said. "You know this neck of the country much better than I do."

"So what? I can hardly get around by myself anymore. If you hadn't come along when you did, I'd still be stuck in my little valley, blunderin' around, trying to live off the land as best I could, knowin' damn well that sooner or later a bear or a painter or somethin' else would come along and make wolf meat of me."

"Yet you stayed on."

"What else was I to do?" Old Bill said bitterly. Turning, he walked off before he made a mistake and gave King a clue to his real motivation in tagging along. He saw the boy unsaddling the horses and joined him. "I'll unsaddle my own."

Zachary, downcast, merely nodded.

"Cat got your tongue?" Old Bill asked.

"I knew his daughters really well," Zach said, indicating Sawyer, who was sound asleep.

"That's death for you." Zeigler gripped the cinch.

"How can you be so coldhearted about it?" Zachary asked. "Didn't you know this family?"

"I did," Old Bill said. "But when you have as many gray hairs as I do, you know that death can strike anyone at any time. Few of us have any say over when and where we'll pass on. It's like rollin' a pair of dice. You never know what will come up."

"I hope I get to chose."

Old Bill smirked. "You and me both, son. You and me both."

In due course the animals were bedded down for the night, Zachary and Zeigler had filled the water skins, and Winona had fixed rabbit stew, courtesy of a fine shot Nate made. Jeremiah Sawyer slept the whole time, until hours after the sun had set.

Nate was sipping a delicious cup of coffee when he heard Jeremiah groan. The man had been tossing and turning ever since he'd fallen asleep, occasionally muttering incoherently. Twice he had cried out, an animal cry of sheer torment, but he had not awakened.

Now Nate saw Jeremiah's face contort into an agonized mask. Jeremiah rolled onto his right side, then back onto his left. His fingers clenched and unclenched as if he were throttling someone in his dreams. His teeth gnashed together so loud it sounded like metal grinding on metal. He started mumbling, the words growing louder and louder.

"I'll save you! I'll save you, girls! No one will hurt you! No one will harm your mother!"

Zachary listened with bated breath from across the fire. "Should we wake him, Pa?"

"No," Nate said, aware that sometimes those in the grip of terrible nightmares lashed out at anyone who tried to bring them around. "We'll wait a bit."

Jeremiah flipped onto his back. He made tiny mewling sounds, like those a frightened kitten might make. Next his mouth worked but no words came out. His hands rose to his throat and he sucked in air as if drowning. Eyelids quivering, he shook from head to toe.

"Are you sure he's not dying?" Zach asked.

As if in answer, Jeremiah sat bolt upright, his eye the size of a walnut, his face slick with sweat. He gazed into the night, his jaw muscles twitching, his hands shaking convulsively. "I'm coming, dearest!" he wailed. "Wait for me! I'm coming!" Propping both palms under him, he went to rise.

Nate guessed Sawyer's intent and intercepted him. Jeremiah took but a single step when Nate seized him around the shoulders and coaxed him toward the blankets. "Easy there, friend. You not going anywhere in the shape you're in."

Jeremiah motioned at the inky forest. "What are you doing? Can't you hear her?"

"Who?" Nate asked while attempting to ease him down.

Sawyer resisted, pushing weakly at his chest. "Yellow Flower! There! See her!" Jeremiah pointed, aglow with excitement. "She's still alive! I only thought she was dead! Please let me go to her!"

"I can't," Nate said.

"You must!" Jeremiah had worked himself into a fever pitch of desperation. He lunged, shoving hard, but Nate held firm. "What kind of pard are you? She needs me. Damn it!"

"Calm down!"

Nate might as well have railed at the wind. Jeremiah struggled fiercely, a virtual madman. What he lacked in brute force he made up for in devilish cunning. He raked at Nate's eyes with his fingernails, and when Nate raised his arms to deflect the blow, Jeremiah jumped to the left to scoot around him.

From two sides Winona and Old Bill closed in. They snared Jeremiah between them and held fast. He kicked and shouted and cursed until he was too weak to open his mouth. As they lowered him down, he burst into tears of abject misery, burying his face in the blankets.

"Will he ever be his old self again, Pa?" Zachary whispered.

"There's no telling," Nate asked. "When a man's spirit is broken, he can lose the will to live."

"Mr. Sawyer is no quitter. He'll be as good as new before too long."

The boy's confidence seemed misplaced to Nate but he held his tongue and was glad he did. For the very next morning he awoke to the uncomfortable feeling that he was being watched, and when he rose on an elbow, he discovered his intuition hadn't failed him.

All the others were sleeping, except for Jeremiah, who had his back supported by the stump and was regarding the brightening sky with intense interest. "Good morning," he said, sounding more like his old self. "Before you say a word, I want to apologize for yesterday. I don't quite recollect everything that happened, but I know I wasn't myself and that I gave you a hard time."

"How are you feeling now?"

"Just dandy," Jeremiah said. "Fit enough to ride. I'd be obliged if you'd let me have one of your horses. I'll get it back to you as soon as I can."

"When we leave, we leave together. I have a hunch we're after the same men you are," Nate said and related the pertinent facts about Buffalo Hump and the Utes.

"It could be the same outfit," Jeremiah said. "If it is, we're better off working together. There are seven of them, every man as mean as a rabid dog."

From a few yards away Bill Zeigler's voice piped up. "You can count me in. I know that I only offered to act as your guide until we got here, but I wouldn't miss this frolic for the world."

Nate King glanced from one to the other. He had deep doubts about taking them. Sawyer's quest for vengeance might endanger them all. And Zeigler couldn't hit the broad side of a barn at 20 feet. Relying on either could prove disastrous.

Refusing both was the logical thing to do. Logic, however, was no match for the one emotion that makes a man do things time and again against his better judgment.

Nate looked at his wife and children. The odds being what they were, he needed all the help he could get. "Fair enough. We ride together."

Old Bill chuckled. "Now the real fun starts."

Chapter Seven

Earl Lassiter wasn't in the best of moods. For one thing, he'd lost a fine tracker and interpreter when Cano's brains were blown out by the Blood. For another, his men were growing more and more restless as they traveled farther and farther north. If they didn't find some plump pilgrims to pluck soon, Dixon and Bear might see fit to strike off on their own.

Holding a bunch of callous killers together for any length of time had proven more trying than Lassiter counted on. There were countless petty squabbles to be handled, days on end when one or the other was in a foul temper and as likely to kill one of their own as anyone else.

The business with Cano had only made matters worse. None of his men cared for the Blood but they had all accepted the breed, more or less, because the breed had some white blood in his veins.

After Cano's death, there had been muttering behind Brule's back. Bear had come right out and said they should do to Brule as he had done to Cano.

Lassiter was inclined to agree. But he couldn't lay a finger on the Blood, nor allow anyone else to do so, until they found someone to replace him, which wouldn't be that simple. Warriors from friendly tribes weren't about to join his band. And warriors from hostile tribes would rather kill them than join.

Hooking up with Brule had been a once in a lifetime fluke, and at first Lassiter had been elated. The Blood was more deadly than a grizzly, more silent than a stalking mountain lion, more brutal than an enraged wolverine. He was the perfect killer, and Lassiter had been thrilled at having him on a short leash.

Now Lassiter knew otherwise. He no longer trusted the Blood. When they were together, Lassiter never turned his back to him. Brule was like a coiled sidewinder, set to strike at the slightest provocation.

Such was the train of thought that occupied Lassiter as he wound down a switchback to a ridge that overlooked a tableland to the north. He heard his name mentioned and looked around.

"Are you deaf?" Dixon asked. "I wanted to know how much farther you think it is?"

"You'll find out when we get there," Lassiter said gruffly, then remembered that he had to keep in Dixon's good graces or he would lose the man. He extended his arm to the northeast. "About a day's ride, I think. If I'm right, South Pass is that way. The wagons come over the pass and make straight for the Green River Valley. Somewhere between the two we should strike paydirt."

"You hope," Dixon said.

"He's not the only one," Ben Kingslow said. "I wouldn't mind having a few dollars in my pocket for a change. After we get this over with, maybe we can head east to the nearest fort. I want to get so drunk I can't stand up."

"We can't go to no fort," Snip said. "We'd be shot on the spot."

"Why, pray tell?" Kingslow asked.

"Have you forgotten what we did to that old Injun and his daughters? And that stubborn cuss and his family? And those three trappers Brule wiped out? Hell, man. Every mountaineer this side of the Rockies must be looking for us."

Ben Kingslow laughed. Of them all, Bear was the densest between the ears, but Snip had his moments. "No one is after us for those killings because no one knows we're to blame," he said. "So long as we keep covering our tracks, we'll be fine."

"Which is why we never leave witnesses," Lassiter said. "Kids, women—you name it. If they see us, they die."

"I don't much like killing sprouts," Bear said.

"Would you rather they squawked and Bridger or McNair came after us?" Lassiter said. "You know as well as I do that neither of those uppity sons of bitches would stand for having a pack of killers on the loose. They'd round up as many men as they needed and stay on our trail until hell froze over or they caught us."

"I don't want that," Bear said, "but I still don't like putting holes in kids. My mama raised me better than that."

Bear was sincere, which made it all the harder for him to understand why the rest of his friends burst into rollicking waves of laughter. "What did I say?" he asked when the mirth tapered off. It provoked another round of mirth.

Annoyed, Bear slapped his big legs against his mount and began to ride past Lassiter. Because he was glaring at the others and not watching where he was going, he nearly rode into the finely muscled figure blocking the way. He reined up in the nick of time.

Instantly the laughter ceased. Lassiter advanced, trying not to let his true feelings show. He resorted to sign language. "Have you found the trail, Brule?"

The Blood's fingers flew. "Yes. Far ahead. I have also found three wagons. There are three whites in the first, four in the second, only two in the third. Six are adults, the rest children. They travel very slowly."

Overjoyed, Lassiter yipped like a coyote, then relayed the news to his men. Only Kingslow also knew the universal hand language of the Indians. "How long will it take us to get there?" Lassiter asked the stoic warrior.

"You will be at the trail before the sun touches the horizon."

Lassiter thought fast. "No, we won't. I can't risk giving ourselves away before the time comes to pay those pilgrims a visit. Find us a good spot to camp for the night. Tomorrow we'll start stalking them."

"As you wish."

"I knew our luck would hold," Lassiter told his eager listeners. "We'll shadow them for a day or two, then help ourselves."

"To the women too?" Dixon asked and smacked his lips hungrily.

"To whatever the hell you want."

Her name was Katie Brandt and she was in love. In love with her husband of only six months, in love with the vast prairie and the regal mountains, in love with the bold notion of venturing to Oregon Country, where few had gone before, and in love with life itself.

On this day she sat beside Glen on the high seat of their creaking schooner and smiled as a yellow butterfly flew past. In front of their team of plodding oxen were two more wagons, the foremost driven by the Ringcrest family, the second the property of the Potters.

"What a grand and glorious adventure this is," Katie said breathlessly. "I'm so happy that I let you talk me into making this journey."

Her handsome husband arched an eyebrow at her. "Oh? For a while there, I thought you would pack your bags and go back east to your folks before you'd set foot past the Mississippi."

"I'm sorry I was so stubborn," Katie said. "I just didn't want to lose you so soon after tying the knot." She had made no secret of her fear. And who could blame her? The tales told about the savages that populated the wilderness were enough to turn a peaceful person's hair white.

"How do you feel now that you've learned all your fretting was for nothing?" Glen asked.

"Like a fool for acting so silly," Katie said. "But need I remind you that we're not out of the woods yet? It's many hundreds of miles to Oregon Country."

"Always optimistic, aren't you, dearest?" Glen said. "I keep telling you that the route we're taking doesn't pass through the territory of a single hostile tribe, but you won't listen."

"Only because I happen to know that hostile tribes like the Blackfeet roam anywhere they so please. We're in Shoshone territory now, but that doesn't mean we won't run into a Blackfoot war party."

Glen laughed. "And here I thought you had a sunny disposition. If I'd known you always looked at the dark side of things, I might never have proposed."

"Is that a fact?" Katie grinned and gave her man a playful smack on the shoulder.

Laughing, Glen Brandt clucked at the oxen. His cheerful demeanor hid a constant gnawing worry. For the truth was that he shared his wife's concern. They were taking a great risk making the trip, so great that he had debated with himself for weeks before committing himself. Many Oregon-bound travelers had lost their lives on the perilous journey and he didn't want his lovely wife to share their horrid fate.

Glen felt confident they would make it though. It was spring, and at that time of the year, the Blackfeet usually stayed close to their own region, busy hunting and stockpiling jerky and pemmican after the long, hard winter.

Plus their small caravan was being led by a man who had made the trip on horseback once before.

Peter Ringcrest had gone to the Pacific Northwest some years ago with Dr. Marcus Whitman's party. Whitman had been sent by the American Board of Commissioners of Foreign Missions to learn whether the Nez Perce and Flatheads tribes were receptive to missionary work. Once they established the Indians would accept them with open arms, Ringcrest had hastened back to the States to fetch his wife and son and anyone else who wanted to go along.

To hear Peter Ringcrest tell it, the Oregon Country justly deserved its reputation as the Promised Land. A mild climate, abundant rainfall, and rich soil made it a paradise for those who eked their living from the earth. Astoria and other growing communities afforded promise to those whose bent was more toward town life. And already the verdant forests were being tapped for their vast reserves of lumber.

"Oregon is heaven on earth!" Ringcrest liked to exclaim, and Glen believed him. He couldn't wait to stake a claim to a choice parcel and build a house that would do his wife proud. Not just any old dwelling or rustic cabin would suffice for the woman he loved.

"Oh, look," Katie said, giggling. "They're at it again."

Glen glanced at the back of the Potter wagon, where the two girls, Tricia and Agatha, were making faces at them. Agatha scrunched up her lively features and stuck out her tongue so Glen did the same. Both girls went into hysterics.

"Aren't they little darlings." Katie sighed. "I can't wait to have a girl of our very own."

"I'm partial to the notion of a son, myself,"

Glen said. "That way, when he's older, he can help out around the farm. Three or four boys would be even better. They could handle most of the chores and give us more time to ourselves."

"Three or four?" Katie said. "How many children would you like to have?"

"Oh, I don't know," Glen said, keeping an eye on a large rock close to the rutted track. He didn't want to break a wheel so early in the journey. "Maybe nine or ten, like my pa had."

"I think we had better sit down tonight and have us a long talk. I like the idea of a large family too, but my idea of large is four or five at the most."

They debated the issue then and there while the sun climbed steadily higher. Toward noon they stopped, as was their custom, in a shaded glade watered by a spring. The oxen were let loose from harness, and the horses tied to the first and third wagons were likewise allowed to drink and graze.

Katie spread out a blanket under a cottonwood and had a small meal waiting for Glen when he was done with the stock. The other couples were similarly occupied nearby. The Potter girls and the Ringcrest boy scampered about like chipmunks, whooping and hollering.

"Isn't life wonderful?" Katie said before taking a bite from a sweetmeat.

"So long as I'm with you, it is," Glen said, folding her free hand in his.

Katie brazenly pecked him on the cheek. As she straightened, her gaze happened to stray to the thickly clustered trees beyond the spring. A patch of brown in the midst of the green foliage piqued her curiosity. For a few moments she studied it.

Then the outline solidified and she gasped, unable to credit her own eyes.

"What's the matter?" Glen asked.

Startled so that she was unable to speak, Katie tried to vent a scream. A chill coursed down her spine, immobilizing her. She could see the cruel face clearly. The man's dark, fearsome eyes bored into hers as if into the depths of her soul.

Glen was sitting up. "What the dickens is it?" he asked and began to turn to look for himself.

The abominable face vanished. Katie leaped to her feet and screeched, clutching herself to keep from shivering. She felt Glen grip her arms and heard their friends running up. Even the children came, cowed into timid silence.

Peter Ringcrest was the first to speak. "What's wrong?" he asked urgently, his rifle in hand. "Why did you cry out, Mrs. Brandt?"

Willing her hand to extend, Katie pointed at the spot. "I saw someone there. An Indian, I think. He was watching us." She paused, the chill spreading. "You should have seen his dreadful eyes! He was a hostile. I just know it!"

Glen grabbed his rifle. "I'll go look."

"No!" Peter Ringcrest said as he anxiously scoured the glade. "If there are hostiles, that's what they would want you to do so they can pick you off. Where would that leave your wife?"

"What do we do then?" Bob Potter asked. A tinker by trade, he was a thin, waspish man whose fear was thick enough to be cut by one of the knives he sharpened for a living.

"We get out of here while we still can," Ringcrest said. "Glen, you collect the oxen. Bob, the horses. Ladies, kindly load everything into the wagons.

We'll cut our stop short. Once we're out in the open, the hostiles won't be able to take us unawares."

The glade bustled with frantic activity. For once the children were quiet, meekly doing whatever they were told. In less than 15 minutes the wagons were rolling, the women handling the reins so the men would have their hands free to shoot if necessary.

No attack materialized. Katie wondered if she had imagined the whole thing, but on reflection she knew there had been a face, that it had been an Indian.

Once clear of the cottonwoods, the pilgrims breathed easier. Glen had been perched on the edge of the seat, cocked rifle in hand. He sat back and said, "Maybe we were lucky. Maybe there was just the one."

"What if he was a scout for a war party?" Katie asked.

"We'll play it safe from here on out," Glen said. "We'll stick to open country, no matter what. At night we'll take turns standing guard and keep a fire going at all times. If hostiles are dogging us, they might give up once they see we're ready for them."

"What if they don't?"

Glen locked his eyes on hers. "Then we won't get to have that big family after all."

"Three days," Earl Lassiter said. "Three stinking days and we haven't been able to make a move."

Ben Kingslow shrugged. "It ain't our fault that they're being so blamed careful. They're just cagier than most pilgrims."

"Damn them all to hell." Lassiter said. "I'll give it another day, two at the most. Then we're doing whatever it takes to wipe them out."

"Sure thing," Kingslow said, having learned long ago it was healthier to agree with anything and everything their leader said when Lassiter was in one of his foul moods.

This time around, Kingslow shared the same sentiments. He was weary to death of plodding along in the wake of the wagons, waiting for the golden opportunity to spring an ambush. But ever since leaving a glade many miles back, the pilgrims never once let down their guard. It made him wonder if they suspected that they were being followed, although he couldn't see how they had guessed.

The gang rode a full mile behind the wagons to keep from being seen. At night, Lassiter allowed a tiny fire only so long as it was well concealed. There was no way in hell, Kingslow reflected, that the pilgrims could have caught on, yet it appeared that they had.

A lithe form appeared, jogging tirelessly toward them.

"Here comes the stinking Blood again," Dixon said. "I wonder what he wants this time? It's still early afternoon. The pilgrims can't have stopped for the day already."

Lassiter reined up and awaited their scout. It bothered him that Brule had become more reticent than ever in recent days. The warrior still did as Lassiter wanted, but now he did so with a marked reluctance, leading Lassiter to suspect that the Blood planned to light out on his own some time soon.

All Lassiter asked was that Brule waited until after they hit the caravan. He'd sneaked a peek at the three wagons and was elated to learn they were heaped high with household possessions and other articles. It was his impassioned hope that one or two of the pilgrims carried a nest egg worth hundreds if not thousands of dollars.

If the latter, Lassiter planned to head east, back to the States, and use his ill-gotten grubstake to set himself up in business in New Orleans. He'd long harbored the notion of having his own gambling establishment or tavern. A few thousand were all he needed to make his dream come true.

Lassiter drew rein to await the Blood. Beside him Bear smacked his thick lips and wiped a grimy hand across his dirty face. "You need a bath," Lassiter said irritably.

"What for?" the giant asked. "It's not August."

"What does August have to do with anything?"

"That's the month I take my bath. My grandma used to say that anyone who takes more than one a year winds up sickly."

"I'd rather you were sickly than rank," Lassiter said and dropped the subject as the Blood halted in front of them. "What have you seen?" he signed.

"The whites have stopped at a stream and are making camp."

"Can we approach the camp without them seeing?"

"No. Again they have picked a spot that gives them a clear view in all directions. There are no trees, no brush, no boulders within shooting range. It is a spot they can easily defend. And again they park the wagons in a circle and string rope to keep their animals inside."

"Damn them!" Lassiter said aloud, then employed sign again. "Do you have any idea why they are stopping so soon? The sun will not set for a while yet."

"I could not get as close as I would have liked," Brule signed, "but it appears one of the little girls is ill. I saw her mother feeling her brow, as if for fever, and mopping her brow with a damp cloth."

"You have done well," Lassiter signed. "Keep a watch on them and inform me of anything new."

"I will."

After the warrior trotted off, Lassiter swung toward his men and relayed the news. "In a way this is a break for us. They'll go slower than ever with a sick brat on their hands. And sooner or later they're going to run out of open country. That's when we nail their hides to the wall."

"It better be soon," Dixon said. "I'm tired of holding back. Hell, Earl, there's six of us. Why don't we crawl up close to them in the dark and blast away? We might drop all the adults with the first volley."

"And if we don't?" Lassiter asked. "If just one of them gets away and somehow makes it to a fort?"

"It was just a thought," Dixon said.

Lassiter was tired of the man's ceaseless belly-aching. He half wished that Brule had shot Dixon instead of Cano, but then he would have been obliged to kill Brule on the spot. Abiding the death of a lowly breed was one thing; the death of a fellow white quite another.

They searched for half a mile to the north and south of the trail, but failed to find any water or a suitable place to take shelter for the night. Having no recourse, they bedded down in the open and made a cold camp.

Ben Kingslow munched on the last of his jerked buffalo meat and lamented the chain of events that had brought him to this low point in his life. A former trapper, and before that a holder of more jobs than he could shake a stick at, he had tired of working like a slave for a living and decided to take the easy way. Only it wasn't as easy as he'd thought it would be.

Bear slurped his coffee and thought of the women in those wagons. He couldn't wait to get his hands on them. Next to killing, the thing Bear liked most was to squeeze a soft female until she screamed.

Dixon sat by himself, his blue cap pulled low over his brow. He was tired of all the riding, tired of all the time they wasted when all they had to do was ride right up to the pilgrims, acting as innocent as could be, and then shoot them down when they lowered their guard.

Snip busied himself grooming his horse, a mare he had taken a fancy to.

Nearest the fire sat Lassiter. He decided to give it three more days. After that they would be too close to the Green River Valley, where many of the trappers congregated, to risk attacking the caravan. Three days it had to be. And then, come hell or high water, those damned pilgrims were going to die!

Chapter Eight

Jeremiah Sawyer practically crackled with impatience when he said, "Why have you stopped? I swear, King, you're slower than a snail. Can't you see that we're wasting precious time?"

Nate raised his head from the hoof he was examining. "Would you rather have one of our horses go lame?"

Instead of answering, Jeremiah glowered at the pack animal responsible for the delay, wheeled his mount, and rode ahead a score of yards to wait for the others.

Old Bill Zeigler sighed and shook his head. "That coon is as high strung as piano wire. He can't wait to get his hands on them who rubbed out his kin, and I can't say as how I blame him."

"Me neither," Nate said. "But you'd think he would be a little less touchy by now."

It had been six days since they had left the

valley Sawyer had once called home. From dawn to dusk they were in the saddle, except for brief stops when their horses needed rest.

Originally, they had followed a faint trail, indistinct tracks only Nate recognized as such. He was by far the better tracker, and thanks to him they had gained rapidly on the gang of cutthroats.

They also had the killers to thank. Apparently the gang had slain three trappers and lost one of their own in the bargain, a breed Sawyer recognized. The trapper's camp had been pillaged. From the amount of prints, and from the five empty whiskey bottles found scattered about the camp, Nate guessed that the killers had spent two days there, possibly more. A costly mistake.

Now the tracks were less than a day old and Nate knew that before too long he would at long last confront the callous butchers who stalked the land. The bloodthirsty fiends had to pay for slaying ten innocent people, and perhaps many more, and Nate was going to see that they did.

It was a confrontation Nate both relished and dreaded. He looked forward to putting an end to their reign of terror, but at the same time he was worried about his family and friends. The odds were such that not all of them would survive, not unless he was very, very careful.

That would be hard to do with Jeremiah Sawyer primed to explode at the first sight of those they sought. Nate had grown increasingly worried about his friend and keenly regretted giving Jeremiah the spare rifle he always packed along on long journeys.

These were the thoughts that filtered through Nate's head as he pulled his butcher knife and pried a small stone loose. Tossing the culprit aside, he lowered the pack animal's leg, gave it a pat on the neck, and stepped to the stallion.

Winona and Zach were talking in hushed tones. They stopped as Nate drew alongside them, and his wife spoke so that only he could hear, "We must talk."

Nate waved to Jeremiah, who resumed tracking with Old Bill as company. Once the pair were well beyond earshot, Nate brought the stallion to a brisk walk, riding so close to Winona that his stirrup brushed her foot. "So what's on your mind, as if I can't guess?"

"What are we going to do about him? He will get us all killed, the way he is acting."

"There's not much I can do. He won't listen to reason."

"Zach and I have an idea," Winona said, and their son nodded vigorously. "Tonight, after he falls asleep, we should jump him and tie him up. Between the four of us we can do it, even if he has regained his strength."

"And then what?" Nate asked. "We keep him trussed up until we've dealt with Lassiter and his bunch?"

"It would seem to be the smart thing to do," Winona said as crisply as ever. "Once we have done what must be done, we will cut him loose and all will be well."

"There are only two problems with that idea," Nate said. "One, we can't do it without him. There are six killers, one of them a full-blooded Blood according to Jeremiah. We're going to need all the help we can get."

"And the second problem?"

"He's liable to hold it against us if we tie him up until it's all over. You've seen the look that comes into his eyes now and again. He's as close to being a madman as a sane man can be and still claim sanity."

"We never should have brought him or old Bill along, husband."

Nate didn't care to be reminded of his mistake. Yet if he had to do it again, he would. His family came first, and with the two men along, he would be better able to protect them. He noticed the position of the sun, some two hours above the western horizon toward which they were headed.

Over a day and a half ago they had come on the grooved tracks of wagon wheels. "The trail to the Oregon Country," Nate had said while noting how the hoofprints of the killers swung westward, paralleling the trail. Initially he had been stumped. Were Lassiter and company heading for Oregon to escape retribution for their acts? Then he had realized that several wagons had passed by a short while before Lassiter's band reached the trail, and he was able to put two and two together.

The cutthroats were after the pilgrims in those wagons.

Nate had pushed the horses as hard as he dared until that very morning. To keep on doing so would exhaust them so badly the animals would be useless for days, in which case Lassiter would get clean away.

But Nate chafed at the delay as much as Jeremiah Sawyer. He looked up to see how far ahead the other two were and was surprised to see only Zeigler, galloping back toward them, and puffs of dust in the distance. "What's the matter?" he demanded as the older man came to a sliding halt.

"It's that danged Sawyer!" Old Bill said. "He's decided you're taking too damn long, so he's gone on ahead."

"He what?"

"I tried to talk him out of it. But he wouldn't listen. He said that he was tired of dragging his heels, that we could catch up when we wanted."

Exasperated beyond measure, Nate lifted his reins, then addressed Winona. "I'll go ahead and stop him. You take your time. There's no sense in running all our horses into the ground." He touched her elbow in parting and was off, the big black stallion responding superbly as it always did. A last glance was all he had of his loved ones; then he buckled down to the task of overtaking the lunatic who would ruin everything.

Fortunately the lay of the land was mostly level. To the north were rolling hills, to the south gullies and ravines. But the wagon trail itself was flat and open so Nate could let the stallion have its head without fear of a mishap.

Presently Nate spotted Jeremiah. Despite the distance, he could see the man flailing away at his mount with the reins, driving the animal relentlessly.

Slowly, the stallion narrowed the gap. The packhorse that Sawyer rode was no match for the black over a long haul. Nate smiled grimly to himself as he cut the yardage in half. Meanwhile, the sun arced into the blue sky. The shadows lengthened.

Jeremiah came to a grade and for the first time

looked back. On spying Nate, he renewed his efforts to spur his horse on. The animal faltered, but didn't go down.

Bent low over the stallion, Nate rode with the accomplished skill of a Comanche. He held the Hawken close to his chest, not that he thought he would have to use it. But a man in his friend's condition was too unpredictable to say for sure.

Loose dirt and small stones spewed out from under the driving hooves of Sawyer's mount. The animal was on its last legs and slipped several times. Jeremiah pounded it furiously with his fist and rifle.

It added fuel to Nate's anger. He didn't believe in mistreating animals and he had never looked kindly on those who did. Some trappers stuck to the philosophy that the only way to master a horse was to beat the animal into submission, but Nate believed that a little kindness went a long way toward accomplishing the same goal.

The black stallion took the grade on the fly. Nate knew that in less than a minute he would catch his quarry. He saw Sawyer's mount stumble, drop to a knee, then rise again. The animal plodded instead of trotted; its head hung low.

Jeremiah Sawyer looked over his shoulder, cursed, and jumped to the ground. He ran toward the top of the grade, his moccasins raising tiny puffs of dust.

Nate didn't bother with the packhorse for the moment. He galloped on past, leaning low, the Hawken clutched in both hands. The summit of the grade was mere yards away when he pulled abreast of Sawyer. "Stop," he said.

A maniacal gleam lighting his features, Jeremiah slowed and swung his rifle, trying to knock Nate off the stallion. Nate had anticipated the swing and evaded it. Then, lashing out with the Hawken, he hit Jeremiah across the shoulders. Jeremiah landed in the dirt, face first.

Nate was off the stallion before Sawyer could rise. He tore the rifle from Jeremiah's grasp and trained his own on the man's chest. Jeremiah froze in the act of pushing to his feet, his face that of a beast at bay.

"Damn you, Nate! You had no right to stop me!"

"I had every right," Nate said, backing up a few strides so he would have room to maneuver if his friend came at him. "The state you're in, Lassiter is liable to kill you before you kill him. And I don't want Lassiter to know anyone is on his trail until we're ready to make our move. That way he won't be on his guard."

"Even if he did put windows in my skull, there's no way he'd know about you and Old Bill," Jeremiah said, rising slowly. He looked at the stallion. "Let me take your horse and go on by myself."

"No."

"Please," Jeremiah said. "For the sake of our friendship, you have to."

"It's because we're friends that I'm not about to let you go riding off half-cocked. Yellow Flower wouldn't want you to throw your life away on her account."

Jeremiah turned red, clenched his knobby fists, and took a menacing step. "How would you know what she'd want? She was my wife, not yours!"

"I knew here fairly well," Nate said calmly. "Well enough to know that she was a lot like Winona. She was as kind as the day is long, and as smart as can be." He noticed that the stallion had stopped shy of the summit and backed toward it. "Yes, she'd want you to avenge her, but she'd never stand still for your committing suicide. And that's exactly what you aim to do."

"You think you know everything," Jeremiah said bitterly, his tone that of a small child caught with his hand in the cookie jar.

"I wasn't born yesterday," Nate said.

The stallion turned as he came up and stood meekly while he grabbed the reins. Jeremiah made no move to interfere. Nate was so close to the top that he only needed to take a few steps to see over it, and curiosity got the better of him. Keeping one eye on the melancholy avenger, he sidled high enough to view the vista beyond.

A wide green valley bisected the trail, running north to south. A river, in turn, bisected the valley. Along its banks grew trees as well as patches of heavy brush. There was no sign of a fire or movement and Nate was about to climb on the stallion when he lowered his gaze to the opposite slope.

Someone was jogging up it toward him. As yet the figure was several hundred yards away, too far for Nate to note much other than it was an Indian. Ducking low, hoping he hadn't been spotted, Nate hastened toward Sawyer.

"Mount up. Quickly."

"What's wrong?" Jeremiah asked, having the presence of mind to obey.

"I think it's that Blood you were telling me

about. He's coming this way."

Jeremiah stopped. Lips quivering, the veins on his temples bulging, he had the look of a bear hound about to bolt after a griz. "Does he know we're here?"

"I can't see how," Nate said. He wagged the Hawken. "Do as I told you. We can't shoot him yet. His friends must be nearby, and they'd hear."

"So what?" Jeremiah said. "I say we end it now."

"It's not open to parley." Nate stepped into the stirrups. To the north stretched a grass covered tract bounded by a low spine. To the south reared a series of small bluffs interspersed with boulders and gullies. When Sawyer had complied, he motioned southward and let the tired pack animal go first.

The arid ground became rocky. Their horses left few tracks. Nate wanted to cover the impressions with handfuls of dirt, but there was no time. Into the nearest gully he went, there to dismount and creep back to the rim. They had sought cover none too soon.

A lithe form stood atop the grade. The warrior looked both ways, then down at his feet. He must have seen Nate's tracks because he promptly crouched and pressed his rifle to his shoulder.

"That's the Blood," Jeremiah whispered at Nate's elbow, his voice full of raw emotion.

Nate looked to see if the other man would do anything rash. Jeremiah had dug the fingers of both hands into the earth and was trembling uncontrollably. "Be patient," Nate coaxed. "Your time will come."

The Blood was studying their tracks. Apparently the prints confused him because he walked around and around the spot where they had clashed.

"He'll find us. I know he will," Jeremiah whispered.

Nate wasn't so certain. Indians differed in ability, just like whites. Some were excellent rifle shots, while some couldn't hit the broad side of a mountain with a cannon. Some, like the Comanches, were natural-born horsemen. Others, like the Blackfeet, only rode when they had to. And in any given tribe, only a handful qualified as outstanding trackers. The rest were no better or worse than the average mountain man.

This one appeared stumped. The Blood strode to the summit again, then back along the line of tracks to where Jeremiah had been knocked down. He scratched his chin, squatted, and shook his head. After a while he made an impatient gesture and jogged on eastward.

"Damn it all," Jeremiah said. "I wanted to make maggot food of the son of a bitch."

"We will when the time is ripe," Nate said, marking the Blood's progress. The warrior never looked back and eventually his silhouette dwindled to a black speck.

Sighing, Nate shifted on his heel to descend. Belatedly, he saw the flick of Sawyer's hands. A spray of dirt struck him flush in both eyes. Involuntarily, he blinked, and it felt as if he had just submerged his head in sand. Tears gushed, blurring his vision. He knew what was coming and tried to leap to one side.

A granite blow landed on Nate's head above

the right ear, and it was as if a bolt of weakness shot through him. His legs buckled of their own accord. He felt another jarring jolt when his head hit the ground. The world had gone black but he was still vaguely conscious, still aware of who he was and where he was. But even that was denied him moments later when another blow hurtled him into oblivion.

Jeremiah Sawyer raised the big rock a third time, then paused. There was a nasty gash in King's head, covered with trickling blood. Another swing might well kill him.

As much as Jeremiah craved revenge on those who had slain his family, he wasn't about to rub out one of his few friends to achieve it. He slowly lowered the bloody rock, took a deep breath to regain his self-control, and cast it aside.

"I'm sorry," Jeremiah said softly. "But I can't rest until the butchers have gone under." He reclaimed his rifle and slipped King's pistols under his own belt. Nate groaned, but made no move to resist.

The black stallion lifted its head as Jeremiah dashed toward it and grabbed for the reins. To his annoyance, the horse pranced backward, out of reach.

"Hold still, damn you," Jeremiah said. Taking a few steps, he lunged. His reflexes were no match for the stallion's, which skipped off, tossing its mane.

Unwilling to waste time chasing the animal down, Jeremiah climbed onto the horse he had been using and rode to the grade. The brief rest had given his mount a chance to catch its wind. It balked a little when he made for the top, but settled down after a sharp kick in the ribs.

Jeremiah rose in the saddle and stared eastward. He couldn't be positive if it was his imagination or not, but he swore that he saw the Blood far, far off, staring back at him. The image vanished when he blinked. Shrugging, he rode on down into the valley. The Blood could wait. First he wanted Lassiter.

The trees were deathly silent when Jeremiah rode up. It was a warning that all was not as it should be. Any prudent mountain man would have proceeded with caution. But Jeremiah rode boldly into the woods. He didn't care if the cutthroats saw him coming. They were going to pay, come hell or high water.

In due course Jeremiah reached the low bank of the shallow river. Rather than seek a spot to ford, he crossed right there. Or rather, he tried to, for no sooner had the horse stepped into the water than it gave out with a loud whinny and commenced struggling to pull its hooves free.

Jeremiah prodded the animal again and again. It tried valiantly to extract itself from the mud bog, without success.

"Come on, you mangy cayuse!" Jeremiah said. "You picked a pitiful time to give out on me."

The animal's legs made great sucking noises as it lifted first one, then the other. Try as it might, it was unable to raise a single limb clear of the mud. Jeremiah was left with no recourse other than to slide off and gingerly pick his way to the bank. He sank with every stride, but not as deep as the horse.

Jeremiah could ill afford to lose his mount. He studied the problem a bit and had decided to simply grip its reins and try to pull it out, when to his ears came the creak of leather accompanied by a low nicker.

Spinning, Jeremiah dashed under cover. As he flattened he saw two riders materialize on the other bank. One was the giant known as Bear. The other was the smallest of the butchers, whose name Jeremiah didn't know.

"I told you that I heard something," the small man said.

"And you were right," Bear said, surveying the vegetation. "But where's the owner?"

"Maybe it belonged to some pilgrim and strayed off," the small man said. "Go fetch Earl while I take a gander."

"Keep your eyes skinned, Snip." The giant nodded and trotted off.

Jeremiah was almost beside himself with glee. He'd caught the killers at long last. It would have been child's play to drop the one called Snip at that range, but Jeremiah held his fire. He was after bigger game.

Snip rode a dozen yards to the south and crossed. A gravel bar provided a natural bridge across the bog. His beady eyes swept the tree line the whole time, and he kept one finger on the trigger of his rifle.

Once on the near shore, Snip drew as close to the stuck horse as he could without endangering his own. He whistled to it, trying to lure it to the bank, but the hapless pack animal had sunk to the points of its hocks and could do no more than whinny helplessly.

Jeremiah was impatient for Lassiter and the rest to appear. He extended the rifle and sighted down the barrel at the same spot where the two cutthroats had appeared. Listen as he might, he heard nothing.

"I wish I had me a rope," Snip was saying. "I'd have you out of there."

Dismounting, Snip walked to the edge of the bog and leaned forward as far as he dared. His fingers brushed the animal's tail. "There has to be a way," he said to himself.

Fifteen feet away, Jeremiah scarcely breathed. He probed the stretch of river for evidence of Lassiter, his body tingling with excitement. Snip hardly interested him. He paid scant attention when the killer paced back and forth as if mulling over how best to free the horse. He didn't give Snip a second look when the man walked to his mount and fiddled with a saddlebag. But he did go as rigid as a plank when Snip suddenly looked in his direction.

The cutthroat wore a mocking sort of smile, as if gloating. It made no sense to Jeremiah until, with a start, he realized that Snip was looking at something behind him. At the same instant he heard a soft scraping noise, as of a bush rubbing buckskin.

Jeremiah knew that if he twisted, Snip would see him. Yet a terrible feeling came over him that, if he didn't turn, he would regret it. For a few moments he wavered.

Suddenly a pair of steely hands swooped down, one closing on the rifle, the other on the back of Jeremiah's neck. He was wrenched into the air and shaken as a terrier might shake a rabbit. And then he found himself staring up into the twisted visage of the huge killer called Bear.

Chapter Nine

Nate King and Jeremiah Sawyer were barely out of sight when Old Bill Zeigler smiled and turned to Winona and the children.

"What has you so happy?" Zachary asked while trying to catch a last glimpse of his pa.

"Life, boy," Bill said. "If you were to live long enough, you'd find that life has a sense of humor all its own. From the cradle to the grave, life is one big laugh."

"I don't think I agree," Zach said.

"Ask me if I care?" Old Bill said, and with deceptive speed he hauled off and rammed the stock of his rifle into the youngster's side, which sent Zach tumbling from the saddle, doubled over in agony.

Winona was so shocked that she sat as one transformed to stone for the few moments it took Old Bill to swing the muzzle of his rifle around to cover her.

"I wouldn't lift a finger against me, were I you," the mountain man said. "Not if you're partial to breathing." He snatched her rifle and threw it down, then stripped her of her pistol and knife. She offered no resistance, which would have been hard to do in any case, with Evelyn in her arms.

"There, now!" Old Bill said, grinning. He moved his mount a few yards away so he could keep track of all three of them. "At long last my patience has been rewarded."

Bewildered beyond measure, Winona saw her son roll from side to side, sputtering through clenched teeth. She wanted to go to him, but was leery of the possible consequences. "We thought you were our friend!" she said.

"Your mistake, not mine," Zeigler said gruffly. "I can't help it if I'm so darned good at actin' that I can fool most any man alive, white or red."

"The whole time you have been pretending to like us?"

"Playing you all for jackasses," Old Bill said. "All these days I've been bidin' my time, waitin' for the opportunity I was sure would come. And it did."

"But why?" Winona asked. It staggered her that she had let herself be duped, that she had been taken in by a man whose nature was akin to that of the killers they chased.

Long ago, as a young woman, Winona had learned that some whites were deceitful, that they secretly harbored strong lusts and perverse longings. Once, when her family had attended a rendezvous, a white man had entered their lodge without permission and tried to have his way with her. Only the timely intervention of her father had stopped him.

The experience had taught Winona to always be on the lookout for such men and to avoid them as if they had the pox. Since marrying Nate, she had rarely been bothered, and as a result she had let down her guard when she shouldn't have. There was really only one man any woman could trust fully and completely, and that was her husband.

"We'll chaw later, woman," Old Bill said. "For now, we have to put a lot of miles behind us before your man comes back. Soon as your boy quits his bellyachin', we'll be on our way, pack animals and all."

Unknown to Zeigler, Zachary King's pain had subsided. He was sore but otherwise unharmed, and he wanted nothing more than to draw his pistol and put a ball through the man's skull. The only thing that stopped him was the rifle Zeigler held on his mother. All it would take was a twitch of a finger as Zeigler fell, and his mother or his sister might pay with their lives for his brash action.

Old Bill glanced down. "I reckon you've moaned and groaned long enough, boy. Why, when I was your age, a little tap like I gave you wouldn't have made me blink. On your feet now and keep your hands where I can see them."

It was the very last thing Zach wanted to do, yet he felt he had no choice. He uncoiled and stood, poised to draw if the mountain man lowered his guard. But Old Bill held that rifle steady on his mother's chest.

"Drop the flintlock and your knife. Then climb on your paint."

Once again Zach complied. His mother gave him a sympathetic look that only made him feel worse. With his pa gone, it was his responsibility to protect the women in their family. And he had failed.

Winona dearly desired to spare her children, so she said, "I am the one you want. Leave Zach and Evelyn here. They pose no danger to you."

"Goodness, you think right highly of yourself," Old Bill said. "I couldn't give an owl's ass about you, Shoshone. You're involved because I can't leave any witnesses."

Confused, Winona said, "But if not for me, then why?"

Old Bill grinned at her son. "For him. Now move out before I take it into my head to shoot the girl."

Both mother and son were confounded by the revelation. Paralyzing fear seized Winona, and she meekly goaded her mare into motion.

Zachary was flabbergasted. He couldn't understand why the old man was going to slay them on his account. "What did I ever do to you?" he asked.

"You hit me, boy."

"That time I walloped you with the rifle when you were fixing to stab my pa?"

"Know of any other time?" Old Bill said brusquely. "That once was enough. I made up my mind then and there that I'd fix you and fix you proper for the hurt you caused me." His voice lowered to a growl. "No one lays a hand on William T. Zeigler and lives to tell of it. No one."

"But he's just a boy!" Winona said, disbelief and fury vying for dominance in her heart. "He was doing what any other boy would do."

"Maybe so," Old Bill said. "And I'd do the same to any other boy."

Winona had known whites to do things that were judged extremely peculiar by the standards of her people, but this, as her husband would say, beat them all. What sort of man would hold a noble act against someone of her son's tender years? Perhaps the horrible tales told about Old Bill stemmed from a kernel of truth. The somber thought prompted her to ask, "Do you eat people? Is that what this is all about?"

Zeigler's eyes twinkled. "Heard that one, have you? I suppose pretty near everyone in the Rockies has."

"Do you?" Winona said.

"I'm not sayin' I do. I'm not sayin' I don't," Old Bill said. "Let's keep it as a surprise for later, after we get to where we're going."

"Where would that be?" Zach asked.

"All in good time, boy," Old Bill said. "All in good time."

Zach saw his mother clutch Evelyn to her and felt a strange lump form in his throat. He gave the lead rope a sharp tug to move the packhorses along. Then he said, "You made a big mistake, mister. My pa will be after us before too long. And I wouldn't want to be in your moccasins when he gets his hands on you."

"Spare me the bluster, brat," Zeigler said. "Your father might be fringed hell on two legs, but I'm no slouch myself. I always stay two steps ahead of everyone else by thinkin' ahead. This time will

be no different. I have a little surprise in store for
your pa that will put an end to the high and mighty
Grizzly Killer forever."

Zachary became so mad, his temples throbbed.
He recollected all the times his pa had warned
him about being too trusting for his own good.
"Trust has to be earned", his father often said. To
take it for granted that someone was dependable
was a sure way of inviting trouble.

Yet Zach had done just that. Old Bill had
seemed so friendly, even after being konked
on the noggin, that Zach had assumed that the
old-timer was a harmless coot. He wondered if
his pa had also been deceived, and he figured
that had to be the case or his father wouldn't
have gone off and left them alone with Zeigler—
unless his pa had counted on him to protect his
mother and sister.

Depressed, Zach glared at the mountain man
and noticed Old Bill staring off at a flock of sparrows winging eastward. "You can see just as well
as we can!"

"Of course I can," Old Bill said. "Fact is, I can
probably see better than the lot of you. My eyes
have always been as sharp as an eagle's."

Zach was quick to discern something else. "You
lied to my pa. You attacked him on purpose."

"Sure did. I was hoping to slit his throat and
take his rifle from him before your ma or you
could interfere, but he was too damned fast for
me."

"It isn't right, what you do," Zach said resent-
fully. "It isn't right to go around hurting others
for no reason."

"Oh, I've got me a dandy reason," Old Bill said,

and he smacked his lips loudly a few times.

"You're vermin, mister, plain and simple."

Old Bill's lips compressed into a tight line. "That's enough out of you, pup. I want you to quit your jawing. I won't stand for being pestered. Just ride along as if you're out on a Sunday jaunt and we'll get along right fine."

Young Zachary King did as he was told, but inwardly he seethed like a boiling volcano. He was not going to let Zeigler harm his father or mother or sister. Somehow, he would turn the tables on their captor.

Brule rarely smiled. It wasn't in his nature to find much amusement in life. But outwitting others always made him feel good. Which was why he smiled broadly now as he trotted eastward along the same rutted track he had been following in the opposite direction for so long.

The warrior had grown tired of the company of whites. Their mindless chatter, their constant bickering, their body odor—all had made him long for the companionship of his own kind. And since that was denied him, he preferred to be by himself.

Brule hadn't bothered to inform Earl Lassiter and the others. That morning Lassiter had sent him off to spy on the whites in the wagons, as usual. Only this time Brule had merely gone a short distance and then circled around to the east. Lassiter and the rest were probably still waiting for him to return and report.

Brule slowed down to study his trail. There was no sign of pursuit, nor did he truly think

Lassiter would be stupid enough to send someone to bring him back.

Brule gave his splendid new knife a pat, then
admired his new rifle. As distasteful as it had
been to associate with whites, he had to admit
that he had benefited greatly. Perhaps he would
do it again one day.

Running on, Brule settled into a steady stride.
He thought of the tracks he had seen at the grade
and of the two whites who had watched him from
the gully without being aware that he knew they
were there. Who had they been? Why had they
fought? Even more perplexing, why had they hid
from him instead of ambushing him when he
came over the summit?

Brule had no burning interest to learn the
answers. If the pair were after Lassiter, it was
Lassiter's problem. He wanted nothing more to
do with the renegades.

Then the Blood came to where a number of
riders and packhorses had come on the wagon
trail from the south. He studied the many tracks
closely, reading them as a white would read a
book. He saw where two men had ridden westward and one had returned. He was able to tell
that another man had then gone after the first.
They were the pair at the grade, he realized.

Five horses had gone south again. Brule guessed
that two of them were heavily burdened pack
animals. The third horse carried lighter weight,
perhaps a child or a small man or woman.
The fourth horse, which was shod, carried a
full-grown man. And the last animal, if the
depth of the mare's tracks were any indication,
was being ridden by a woman. Since this horse

wasn't shod, Brule suspected the woman to be an Indian, which changed everything.

Brule had not been with a female in many sleeps. White women revolted him; they were puny, pale whiners, about as attractive as slugs. He did not know of a single warrior of any tribe who had taken a white woman as a wife because they were so widely regarded as unable to adapt to the Indian way of life.

Lassiter had surprised Brule by telling him that white women felt the same way about Indian men. In Brule's estimation it was typical of white women that they were too stupid to appreciate worthy mates. He, for instance, was a skilled fighter and hunter. If he had a wife, she would never want for meat or hides. And the many coup he earned would bring honor to their lodge. Any woman in her right mind would leap at the chance to be his mate.

Brule straightened and scowled. He must not think about such things. Being an outcast, he would never know the joy of having a Blood wife, never rise in standing in his tribe to one day be a war chief as he had always dreamed of doing.

But just because a Blood wife was denied him did not necessarily mean Brule couldn't have another. Any Indian woman would do. And here was one ripe for the taking.

Brule gazed eastward. It had been in his head to travel to the prairie, but another idea appealed to him. Swinging to the south, he trotted on the trail of the three riders.

A cool breeze on his face was the first sensation Nate King felt upon reviving. He lay still a few moments, his head racked by drumming pangs, trying to remember what had happened. When he did, he shot up into a sitting position and winced as the torment worsened. Blinking, he looked around.

The sun crowned the western horizon. Soon twilight would descend. Jeremiah Sawyer was gone. The black stallion stood 50 feet off, nibbling at a small patch of brown grass.

Nate carefully ran his fingers over his wound. A coat of slick dry blood matted his hair and clung to his ear, cheek, and neck. He rubbed his cheek but the blood wouldn't come off. Retrieving his hat and Hawken, he slowly stood, and in doing so he discovered that both of his pistols were missing.

The stallion saw him shuffling forward and walked over to meet him. Nate leaned against the big black for support, stroking its neck. "Good boy," he said softly.

Nate donned the hat, gripped the saddle, and pulled himself up. For a few moments the landscape seemed to dance as if alive, and he thought he would lose his hold and fall. Forking a leg, he slumped down on the stallion's neck and breathed deeply while regaining his strength.

At length Nate straightened and rode up out of the gully. At the Oregon Trail, he drew rein. From the tracks it was clear that Jeremiah had gone into the valley. Nate had to make up his mind whether to go after him or to rejoin his family.

Nate told himself that he was under no personal obligation. Jeremiah had been a friend, but that had been a totally different Jeremiah Sawyer, a man very much like Nate, a fellow free trapper who had taken an Indian wife and become a devoted husband and father. Unlike the majority of trappers, who took wives for a single season and then cast them aside or merely indulged when they could pay the price, the two of them always regarded their marriages as seriously as they would if they were wed to white women. It was no wonder they had become close friends, they were so much alike.

But as far as Nate was concerned, Jeremiah had severed the ties that bound them by trying to beat in his head with a rock. He shouldn't bother trying to save Jeremiah from himself. The man had made his choice and had to live with it.

Nate lifted the reins and went to head eastward. To his mind's eye appeared an image from the last rendezvous, when the two families had sat around a fire late at night swapping tales and joking. He remembered Jeremiah passing a whiskey jug to him after taking a long swig, and how they had both laughed when little Evelyn got a hold of Winona's nose and wouldn't let go.

"Damn it all," Nate muttered, turning the stallion. He went over the summit at a gallop, no longer caring about stealth. He couldn't just ride off and leave Jeremiah to face the killers alone, no matter what had happened.

Nate was grateful that Winona and the children were safe. Should anything befall him, Bill Zeigler was on hand to help Winona reach their cabin. He could rest easy and concentrate on the renegades.

Suddenly Nate spied several large black birds wheeling high in the sky above the river. "Buzzards," he said aloud and rode faster until the cottonwoods closed around him. Here he halted and secured the reins to a low limb.

Never take anything for granted—that was the creed Nate lived by, and he applied it by crawling through the undergrowth to a vantage point that afforded an unobstructed view of the river. He could see the vultures, seven in all, swooping steadily lower. Toward what? he wondered, then saw a bulky form lying at the water's edge. It was too big to be a man.

Nate bided his time. Several buzzards landed, one on top of the carcass. Its hooked beak tore into the hide as neatly as a knife, ripping an opening so the scavenger could get at the juicy flesh underneath. Strips of red meat were ripped off and greedily gulped.

Nothing else moved along the river. Nate searched the shadows long and hard. He wouldn't put it past Lassiter to try to lure him into a trap, but after ten minutes he grew convinced the coast was clear.

Still, to be safe, Nate hugged the ground as he snaked close enough to identify the carcass. He believed it was a horse, but he had no idea it would turn out to be the packhorse, partially buried in mud. Someone had slit the animal's throat and left it to meet a slow, grisly end, its lifeblood pumping into the bog in which it had been stuck.

Rising, Nate stalked as close as he could without sinking. There was no trace of Jeremiah. And with the sun gone, it would soon be too dark to track. He decided to try anyway, since his friend's life was at stake, and he turned to hurry to the stallion.

A guttural groan fluttered on the wind, arising somewhere to the north of where Nate stood. He walked toward the source, scouring the brush at ground level. Under a massive willow, he stopped to listen. Time passed and the groan was repeated. Only it came from above.

Nate tilted his head back and gasped. He had witnessed many gruesome atrocities since taking up residence in the untamed Rockies, but few equaled the ghastly savagery Jeremiah Sawyer had suffered.

The renegades had stripped him and peeled his skin from his body as if he were an orange. His fingers and toes had been hacked off, his ears smashed to a pulp, his nose sliced down the middle. Then they had tied a rope to his wrists and hauled him ten feet off the ground. As if that wasn't enough, someone on horseback had thrust a knife into his gut and left the knife there. A loathsome pool of blood had formed under the doomed man.

Quickly Nate scrambled into the tree. Working from branch to branch, he reached the limb to which Jeremiah was tied. He hesitated before applying his knife, then did. He tried to catch the rope before Jeremiah fell. The weight was too much for him, the rope searing his palms so badly he had to let go or lose all his skin. He winced when his friend smacked wetly into the pool.

Clambering swiftly down, Nate dashed over and knelt. Jeremiah's good eye closed and he was breathing heavily. Nate touched his head and almost jumped back when Jeremiah's lid snapped wide open.

"Nate?" The word was croaked, Jeremiah's pupil dilated and unfocused.

"I'm right here," Nate said, reaching for a hand that wasn't there. He didn't know what else to do so he put both his hands on Jeremiah's head.

"You were right all the time. I should have listened." Jeremiah licked red froth from his lips. "The Blood ran off on them. They were hunting for him when they saw me. Tricked me, the bastards. Made me think one of them was going back for the rest when all the time he was circling around behind me."

"Don't talk," Nate said when his friend took a breath. "You should lie quietly."

"For how long?" Jeremiah said weakly. "You have no idea of the pain. It's worse than I can describe."

Nate swallowed his building grief and said, "I wish there was something I could do."

"There is."

"What?"

"Kill me."

"No," Nate said.

"You have to. I hurt so bad. Please."

"No."

"You know I'll die anyway," Jeremiah said, tears streaming from the corners of his eyes. "Don't let me suffer. Deprive them of that, at least."

"I—" Nate said, but couldn't finish. He knew what he had to do but he couldn't bring himself to accept it.

"I'm waiting," Jeremiah said forlornly.

Nate lowered his leaden right hand to his butcher knife, then froze. The thought of burying the blade in his friend's ribs was one he couldn't abide. He didn't care how close the renegades were. He picked up the Hawken and thumbed back the hammer. As Nate lightly pressed the muzzle to the other man's temple, Jeremiah twisted his neck.

"I don't blame you, pard. You did all you could." Jeremiah coughed. "Just do me one favor."

"Anything."

"Make them pay."

"You have my word," Nate King said huskily, then stroked the trigger.

Chapter Ten

Katie Brandt was in the process of making a pot of fresh coffee when a shot echoed across the darkening valley. She glanced anxiously up at her husband, who was mending harness while seated on the tongue of their wagon. "Was that a shot?"

"It was," Glen said, standing. Against the wagon leaned his rifle, which he picked up.

"But who could be shooting? We're all here."

That they were, the Ringcrest family across the clearing by their wagon, the Potter clan at ease on a blanket spread out on the soft grass.

"Your guess is as good as mine," Glen said.

"Do you think it might be hostiles?"

"Mighty careless hostiles, if it is," Glen said. "Indians don't like to advertise their presence. It could be a trapper shooting his supper. I doubt he has any notion we're here."

Katie stood, flashing her teeth in joy. "Do you

really think so? Oh, I do so hope you're right! It's been ages since we talked to anyone besides our companions. Wouldn't it be nice to have a guest in camp? Maybe you should go see."

The idea disturbed Glen. It was bad enough that they had been stuck in a small clearing on the west side of an unnamed valley for over a day while repairing Peter Ringcrest's broken wheel. Hemmed in by trees, they were sitting ducks for savages inclined to deprive them of their lives or their belongings or both.

Six days had gone by since Katie had seen the Indian. So far they had seen neither hide nor hair of any hostiles. The others were of the opinion that they had been needlessly worried, but Glen didn't share their outlook. He had a nagging feeling that they were all in grave peril. And if his hunch was right, it would be stupid of him to go off alone.

At the same time, Glen had no desire to appear yellow in front of his new bride. So when no one objected to her proposal, he started for the ring of vegetation.

"Hold on," Bob Potter said. Like Glen, he had grabbed his rifle and stood peering into the woods. "Maybe you should wait until we know who is out there."

"We'll never know who it is if one of us doesn't look," Peter Ringcrest said. "And we'd better do it before it's too dark to be abroad."

"I'll go," Glen said, secretly hoping someone would stop him. No one did though, so he squared his shoulders and strode into the trees. Thanks to the glow cast by the trio of cooking fires, the area was lit up as bright as day for all of five paces.

Then the darkness closed in like a murky veil and he could hardly see his hand in front of his face.

Glen was surprised that Katie had suggested he go. Usually she couldn't bear to have him stray out of her sight. He knew she had been embarrassed by her show of fear at the spring and further embarrassed when hostiles failed to materialize. Just the night before she had confided that she was beginning to think it had been a friendly Indian she scared off by acting like a ten year old.

Was she trying to prove she could cope when alone by having him search for the shooter? Glen didn't know, but it was the only logical explanation. Then again, as he'd learned during the short time he'd been married, trying to figure women out was guaranteed to give a man a headache.

Glen halted and listened. The shot had come from the vicinity of the river but he heard no other sounds from that direction. Being by himself in the dark brought gooseflesh to his skin. Steadying his nerves, he slowly advanced.

Seconds passed, and Glen thought he saw something move off to the right. Leveling the rifle, he said quietly, "Who's there?"

No one replied.

Chalking it up to his imagination, Glen went on. He held the rifle tucked tightly to his side, ready to fire at the vaguest hint of a threat to his life. Every few steps he stopped to look around. His skin crawled as if covered with thousands of bugs and his hands became clammy with sweat.

Glen covered 50 or 60 feet, then stopped. There was no need for him to go the whole mile and a half. None of the others would ever know if he simply waited a suitable interval and then returned to inform them he had not seen anyone. What harm could it do? he asked himself.

Five minutes went by. Glen began to feel guilty. He had told his wife he would go see, and here he was cowering among the cottonwoods. What sort of husband would deceive his wife? What kind of man had he become if he was so willing to lie to his friends?

Glen hiked deeper into the trees. An owl hooted to the south and was answered by another to the north. Yet another hooted to his rear.

That was strange, Glen reflected. He'd seldom heard so many owls sound off at the same time. It brought to mind stories he had been told about the uncanny ability of Indians to mimic animal cries. Turning, he sought some sign of the nocturnal birds of prey.

Above him, something rustled. Glen heard a creak and looked up in time to see a vague form swooping down on him from a branch. He tried to bring the rifle up but the form slammed into him before he could. The breath whooshed from his lungs as he crashed onto his back with a heavy weight astride his chest.

Glen was aware he had lost his rifle. He attempted to lift his arms but a knee kicked him in the gut, rendering him as weak as a kitten. Footsteps converged and his arms were seized. It all happened so fast that he was being held upright between two men in buckskins before he quite collected his wits.

"Well, what have we here?" said a tall specimen with a face as hard as iron. "You should have stayed in the States, pilgrim. The climate out here isn't good for your health."

Others laughed, and Glen realized there were five men, all told. "Who are you men? What do you want?" he demanded. He assumed they were trappers who had mistaken him for a prowling Indian and would release him at any moment.

The tall man tapped Glen's head. "Not too bright, this one." He poked Glen in the chest. "The name is Lassiter. I've seen you before. We've been following your little caravan for a while now."

"Why didn't you show yourselves?" Glen said. "We wouldn't shoot at white men. I'm Glen Brandt, and you can take my word for it that all of you would have been welcome to enter our camp at any time."

A tall man laughed. "Now ain't you just about the friendliest idiot I've ever run into!"

"Idiot?" Glen said.

Lassiter shot Bear a sharp glance, then put on his best smile and gave the young man a friendly pat on the shoulder. "Don't mind him. He's been hit once too many times on the head. His thinker is puny." Gesturing for Dixon and Kingslow to let Brandt go, he said, "I'm sorry for the rough treatment. We didn't know if you were friendly or not, and a body can't be any too careful in the wild."

"Believe me, I know," Glen said, happy the mistake had been remedied. He rubbed his sore stomach. "It's my fault. I shouldn't have been creeping about in the dark, but we've been afraid of tangling with hostiles ever since my wife spotted a savage."

"Hostiles, you say?" Lassiter said. "If that's the case, maybe we should join forces. We're heading west too. With us along, you'd be better able to protect your womenfolk."

"There's an idea!" Glen said. With five more rifles to rely on, his party could drive off any number of hostiles.

Because of the darkness, the young farmer couldn't see the sly grins that nipped at the mouth of every man there except the giant. Bear was befuddled by the talk of joining the pilgrims on their trek. After days and days of considering how best to wipe the pilgrims out, it was incomprehensible to him that Lassiter was acting so friendly.

"I don't get it," Bear said. "I thought you told us—"

Lassiter knew Bear well enough to foresee his blunder. Giving Bear a playful but hard elbow-jab in the ribs, he forced a laugh and said, "Yes, I told you that we should swing on around the caravan and go on by ourselves, but I've changed my mind."

"Oh," Bear said dully, still at a loss to understand. But the cold look Lassiter gave him kept him from opening his mouth again.

Glen Brandt had paid no attention to the exchange. He had walked over to his rifle and picked it up. Delighted by his stroke of good fortune, he clapped Lassiter on the back and said, "Follow me. I'll hail the camp so they don't open fire."

"We'd be obliged," Lassiter said. He cannily waited until the young innocent had taken a few strides, then said, "Hold on just a second. I have to send someone for our horses."

Gesturing for his men to gather close, Lassiter

whispered, "Bear, you fetch the animals and keep your mouth shut. I don't want you spoiling things."

"What about that shot we heard?" Dixon asked.

Snip stared toward the river. "That's right. It must be a friend of that guy we strung up."

"We'll worry about it later," Lassiter said. "Right now the pilgrims are all that matter. Keep your fingers on your triggers and be ready to follow my lead."

Glen had stopped to wait for them. He wondered why they saw fit to speak so quietly. "Is everything all right? You're not changing your minds, are you?"

Lassiter faced him, smiling. "Not on your life. Lead the way. We'll be right behind you."

It never failed to amaze Lassiter how gullible some folks could be. They were too damned trusting for their own good. They assumed everyone was as meek as they were, when anyone with half a brain knew that it was a dog-eat-dog world, every man for himself. The survivors were those who trusted no one, who preyed on weak fools like Brandt just as wolves preyed on flocks of sheep.

Lassiter was in such good humor that he whistled to himself as he strolled in the wake of the pilgrim. At the back of his mind was a speck of unease over the shot they had heard, but he put it from his thoughts for the time being. They would deal with whoever was out there just as they had dealt with Jeremiah Sawyer.

Presently fires flared in the night. Lassiter saw figures moving about, men, women, and children. The sight of the women made his mouth water.

Glen waved an arm and shouted, "I'm coming

in! And I'm bringing friends! Whatever you do, don't shoot!"

In the clearing, Katie Brandt saw the startled looks on the others. They were thinking the same thing she was—it might be a trick of some kind. Peter Ringcrest and Bob Potter moved closer to the edge of the clearing, their rifles at the ready. Katie joined the women and children at the Potter wagon. The girls hid behind their mother's skirt while little Charley Potter had found a stick which he held as if it were a club.

Then Glen appeared, grinning happily. "We won't have to worry about hostiles any more," he said. "I've met some trappers."

Katie's heart leaped into her throat at the sight of their saviors. They were as cruel looking a bunch as she had ever set eyes on. The tallest, in particular, gave her the same gaze she might give a haunch of beef she was fixing to buy. It sent a shiver down her spine.

"This here is Lassiter," Glen said. "There's one more but he went to get their horses."

Lassiter offered his hand to the men. He listened with half an ear as they told him their names, his eyes lingering on the three women. The youngest was a genuine beauty, a vision of loveliness made real. Often he had dreamed of women like her, but never in his wildest cravings had he ever expected to make love to one.

"I'm pleased to meet all of you," Lassiter said. He was also pleased to see Dixon, Kingslow, and Snip fanning casually out to either side. "Hope we didn't spook you folks none."

"Not at all," Peter Ringcrest said, setting the stock of his rifle on the ground. "As the Bible says, we must love our neighbors. Make yourselves comfortable. We have plenty of coffee to share."

Dixon looked expectantly at Lassiter but Lassiter gave a single shake of his head and moved over to a fire. Sitting cross-legged, he accepted a tin cup and grinned at the young woman, who came over to pour for him. "That's right nice of you, ma'am," he said.

"My pleasure," Katie said, although her insides were balled as tight as a fist. Her every instinct shrieked at her to get as far away from the newcomers as she could, but she dismissed the feeling as childish. The other four had also sat down and were being just as gracious as their leader.

Lassiter made a show of scanning the wagons and the livestock. "It's mighty brave of you to be heading for the Oregon Country with as small a party as you have," he said, then took a sip. The coffee had been sweetened with sugar, a rare treat. He figured there must be bags of the sweetener in the wagons, enough to last him a year. And who knew what else?

"Have you been there?" Peter Ringcrest asked.

"Can't say as I have," Lassiter said.

"Well, I have," Ringcrest said, "on the Lord's work. And I'm here to tell you that mortal man hasn't set eyes on prettier land anywhere. It's as if the Lord gave the land his personal blessing."

Lassiter arched an eyebrow. "From the way you talk, I gather you're a religious man."

"I'm a missionary," Ringcrest said stiffly. "Dr. Whitman and I are associates."

"Who?"

"Marcus Whitman. Surely you've heard of him?

He was quite the sensation at the rendezvous."

"Must have been a rendezvous I missed," Lassiter said. The fact was that he had heard of Whitman and the holier-than-thou types who were determined to convert the Indians whether the Indians wanted to be converted or not. Their gall put a bitter taste in Lassiter's mouth.

"We're the first of a wave of settlers who will stream to Oregon now that the way has been opened," Ringcrest said. "Dr. Whitman expects that within ten to fifteen years the territory will be able to apply for statehood."

"How nice," Lassiter said dryly.

"Maybe sooner, once all the tribes forsake their heathen ways and accept Christianity," Ringcrest said.

"Maybe you should keep in mind that a lot of mountain men share those heathen ways, as you call them," Lassiter said.

"To the ruin of their eternal souls. It behooves all of us to anchor ourselves in the Bible and not allow temptation to carry us adrift on the wayward seas of life."

Lassiter swallowed more coffee to relieve the bitter taste, then said, "Whatever you say, Parson." He could tell by the way some of his men were fidgeting that they were growing impatient, and he didn't blame them. But the young woman and Bob Potter still regarded them suspiciously and he wanted all of the pilgrims off their guard when he made his move. "Are all of you missionaries?" he asked.

"Goodness, no," Glen Brandt said. "I aim to be a farmer, and Bob is a tinker by trade. If your knives need sharpening, he's the man to see."

"Do tell?" Lassiter said, brightening as an idea occurred to him. Pulling out his butcher knife, he extended it, hilt first. "Then here you go, mister. I reckon all of us could use our blades honed." He glanced meaningfully at his men. "All of us."

Ben Kingslow was quickest to deduce Lassiter's motive. "Ain't that the truth," he said. "Here's my knife too. I want an edge sharp enough to split a hair."

In short order Bob Potter had all their knives. He acted bewildered by their request, as if it was the very last thing he had expected them to do. His wife held his rifle since he had his hands full. "Mark my words, gentleman," he said. "When I'm done, you'll be able to shave with these."

"Have at it," Lassiter said, and he had to down more coffee to keep from laughing when the pilgrim headed for his wagon. The young woman, Katie, was still watching them warily, so he said, "First you share your coffee. Now you take care of our knives. We'd like to show our appreciation by doing something for you."

"There's no need," Ringcrest said. "Sharing is reward in itself for those who walk in the steps of the Lord."

"There must be something we can do," Lassiter said. "If we're going to travel together, I insist on doing our part to help out. We can hunt and cook for you."

"You cook, Mr. Lassiter?" Katie asked skeptically.

"Sure, ma'am."

"Most men regard cooking as womens' work. They won't touch a pot or ladle with a ten-foot pole."

Lassiter could be a charmer when he wanted, and he was his most disarming when he said, "Heck, Mrs. Brandt. When a man lives by his lonesome in the mountains, he learns soon enough which end of a ladle is which." He was pleased when she grinned and turned away. At last the pilgrims were all convinced that he and his men were friendly. The fools.

"Matter of fact," Lassiter said, "tomorrow, for supper, we'll fix venison like you've never tasted before. You just leave the hunting, carving, and everything to us."

"Why, aren't you the perfect gentlemen?" Ringcrest's wife said.

"We try our best," Lassiter said. Lowering the cup, he held his right hand close to his thigh and wagged a finger at Dixon, who nodded and slowly stood. Kingslow shifted so he was facing Bob Potter. Snip swiveled so he could keep his eyes on Ringcrest, who was talking to his son.

It was a moment Lassiter savored. He was about to educate the unsuspecting pilgrims in one of the harsher realities of life, a lesson they would never forget during the short span allotted them on earth. It tickled him, having hoodwinked them the way he had. It confirmed his own opinion that he was smarter than most men.

Katie Brandt stepped to her husband and took his hand. As nice as the trappers were being, she couldn't shake a troubling feeling that all was not well. Looking at Lassiter made her uncomfortable, as if she were gazing at the visage of a mad dog about to pounce.

Glen grinned at her. He knew her well enough to sense that something was amiss, but not well enough yet to pinpoint the cause. Squeezing her hand, he said softly, "What has you worried? Everything will be all right now that these men are here to help us."

"I hope so," Katie said softly so only he would hear.

Lassiter saw them huddled together and casually draped a hand on his rifle, which lay propped against his leg. "Well, I guess now is as good a time as any."

"For what?" Peter Ringcrest asked.

"For this," Lassiter said and shot the missionary through the chest. He acted so swiftly that none of the pilgrims had time to react. Then Mrs. Ringcrest screamed and Potter's wife shrieked. Potter started toward him with a knife in hand, but drew up short when Ben Kingslow covered him. Young Glen Brandt went to lift his rifle, but froze when Dixon trained a muzzle on his wife. The children merely gawked, too stunned to think.

Lassiter rose and moved to the fallen man. Ringcrest still lived, his eyes wide in astonishment, his lips working feebly.

"Why? In God's name, man, why?"

"I wanted to," Lassiter said. He kicked the missionary in the mouth, then smirked when blood spurted out and Ringcrest writhed in agony. "You like to go around preaching love for all. Me, I like to go around doing as I damn well please. And it pleases me to take your life and everything else that belongs to you."

"You monster!" The howl of outrage came from little Charley Ringcrest, who launched himself at Lassiter with his stick upraised. Lassiter got his arm up to deflect the blow. Spinning, he backhanded the boy across the face. Charley fell onto his side, gritted his teeth in fury, and rose to attack again.

Snip shot the boy through the head at near point-blank range. The back of Charley's skull exploded outward, showering gore and brains all over Mrs. Ringcrest, who promptly fainted.

"Anyone else care to die?" Lassiter said, regarding each of the pilgrims in turn. "I'd rather keep you alive for a while, but I'm not going to force you to live longer if you don't want to."

"You bastard!" Glen Brandt growled.

In two strides Lassiter reached him and struck with all his might. His fist crunched into the younger man's cheek, splitting the flesh and flattening Brandt where he stood. Katie made a move to help, but Lassiter wagged a finger at her. "Don't even think it."

Katie blanched, scared to the core of her being, her wits scrambled by the terrible turn of events. "What do you want with us?"

"Why, I should think that would be obvious," Earl Lassiter said, reaching out to stroke her long golden hair. His sadistic laugh wavered on the night wind.

Chapter Eleven

Winona King kept hoping against hope that her demented captor would turn his back or otherwise give her an opening she could exploit, but the crafty mountain man never did.

Until half an hour before sunset they wound southward along the same route they had followed north. Zach and she were leading packhorses; Bill Zeigler was bringing up the rear, far enough back to drop either of them if they tried anything.

Zach was also alert for a chance to do something, although he had no idea what. Dashing off into the undergrowth would be pointless. He'd escape, but it would leave his mother and sister in Zeigler's clutches. He had to slay the man, a hopeless task without a weapon.

Old Bill reined up on the north side of a narrow creek. "This is far enough for today," he said. "I want both of you to climb down. And don't try anything. I know all the tricks there are. You'd only get yourselves killed."

Zachary eyed a parfleche draped behind his saddle as he dismounted. It contained, among other things, a small knife he used when whittling. Somehow he had to get his hands on it.

Zeigler had climbed down and moved to a convenient log. His rifle was pointed right at Winona. "Here's the way it will be. You'll fix supper, squaw. The brat will go gather wood for our fire. But first you put that cradleboard down over here by me. Keep in mind that if either one of you gets any contrary notions, I'll shoot the papoose. And don't think I won't."

Helplessness and frustration seared Winona like red-hot coals. She obeyed, giving her precious daughter a kiss as she straightened up. "If you harm her—"

"Oh, please," Zeigler said, cutting her off, "save your threats. You're in no position to do a damn thing, and you know it. And you don't want to get me riled."

Winona gazed toward the Oregon Trail. How long would it be, she wondered, before Nate showed up? Would he suspect what had happened? Or would he ride blindly into Zeigler's sights and be cut down before she could warn him?

"Get crackin' with them vittles, Shoshone," Old Bill said. "All this ridin' has given me a powerful appetite."

"What would you like?"

"We have some jerked deer meat left, as I recollect. Fix me a stew and throw in some of that

tasty pemmican of yours." Old Bill glanced at
Zach. "What are you waitin' for, boy? I told you
to collect firewood. And get a lot of it. I aim to
keep the fire going all night long."

From the old trapper's expression, Winona
knew that he had something devious in mind in
case Nate came. She absently went about making
the meal, the whole time racking her brain for a
way out of the predicament. Zach brought four
loads of dead wood, which wasn't enough to suit
Zeigler. He made Zach bring two more.

Old Bill walked to his horse and produced a
coiled rope. Throwing it at Winona's feet, he said,
"Now tie the brat's ankles so he won't try to sneak
off."

It was senseless to argue when staring up the
barrel of a heavy-caliber flintlock. Winona reluctantly did as she was bid, then resumed stirring
the stew. Evelyn began to fuss, so Winona started
to go to her. But she was stopped by a curt command.

"No you don't!" Old Bill said. "My stomach is
more important than your sprout. Finish with
my supper. Then you can rock her to sleep or
whatever the hell you have to do."

Gloom gripped Winona's soul, a feeling that if
she didn't act soon, she would lose those who
meant more to her than life itself. Her husband
and children were her reason for living.

Winona tested the broth with her fingertip. It
was nearly done. She glanced at Old Bill, who
was staring glumly at Evelyn as if he was of half
a mind to shoot her.

Zachary also noticed and automatically tried to
take the mountain man's mind off his sibling. "So

how many folks have you killed over the years, Mr. Zeigler?"

"What's it to you?" Old Bill asked.

"I'd just like to know if the stories are true," Zach said.

"Live to be my age and you'll learn there's always a kernel of truth behind every tale," Old Bill said. He sank onto the ground and leaned against the log, the rifle draped across his thighs. "I reckon I've killed thirty people or thereabouts. Not countin' Injuns."

"Killed them how? Did you eat them?"

Old Bill laughed. "You keep harking back to those rumors about my being a cannibal. How come? Are you afeared I'm liable to plunk you in a pot and boil you alive?"

"I'm just curious," Zach said, glad that the old killer had taken his eyes off of Evelyn.

"Ain't you ever heard about what curiosity did to the cat?" Zeigler said. "A person should never go pokin' his nose in where it doesn't belong. Someone might up and lop it off."

The stew had come to a boil. Winona dipped the ladle in and tasted it. Her stomach was so empty it growled, but she ignored the pang. Using a small cloth, she gripped the metal handle and went to carry the pot over to Zeigler. Once she was close enough, she intended to toss the contents in his face, wrestle the rifle from his grasp, and shoot him between the eyes.

"What the hell do you think you're doin'?" Old Bill said. "Just leave the pot there and fill a bowl. It's not like we're at one of those fancy inns where they serve your food in bed."

Winona had no idea what he meant, but she

offered no objection. To rush him would prove fatal; all he had to do was lift his rifle and squeeze the trigger. She rummaged in a parfleche for a wooden bowl, filled it full to the brim, and carried it over in both hands. It was in her mind to hurl the contents into his eyes. As if he guessed, he squinted at her and elevated the rifle in her direction. She had no choice but to gently deposit the bowl beside him, then back away.

"Smart squaw," Old Bill said. "You'd be pushing up grass tomorrow if you'd done as you wanted."

Winona indicated the cradleboard. "May I hold my daughter now?"

"Suit yourself. Over there by the brat."

Bending, Winona scooped her hands under the cradleboard and was rising when Zeigler's foot lashed out, catching her in the shoulder. Knocked off balance, she fell to one knee and listened to his laughter.

"Ma, are you all right?" Zach cried.

"Of course she is, sonny," Old Bill said before she could. "A little tap like that won't bother no squaw. She's used to being slapped around by her men."

Zach was livid. "My pa has never laid a finger on my ma."

"Don't blame me if he's weak kneed. The only way to keep a woman in line is to beat her whenever she acts uppity. I know because I had a few wives in my younger days. Wasn't a one of them who didn't give me sass, but only once." Zeigler spooned soup into his mouth, then spoke while chewing. "Your pa could do with some lessons in how to handle women."

Winona held her hand out when her son opened his mouth to reply. She feared Zach would antagonize the mountain man into shooting. "I will get your soup."

"I'm not hungry, Ma."

"You will eat anyway. You must keep your strength up." Winona filled bowls for both of them. Although she had no real desire to eat, she did so to set an example for her offspring, who, once he had tasted the stew, downed it with relish.

Winona attended to Evelyn next. It was Indian custom to wean children at a later age than was common among whites, and Evelyn was at that age. Winona fed her some soup after mashing the jerky to a soft consistency.

Old Bill polished off his supper slowly, cast the bowl down, and belched. "Not bad, squaw," he said. "I have half a mind to keep you around just so you can fix me fine vittles every day. But we both know that wouldn't be too bright, would it? You'd gut me the first chance you got, wouldn't you?"

Winona knew better than to answer.

"That's all right. Don't say a word. The truth speaks for itself." Old Bill settled back. "Well, now that the eats are out of the way, I want you to tie your boy's wrists nice and tight. And I mean nice and tight. I'll be checking, so don't try to trick me."

The fleeting panic in Zach's eyes tugged at Winona's heart, but she had to do as bidden. Besides, something told her that Zeigler was in no great hurry to kill them. He might even wait until they reached his dugout. Covered by his rifle, she secured her son's arms. "I am sorry, Stalking Coyote," she whispered. "Do not give up hope."

Old Bill stood. "Now I want you to take that last piece of rope and tie your own ankles together."

Once more Winona obeyed. The mountain man walked toward her and she quickly pressed Evelyn to her bosom. Old Bill merely tested the knots, did the same with Zach, and nodded.

"You did a right fine job. Both of you lie on your sides."

Afraid that she had made a dreadful mistake and that Zeigler was about to abuse them or worse, Winona sank down, but balled her fists to strike when he came close enough. Zach was also coiled.

"Wouldn't want you to catch your death," Old Bill said. From their supplies he obtained two blankets. "These will keep you nice and warm until morning."

Winona lay still as Zeigler spread the blanket over her from her neck down. She noticed that he took particular care to tuck the edges under her feet. His intent was plain. He wasn't concerned about their comfort so much as he was about concealing the fact they were bound. To anyone surveying the camp, it would appear they were sleeping soundly.

Old Bill covered Zach, then straigthened up. "There, now. If you pa shows, he won't suspect a thing." He jabbed the boy with his rifle. "Don't try to throw the blanket off, brat. I'll be watching you the whole time."

Mother and son lay there and watched their captor tramp off into the undergrowth near the trail of tracks they had left. The fire crackled and snapped, casting light to the trees but no farther.

"Ma," Zach whispered. "What are we going to do? Pa will ride right into the buzzard's trap."

"I might be able to free my ankles without Zeigler noticing," Winona said, "but I will not escape without you. Do you think you can loosen your bounds?"

"I'll try my darnedest."

Many minutes passed. Winona waited as her son grunted and squirmed, and at length he gave a deep sigh.

"I'm sorry, Ma. I've tried my best, but all I've done is rubbed the skin off my wrists and gotten my arms all bloody."

"Then one of us must stay awake at all times. And when we hear your father coming, we must cry out to warn him."

Zachary frowned. He was upset that he had allowed himself to be trussed up, even more upset that he hadn't thought of a way of turning the tables on the sly old fox who had abducted them. "You can sleep first, if you want. I'm not very tired."

"Wake me when you can no longer keep your eyes open," Winona said. Making herself comfortable, with Evelyn tucked at her waist, she tried to relax so she could doze off. She didn't think she would be able to, not with Zeigler lurking out there somewhere, watching them, but her exhaustion and the comforting crackle of the fire lulled her to sleep.

Unknown to Winona King, another set of eyes was fixed on her as she fell asleep—a dark, stony set that belonged to Brule the Blood.

Brule had caught up with the travelers an hour before sunset and dogged their footsteps until they camped. It had been his intention to slay the white man, the boy, and the small girl at the first opportunity, then to have his way with the Shoshone. But it had soon become apparent that something was amiss. The white man made it a point to always hold a rifle on the others. By the actions and expressions of the woman and the boy, Brule discerned that they were being held captive. His insight was proven to be right when they were bound.

Brule did not know what to make of it. This was a new experience, and he resolved to study the situation to learn why the old trapper had taken the woman and children prisoner.

The mystery was compounded because the tracks told Brule that the white-eye, the Shoshone, and the breeds were all part of a party that had trailed Lassiter's bunch northward for quite a few sleeps. Two men in that party had gone on ahead; they were the ones who had fought at the grade and then hid from him in that gully.

How did the woman and children fit into the scheme of things? Was she the wife of one of the whites? Or had she been held at gunpoint the whole time, forced to ride along whether she wanted to or not? And why had the old trapper gone to hide in the brush near the trail? Was the trapper expecting the other two to show?

There were so many questions, and Brule was unable to answer a single one. He wanted to solve the mystery. So, for a while, he would content himself with shadowing them. Perhaps he would learn the answers.

Brule leaned back against a tree trunk, folded his arms, and permitted himself to doze off. Every now and then he would snap awake to look and listen. He saw the boy keeping watch and, later, the mother. Of the old trapper there was no sign, but Brule knew exactly where the man was concealed and could have slit the man's throat whenever he wanted.

A pink band framed the eastern sky when Brule roused himself and crept 100 yards along the creek to quench his thirst. He was hungry, but suppressed the need. There would be plenty of time to eat later. He hurried back.

The old white-eye had returned to the camp. The Shoshone was untying herself. Soon she had the boy untied too. While the boy fed limbs to the fire, the woman busied herself making breakfast.

Brule found it hard to maintain his self-control while they ate handfuls of pemmican and drank cups of coffee.

Shortly after sunrise they were mounted and bearing to the south once again, the old one bringing up the rear as before. Frequently the white man glanced over his shoulder as if expecting pursuit.

Traveling on a parallel course, Brule had no difficulty keeping them in sight. They rode no faster than a brisk walk. At midday they stopped briefly to water their animals and munch jerky. The woman breast-fed her daughter, and Brule imagined what it would be like to take the little one's place.

By late afternoon they were among rolling foot-
hills. Beyond loomed sawtooth ridges and high,
jagged spires. They climbed steadily until it was
almost dark.

Brule had learned nothing all day. He was
growing tired of their plodding rate of travel
and debated whether to finish the white man
off before it grew too dark. Either that or he
had to go in search of food to tide him over until
morning.

Deciding there was all the food he needed in
their camp, Brule placed a hand on the hilt of
his wonderful new knife and began to rise. Then
he stopped because the most remarkable thing
happened.

Winona King had made up her mind to break
free of Zeigler's grasp, no matter what. She was
convinced that as each day took them farther
and farther away from Nate, so too did each
day increase the chances that she or her children
would be harmed.

During the afternoon Winona had contrived to
whisper to Zach, but was thwarted when Old Bill
refused to let them ride close to one another.

On a belt of grassy land halfway up the side of
a ridge, Zeigler called a halt for the day. A small
spring was nestled under a short rock overhang
that bordered the grass. Here Winona watered
the horses under the mountain man's hawkish
gaze while Zach gathered wood.

Old Bill sat perched on a waist-high boulder,
scratching himself, as Winona tethered the animals. Out of the corner of her eye she saw that
he couldn't take his eyes off her, that her every

movement came under close scrutiny. So it came as no surprise when he cleared his throat.

"You're a fine figure of a woman, Shoshone, if I do say myself."

"My husband will be glad to hear that you think he has good taste," Winona said.

Zeigler snorted. "It would be best for you to forget you ever met him. Nate King ain't your man anymore. I am."

"I am Grizzly Killer's forever," Winona said with a toss of her head. "I will never lie with another man. If he were to die, I would never take another husband."

"It's not like you have any choice," Old Bill said. "What I want, I take. And I want you." He strode toward her, leering.

Winona sensed the moment of truth had arrived. She was thankful that little Evelyn was yards away, propped in the cradleboard against a boulder. Squarely facing Zeigler, she said, "No man has the right to force himself on a woman. I will not let you put your hands on me."

"Ask me if I care about how you feel?" Old Bill said. Halting, he leveled his rifle. "I think I'd like to see how you look without that buckskin dress on. Take it off."

"Never."

Old Bill swiveled so his gun was fixed on Evelyn. "The dress or your daughter? Which will it be?"

"You are a despicable man," Winona said, backing slowly away. She cast about for a weapon—a rock, a club, anything. But there was nothing.

"Despicable?" Old Bill said. "Mercy me. Your husband has taught you better English than I use myself. Do you squeal in English?"

"Squeal?"

"You know," Zeigler said, his eyes straying to a point below her waist. "I sure do like it when a female squeals. Sets my blood to boilin'."

Winona suddenly bumped into one of the horses. She stopped and looked to the right and left, ready to bolt if he came one step nearer. The distinct click of the rifle hammer rooted her in place.

"I'm not playin' any games," Old Bill said, taking a bead on the cradleboard. "Either start strippin' to your birthday suit or you can kiss your bundle of joy good-bye."

Winona felt her mouth go dry. She had nowhere to run, no way to fight, even if her daughter's life wasn't at stake. "Do not hurt my child," she said.

"Then don't keep me waitin', damn it."

Desperate to avoid the inevitable, Winona reached up and fiddled with the neck of her dress, pretending to be loosening the strings of beads that encircled her throat. In reality, the only way for her to undress was to pull the buckskin garment up over her head.

Old Bill had the feral air of a wild cat about to swallow a minnow. He licked his lips and grinned wickedly, feasting on her turmoil. "It's been too long since last I had me a woman," he said. "Please me and I just might keep you alive so you can service me on a regular basis. What do you say?"

"I would rather be choked to death," Winona said before she could stop herself.

"That can be arranged, bitch," Old Bill said. "Hurry it the hell up!"

Despair tearing at her, Winona bent down to

grip her dress. Abruptly, past the mountain man, a small figure moved into sight. It was Zach, with a thick length of branch in both hands. Her son whipped the branch overhead as he charged and let out with a Shoshone war whoop.

For a man well into his sixties, Bill Zeigler had the reflexes of a 20 year old. He spun at the first note of the outcry, his rifle pointing at the boy's midsection.

"No!" Winona said, and flew at the mountain man like a tiger gone berserk, her fingers formed into claws to rake his face and eyes.

Old Bill glanced at her, realized she couldn't reach him before he could shoot, and faced Zach again. He expected Zach to swing the club. He figured he had plenty of time to kill the sprout and deal with the squaw. He was wrong.

Zachary King had learned to fight from a man whose survival skills were unsurpassed. His father had bested grizzlies, wolverines, painters, wolves, bobcats, hostiles, and renegade whites. With gun, knife, and tomahawk, Nate King was extremely skilled, and he had diligently tried to pass on some of that prowess to his son.

Even more importantly, Nate had seen fit to teach his son about unarmed combat—how to use his fists and feet as white men did, how to grapple and wrestle as Indians did.

If there was any one point Nate had stressed the most, it was always to do the unexpected. A close second had been that when Zach found his life hanging in the balance, he had to do whatever it took to win.

So as Zachary King hurled himself at Old Bill Zeigler, he did the last thing the mountain man would ever have anticipated. Instead of striving to bludgeon a man bigger and stronger than him, Zachary took deliberate aim and threw the club with all his might.

At that very instant, the rifle blasted.

Chapter Twelve

Nate King was fording the shallow river when shots rang out to the west, punctuated by screams of mortal terror. Jabbing his heels into the flanks of the stallion, he galloped up onto the bank and on into the cottonwoods. Once again his pistols were wedged under his belt. The loaded Hawken was in his left hand.

Jeremiah Sawyer had deserved a proper burial. Nate had delayed his pursuit of the cutthroats long enough to dig a grave deep enough to insure scavengers wouldn't unearth the body later. As a crowning touch he had added a crude cross fashioned from a broken branch, using whangs from his buckskin shirt to bind the pieces at the right angle.

Then Nate had climbed on the stallion and headed across the river to see if he could pick up the trail of Lassiter's gang before it was too dark.

Now, racing through the woodland, ducking branches and weaving among trunks, Nate recalled the recently made wagon tracks and feared for the safety of the poor pilgrims bound for the Oregon Country. Lassiter would give them the same treatment as Jeremiah.

Nate couldn't allow that to happen. He had covered over a quarter of a mile and was scouring the west side of the valley for the killers when he came upon a small knoll. Going up and over rather than around, he was shocked to see five horses tethered below and a giant of a man in the act of untying them.

There was no doubt as to whether it was a member of Lassiter's bunch. Immediately on seeing Nate, the giant tried to bring a rifle into play.

Streaking down the knoll, Nate was beside the man in a flash. He should have shot then and there. But he had the notion to take the giant alive in order to get certain questions answered. So he drove the stock of his Hawken against the giant's skull. It was like striking an anvil.

The man bellowed in pain and staggered, but didn't go down. Nate wheeled the stallion and closed in to deliver another blow. The giant had dropped his own rifle and appeared defenseless. Nate should have known better.

Whipping around, the giant swung his mallet of a fist, clipping the stallion on the point of its chin. A punch from a normal man would hardly have fazed it. This man stopped the horse in its tracks. Wobbly legs swaying, the stallion almost went down.

Nate raised the Hawken to swing again. The giant, moving with astonishing speed for a man of his bulk, leaped and grabbed hold of the front of Nate's shirt. The next moment Nate sailed over the head of his horse and crashed down on his stomach in the high grass.

Woozy from the impact, Nate tried to stand and turn. He was only halfway erect when fingers gouged into his shoulders and he was flung a dozen feet against the knoll. In the bargain he lost the Hawken. Dazed and winded, Nate twisted and saw the giant lumber toward him.

"Any last words, you son of a bitch, before I snap your spine like a dry twig?"

Nate kept his breath for saving his life. The giant lunged at him and he scrambled aside, then pushed upright. His right hand fell on a pistol and he drew, his arm a blur. Yet as fast as he was, the giant was faster.

Arms like coiled bands of steel closed around Nate. He was hoisted off the ground and found himself nose to nose with the puffing giant, who grinned and squeezed.

"I'm fixing to crush you, mister!"

Nate didn't doubt it. Shakespeare McNair had once told him about large snakes in Asia or Africa that crushed prey in mighty coils, and it seemed to him that he was about to suffer a similar fate. He surged against the man's arms, but as powerful as he was, he couldn't budge them.

The giant laughed and a lancing spasm racked Nate's chest. Then another. He was unable to take a deep breath and swore his ribs were about to collapse, splintered into fragments.

Nate couldn't use his arms or hands. His feet dangled uselessly and he couldn't get a grip on his weapons. The giant smirked, sensing victory.

And that was when Nate drove his forehead into his foe's nose. Cartilage crunched, blood sprayed, and a moment later, Nate was free.

The giant tottered backward, a hand covering his shattered nostrils. He acted more shocked than hurt.

To give the human bear a moment's respite was to invite disaster. Nate took two steps and dived. His arms looped around the giant's ankles. He heaved, felt the man's legs start to give, and heaved again. The smash of the heavy body hitting the earth was like that of a felled tree.

Nate rolled to the left, out of the giant's grasping reach. He was upright first and waded in with fists flying. A right hook caught the giant on the jaw, but did nothing more than make him blink.

Rumbling deep in his chest, the huge man sprang, swatting Nate's left jab aside. Again those massive arms coiled around Nate and lifted him into the air.

"You die!"

Spit and blood splattered Nate's face. He tried to slam his head against the giant's mouth but the man was prepared and jerked away.

"Not this time, bastard!"

Undaunted, Nate tried another tack; he rammed his knee into his adversary's groin, not once but three times in swift succession.

Sputtering, the giant released his hold and shambled off to the left, his enormous hands spread protectively over his privates.

Nate drew his tomahawk. He no longer cared about taking the man alive. Darting forward, he slashed at the giant's neck but the killer sprang out of harm's way and flourished a long knife, which he waved in tiny circles.

"It takes more than you've got to rub me out."

The Shoshones believed that warriors should never talk in the heat of battle, a belief shared by Apaches and others. Talking distracted men at crucial moments. It was considered the hallmark of poor fighters. Yet this man, gabby as he was, had proven to be as masterful a fighter as Nate had ever encountered.

Circling, Nate sought an opening. He had to be wary of the giant's greater reach and strength. Twice he feinted, but was unable to pierce the other's guard. The tomahawk and knife rang together like small bells, clanging with each strike.

Blood seeped from the giant's smashed nose into his mouth and he kept spitting it out to one side. Nate watched closely, his legs coiled like springs, and when the giant spat again, he dove, aiming a vicious swipe that would have ripped a thigh wide open. But the giant slid to the left with the agility of a mountain sheep.

The strain of all Nate had been through began to take its toll. His head ached abominably from the clout Jeremiah had given him, and his aching lungs strained to catch a breath. He had to end the fight quickly or the giant would end it for him.

As if sensing Nate's weakness, the huge man stalked in for the kill, swinging the knife like a sword, slashing high and low, seeking to penetrate Nate's guard. Nate retreated under the onslaught, parrying furiously, his fatigue rendering the heavy tomahawk more unwieldy than it would ordinarily be.

Having to focus on the giant to the exclusion of

all else, Nate had no idea what was behind him as he retreated step by hasty step. He suspected he was being forced back toward the forest. Confirmation came when tree limbs appeared overhead. Moments later he backed into a bole.

Evidently the giant had been waiting for that to happen. Snarling like an animal, he lanced his knife forward, seeking to pin Nate against the trunk. Nate wrenched aside, but not quickly enough. He nearly cried out as the keen blade sliced through his shirt and skin, drawing blood.

Skipping to the right, Nate crouched to meet the next attack. The wound was shallow but it stung like 1,000 bee stings at once.

The giant slowly turned. Wearing a mocking smile, he advanced, his arms constantly in motion as he flipped the knife from one hand to the other. His strategy was transparent. He would keep Nate guessing until the very last instant, then finish Nate off with a swift stroke.

That wasn't going to happen. Nate knew the giant expected him to keep on defending himself with the tomahawk, knew that the very last act the giant would expect was for him to snap back his arm and hurl the tomahawk in an overhand toss, yet that was exactly what he did. And he also knew, even as the smooth haft sped from his fingers, that the giant would easily dodge the tomahawk or deflect it. The latter proved to be the case.

Then, at the exact moment that the giant's knife arm was bent halfway around his body from the swing, Nate sprang, drawing his own blade as he did.

The giant's eyes widened to the size of walnuts

and he desperately tried to cover himself with his other arm.

Nate reached him first. Or rather, the knife did. It sank neatly between two of the giant's ribs, ripping through flesh and muscle with astounding ease, all the way to the hilt. Nate twisted, holding on tight as the giant tried to back out of reach. The man grunted, streaked his knife arm overhead, then stiffened, gasped, and melted as if made of soft wax.

Leaping back in case the giant tried to nail him while falling, Nate held his dripping blade at waist level. He was eager to finish his enemy off, but there was no need.

With a puzzled expression on his face, the giant eased onto his buttocks and sat there with a hand over the wound. He blinked and looked at Nate. "Damn. Never figured a runt like you would be the one—" Breaking off, he stiffened, then sagged onto his back.

Nate stepped nearer, prepared for any tricks.

"I want," the giant said weakly. "I want—"

"What?" Nate finally spoke, but he was destined to never know since the man expired with a drawn, strangled breath and went limp.

Nate took a deep breath to steady his racing pulse. He had been in more violent clashes than he cared to think about since settling in the Rockies, but few adversaries had pressed him as hard as the giant. "Whoever you were," he said softly, "you were as tough as they come."

The nicker of a horse reminded Nate there were more cutthroats abroad in the night. Shaking his head to clear his thoughts, he hastened to the animals. The stallion was grazing. The other five horses looked at him, but made no move to flee.

First Nate rounded up the two rifles. It turned out the giant had also owned a Hawken, the same caliber as Nate's. He put it in his bedroll. Next, taking the lead rope in hand, he mounted the stallion and rode to the south even though the shots and screams had arisen to the west.

There was a reason. Nate figured that he had all of the horses belonging to Lassiter's band of bloodthirsty killers, and he wasn't about to let them get their hands on the animals. He rode several hundred feet, slipped from the saddle, and secured all six horses.

After making sure his guns were loaded, Nate ran west. It wasn't long before fingers of flame appeared in the night. They took on the size and shape of three campfires spaced about 30 feet from one another in the shape of a circle. The pilgrims, Nate guessed, since only greenhorns would bother to build three fires where one would suffice.

Slowing, Nate worked his way as silently as a Shoshone warrior to a large fallen log. Kneeling, he studied the layout of the camp and the figures moving about.

A tall man with his thumbs hooked in his belt was strutting about as if he owned the valley. It had to be Lassiter, Nate guessed. Nearby two hard-hewn characters in buckskins were covering a cluster of frightened pilgrims. A fourth killer was visible in one of the wagons, sorting through belongings in search of plunder.

Of the pilgrims, two were bawling women. A third female, younger and fairer of form, was glaring at Lassiter. A young man stood beside her, his hands in the air. Another man stood meekly next to a wagon wheel, three children grasping his legs in fear.

Nate shifted, then choked off an oath. Two bodies lay in spreading red pools—that of a man in homespun clothes and that of a small boy, a child no older than Zach.

"Even children," Nate whispered to himself, horrified. The sight chilled him to the bone. No matter how long he lived in the wilderness, no matter how much slaughter he beheld, he found it impossible to regard wanton butchery with anything other than total loathing. Some of his fellow trappers had no such qualms. To them, death was so common an occurrence that it hardly deserved a second thought. They could stare at heaps of bodies killed in a raid and not be moved in the least.

Not Nate. He burned with sheer rage on seeing the child. Only the worst sort of men could do such a thing, men with no morals, no scruples, no conscience. Men as hard as the mountains themselves. Men whose hearts had changed to stone.

The thought gave Nate pause. Was it proper to even call them men when they were more akin to the savage beasts that shared the land they roved? Anyone capable of shooting an innocent child in cold blood was the scum of the earth, despicable beyond redemption, as soulless as a grizzly or a fierce painter.

Nate raised the Hawken and extended it across the log, making it a point not to let the barrel scrape the rough bark. He tucked the stock to his shoulder and took precise aim at Lassiter.

According to Jeremiah Sawyer, Earl Lassiter was the brains of the bunch. Kill him and the rest would be thrown into fleeting panic, giving Nate the time he needed to pick them off one by one.

Without warning, Lassiter turned and stepped to the wagon being ransacked. The short man inside said something. Nodding, Lassiter climbed in.

Nate held his fire. He wanted a clear shot, and he only caught glimpses of the cutthroat leader as he moved about under the canvas.

One of the men guarding the pilgrims, a killer wearing a blue cap, reached out to stroke the young woman's hair. She recoiled and slapped his hand. In retaliation, the man smacked her with such force she stumbled back against a wagon, which spurred the young man beside her into lowering his arms and moving toward the killer.

Nate saw the man in the blue cap train his rifle on the husband. A wicked gleam lit the killer's visage. In another second he would fire, slaying the husband in front of the young wife's eyes.

Nate couldn't allow that. Swiveling, he glued the front bead to the killer's chest, lined up the rear sight with the bead, and stroked the trigger.

The man in the blue cap, unknown to Nate King, was Dixon. The lead ball tore into his chest, passed completely through a lung, and burst out his back between the shoulder blades. The impact lifted him off his feet and flung him to the grass, where he convulsed briefly, trying to marshal his fading willpower. The last sensation he experienced was that of a black hand enfolding all he was in its inky grip.

Ben Kingslow had been standing near Dixon when the shot shattered the night. Instantly he crouched and snapped return fire at a cloud of gunsmoke in the woods.

Nate King, already on the move, heard the ball smack into the top of a log and ricochet off. He darted into a thicket and bore to the left.

Inside the wagon, Earl Lassiter leaped up at the booming crack and jumped onto the front seat. The shot had come from in the trees, not in the camp. He saw Dixon down and dead and Ben Kingslow rapidly reloading. "How many? Where are they?" he shouted.

Kingslow had no idea and pivoted to say as much.

By then Nate had raced over 15 feet. His right hand flashed to a pistol and it cleared leather in a practiced draw. One handed, he sighted at the killer who was reloading, then fired, rushing his shot.

This time Nate's aim was off. Kingslow was in the act of pulling his ramrod out when the shot caught him high on the temple. It was like being pounded by a hammer. The next he knew, he was lying on his back, stunned, his rifle no longer in his hands. He groped for it, rising onto his elbows.

Of the pilgrims, Katie Brandt was first to regain her senses after being startled by the gunfire. Belatedly she realized that whoever was out there was trying to help them. One of their captors was dead, another severely wounded. They would never have a better opportunity to turn the tide.

"Glen! Bob!" Katie shouted. "We have to help!"

Kingslow was almost to his knees when a hell-cat in the guise of a young woman flew into him, her nails raking his cheek and neck. He tried to shove her away but Glen Brandt was on him a heartbeat later, slamming fists into his face and head. Kingslow grabbed for his knife, felt his wrist grabbed in turn as the knife came clear.

Glen saw his wife seize the killer's wrist and leaped to her aid, adding his hands to hers. Both of them bent and shoved upward simultaneously, shearing the blade deep into the cutthroat's stomach at a 90-degree angle.

All this while, Nate had continued circling, hoping for a clear shot at Lassiter. Suddenly the leader and the short man spilled from the wagon and sprinted into the cottonwoods.

Of Nate's three guns, only one pistol was still loaded, which didn't stop him from speeding in pursuit of the renegades. He bounded past a tree and saw the short killer ten feet off, fleeing.

Snip sensed someone was behind him and whirled. He fired from the hip, and had he been a shade steadier, he would have put a ball through his pursuer's gut.

But as it was, Snip missed, and Nate immediately pointed his pistol and fired. At that range, the .55-caliber had the wallop of a cannon. Snip's head dissolved in a geyser of brains and gore.

That left only Earl Lassiter, who fled through the forest as if demons were on his trail. He'd glanced back in time to see Snip meet his Maker. The glimpse he had of the big man who was after them was sufficient to tell him who it was: Nate King, a close friend of Shakespeare McNair's and

Jim Bridger's. He knew King was a free trapper whose reputation for honesty and courage was unmatched by any save the other two living legends.

Nate King! Lassiter fumed as he fled. Of all the cursed luck! He couldn't understand how King had learned of his band. Then he recollected seeing Jeremiah Sawyer and King together at a rendezvous. There had to be a connection, and Lassiter would ponder it later. For now he had his hide to save.

All his guns empty, Nate sped in the killer's wake. He pulled his knife and reversed his grip.

Lassiter was running flat out, glancing back every few yards. The next time he did, he neglected to check the ground in front of him first.

Nate saw the murky outline of a small boulder. He poured on the speed as Lassiter tripped and sprawled forward. Lassiter landed on his hands and knees, and like a coiling serpent he spun around and began to jerk up his rifle. By then Nate was less than eight feet away. His supple body flowed into a smooth, superbly coordinated throw. The butcher knife cleaved the air straight and true.

Earl Lassiter's final sight was of a dully glittering blade as it thudded into his chest.

Chapter Thirteen

It was Zachary King's hurling of the club that saved his life. As he threw, he naturally shifted his body into the direction of the throw. The slight movement was just enough to throw Old Bill Zeigler's aim off.

The bullet missed Zach by a hair. He never slowed his charge, and he was on Old Bill a second before his mother. The mountain man roared and snapped his rifle on high. But between Zach and Winona, they brought him crashing to the earth.

Winona fought in a frantic frenzy for the lives of her children. She gouged her nails into Old Bill's right eye as he tried to elbow her in the face. His howl was fearsome. She saw him let go of the rifle and grasp the hilt of his knife. To stop him from using it, she clamped her hands on his forearm and held fast. "Zach! Get his pistol!" she cried.

Young Zach spotted the butt jutting from the top of Old Bill's belt. He made a grab for it, but was given a swat that sent him tumbling and set his ears to ringing. When he pushed to his feet, he was terrified to find Old Bill on top of his mother, choking the life from her with one hand while striving to pull his knife with the other.

Winona tossed and bucked, trying to dislodge the demented mountaineer while simultaneously attempting to prevent him from unlimbering his blade.

In a twinkling Zach rushed to help her. Balling his fists, he barreled into Zeigler and delivered a flurry of blows that would have rendered the older man senseless if Zach had been a few years older. As it was, all he succeeded in doing was drawing Old Bill's wrath.

Zeigler's rage was such that he no longer entertained the notion of keeping mother or son alive. They had hurt him badly, and for that they were both going to die. He cuffed the boy, knocking him to his knees, then clasped both hands around the mother's slender neck.

In a moment of panic Winona grasped his wrists and urgently tried to pry the man's hands from her windpipe. She was so concerned about being strangled that she forgot all else.

Not so with Zach. He had the presence of mind to remember the pistol and knife. Diving at Zeigler's waist, he pretended to snatch at the pistol with one hand and when Old Bill lowered an arm to block him, he seized the knife instead.

Old Bill didn't feel the blade slide from its sheath. He did feel a strange tingling in his innards though, and he looked down to discover seven inches of cold steel planted in his abdomen. Wailing like a banshee, he leaped to his feet. As he did, Zach ripped the knife loose.

"Damn your bones!" Old Bill said, staggering backward. He told himself that this couldn't be happening to him, that a brat and a miserable woman couldn't be getting the better of him. He tried to stop the crimson spray shooting from his ruptured gut, but it was like trying to plug a cracked dam. Looking up, he sought his rifle, but Winona King held it.

"Oh, no," Old Bill said and clawed at his pistol.

"Oh, yes," Winona said. She shot him in the face.

The lanky frame of the grizzled madman did a slow pirouette to the ground. It wound up on its back, blank eyes fixed on the heavens.

Zach stared at the neat hole in Zeigler's forehead. The thought of how close they had come to dying caused a tiny shudder to ripple down his back. "We did it," he said numbly. "We're safe now."

Stepping over to him, Winona draped an arm across his shoulders. "Yes, we are," she said, struggling to catch her breath after her ordeal. "Tomorrow at first light we will head north to rejoin your father."

"He should have been back by now, shouldn't he?" Zach asked.

Winona thought so, but she wanted to spare her son any more anguish than they had already been through. "I would guess that he is busy tracking down the men we were after. There is no need to worry about him. Your father can take care of himself better than any man I know."

"That's why he's the best there is at what he does," Zach said proudly. Remembering the knife in his hand, he squatted to wipe the blade clean on the grass. Behind him there was the barest whisper of movement, so faint that he thought it was the wind, that the breeze had picked up, and he turned to let the cool air fan his face.

Eight feet away stood a swarthy warrior holding a rifle leveled in their direction.

"Ma!" Zach exclaimed, bouncing erect.

Winona whirled, bewildered by her son's outcry since the danger was past. Then she set eyes on the warrior and knew by the style of his hair that he was a Blood. "Get behind me," she said, remembering that Jeremiah Sawyer had told them about a certain Blood who rode with Earl Lassiter. It was too much of a coincidence not to be the same person.

"I'll protect you, Ma," Zach said, moving in front of her.

Grabbing her son's arm, Winona swung him around to her rear. The Blood regarded them with a hint of amusement and something else. He took a step, then gestured curtly for her to drop the rifle. It was empty anyway, so she did.

Brule the Blood had seen the white man slain. He had admired the woman's fierce resistance, which made her all the more desirable since Blood men looked for fighting spirit in their women. Being fully aware of her battle prowess, he was not about to give her the chance to do to him as she had done to the white man. Keeping her covered, he took several strides.

Winona tried a bluff to buy time. "Who are

you?" she signed. "What do you want with us?"

Brule hesitated. To answer, he would have had to cradle the rifle in his elbow. Since the woman was unarmed, he saw no reason not to. The child in the cradleboard certainly posed no threat, and the boy couldn't possibly reach him with the knife before he could get off a shot. "I am in need of a woman," he said. "I have chosen you."

This new threat, coming as it did immediately on the heels of the other, took Winona off guard. She had no idea what to do. A Blood warrior was many times more deadly than Zeigler had been. But she had to do something. Then fingers tugged at her dress. Zach had sidled next to her leg and was giving her a devilish grin.

"Tell the boy to drop the knife and move aside," Brule signed.

Zach was fluent in sign language. He chuckled and said in English, "I don't have the knife any more, you idiot. I exchanged it for this." Sliding to the right to be clear of his mother, he extended the pistol he had taken from Old Bill.

Brule the Blood took one look and swept his rifle up.

A single shot echoed off the high peaks.

Not quite 24 hours later three riders and a child in a cradleboard met on a pine covered ridge.

Nate King had nearly ridden his magnificent black stallion to exhaustion in finding his family. "It's over," he said after greeting them warmly. He looked around. "Where's Old Bill?"

Winona explained, then told about the Blood. "Your son never lost his nerve. He did as you taught him. You should be very proud."

"I am," Nate said, ruffling Zach's hair. His gaze strayed to his wife's mare, to a pair of fresh scalps hanging from a rawhide cord strung across its back. "What are those?"

"I thought Two Owls would need proof to show his people."

"It's downright spooky," Nate said.

"What is?"

"How much we think alike." Twisting, Nate pointed at five scalps dangling from his saddle.

Zach walked over to examine them. "Does this mean the Utes will leave us alone, Pa? Does this mean we can go on living where we always have?"

"It sure does, son," Nate said, and he recalled an old saying his grandfather had been fond of. "There's no place like home."

ATTENTION WESTERN CUSTOMERS!

SPECIAL TOLL-FREE NUMBER
1-800-481-9191

Call Monday through Friday
10 a.m. to 9 p.m.
Eastern Time
Get a free catalogue,
join the Western Book Club,
and order books using your
Visa, MasterCard,
or Discover®.

Leisure
Books

GO ONLINE WITH US AT DORCHESTERPUB.COM